the
Obsession

DEDICATION

To everyone who loved this book the first time around, I hope you enjoy it even more now. This book was and continues to be a rollercoaster ride every time I go through it.

CHAPTER ONE

Santa Barbara, California

MONDAY, NOVEMBER 3

Tristan was a freak. His mother even said so, didn't she? It's what she called him when she saw him touch himself around other boys anyways.

So, it was no wonder whenever Collin walked into the classroom he had to do what came naturally. Smirking, he crept lower in his chair and let his fingers toy with one of the many small, hooped earrings lining the shell of his right ear.

Collin, a stunning young man with dark eyes and auburn hair, cut in wispy collar-length layers around his face, strolled into the university classroom and went for a seat at the desk in front of him. His light t-shirt pulled across his wide shoulders and his jeans hung low at his narrow hips by a thick, brown belt. A hunter-green backpack spilled off the side of his back to fall onto the linoleum floor beside him.

Tristan's cock swelled as he focused on Collin. Mesmerized, his blond hair, long enough to cover his shoulders, draped over his face while he watched the graceful movement of the six-foot tall, muscular body sitting in front of him. How many times had he called out Collin's name? A hundred? Maybe. He'd pleasured himself at least that many times fantasizing about him back at his dorm room.

He kept his gaze on the back of Collin's head while he snuck his hand under his black t-shirt and into the front pocket of his jeans. He was smart, wearing his pants on the baggy side and underwear made of thin, knitted silk—snug, but able to stretch in just the right places. It allowed him to do what he needed whenever the desire arose.

His fingers ran a soft circle over the head of his erection, feeding his need, washing a wave of pleasure over him like a warm bath. His breath quickened. Stopping for a moment, he took a fast glance around the class to see if anyone noticed him.

Students filled all fifty desks, waiting patiently for the professor to begin.

No one noticed. A soft smirk played on his face, lifting one side of his lips, exposing the dimple in his cheek. They never noticed. He was invisible.

Closing his eyes for a moment, he reached a little lower, letting his fingers play along his shaft. Tiny pulses rocked his body, made him yearn to move his hips. But he couldn't. That would have to wait.

As the professor took the podium and started the day's sociology lesson, he reached a little deeper. This time, his fingers found the base of his erection. He pressed down hard at first, letting the sensation take him for a moment to a place of calm excitement, and started a steady, soft rhythm of stroking, up and down, over and over. The soft touch over thin cloth sent shivers through him without sending him over the edge too quickly, allowing him to drag it out for sometimes hours at a time.

His vision dazed as pleasure surrounded him, cradled him, made him whole. What was the professor droning on about? No matter, he only wanted to feel anyways.

A movie played in his mind. Collin was the star. The object of his desire crawled under his desk and everyone else disappeared. His lean body sat naked while Collin took him in his mouth, sucking, licking, and flicking his tongue over his firm cock. A shiver raced over his spine, and he let out a soft moan.

The dream vanished and he ceased the hand movement. Did anyone see him? His gaze darted around the room, taking in the sterile desks and white walls and students, sitting like zombies in a graveyard. No, he was still invisible.

As he resumed the rhythm of his fingers, he lost himself to the vision. He moved his fingers quicker, pressed harder and circled the spot just under the head. Oh, how he wanted to move. How he wanted to moan and gasp. But he couldn't. Controlling it was half the fun.

He trailed his fingers lower as need heightened inside him to a thrumming crescendo, pressing round groves against his sac. He loved fondling this part of his body when it tightened with arousal, loved the sparks it sent through him. He'd do this all day if he could and some days he did. And why not? His mother wasn't around anymore to make him stop, was she?

Leaning to the side, he reached lower, underneath, pressing hard between his sac and passage. A shudder rolled through his body. His hips twitched, itching to thrust, but he caught himself.

He closed his eyes again as he brought his fingers back up and squeezed the tip of his cock. A pulse of sensation raced through him, making him swoon.

He did it again, bringing himself dangerously close to the brink. Time to slow down. He was there. Right where he wanted to be. The height of sensation without going over the edge.

The movement of his fingers teased him in his jeans, dancing along his shaft, pressing at the right place but never enough to satisfy.

"Hey, got a pen I can borrow? Mine died." Twisted around in his seat, Collin faced him, holding up a black pen.

Tristan halted all motion and stared at his pen. His heart hammered in his chest. Could Collin hear it?

"You okay? You look sort of flushed, like maybe you have a fever or something."

3

Keeping his fingers pressed to his erection, Tristan focused on the heat they gave off. What did he want? Oh, yeah. "N-no, I'm okay. Uh, yeah, I have a pen."

"Cool." Smiling, Collin dropped his hand to his side.

Leaning down, Tristan reached into the outside pocket of his black backpack.

A barrage of silver necklaces dangled from Tristan's neck and the silver-balled bracelets he wore on his wrist caught on the zipper. "Shit," he whispered. He yanked his hand out, dove it back in and pulled out a pen. The movement pressed his fingers harder into him. A jolt of pleasure rocketed through his body. "Uh..."

"You okay? I mean, you didn't, like, pull your back out or anything, did you?"

Straightening, Tristan held out the pen to him and shook his head. His gaze roamed over the angles of the striking face he'd only seen from far away, resting on perfectly formed lips.

"Hey, thanks." After taking the pen, Collin smiled and turned back around.

Heartache and longing threaded through Tristan's body and gnawed at his insides. The second he'd seen Collin for the first time he'd fallen in love. He knew it. It had hit him so hard he'd lost his breath and couldn't move. He let out a long, soft sigh. If only he could talk to him, get close to him somehow.

Tristan's erection pulsed against his fingers, beckoning to him. This would have to do, a stolen moment because of a dead pen. Furrowing his brows with a soft huff, he hung his head. Collin would be his, but only like this, in fantasies and dreams. He should just get used to it.

Tristan stroked slowly and sensually against his seeping cock. He ran his fingers down and up, under his sac to the tip of his shaft, pinching and swirling at will as they went. The delicious sensation swept away the pain, the hunger, for the living, breathing body sitting so close ahead of him. He gazed at Collin with a slack mouth. Collin wrote notes with his pen while he touched himself under the desk.

Collin wrapped his fingers around the pen—surrounded it on all sides, caressing it, embracing it.

A sharp heat filled Tristan's chest. If only he were that pen. If only Collin touched and held him like that. His vision blurred, an ache shooting through his chest.

He blinked, his heart stinging. Crying wasn't allowed. His mother had made sure of that. But the moment with Collin overwhelmed him more than he let himself believe and all the stroking in the world wouldn't soothe him.

Ripping his hand out of his pocket, he swiped at his eyes and rose from his seat.

All eyes focused on him.

Tristan glanced around the room at the pale faces sitting under florescent light. He shifted his gaze to the professor, slapping a marker to his palm, waiting.

"Mr. Tolken, are you going somewhere?"

He focused on Collin.

Collin smiled up at him from his seat. "Dude, what're you doing?"

With his legs itching to run, Tristan leaned over, snatched his backpack, and raced out of the room. The heavy door slammed behind him.

He ran into the sunlight, through a courtyard filled with palm trees and a manicured lawn, passed the rigid angles of modern buildings mixed with the stucco curves and red tiles of Spanish revival architecture, across cement steps and cobblestone paths, until he reached the landing of his dorm building. The faint scent of the ocean filled the air around him.

He looked up at the curved structure, maybe four stories high, all cold, modern lines and uninviting, but it was his home. Rose bushes towered over him from either side of the door, bearing fat reddish-pink blossoms. Panting, he strode to the glass of the front door, opened it, and stepped inside. Other students milled about in shorts, jeans, and t-shirts. He tilted his head away from them and trudged through the common area. He needed to be alone.

After striding to the elevator, he pressed the up button. As he waited, he pushed his hand into his pocket. He stroked himself into arousal, toying and teasing his cock until it grew sensitive again.

The ding of the elevator rang in the hallway, and he stepped through steel doors as they opened. The doors slid shut. He was alone. Stroking hard on himself, leaning against the elevator wall, he thrust his hips and moaned out loud. Sweet pleasure rushed over him. His eyes clenched shut and his brows tensed.

Another ding sounded and he ceased all motion, except for his fingers. He let them stroke and tease as he walked the hallway to his room. The smell of mildew rose from the carpet to fill the air around him.

When he arrived at his door, he removed a key from his backpack, unlocked it and stepped inside. He dropped the backpack to the floor and strode passed a set of closets and a bathroom to his twin bed, sitting against the wall. He glanced at two laminate desks with wide bookshelves hanging on the wall above them. The desks and bookshelves sat on either side of a window—one was empty while the other housed his computer and books.

Mini blinds came down halfway inside the wood window frame, letting a rectangle of sunlight spill over the gray carpet and a small refrigerator. His gaze moved to the plain headboard of the white bed framing a bare mattress on the far wall while he undressed down to his silk underwear. Those he left on until the very end.

He climbed onto the navy-blue bedspread of his bed, lay on his back and looked down on his tortured cock, straining to break free from the confines of the smooth cloth binding it. He ran his fingers along his shaft, all the way down to the crevice between his legs and back up again, pressing hard along his sac. After a few strokes he used his palm, rubbing long and even while he thrust his hips.

Tingling filled his groin. He arched his back and gasped as his need begged to go harder, faster. No, he wouldn't, he never did, not until he satisfied his craving for sensation.

Muffled clanking and tinkling snaked into the room from the direction of the door. Holy shit, was someone trying to get in? His gaze darted around the room. What should he do? *Shit, I'm trapped like this!* He shoved the covers down and scrambled underneath them. Holding his breath for a moment, he stayed motionless as the door popped open and footsteps filled the room.

"Hey, would you look at who I have for a new roommate?" Collin stood at the edge of his bed with a large duffle bag slung across his shoulder and his backpack in his hand.

Tristan's heart about stopped. "Uh, C-Collin, what are you doing here?"

A soft smile curled Collin's lips and he took a seat on the opposite bed, setting the duffle bag on the floor. "Well, I had a problem with my apartment and decided I'd be better off in the dorms this year and this one had an opening. So here I am. Your new roommate." He held out his arms like he was part of a vaudeville act. Dropping his arms back down, his smile waned and his brows lowered. "Sorry I didn't knock first. The RA downstairs gave me a key and just told me to come on up. Hope I didn't wake you. Uh, how'd you know my name? My last name is Stanley by the way, and what's yours?"

"N-no you didn't. Um, I-I don't know how I knew your name. I guess I must have heard someone call you that. I'm, I'm Tristan." He brushed his palm against his erection, reminding him of his arousal, then skimmed his tongue over his lips, his gaze drawing to Collin's mouth.

"Oh, Tristan, huh? Hey, why'd you leave class like that? I didn't even have time to give you your pen back." Leaning down, Collin dug around in his backpack.

"Oh, y-you can keep it. I have plenty." Tristan's vision glazed over for a moment as he probed and pinched at the head of his erection, sending sweet pulses into his body. It was the only way he could keep fear from paralyzing him. "Uh, I left because I—had to go to the bathroom."

Collin straightened. "Really? That's pretty funny. You must have had to go bad." He let out a soft chuckle. "Uh, thanks for the pen." He stood up from the bed. "Well, I better unpack. Then maybe you and I can get a bite to eat."

Tristan's fingers stopped again. "A-a bite to eat? You mean with you?"

A short laugh escaped Collin. "Yeah, I figure if we're going to be roommates we better get to know each other. You know, talk about what pisses us off and stuff so we can be better roommates." He stepped toward the closet on his side of the room. "I'll just unpack my clothes for now and be done in a few."

Tristan rolled onto his side and placed his hands between his thighs, resuming light stroking over his erection, swaying his hips forward and back, but not enough for his new roommate to notice. His heart thrummed in his chest. How could he have been so incredibly lucky? And how was he ever going to get through this? He couldn't eat with Collin sitting at a table with him. Let alone, sleep in the same room?

Tristan pressed his face into the pillow, stifling a moan. His sensitivity heightened. What would doing all those things with Collin be like? How would he ever contain himself? He stopped his fingers and clenched his teeth. He was too close.

Raking a hand through his straight, long bangs, Collin stepped back to his bedside. "Ready for some chow?"

Tristan rolled to his back. "Now?"

Collin shrugged. "Sure, why not? You don't exactly look like you've got a class or anything." He chuckled. "You're not even dressed." He pointed to Tristan's clothes lying in a heap on the floor.

Glancing at his clothes, Tristan said, "Uh, yeah." He thought for a moment. If he got out of bed now, Collin would see his hard on. "Collin? Could you give me a minute? Maybe wait outside?" He winced. The request might sound odd.

Collin furrowed his brows. "Yeah, sure." He turned and walked toward the door.

The click of the door opening and the soft thud of it closing filtered into the room. Tristan pressed hard on himself, rubbing fast over his erection. His breathing became ragged as he brought himself to the raw edge of climax. He stopped. Desire surged inside him, but he let it pass. He'd wait. He always waited.

He climbed out of bed and dressed, pulling his black t-shirt down over his body and lifting his jeans up over his firm cock. A quick rap rippled into the room.

"You coming?" Collin's voice called out from behind the door.

Tristan smirked. Not yet. He felt for his wallet in his back pocket. It was there. He started for the door and stopped again. His chest squeezed. *Collin is my roommate.* Stuffing his hand into his pocket, he let his fingers stroke him into tranquility. It'll be all right, as long as he felt the tension coiled inside him, his fears would be kept at bay.

Stepping to the door, Tristan opened it. "Ready."

Collin grinned. "Okay, so let's get out of here." He turned to stroll down the hallway.

Walking beside his new roommate, Tristan stole glances at the stunning angles of his face, the nicely sculpted cheekbones, the high forehead, the little bump in a nose that was neither too big, nor too small. He continued to tease his erection with his fingers.

They stopped at the elevator. "Where do you want to go?" Collin pushed the down button.

Tristan looked at the floor. Need churned inside him. "I don't care. Wherever you want to go."

The elevator doors slid open, and they stepped inside. "Okay, how about that burger joint on Main?"

With a nod, Tristan's erection pulsed. A short gasp escaped his lips.

"You okay? We don't have to eat hamburgers if you don't want."

Tristan stopped his fingers. He couldn't look at Collin. He fought to ease his breath. "I'm okay. Hamburgers are fine."

The elevator opened at the main floor and the two stepped off and strolled through the common area, passed vinyl couches, coffee tables and a television, to the front door.

With a faint grin on his face, Collin opened the door and held it for him to pass.

Tristan glanced up. Why was Collin being so nice? People weren't usually nice to him. No, they could be downright mean.

They walked across campus under midday sun and blue sky, passed a mission-style building with arched doorways and bougainvillea vines straining to reach the roofline. The simple lines of modern architecture rose up in the distance within the backdrop of the chaparral-covered Santa Ynez Mountains.

"So, where you from?" Collin walked with an easy and care-free gait.

Tristan refreshed the rhythm of his fingers, calming him. "Uh, I'm from Utah. Salt Lake."

"Really? You're not Mormon, are you?"

Tristan nodded.

"Oh. Do you actually practice all that stuff?"

"Not anymore." Not since he'd been in southern California had he even thought about his religion. It condemned young men like him in so many ways.

"I'm from a little east of here, Arizona." Collin squinted in the sunlight.

"Yeah?"

"Yeah, Phoenix."

Tristan glanced up. They came upon the front doors of a plain brick building housing the local hamburger joint.

"Here you go, Big Fred's." Smiling, Collin held the glass door open for him again and gestured. "After you."

Strolling inside, the aroma of beef and grease caught Tristan's senses. Quite a few students were already eating at diner-style tables and chairs. He walked across a checkered floor to the front counter where a teenager waited to take their orders.

Collin stepped up behind him and looked over Tristan's shoulder, being a good two inches taller than him.

Collin's breath puffed on the back of his neck. A shiver raced down his spine. His sensitivity skyrocketed. He stopped his fingers and pressed hard, wincing as a pulse of pleasure jolted him. Oh God, he wanted to climax, right then, right now. But he'd let it pass.

"Can I help you?" The boy behind the counter lifted his brows as he studied Tristan.

Collin planted his hand on Tristan's shoulder.

With a hard swallow, Tristan's body trembled.

Leaning over him, Collin said, "Yeah, I'll just have your number one with a soda." He turned his head to Tristan. "What did you want?"

"Uh, um, I'll just have the same," Tristan said. He didn't care what he ordered. He had to get out of Collin's grasp or his heart would explode.

Collin squeezed his shoulder and his breath whispered across Tristan's ear, sending a shiver down his spine. A soft huskiness filled Collin's voice. "You all right? It feels like you're shivering. Maybe you do have a fever."

Gasping, Tristan stepped forward out of his reach. "No, I-I'm fine." He twisted to face Collin, resuming the stroking on his erection. "Just hungry, that's all. Guess I get sort of shaky sometimes."

Collin frowned and narrowed his eyes at him. "Okay." He glanced at the counter. "Hey, there's our food."

They went to the counter, paid for their meal, and picked up trays of food in little cardboard boxes.

Tristan followed Collin to a square table by a window and sat down.

Sitting next to Tristan, Collin took a sip of his drink from a straw. "So tell me, what sort of things piss you off?"

Tristan trailed light circles over his shaft with his fingers, comforting him. "I don't think anything does." He picked up his burger with his unoccupied hand and took a bite.

"Oh, come on. Everyone gets irritated by something."

Thinking for a moment, Tristan chewed. "I guess I don't like bullies."

Collin chuckled. "Bullies, huh? I don't think anyone likes them." He wrinkled his brows. "Why, have you been bullied a lot or something? I mean, I guess it's sort of a strange thing to bring up. Are you right out of high school?" He ate a fry and took another sip of soda.

Tristan glanced up at him. "No, I'm actually starting my fourth year here. I turned twenty-one over the summer."

"Yeah? Me, too. I mean I'm twenty-one. I just finished my Bachelor's at NAU and decided to come here to the illustrious Cal State to do my Master's. I'm on a bit of a fast track, you could say." Collin looked into his eyes. "You never answered me about the bullies."

Tristan swallowed down some hamburger. "The answer is yes. I have been, sort of, bullied." He ran his fingers faster along his erection, shutting down painful memories of being called names, of always being on the outside.

Memories of Sean, his best friend, shoved through. In his senior year of high school, he'd kissed him in a drunken moment at a party. Tristan winced at the memory, his friend's anger, how Sean told everyone what he was and the beating that followed. He ran his fingers fast and hard. A wave of pleasure washed over him, ripping him from the memory. He lowered his free arm across the table.

"Hey, Tristan." Reaching across the table, Collin placed a hand on his forearm.

Tristan's gaze dragged to Collin's face, and he slowed the fingers over his shaft.

Collin released his forearm and sat back, wrinkling his forehead. "You looked like you checked out for a minute there. Are the memories that bad?"

Tristan stared at him. *Why did he care about me?* No one had shown him any concern for years. "I-I guess so."

Leaning forward, Collin set his elbows on the table and gazed into his eyes. "Do you want to talk about it some time? I mean, probably not here, out in the open. We could talk about it back at our room if you want. I'm a psych major. My Bachelor's is in psychology, and I plan on getting a PhD soon enough. I'm pretty good with stuff like that. I even work on the student suicide hotline sometimes."

"Y-you do?" Should he take Collin up on his offer? But he wasn't used to letting his ugly secrets out. "Um, sure, maybe."

Looking him over as if assessing him, Collin said, "You don't have to talk to me if you don't want to. I just thought it might help." His focus rested on the hand inside Tristan's pocket. He pointed to it and grinned. "Hey, do you ever take that hand out of your pocket?"

Tristan froze. Could he pull his fingers out and still talk to him without being terrified? Looking down at his lap, he willed his hand to come out. Slowly, letting his fingers hover for a moment, he removed them from their position over his erection. He slid his hand out from his pocket and rested it in his lap, still over the solid flesh below, a security blanket. "It's just a strange habit I have." He brought his gaze up to meet Collin's.

Collin's gaze locked with Tristan's and he flicked his tongue over his lower lip. Clearing his throat, he straightened in his chair. "Yeah, that is strange."

As his gaze took Collin in, heat flared over Tristan's skin. He absently closed his legs and pressed on his groin with the heel of his hand. A dull pleasure washed up from his lap.

Collin's gaze flicked downward.

Watching Collin, Tristan pressed a second time and held it, leaning forward.

Collin dragged his gaze away from Tristan's crotch, squirming in his seat. "Uh, wh-what are you majoring in?"

"Art." Tilting his head to the side, he pressed down harder.

Collin adjusted his jeans. "Ah, art. You must be an artist then?"

With a smile, Tristan released the pressure on his shaft. "Yeah, I want to be an illustrator."

"What sort of things do you like to draw?"

Tristan tensed his brows. He couldn't tell him what he really liked to draw. Telling another man you like to draw guys naked in sexual positions just wasn't a good idea in his experience. "Portraits, mostly."

Collin took another bite of his hamburger. "Yeah? Maybe you could do my portrait sometime."

An image of Collin naked flooded Tristan's mind. Collin, posing just for him. He let his palm rest over his erection, enjoying the heat. "Sure." He struggled to find something else to focus on. "Hey, why are you taking an undergrad sociology class if you're a graduate?"

A sly smile spread over Collin's lips. "Well, believe it or not, when I took it at NAU I got a shitty grade. So I'm just repeating it to strengthen my overall GPA."

Taking a sip of soda, Tristan nodded. "I didn't know you could do that after the fact."

"Well, technically I didn't quite graduate. I have to finish this class and then they'll let me graduate. It's a long story and a bit of a logistics nightmare, but the university let me into the graduate program anyways." Collin looked away for a moment, then a smirk spread over his mouth. "I don't want to brag or anything, but I'm a bit of a prodigy." He patted himself on the head. "Got a genius IQ."

Tristan widened his eyes. "Oh, wow." It figured. He was not only good-looking, he was incredibly smart, too.

Collin burst forward in his seat. "Oh." He glanced at a watch around his right wrist. "Shit, I have a class to get to. I'll catch up with you later." He grabbed his soda, shoved a few fries in his mouth, stood up and jogged toward the front door.

Tristan's gaze chased after him. His heart ached. He didn't really want him to go, even if it did put him in a tailspin.

Collin stopped at the door and waved before opening it and stepping outside.

Tristan looked down into his lap. He didn't feel much like eating anymore. He did have two more classes today. Thankfully, one was a two-hour art class he could lose himself in. He rose from the table and shoved his hand into his pocket, starting the slow stroking and teasing he craved, then left the restaurant. He'd fall back on his old soothing habits and feel delicious tension until tonight. Then he wouldn't have to feel the aching in his chest for someone he could never have.

CHAPTER TWO

After closing his book, Tristan rose from his desk at the foot of his bed and stretched. He was tired of studying and waiting for Collin to come back. Where had he gone, anyways? It was after eleven already. He knew Collin didn't do something brash like move out. He glanced at the desk on the other side of the room. A new laptop computer rested on it and a myriad of books filled the once-empty shelves above it.

He looked over Collin's vacant bed, stepping toward it. A green duvet covered the top and ivory sheets peeked out from underneath. There were even some silly posters of Albert Einstein, Sigmund Freud, and Carl Jung on the wall above his bed.

It was time. Time to give his body what he'd promised it all day. Release beckoned him. He climbed onto Collin's bed and sprawled out over the green duvet on his back. This was going to be good, perfect even. He had new visions of Collin to think about, plus he'd do it right where Collin would sleep tonight.

He pulled his t-shirt up over his head and flung it to the floor. His erection ached as he unfastened his belt and jeans, exposing his underwear-bound cock. He'd been stroking and teasing steadily with nimble fingers while he'd studied. He rubbed his palm in long, hard strokes over his erection. As he came up over the tip, wetness slicked his palm. He looked down. His cock seeped, soaking a large spot in his underwear. A faint smirk spread on his lips. It was an intense day.

As he stroked, his need rushed to a sharp tension, making him gasp in pleasure. He thrust his hips, letting an urgent moan escape. He snuck his hand beneath his briefs and freed his thick cock. He squeezed hard on it and brought his other hand down to fondle his tight sac. Climax roared to a raw edge. He clenched his teeth.

Jingling rang out in the room and the door creaked as it swung open.

Tristan's heart jolted. Trembling, he jostled his erection back into his underwear and fastened his jeans. He scrambled to the edge of the bed, necklaces swaying, just as Collin walked to it.

Collin looked down at a bare-chested Tristan. "Oh, hey. How are you?"

Tristan stared up at him, wide-eyed and slack-jawed, panting.

Tilting his head, Collin tensed his brows, eyeing him. "Uh, what are you doing on my bed?"

"Um, I um, I just—"

"Guess you're not used to having a roommate." Smiling, Collin dropped in next to him.

"Uh, no I'm not. I had a s-single room until this year." Tristan's trembling worsened. He couldn't look at Collin with him sitting so close. He focused on his hands, wringing around each other as if they had nothing better to do. *Oh no, I forgot to buckle my belt...*It hung slack in his lap.

Resting his hand on Tristan's thigh, Collin said, "You sure you're not sick or something? Cause you sure were flushed when I came in and I can feel you shivering from here."

Tristan gulped hard. The heat from Collin's hand seared into his groin. His dick pulsed. If only there was something more between he and Collin. A shudder ran down his spine. "N-no, I'm not sick."

"Look at me."

"What?" Tristan's heart jolted. "N-no."

Sighing, Collin reached his arm up and pressed the inside of his forearm against Tristan's forehead.

Clenching his eyes shut, Tristan bit his lip. Damn it, he couldn't shove his hand in his pocket, Collin might see him.

"Hmmm, you don't feel all that hot." Collin dropped his arm to his side. "My mom always used to do that, take temperatures that way. It works."

"Uh, r-really?" Tristan fisted his hands. If only Collin would touch him again in any other way.

"Yeah. Hey, why are you shaking so much if you don't have a fever? I don't make you nervous, do I?" Collin shifted on the bed to face him, lifting a leg onto the mattress.

Tristan jumped from the bed, stepped the short distance to his own bed and threw down the covers, exposing baby blue sheets. "I'm tired. I need to get some sleep."

Leaning forward, Collin rested his elbows on his thighs. "Why? Do I make you nervous?"

"Y-you don't. I just need to get some sleep." As Tristan glared at his bed, he willed his breathing to slow, his body to relax, taking deep breaths. He twisted and strode to his closet and pulled out a white terry-cloth bathrobe, then threw it over his shoulders. Sighing, he toed off his tennis shoes and kicked off his jeans. Wrapping the robe tightly around him, he padded back to his bed.

"Dude, nice robe." A soft grin curled Collin's generous lips as he gazed up at him.

Tristan glared at the white planks of his own headboard. "Don't mess with me, okay? I've had a—a rough day." He pursed his lips. *He thinks I'm an idiot.* His eyes stung with the threat of tears. He blinked them back.

Collin stood and planted his hand on Tristan's shoulder. "Hey, I'm sorry, man. I didn't mean anything by that. It's really a nice robe, seriously. Just not something most college guys wear to bed, you know?"

With Collin's hand searing heat into Tristan's shoulder, Tristan said, "Then please, just leave me alone. I need to get some sleep, okay?"

"Sure." Collin squeezed his shoulder, then stepped to his desk.

Tristan said, "Aren't you going to bed?"

Stopping, Collin said, "Right now?"

"Yes. It's late. We have class in the morning, remember?" Tristan studied him.

Collin stole a peak at him. "Yeah, sure. I'll go get ready." He walked into the bathroom and shut the door.

Tristan freed a loud exhale, peeled off his robe and climbed into bed. How he ached, physically and emotionally. He rolled to his side, facing the wall and tucked his hands between his thighs, arcing his thumb across his softened cock, making it fill with need. Just wait. Wait until Collin was asleep, then he could give himself what he craved.

Collin strolled out from the bathroom, shut off the light switch on the wall and climbed into bed. A faint light poured in through the window between their desks, through the slats in the blinds. The sound of rustling sheets filled the air as Collin moved his limbs in his bed. After a few minutes, his breathing grew deep and steady.

Good, he's asleep. Slowly, quietly, Tristan lowered his briefs and exposed his firm cock. His hand rubbed long, hard strokes over it, circling the tip with his thumb, spreading a pearl of pre-cum over the head. He shuddered as delicious tension coiled in his gut. A soft gasp escaped him and he clenched his teeth.

He moved his hand in quick, jerking motions over his shaft. Letting out a soft whimper, he shoved his face into his pillow and bit it, stifling a moan.

Pounding rushed his ears. Intense tingling flooded his cock. His peak surged in a tumult of sensation. Brutal contractions sent harsh waves of pleasure rocketing through his body, again and again, as cum spurted into sheets, over fingers, onto his stomach.

His toes curled and cramped. As his climax slowed and his body relaxed, he parted his teeth, letting the pillow fall from his mouth.

Rustling filled the air. Soft, muffled gasps wafted through the room.

Is that Collin? Carefully, Tristan rolled, twisting his head to look at Collin's bed.

Collin lay on his side, back to him. His sheets and comforter quivered in the glow filtering into the room. His body stirred and went still.

Rolling to his side, Tristan stared at the wall. Did Collin just jerk off, too? A faint grin spread over his lips. No way.

Collin flung his covers down, jumped out of bed and jogged to the bathroom.

Tristan pretended to sleep until the click of the bathroom door closing and water running snaked through the room. Oh my God, he must have. Why would he do that? Had Collin heard him and decided to do it, too? Heat swept through his cheeks. How could he possibly face him tomorrow? He snuck his sticky fingers to his lips and licked them off.

Bitterness mixed with salt to glide over his tongue. Bringing his hand back down, he rubbed it over his stomach and spent cock, getting as much of his fluid as he could before lifting it back up to his mouth. He lapped and licked at his palm and fingers. How he loved this taste.

A click sounded and the bathroom door opened.

Tristan held still, feigning sleep as Collin crept back to his bed and climbed under the covers. A soft sigh escaped Tristan as he drifted off to sleep, satiated for the moment.

CHAPTER THREE

TUESDAY, NOVEMBER 4

Tristan stepped out of a tiled shower with a white towel wrapped around his waist and looked at his cell phone, sitting on a glass shelf over the sink. Good, he still had a half-hour before class. His damp hair hung in a heavy mop over his shoulders, dribbling water onto his toned chest and back.

He unfastened the towel and let it drop to the linoleum floor. Leaning down, he took hold of a pair of silk briefs and slid them up his legs and over his groin. His cock filled as the sleek material engulfed it, caressed it. A familiar ache started inside him. He let his fingers brush over the thin cloth, stroking his erection with a light touch.

Closing his eyes, a soft moan escaped his lips. He should stop. Collin was still sleeping in bed. Oh, but Collin did this, too, didn't he? Didn't he hear Collin doing it last night? His cock pulsed, sending pleasure rippling into his body. He couldn't start this early. It was too much and now he had a roommate to deal with.

He opened his eyes and cleared his throat. He needed to focus on getting ready and out the door. He glanced at himself in the mirrored medicine cabinet, hanging over the sink, taking in his deep blue eyes. Probably the only thing he'd gotten from his dead father since his mother's eyes were brown. He opened the cabinet and found his comb. Bringing it to his hair, he slid long strokes through it, careful to keep the teeth from snagging his earrings, and untangled a mess of snarls.

After putting the comb away, he bent over to a heap of clothes on the floor. His necklaces swayed off his neck and the bracelets jingled over his wrist. He grasped a black, collared shirt and looked through the heap for a pair of jeans. Where were they? He found yesterday's jeans, but he couldn't wear those. They were soiled. They must be in his laundry basket.

He straightened, opened the bathroom door, and peered into the room at Collin's bed. Was he still asleep?

Collin lay on his side, motionless.

Tristan crept out into the room and to a plastic laundry basket tucked inside his closet. He bent down and fumbled through it for a cleaner pair of jeans. *There they are.*

"Nice underwear."

Gasping, Tristan lurched up with the jeans clutched in his hands and covered his groin. The legs of the jeans dangled down in front of him. "Uh, C-Collin, you're up." He stared, wide-eyed, at the clothes hung in his closet, then peeked at him.

Collin raked his hand through sleep-mussed hair. Dark boxers hung over his hipbones. "Yeah, I have a class in an hour." He let out a slow yawn. "You've got some style in clothes, man. I don't think I've ever seen a guy wear underwear like that unless they were dancing in one of those shows in Vegas." A soft chuckle escaped him. "Hey, you're not one of those male dancers, are you? Like, a male stripper?" He slapped Tristan's ass.

Tristan's hips jerked forward with the force of the slap. Heat swarmed his face, and he clenched his jaw. He faced Collin, but glared at the floor. "Don't say things like that. Why can't you keep your comments about my stuff to yourself?"

Collin clapped his hand on Tristan's shoulder. "Dude, I'm joking. Don't be so sensitive."

Flinging Collin's hand off his shoulder, Tristan locked his gaze on Collin's. "I don't think it's funny. I don't like being bullied, remember?" How the hell did he blurt that out? How could he accuse Collin of something like that?

Collin's face tensed for a second, then he sucked in a deep breath. "Shit. I'm sorry. I didn't think of it like that. I really was only making a joke." Collin blew out an exhale. "I'm really messing this up already, aren't I?" He planted a hand on his hip and studied him.

"Uh, well, no, you're not messing anything up." Tristan shifted his stance, stealing a peek and him. His chest tightened and his gaze wound to Collin's mouth.

Skimming his tongue over his lips, Collin grasped Tristan's bicep. "I like being your roommate and I don't want you to hate me already."

Tristan knitted his brows. A steady ache grew in his chest. "I don't hate you, not at all. I..." The ache intensified, swallowed him. "I have to get dressed." Jerking his arm free from Collin, he stumbled over his jeans and into the bathroom, slamming the door shut behind him, then fell to his knees on the floor, puffing out heavy breaths. What was that? Was he imagining things? Did Collin somehow like him? What was it that had happened last night anyways? Did Collin really jerk off with him?

A rap on the door filled the bathroom. Collin's muffled voice drifted into the room. "Hey, I'll see you later this afternoon, okay? I'll be here studying."

Tristan rubbed the heal of his hand over his chest. "Okay."

A FEW HOURS LATER, Tristan unlocked the door on his dorm room. His hands trembled. Was Collin here yet? Removing his key, he stepped into the room and shut the door behind him, his stomach grumbling. Maybe the soup he had for lunch in the cafeteria didn't sit too well with him. Or was it nerves?

"Hey, Tristan." Collin stood from his desk at the far end of the room and stretched his arms high above his head.

Tristan's gaze rose from Collin's bare feet, over his jeans, to the patch of taut stomach peeking out from under a red t-shirt, then up to Collin's stunning face. He dropped his mouth open as heat rushed his cock. Stuffing his hand in his front pocket, he cleared his throat. "Uh, hey." His heart ached and his chest tightened.

Collin dropped his arms. "Done with classes yet?" He swung his arms at his sides.

"Um, yeah."

"Did you have lunch?" Collin stalked toward him.

Tristan nodded. "Uh-huh." He looked down at the floor and teased his fingers over his shaft, letting the sweet sensation soothe him.

"Shit. I was hoping we could eat together today." Collin stopped in front of him. "We should talk."

"Uh, t-talk?" He rubbed his fingers harder and squeezed the head of his erection. His breathing quickened with the pleasure filling his body.

Tensing his brows, Collin opened his mouth as if to speak, then shut again. He grabbed Tristan's bent arm, under the shoulder.

Tristan's stroking ceased. Why did Collin have to grab *that* arm? He worried his lower lip and pressed hard on his aching cock.

Collin's voice became soft, sensual. "I just wanted to make sure there wasn't anything...bad between us. I didn't quite tell you the whole story of why I'm here and I wanted to clear the air."

Tristan's gaze cut to his face. "What do you mean you didn't tell me the whole story?" His pulse quickened as his mind reeled with possibilities, none of which he could put into words.

"Please, come sit down with me." Collin tugged at his arm

and led him to his bed, then freed him, slid Tristan's backpack off his shoulder, and set it on the floor.

Tristan stood in a daze, watching Collin's movements.

Sitting at the edge of the bed, Collin patted the spot next to him. "Sit, please."

Tristan ran his fingers in circles over the tip of his cock, heightening his sensitivity, calming the butterflies swirling in his stomach. He stared at his lap. There was no way he could look at Collin, not now. "So, what is it?"

"Well, I'm not here just because my parents decided to put me in the dorms." Collin scrubbed his hand over his face.

Rocking forward, Tristan rubbed faster over the head of his cock. A pulse of pleasure rippled through him, and he shut his eyes for a moment. "And?"

A sheepish grin spread on Collin's lips. "And, well, I sort of pissed off my last roommates and they kicked me out. I couldn't find anyone else who wanted to get a place with me, so here I am, in the dorms."

Tristan let out a soft sigh. "Is that all?"

"Don't you want to know *why* they got pissed off at me?" Collin dipped his head, peeking at Tristan's face.

Twisting his head, Tristan said, "I don't know. Does it really matter?"

Collin grabbed Tristan's chin and turned his face toward him.

A sharp gasp escaped Tristan. He stared at the far wall, behind Collin. His heart hammered in his chest and he pinched his cock.

"Look at me, Tristan," Collin fixated on him.

"W-why?" Tristan took a hard swallow. He was way too close for that.

"Please, just look at me."

Tristan furrowed his brows, his stomach clenching, trembling starting up inside him. "I-I can't." He chanced a glance at him.

"Why not?" Collin's gaze searched his face.

"B-because I just can't." Tristan pursed his lips.

"Listen, you don't have to be afraid of me."

"I'm not." Tristan huffed.

"Yes, you are. Why else would you be shaking like this and looking like a fucking deer stuck in a car's headlights?" Sighing, Collin released the hold on Tristan's chin.

Tristan hung his head, his gaze darting to the floor, Collin's feet, Collin's knees. "I'm not." His voice wavered and his vision blurred. "Shit." He couldn't take much more of this. He jumped from the bed and raced to the bathroom, slamming the door behind him.

With his shoulders heaving, Tristan's his breath hitched. He slapped his hand to his mouth and bit the fleshy part of his thumb, willing the tears away. Falling back onto the door, he ripped his hand out of his jean's pocket and shoved it into the top of his jeans, beneath his silk briefs. He stroked hard over the solid flesh of his cock, thrusting his hips. He had to make it go away. The pain had to go away. Need flared in his shaft. His climax rushed to the edge.

Pounding jiggled the door and thrummed in his ears. "Tristan, please come out and talk to me." Collin's muffled voice carried through the door.

Tristan shook his head. "N-no..." He jerked his cock with his palm, his breath growing ragged.

"Tristan? Please, if you won't come out, then let me come in. Let me help you. I'm sorry, I didn't mean to scare you like that."

With a hard blink, a hot tear tumbled down his cheek. His body went rigid. His knees locked. His teeth clenched. Sharp gasps ripped from his throat. He squeezed and jerked himself. Release seared into his cock, cum spurting over his fingers, into his underwear. Sweet contractions pulsed through his body, bringing surrender, calm, euphoria. He slowed the stroking and his breathing relaxed.

"Tristan?" Collin's voice raised in pitch.

Tristan slid down the door until he sat on the linoleum floor with his knees drawn up and his eyes glazed over in a post-climax haze.

A thud reverberated on the door and shook him from his stupor. Snatching a towel from the floor, Tristan shoved it into his jeans and cleaned himself off.

"I'm coming in, damn it. You better not have done anything stupid," Collin shouted.

Another thud and the door wrenched open a crack.

Tossing the towel away, Tristan scrambled for the glass shower stall at the other end of the bathroom on his hands and knees. Quickly, he licked any remnants of lust from his palm and fingers.

The door slammed open, and Collin stood, panting in the doorway. He scanned the bathroom, then stomped to Tristan, sitting in front of the shower with his legs bent sideways in front of him.

Tristan peeked up at Collin from under a mess of his long bangs.

Collin fell to his knees in front of him, then placed a palm on Tristan's cheek. "Are you okay?" As he looked Tristan over, his brows wrinkled.

Tristan nodded, gazing at Collin, then skimmed his teeth over his lower lip.

"What the hell were you doing in here?" Collin glared at him, then swept his gaze over Tristan's body a second time.

"N-nothing."

"Nothing? For fuck sakes, I thought you might hurt yourself or something. God damn it, Tristan, what the fuck is wrong with you?" Collin's gaze hardened.

Tristan shrank inside and hugged his legs to his chest. Pain and nausea rolled inside him. Visions of his mother invaded his mind, of threats, insinuations, abuse. He shook his head and shut his eyes tightly against it. His faint voice cracked. "No, Mom. I'm okay. Really, I'm okay."

"What?" Collin crept closer to him until their knees touched, placing a hand on Tristan's shoulder. "Holy shit. Did your mother do something to you?"

Tristan shook his head, his body trembling. He released his arm from around his knee and reached down to find his pocket.

Snatching Tristan's wrist, Collin yanked it up. "No, no pocket this time. Talk to me."

He bowed his lips down and creased his brows, then fixated on Collin. "Let go of my hand."

"No." Collin tightened his hold.

Tristan's eyes pricked and his vision clouded. Emotion threatened to overwhelm him, then heat swarmed his chest. *Too much.* "Let go!" Ripping his hand free from Collin's grasp, he rammed him with the heels of both palms using all his might.

Collin flew backward and landed on his back in the doorway. He lay there for a moment, staring up at the ceiling with wide eyes.

Plunging his hand into his pocket, Tristan rubbed hard over his cock, feeling sweet sensation returning to wash it all away. Closing his eyes, he lost himself for a moment.

Groaning, Collin rose up to sitting with his legs stretched out in front of him.

Tristan opened his eyes and his gaze caught on Collin. "Collin? Oh no." He scrambled forward to sit on tucked legs at Collin's feet. "I-I'm sorry, so sorry. I didn't mean to hurt you or anything."

Collin rubbed the back of his head and looked at him. "Really? Could've fooled me." He sighed. "Fuck, dude. Do you really hate me that much already?"

"I don't hate you. Quite the opposite." Oh no, why did he say that? Gasping, he slapped his palm over his mouth. "I-I mean, I, uh, like having you as a roommate, too."

Collin lowered his brows. "Listen, I have sort of a history of pissing people off and clearly, I've pissed you off already. I tend to be pretty blunt and maybe a bit, uh, pushy. It gets me into trouble, I think."

With a nod, Tristan glanced at the door, focusing on the tease of his fingers on his erection.

"I, uh, want to get to know you for some reason." Collin let out a soft chuckle. "I think I can help you and this thing, whatever it is, that's messing with you." He shifted. "If you'll let me."

Tristan furrowed his brows and rubbed his fingers hard over his shaft, swirling the tip, sending sweet pulses to calm him. "You really want to help me?" But he was a freak, wasn't he? Could he be helped? He focused on Collin's dark eyes.

"Yes." Collin placed a hand on Tristan's knee.

Tristan swallowed hard. Could he let Collin in? Would Collin hate him if he knew his secrets? He gazed deeply into his eyes. What did he see there?

"I, um, I like you." Collin's face flushed.

Gasping, Tristan's gaze darted down to the floor. Did he really hear Collin right? He liked him? How? As a friend, yes, that must be it, just friends. He raced his fingers over his erection under his pocket. Sweet pleasure reached around him to calm his nerves.

"Did you hear what I said?" Leaning forward, Collin squeezed Tristan's knee.

"Huh?" Tristan's gaze returned to his face. "Uh, yeah, I heard it."

Collin looked around them as if searching for something, then focused on Tristan. "Can we talk now?"

"We did, didn't we?" Tristan arched a brow.

Releasing a long exhale, Collin raised his knees and wrapped his arms around them. "I mean really talk."

Tristan pressed his fingers harder on his shaft and squeezed the head of his cock. "Um, sure."

"Okay." Grunting, Collin pushed himself up and straightened.

Tristan's gaze followed him.

Stretching a hand down, Collin wiggled his fingers. "Come on."

With a hard swallow, he took Collin's hand and allowed him to pull him up from the floor and lead him to Collin's bed.

Collin sat on the edge.

Sitting beside him, Tristan tried to pull his hand away, but Collin tightened his hold.

"Does that make you nervous?" Collin eyed him.

"What?" Tristan lifted his brows.

"Holding my hand?" Collin held their entwined hands up between them.

Tristan's heart pounded and he squeezed his cock from inside his pocket, sending a ripple of sensation through his body. How did he feel about this? "I-I don't know."

"I just thought it might help you to talk to me, you know?" Collin brushed over Tristan's forearm with his free hand, caressing it. His gaze followed the movement of his fingers over Tristan's arm. "I read in one of my psych books that physical contact like this can really help people open up, sort of lessen their anxiety about it," he said, his head tilting.

A deep ache flooded his heart. Collin's touch enflamed his desire. He yearned to kiss him, ravish him, make love to him. But how would he even do that? He was still a virgin. He circled his lips with his tongue and his breath quickened. "Wh-what do you want to talk about?"

Tensing his brows, Collin focused on his face. "How about we start with what it was like for you growing up."

"Growing up?" Tristan fell into a daze, letting his fingers dance over his erection, keeping the nightmares of his childhood from devouring him. Delicious pleasure burst forth, making his sensitivity heighten.

"Tell me about it, your family and stuff," Collin narrowed his eyes.

"Um, well, I never knew my father. My mom said he died when I was born, but never said how." Tristan's throat went dry, and he swallowed.

Collin gave him a single nod. "Go on."

"I don't have any brothers or sisters. It was only me and my mom. My mom worked a lot and, well, she drank a lot." Pain threatened to take control of his emotions. A shrill voice rose up in his mind. *You're a fucking freak, Tristan! A good-for-nothing freak just like your father!* He squeezed Collin's hand and quickened his fingers over his aching cock. The threat of release teased and soothed.

"It's okay. Did she hurt you? I mean, physically?" Collin leaned forward.

Tristan shrugged. "I suppose so. She hit me once with a frying pan."

With a gasp, Collin said, "Shit, where?"

Tristan's gaze locked on Collin's, and he pulled his hand out of his pocket to point at the back of his head. "Right here."

Still grasping his hand, Collin reached up with his free hand and placed his palm on Tristan's head, then rubbed up and down. "You got a lump there. Damn, is that from when she hit you?"

With a nod, Tristan said, "She gave me a concussion and I was in the hospital for a while. But I'm okay now."

Collin fixated on him, his brows knitting, his lips parting. "Didn't anyone call child protective services?"

Shifting his gaze to his lap, Tristan let his hair fall over his face. "It was my fault. I deserved it. What I did was, was not right. I-I told them I fell."

Collin wrapped his arm around Tristan's shoulders and drew him into his chest

With Tristan's heart fluttering, a wave of nausea twisted in his gut. He plunged his hand into his pocket and squeezed hard on his softened cock, letting pleasure sear through him. Need surged to the surface to comfort him.

Placing his forehead on the side of Tristan's head, Collin said, "There is absolutely nothing you could have done that would warrant your mother hitting you with a frying pan. Nothing."

Tristan lifted his brows. "Not even jerking off in front of other boys?" *Did I say that out loud?* "Oh, shit." His heart raced and he fought to catch his breath. Glancing up at Collin, he ripped free from his grasp, then jumped up and ran toward the door. "I'm sorry. I shouldn't have said that."

"Tristan!" Collin raced him to the door and flung his arms around him from behind.

Tristan clawed at the doorknob.

Seizing Tristan's hands, Collin jerked them up to Tristan's chest.

He thrashed in Collin's hold. "Let me go. I can't talk about this anymore."

"Shh, it's okay." Collin tightened his hold and twisted him around, pinning Tristan's arms between them.

Their gazes locked.

A shiver raced down Tristan's spine, his heart beating out of control. *Oh God, I'm in Collin's arms. Collin's!* His cock ached and swelled to an unbearable level. His body shook, knocking his knees together. He heaved in deep breaths of air and squirmed.

"Tristan, relax, please. Don't fight me." Collin leaned in, his face coming close until their noses almost touched. His gaze dropped to Tristan's trembling lips. "It's okay, it's...um..." Diving forward, Collin claimed his mouth in a desperate kiss.

Stumbling back, Tristan took Collin with him until they hit the door.

Collin pressed his body flush against Tristan's, his mouth planted on Tristan's, parting his lips with his tongue, deepening the kiss.

Letting out an urgent moan, Tristan's passion released, focused on Collin's mouth, on the sweet taste of the one he loved. Heat shuddered over his skin and his knees buckled.

A groan of pleasure rippled from Collin's mouth as he licked at Tristan's lips and sucked on his tongue. He thrust his hips, grinding his cock on Tristan's erection through their jeans.

Delicious pressure and friction sparked into his hard cock. Sensitivity burst forward, tightening his sac, bringing on the peak of urgency. He thrust once against Collin and climaxed, hot wetness coating the inside of his briefs, crying out as each violent contraction sent pleasure screaming through his body.

Drawing away, Collin furrowed his brows and looked him up and down.

Tristan shuddered as the last of his release pulsed through him. As the haze of climax lifted, his pulse skittered. *Oh no, what just happened? What fucking happened?* His eyes grew wide.

"Dude, did you just do what I think you did?" Collin cocked his head.

Biting his lower lip, Tristan twisted his head to stare at the wall next to him. He had to get away. Now. His vision blurred and his chest heated. In a snarl, he said, "Let me go, Collin."

Raising his arms up, Collin took a few steps back.

Tristan whirled around, snatched the doorknob, twisted it, and flung the door open. He tore down the hallway as his emotions raged a war inside his body.

He flew down set after set of stairs, tossed a glass door open and dashed across lawn and pavement, passed trees and students into stucco shops and offices with curved archways.

Air burned inside his lungs with each breath. His legs ached and sweat broke out over his skin. He had to stop. He searched for a safe place. An alley, dark and filled with trash, came into view in the early evening light.

Perfect. He ran into the alley and slowed to a fast walk, then paced back and forth, from brick wall to brick wall with his hands planted on his hips, panting. He tensed his face. How the hell did that happen? Why did he let himself get so out of control? He shouldn't have told Collin that. Not that. Not about what he did. Not about what he still does, even now.

His breath hitched. *He hates me now, doesn't he?* There's no way Collin would ever look at him or talk to him again. A lump formed in his throat and his eyes stung. He looked down at a rusty can floating in a pothole puddle in front of him. With a growl, he lunged forward and kicked it.

The can flung against the wall. A loud ting rang through the alley as the can hit and ricocheted into a mound of open garbage bags and stink. Flies scattered.

He blinked. A hot tear tumbled down his cheek. Furrowing his brows, pain ate away at his heart, ravaging him from the inside out. He clenched his teeth and plunged his hand into his pocket. Wetness soaked through the inside to smear his fingers.

He rubbed hard on his cock, bringing his hand in and out of his pocket, in a desperate attempt to lose himself in sensation. The lump in his throat grew. Fresh tears filled his eyes. A sob caught in his chest. *Help me, please, someone help me.*

Dropping to his knees, he fell forward onto one outstretched palm. His breath became jagged, forcing his shoulders to shake. His body trembled and jerked. His arm buckled and down he went, head first, to the pavement.

A smack filled the air as his forehead hit and his body went limp, his chest resting on his thighs. As the ache in his chest overwhelmed him, he wept.

CHAPTER FOUR

WEDNESDAY, NOVEMBER 5

P ressure poked at his ribs, rocking his body back and forth. "Hey, you there. Get up," a rough male voice said.

Tristan fluttered his eyes open and rolled to his back, then tried to focus. Sunshine blinded him. He clenched his eyes shut and brought his hand up to shield his face. Where was he? What time was it? Oh no, Collin. His mind flooded with the memory of the kiss and his sudden climax. *Collin kissed me... Why?* Heat flooded into his cheeks.

"I said get up," the voice said.

Tristan looked up.

The clear outline of a policeman stood over him.

Sharp pain thumped in Tristan's forehead. He gasped and rolled to his side, bringing his knees up to his chest. "Oh, shit."

"Have a little too much to drink last night?" The policeman shifted his stance. A voice squawked commands from a tiny receiver on his shoulder.

"Um, yeah." It was as good an explanation as any. Tristan fingered his forehead. Crust covered a tender lump just under his hairline.

The policeman crouched beside him. Patches of salt-and-pepper hair peeked out from under his hat. His light blue eyes peered at him. "Let me see your head, kid."

Tristan let his arm fall to his side.

The policeman parted Tristan's long bangs and studied Tristan's wound. "Not too bad, just a bump on the head." He drew his hand away and blew out a long exhale. "You were lucky I found you. You did a really stupid thing, passing out in an alley all night like that. You could have been killed."

With a nod, Tristan said, "I'm sorry." All night?

"Yeah, well, take this as a lesson and don't do it again. Watch your drinking." The policeman stood up straight. "Go home, kid. If I find you out here again, I'll haul your ass off to the drunk tank. Got it?"

"Yes, sir." Tristan's head pounded as he climbed up to standing. He swiped his hands over his shirt and jeans, brushing off dirt and debris, then glanced at the policeman, standing with his hands on his belt. "Um, what time is it?"

A soft chuckle rumbled in the policeman's chest. "About eight AM."

Tristan nodded. "Oh, thanks." That gave him an hour to get to class.

———

AN HOUR LATER, Tristan hurried across the lawn, passing neat rows of blue-globed agapanthus flowers, to the squat brick building housing his sociology class, raking his fingers through wet, disheveled hair, a last-minute attempt at getting the rest of the snarls out of it. Thank God Collin wasn't in their dorm room when he'd gotten home. How the hell was he going to face him in class? Maybe he'd just sit on the other side of the room today.

His stomach grumbled as he walked, hunger gnawing in his gut. Too bad he hadn't had time for breakfast. Well, at least he'd been able to take a quick shower and change into a new pair of jeans and t-shirt.

He stopped at the door to his classroom and tugged the handle. The heavy, metal door opened, and he stepped inside.

With his heart hammering in his chest, he scanned the crowd of students chatting and sitting at desks. Was Collin here? He hung his head. *Everyone's staring at me.* He strode to a desk in the back and slipped into the chair behind it, dropping his backpack behind him, then unzipped the pack and fumbled through it for his pen and notebook. Silver necklaces swayed over the dragon design on his dark t-shirt. Glancing up, he brought the things to his desk.

Collin stepped through the doorway, talking with a pretty blonde. His khaki cargo pants stopped just below the knee and a white polo shirt pulled tight across his shoulders.

Tristan's pulse kicked up. *He kissed me and I fucked up.* He wrinkled his brows and gnawed his lower lip, focusing on his notebook. He clenched and unclenched his fists in his lap. *Please don't look over here.*

"Tristan." Collin's voice was soft.

He stared at his desk.

Collin crouched down beside him and peered up at his face. "What happened to you? You look like shit."

Twisting his head, Tristan stole a peek at him, then came back.

"Holy shit, dude, what happened to your head?" Collin placed his hand on the denim covering Tristan's knee.

A soft gasp whispered from Tristan and his body tensed as Collin's touch shivered through him. "Leave me alone, okay? I-I can't talk right now."

The professor entered the room and set a folder of papers on a podium at the front of the class. His voice rang out in the room.

"Okay. But we *will* talk later." Collin rose and slid into a seat at a desk a few rows ahead of him.

Tristan frowned. Talk later? What did that mean? He couldn't take much more. He opened his notebook and tried to pay attention to the professor, but his gaze kept floating to the back of Collin's auburn head and heat rushed his groin, his cock swelling and aching. The urge to touch himself heightened inside him, a persistent itch screaming to be scratched. He dropped his hand into his lap. The heat and slight pressure made his hard shaft jerk and pulse. *No. Focus on the lecture for once.*

As the professor droned on, an inner battle waged between his head and hand. He brushed his fingers over the fabric of his jeans, bringing a tickle to his shaft. He let them skim up to the head and press down. A sweet wave of pleasure rippled through him. He closed his eyes while he lost himself in the sensation. *Stop.*

He crept his fingers to the side and caressed the seam of his pocket as if waiting for the right time to strike. The ache in his groin filled his senses and his breathing quickened. *Don't do it. Don't think about it.*

He raked his teeth over his lower lip as he dipped his fingers into his pocket. They rested over hard flesh and waited, heat and need flooding his body. *Okay, just a little. No one will see. No one will know.*

Leaning to the side, he dug his hand in deep under his tightened sac and rubbed up hard. Intense pleasure washed over him, numbed his fears, his shame, his self-loathing. His jaw grew slack, and his vision glazed over. He did it again, down and up, stroking harder through the thin fabric. Sensitivity rushed to the surface, feeding his hunger, his craving.

The classroom vanished. He stood with his back up against the door and Collin's hard body pressed solidly against his chest and hips. Collin sucked and licked at him in heated kisses. Urgency filled his body. He needed to thrust and moan, but he held still, swirling and teasing the head of his cock. Tiny pulses rocked through him. This was where he wanted to be. Nothing else mattered.

"That's it for today. I'll see you all on Friday." The professor slapped his book shut and walked from the podium.

All around the class, students rose and put their things away in packs, hushed voices swelling to fill the air.

Tristan teetered at the sweet edge of release and tugged his hand out of his pocket to toss his notebook and pen into his backpack and zip it.

"Hey, you got another class now?" Collin stood, looking down on him with his arms crossed on his chest, his brows creasing.

"Uh, I have an art class in a couple of hours." Tristan straightened, swung his pack over his shoulder and shoved his hand into his pocket, letting his fingers squeeze and play along his shaft.

Collin's gaze rested on his forehead he and lifted his hand toward Tristan's head.

Ducking away, Tristan said, "Don't."

Collin focused on Tristan's hand-filled pocket. His voice became soft, gentle. "I want to talk to you. We need to talk about what happened, but I'm supposed to meet with Jessica, my advisor, to go over my psychology thesis. Promise me you'll come back to our room after your art class." His gaze shifted to meet with Tristan's.

With his heart hammering, an ache flooded Tristan's chest. He pressed harder on his erection, attempting to numb all the feeling inside him. "Okay, I promise." He dipped his head.

"What time is it over?" Collin asked.

Tristan's attention drew to him. "Three."

"I'll be expecting you no later than three-fifteen then. Got it?" A thin-lipped smile spread over Collin's mouth.

"Yeah." Tristan dropped his gaze to the floor between them.

Turning, Collin jogged toward the exit door.

Tristan thrummed his fingers over his shaft, releasing the tension coiled up in his groin. He needed this. And he needed some food.

39

AFTER EATING LUNCH, Tristan stepped into his dorm room, shut the door and rubbed his belly with his free hand. The cafeteria meatloaf was good today, satisfying. He strolled to his bedside and let his backpack slide off his shoulder to the floor, taking a quick glance at his bed. When would Collin return?

He thought a moment, letting his fingers play over his erection through the pocket lining. Did he have time? Surely Collin wouldn't be back before one if he couldn't talk before art class. And what if something happened between them again?

With a shiver at the thought of Collin's body pressed up against his, he gave the head of his erection a quick squeeze. A low moan floated out from his throat as his shaft pulsed with urgency. He pressed harder, faster, heightening the sweet need to a new level. He had time and he had to be ready if something did happen between them. He couldn't look Collin in the eye if he lost control again.

Quickly, he unfastened his belt and jeans and dropped them to the floor, then stepped out of them, tossed his covers aside and crawled between baby blue sheets. This time he'd be ready if Collin decided to come back early. At least he would be covered.

Laying back on his pillow, he pushed long strokes over his brief-bound cock with his palm, all the way down under his sac and back up to the tip. The friction was exquisite, just enough to tease and make him yearn for more.

He thrust his hips in time with his palm, sliding up and down, over and over. His sensitivity heightened to a raw edge. He stroked quicker, harder, squeezing and swirling the tip and let out long, soft moans as his need built. Release came rushing forward, but he ceased all motion and kept perfectly still, letting the feeling pass.

Then, he shucked his briefs down his thighs, freeing his weeping cock. Bringing his palm over his shaft, he ran his thumb over the tip, swirling a bead of pre-cum over the head. A delicious pulse raced through his body. Gasping, he arched his back, then whimpered, "Collin..."

Visions of Collin flooded his mind, and he was once again pinned against the door with Collin's taste in his mouth, Collin's cock pressed against his, grinding over his groin. He jerked over his shaft and the head of his erection. The sensitivity in his groin heightened to a delicious peak. His sac tightened and his toes curled, teeth clenching. Crying out, his climax erupted out of him, washing waves of pleasure through his body, painting ribbons of cum onto his stomach and into the sheets with each sweet contraction.

The pleasure dulled and he slowed his hand to a stop. He lay panting with his eyes closed and his mind in a satiated daze for a few moments.

Collin. What would he say to Collin later? He flashed his eyes open and flung the sheets off him. As he brought his hand to his lips to lick globs of lust from his palm and fingers, he tensed his brows. His chest tightened as he lapped at his hand. Would Collin make him admit what really happened? Would Collin see what a freak he really was? Oh no, he couldn't tell him. He couldn't find out. *And why did he kiss me?*

He snuck his hand back down, swiped cum off his stomach, and brought it back up to his eager tongue once again. What would Collin's taste like? He closed his eyes, imagining the taste in his mouth was from Collin.

Tingling knotted in his groin. *Stop it.* He had to calm himself and not get worked up again. With a sigh, he skimmed his briefs back up and climbed off his bed. His gaze landed on the clock above the window. Almost one, he had ten minutes to get to art class. If he could only keep his mind on drawing, he'd be fine.

CHAPTER FIVE

A fter his art class, Tristan made his way across campus, hanging his head. It was near impossible to sit and draw without a hand in his pocket, but he'd done it. A frown swept over his lips. Would Collin really be waiting for him back in their room? His heartbeat grew faster. He planted his fingertips at the entrance to his pocket. No. He couldn't do this now. He had to talk to Collin first.

Tristan trudged through the doors to the dorm, through the common area, and stepped into the elevator with his pulse quickening. Why did Collin kiss him? What the hell was going on between them? The elevator doors opened, and he made his way down the familiar hallway. The musty smell surrounded him.

"Hey." Another student walked by him.

Clenching his jaw, Tristan focused on the gray carpet covering the floor. He stomped to his door and inserted the key.

The door swung open. "Hey, Tristan." Collin's raised arm hung on the edge of the door jamb, and he stepped sideways, waving him into the room.

He glanced up at Collin's stunning face, racing his hand to his pocket entrance, then stopped, hovering, fingers twitching for a moment. He dropped the hand to his side. Walking into the room, his nerves took on a raw edge as he strode to the other end and set his backpack down on his desk.

Collin stepped up behind him and placed Tristan's key on the desk and his hand on Tristan's shoulder. "I was worried you wouldn't come back like you promised."

Fisting his hands, he fixated on his desk. In a soft voice, he said, "I live here, remember?"

Collin let his arm fall to his side. "Yeah. You seem really pissed at me."

Blinking hard, Tristan fought to calm his rolling stomach. "No, I'm not. I'm just—"

"Do you like me, Tristan? I mean, at all?" Collin's voice wavered.

Tristan shook and he clenched his eyes shut for a second. *I should turn around. I should face him right now.*

"Well?"

In a whisper, Tristan said, "Please don't ask me things like that. You know I do." Biting his lower lip, he held his breath.

"Turn around and look at me then." Collin tugged on Tristan's shoulder, turning Tristan to face him.

Tristan focused on the white shirt covering Collin's chest and drew a deep inhale, then forced his gaze up to Collin's and dropped it again, clenching his teeth.

"I'm sorry I kissed you. I suppose I shouldn't have done that." Collin squeezed his shoulder, his brows wrinkling.

Pain pierced Tristan's chest. He locked his gaze to Collin's. What had he meant by that? "No, don't be sorry. I-I liked it." His heart beat a frantic rhythm in his chest.

Collin tensed his face. "Then why did you run away like that?"

"Because I was scared and um, embarrassed." Gasping, he brought a hand up to cover his open mouth. Why was he admitting to all this?

"It's okay. You can talk to me. I don't want you to be scared."

Collin wrapped his arms around Tristan's shoulders and drew him into his chest.

Tristan closed his eyes, savoring the gentle embrace. He raised his arms, hesitated, then surrounded Collin's waist. Words, thoughts, and visions scrambled in his mind. His legs twitched as if preparing for flight.

"See, I'm not that scary after all, am I?" Collin brushed his hand up and down Tristan's back.

Tristan's voice cracked. "N-no." He cleared his throat.

"So, I guess you did, uh, come when I kissed you?"

Adrenaline came at him from all sides. *Get out of here. Don't say a word.* He shoved at Collin's hips.

Collin tightened his hold, imprisoning him in his arms. "Relax, don't run off on me again."

Shaking, Tristan shoved a hand into his pocket to fondle his cock. There was no other way.

"Take your hand out of your pocket." Collin gently tugged at Tristan's wrist.

Clenching his jaw, Tristan said, "I can't. You don't understand. I need this. I have to—"

"You masturbate to soothe yourself. I know. It's like a baby with a pacifier."

Tristan gasped. "What?" He pulled away and his gaze darted over Collin's face.

Seizing Tristan's shoulders, Collin held him steadily in front of him. "You heard me. Do you really want me to say it again?"

"I...no." He furrowed his brows and rested his fingers on the erection, now aching just under his pocket lining, and swallowed hard.

"Let me help you." Collin grasped Tristan's wrist once again, and gently pulled his hand out of the pocket of Tristan's jeans.

Tristan hung his head and shut his eyes, shaking as his pulse quivered in his chest.

"Have you ever been with anybody?" Collin dropped his head to peer into his face.

Shaking his head, Tristan mumbled, "No."

Pursing his lips, Collin shifted his stance and studied him. "Would you like to be?"

Lifting his head, he gazed deeply into Collin's stunning, brown eyes. "Yes."

Collin's gaze softened. "I wouldn't mind being with you."

An unbearable ache grew in his chest, in his gut. Did he really hear him right? "Why?" His eyes pricked and his lip trembled. He breathed in deeply, attempting to calm himself.

"Tristan, please, don't cry." Collin rested his palm on Tristan's cheek.

Looking away, Tristan bit the side of his lower lip. "I'm not."

Leaning close, Collin kissed his eyes, one after the other. "It's like I've been saying all along. I like you. I'm...I don't know, enthralled by you."

"But why me?" His gaze flickered back to meet Collin's, holding his arms down stiff at his sides. He had to find a way to look at him, to listen to him, without losing his mind.

With a shrug, Collin said, "Why not?" His gaze roamed over Tristan's face, his hair, his chest. "You're a really good-looking guy and quite frankly, you turn me on. Obviously, you like guys, right?"

Tristan nodded and knitted his brows. "I've always liked guys, but I thought that was wrong."

"Depends on who you talk to." Collin released him and grasped his hand. "Come lay down with me and we'll talk."

A shiver played over Tristan's spine. "Lay down? With you?"

Collin offered a soft smirk. "I won't bite, and I promise not to do anything. Well, unless you want me to."

Puffing out long exhale, Tristan gathered his courage. "Okay." He let Collin guide him to his bed.

Collin climbed up and laid on his side, making room for Tristan, then patted the empty space in front of him. "Come on."

Tristan hesitated, then climbed up on the bed to lie on his

back beside him, his gaze wandering up to Collin's gorgeous face, so close to his own.

"Is it okay if I touch you?" Collin smiled, a wide, lazy smile. "I mean, more than I have already?"

Nodding, Tristan focused on Collin's face. "Yes."

Collin rested his palm on Tristan's stomach.

He let out a soft gasp as heat rushed his groin. Desire flooded through his senses and stunned him for a heartbeat, his cock hardening.

Trailing his hand over Tristan's stomach in a swirling motion, Collin's gaze remained fixed on Tristan's eyes. "Tell me why you think you touch yourself all the time."

Tristan squirmed, heat tingling up his neck. Collin's touch felt good, soothing in an altogether different way. "Do I have to talk about that?" A soft huskiness filled his voice.

With his breath quickening, Collin said, "I'd like you to. It's supposed to help you get over it. If you talk about it." Collin dropped his gaze to Tristan's mouth and skimmed his tongue over his own lips.

"I...I don't know. I just always have, even though the damned Mormon Church forbids it." The yearning for his obsession scurried forward. He couldn't even talk about it without wanting to do it. He snuck his fingers into his pocket and rested them over his erection.

Collin glanced toward Tristan's hand. "It's okay. I don't mind." He fixated on Tristan's movements in his pocket. "They forbid masturbation?" He chuckled. "That's ridiculous."

Squeezing the head of his cock, pleasure rippled through Tristan. With Collin's hand on him and his own teasing his shaft, his senses reeled. A soft moan escaped his lips.

Reaching up higher, Collin brushed over Tristan's nipple and circling it through the thin fabric of his t-shirt.

Tristan's body jerked as pleasure pounded forward, heightening his sensitivity to the brink of release. "S-stop, Collin. Stop touching me."

Lifting his hand, Collin said, "Are you okay?"

Tristan dropped his mouth open and darted his gaze over the area around the bed, the wall, the ceiling. What should he do? Should he run again?

Rolling over on top of Tristan, Collin held him down and wrapped a bent leg over Tristan's waist. He pressed his cheek against Tristan's. Hard flesh under his jeans pushed against Tristan's hip. "You look like a cornered animal. Relax, you're safe with me. I promise."

Tristan willed his heart to settle, his hand to remain motionless, his body to keep from climaxing right this instant. The heaviness of his breath raised and lowered Collin over his chest. "Wh-what's the matter with me, Collin?"

Collin propped up on an elbow and looked down on him. "I suspect you've been abused, not just with a frying pan." A faint grin hovered on his lips. "Can you tell me more about your mother?"

"What, now?" Tristan's cock ached with need. Anything could set him off right now, anything. He stilled and focused on breathing.

"Well, what do you want to do?" Collin lowered his brows. "Maybe it would help if we got rid of some of your tension." He dipped his head, placing heated kisses on Tristan's mouth, sliding his tongue along the seam of his lips, parting them.

With a low moan, Tristan rocked his hips against Collin.

Collin yanked Tristan's hand out of his pocket and stuffed his own hand down Tristan's jeans and into his briefs. He stroked hard over his erection with his palm, circling the head, again and again.

Tristan bucked and fought to keep his mouth pressed to Collin's, their tongues tangling. Surrendering, he hooked his arms around Collin and broke the needy kisses. "Oh, shit." Intense tingling and humming filled his cock. His peak hit with brutal force, delicious spasms rocking his body as cum erupted into Collin's palm and fingers, his body shuddering with each pulse.

Collin stayed on him, kissing and nipping at his neck, until it all slowed. Panting, he lifted his head and gazed at Tristan with blown pupils and hooded eyelids. "Feel better?"

Seizing Collin, Tristan yanked him down on top of him, and plunged his face into his neck. "Damn it, why did you do that?"

Collin placed a kiss on the side of his head. "Because you needed it. There was no way you were going to lay on this bed with me, playing with yourself, and be able to talk to me unless you came. And so, I made you." He swiped the top of his sheets with his hand, cleaning it.

"So you think you can just do that to me whenever you want?" His voice quivered. He tightened his desperate hold on Collin as if letting go would make the world crash down on him. How he'd wanted Collin to do that, fantasized about it even, but he wasn't ready.

Collin rocked his hips, his hard cock pressing against his pelvis. "You can do that to me."

A jolt shook him from his thoughts. *Should I?* Craving rose inside him as if he'd never been satiated. As his heart beat a frantic rhythm, he stared at the ceiling, unable to move.

"Tristan?" Collin made to lift up, but Tristan held him down. "Are you crying again?"

"No, I wasn't crying before either." Tristan huffed.

Collin skimmed his hands over the top of Tristan's head. "It's okay. If you don't want to do it, that's okay, too."

"That's not it. I just...I've never done anything like this." Tristan raked his teeth over his lower lip. *And when I did do anything remotely close to this, it didn't end well.*

"Let me up for a minute and promise me you won't bolt on me." Collin squirmed in his hold.

Tristan released him.

Raising himself on both elbows, Collin shifted to lay his whole body over Tristan's, chest to chest, hip to hip.

Tristan darted his gaze around the room, taking in the wall, the ceiling, then back to the wall.

"Look at me for once." Collin brushed his knuckles over Tristan's cheek. "You remind me of a frightened rabbit or something."

Heat filled Tristan's chest and he glared at him. "I am not a frightened rabbit."

Letting out a soft chuckle, Collin planted a quick kiss on his lips. "Sure. You know, you really did a number on me."

"What do you mean?" Tristan arched a brow, peeking at him.

"I'm so fucking hard right now I could come any second." Closing his eyes, Collin thrust his hips, pressing his solid dick to Tristan. "Damn..."

Tristan's cock swelled against Collin's. "Y-you mean I really do turn you on?"

"Fuck yeah." Collin continued rocking his hips, then he worked his hand down to cup Tristan's ass and urged their hips tighter together. His breath grew ragged.

Tristan's brows tensed as sweet sensation returned to his hardening cock. Maybe he *could* jerk him off. Maybe he was ready for it, for all of it. He looked up at Collin, gazing back down at him with darkened eyes. In one swift move, he seized the back of Collin's head and pulled, crushing their lips together. He opened his mouth and thrust his tongue between Collin's lips, probing and penetrating him the only way he knew how.

Collin thrust harder, faster, against Tristan, meeting his intensity. He caressed and kneaded Tristan's flesh through his shirt, groaning. In a raspy voice, he said, "Do it, Tristan."

Tristan snuck his hand downward.

Tilting his hips to the side, Collin let him go at his belt and jeans.

With trembling fingers, Tristan unbuckled Collin's belt and unfastened his jeans. He plunged his hand into the depth of Collin's groin, between cloth and soft skin, to grasp his seeping cock.

Collin let out a sharp gasp and gave his hips a hard thrust.

As Collin's erection pushed through Tristan's palm, it

twitched. Tristan tightened his hold and stroked him the way he'd stroked himself, so many times before. Release wound tight in his groin, his dick aching. The impossible was happening, here, now. He lost himself in the sensation of Collin rocking against him, of his tongue exploring Collin's mouth, of Collin's cock in his palm.

"Shit. Faster, Tristan." Collin clutched at the pillow on either side of Tristan's head, and he clenched his teeth, his body growing rigid, deep moans spilling out of him. "Oh, fuck."

Tristan jerked his hand over Collin. As Collin's cock pulsated in his palm, hot wetness erupted over his palm and fingers. His heart fluttered as he watched Collin's orgasm and his second climax rushed to the sweet brink.

Panting, Collin slowed and relaxed over his body.

Tristan rutted his aching cock against Collin's hips, willing him to keep moving, keep the intensity of the moment from waning. He was so close again. It couldn't be over, not now. "C-Collin, please."

Collin lifted his head and peered at him. "Again?"

Nodding, his breath came in ragged bursts. If only Collin would touch him, would kiss him, now. "Please?"

With furrowed brows, Collin said, "Yeah, sure." He dipped his hand back into Tristan's briefs and wrapped his fingers around his stiff cock, fixating on him.

He jerked his hips up, forcing his shaft through Collin's fist. As he closed his eyes, he released a throaty moan and lost himself in Collin's touch.

Collin watched, wide-eyed, while he pumped Tristan's cock. After licking his lips, he dropped down and pressed a heated kisses on Tristan's mouth.

Tristan slanted his mouth against Collin's taking him again and again. Pleasure heightened to a sharp edge. He clung to Collin as a second peak rocketed through him, bringing intense waves of sensation, releasing the need coiled inside him. A shiver pulsed his body as it slowed, and he opened his eyes.

Collin studied him.

Warmth swept up his neck and he flicked his gaze to the ceiling once again. "Don't look at me like that."

"Like what?"

"Like I'm some kind of freak!" His heart jolted and he thrashed in Collin's hold, trying to free himself for escape. "Let me go."

Pinning Tristan's arms above his head, Collin stayed on him, throwing his body weight over him. "Stop fighting me, damn it."

"Let go!" He squirmed and wriggled his arms.

"Stop it!" Collin's voice thundered in the room.

Wide eyed and panting, Tristan ceased all motion and stared up at him.

"Stop trying to run from me. I don't think you're a freak. When are you going to get that through your head? God damn it, Tristan, I like you and I want to help you." Collin's gaze searched his face.

Tristan gulped hard. "No one's ever wanted to help me. No one's ever even liked me. Why should I believe you? Why should I—"

"Because I'm here and I'm not letting you go." Collin tensed his brows. "Let me, please."

"But why?" His voice cracked. His eyes stung and his vision clouded. "I'm not n-normal. I'm, I'm a f-freak..." A hot tear rolled down the side of his face.

"I don't know where the hell you got that idea, maybe that stupid church, but you are not a freak. You might be a little messed up, but definitely not a freak. There are far worse things than what you've been doing, believe me." Collin looked far away for a second, then focused back on Tristan.

He snuck his lip between his teeth and sniffled. "Collin?"

"What?"

"I'm scared." Tristan's breath caught. Was it possible Collin was for real right now?

Collin released Tristan's hands and brushed his knuckles over

Tristan's cheek, wiping the trace of the tear away. "Why are you so scared of me?"

With Tristan's gaze shifting to the wall and coming back again, he whispered, "I've thought about being with you for a long time."

"You have?" A faint grin played over Collin's lips, then waned. "Tel me more. How long have you thought about me?"

Tristan tilted his head and focused on the wall. How could he tell him the truth? "Uh, I don't know."

Collin shifted to put himself in his view. "Talk to me. Answer my question."

"Well, ever since I first saw you in sociology, I guess." Tristan clenched his eyes shut. Would Collin do something mean now? But why would he do that? His heart pounded in his chest, and he opened one eye, peeking at Collin.

Collin's eyes grew wide. "Really?"

Opening both eyes, Tristan nodded.

"So you, like, have a crush on me?" A full-on grin crept over Collin's mouth.

Tristan squirmed and twisted his head the other way, shifting his gaze to the center of the dorm room. In a faint voice, he said, "Yes."

"What? Look at me." Collin grabbed Tristan's chin and brought him back. "What did you just say?"

"I didn't say anything." He knitted his brows as his chest tightened. How could he possibly admit his feelings and look him straight in the eye at the same time?

"Tell me, please. It's okay, it really is. I want you to be comfortable with me. And I think the only way that can happen is if we get these sorts of things out in the open." Collin gazed deeply into his eyes.

"I-I this is too much for me. I can't talk to you about this right now. It's too much." Trembling started up inside him and his pulse quickened.

"But you do, don't you. I'll admit it. I noticed you in class." A wide smile played on Collin's lips. "I always thought you were, I don't know, hot." He let out a soft chuckle.

Tristan's breath snagged and his gaze searched Collin's face. Could he really believe what was happening? Could he really believe what Collin said? "You did?"

"Yeah. I can't tell you how fucking surprised I was to find out you were my roommate. Holy shit, dude." Collin's smile faded. "Bet you're surprised I'm not straight, huh?"

Tristan nodded, his heart blooming with warmth. He had absolutely nothing to say to that.

"Well, I'm not totally gay." Collin traced circles on Tristan's shoulder. "I like to think of it in terms of not having a gender preference. I like people for who they are, not their gender, get it?"

Tristan nodded again, his eyes widening and his mouth growing slack. How was this real right now?

"My mom is actually, well, she lives with another woman." Collin shook his head once as if affirming his statement. "Yeah, she married my dad and they lived together for years, even had two other children besides me. I have an older sister and a younger one. But they got divorced a few years ago and then my mom just took up with this lesbian woman."

He chewed his lower lip a moment, thinking. "S-so your mom, does she know that you, um, that you're like that?"

Collin shrugged and shifted his gaze to his fingers, still running absent patterns over Tristan's shoulder. "Sure. It's no big deal. I guess I'm like her in a way. We understand each other and we're actually pretty close."

"And what does your dad think about all this?" Tristan's chest relaxed and his heartbeat calmed. Could it really be that having feelings for the same sex wasn't such a twisted thing after all?

"Well, of course he was pissed off when my mom left him. But he told me once that it was much easier knowing she was with a woman than with another man." Collin lifted the edge of his mouth.

"But does he know about you?" Tristan watched him.

Collin looked deeply into his eyes. "Yes, he knows about me and it's not a big deal. He seemed, I don't know, a little weird about it at first, but he's okay with it now. I'm not always with guys though. I've had girlfriends, too."

"You have?" His heart pricked, then his breath caught. He didn't want to think about him being with anyone else. It was painful.

"Yes. Does that bother you?" Collin eyed him.

Tristan slowly shook his head. He couldn't admit to that.

"Then why the hurt look on your face?" Collin planted a quick kiss on his lips.

Tristan glanced away, then focused on him. "I guess it does sort of bother me." What *were* these feelings he was having?

"Why?" Collin wrinkled his forehead, and caressed Tristan's shoulder.

"It hurts to think about you being with anyone else." He freed a soft gasp. Did he really just say that?

Collin skimmed his index finger over Tristan's lips, then kissed him. "Well, I'm not with anyone else now, am I?"

Heat swept up Tristan's neck. "No." He was so not used to talking about things like this. How was he supposed to be okay with it?

"Then let's get cleaned up. I want to hear more about you." Collin tapped Tristan's nose with his finger.

CHAPTER SIX

C ollin stepped out of the bathroom, rubbing his damp hair with a towel, his bare chest gleaming in the glow of the overhead dome light and his gray sweatpants hanging low on his hips, showing the band of his boxers and a generous bulge.

Turning around in the chair at his desk, Tristan took a hard swallow. Would he ever get used to having Collin this close? He ran his fingers through the ends of his damp hair and crossed his arms over the dark fabric of his shirt.

"So. Now that we're all cleaned up, you want to grab some dinner in the cafeteria?" Collin walked toward him with a wide smile on his face.

"Um, sure." Tristan bent down, unzipped his backpack, and fished through it for his leather wallet. Warmth rested on his neck.

"You can tell me more about yourself while we're eating. I want to know everything about you." Collin squeezed his neck.

Tristan straightened with his wallet clutched between his thumb and fingers, then lifted his gaze to Collin's face. "I don't know if I can tell you what you want to know while we're eating."

Nodding once, Collin said, "Well, tell me whatever you want then." He walked away, grabbed a white t-shirt from his bed and slid it over his head and torso. "Ready?" He focused on Tristan.

"Yeah." Tristan stood up and strolled toward the door. As he passed Collin, a firm hand wrapped around his arm. His breath stopped in his throat.

"Kiss me." Collin tugged his arm.

Tristan faced him, his attention drawing to Collin's lips. He leaned in.

Collin's warm mouth claimed his in a lingering kiss, then he grinned. "Okay, now we can go." He tangled his fingers in Tristan's and pulled him along as he headed for the door.

When they reached the door, Tristan wriggled his hand in Collin's grasp. "Collin," he whined.

"What?" Collin lifted his brows at him.

"We can't go down there holding hands." A faint grin spread over his lips despite himself. He dropped his gaze to the floor.

"Why not?" Collin tightened his hold on his hand.

"What are people going to think?" Tristan peeked at him.

"They'll think we're together. We are, aren't we?" Collin ducked to peer into his face. "Tristan?"

He smiled a full on, happy smile. "Yes." He couldn't believe it. He was with Collin. He let his gaze rise to meet Collin's beautiful, smoky eyes. "But—"

"This is a university campus in Southern California, probably the most liberal state in the US. I'm sure it's not the first time two guys held hands down to the dorm cafeteria and I'm sure it won't be the last." Collin used his free hand to turn the knob on the door and open it. He tugged on Tristan's hand.

Standing steadfast, Tristan's heart kicked. But what if someone wasn't all right with it?

"Come on." Collin yanked his hand, heaving him into the hallway.

Tristan stumbled and stopped beside him. "You sure no one will say anything?" A frown replaced his smile.

"If they do, I'll beat the shit out of them. How's that?" A smirk played over Collin's lips.

Tristan nodded. "Okay." He had Collin now to protect him. His heart warmed.

"Good, I'm starved." Collin led him to the elevator.

Tristan followed Collin into the cafeteria with his head hanging and his hair blanketing his face. He lifted his gaze from the tile floor to glance from side to side. Did anyone notice them? A few absent glances came his way, but no one stared at least.

Collin pulled him along, passed round tables with dark, plastic chairs and bulletin boards hung on the walls. Toward the back of the room, stainless steel counters hid bars filled with tubs of mashed potatoes, chicken, pasta, and an assortment of other food. A round pizza display tucked into the corner and a salad bar sat at an angle out in the open next to a table with a cash register.

Collin led him to the tubs of food at the end.

A young man, maybe a few years younger than Collin and Tristan, stood behind the counter with a chef hat on his head and a white apron covering a dark t-shirt. "What can I get you?" He glanced at Collin's hand entwined in Tristan's.

"I'll have the special." Collin squeezed Tristan's hand and leaned over to him. "What do you want?"

"Um, I think I'd like some pizza." Tristan's body relaxed. It wasn't so bad after all.

"Pizza's self-serve over there." The young man pointed to the pizza display.

"Oh, yeah." Tristan nodded and pulled his hand out of Collin's grasp as he left for the display. He knew that. He still wasn't thinking so clearly. He grabbed a plastic plate, opened the glass door of the display, took out a piece of pepperoni pizza and slapped it on his plate. His attention turned to the soda dispenser, along the wall a few feet away, then he grasped a plastic glass and filled it with ice and soda.

Collin came up behind him with a plate piled high with mashed potatoes and baked chicken. "Yum, yum, huh, Tristan?" A wide smile spread over his face as he poured his soda.

Tristan waited for him to finish, and they paid for their meal at the register.

"Come over here." Collin ticked his head and headed off toward a table in a corner of the room.

Tristan followed and dropped into a chair with his back to the room, next to Collin.

"See? No one said a word, did they?" Collin stuck a fork into his mashed potatoes and stuffed it into his mouth.

Tristan leaned toward him. "No, but they noticed us."

After swallowing, Collin said, "So?" He picked up his soda and took a sip from a clear straw. "They were probably looking at how hot you are." A smirk spread over his mouth.

Tristan dropped his gaze to his plate. "Oh, shut up." Heat crept into his cheeks.

"You going to eat that pizza or just look at it?"

Tristan tried to glare at Collin, but a grin took it away. He lifted the pizza to his mouth and took a bite.

"So, your mother was a drinking Mormon, and your father is dead." Collin eyed a piece of chicken stuck to his fork as he held it in the air.

Tristan stopped chewing and stared at him. "What?" Did he really just say that?

Collin set his chicken back down on his plate and leaned forward. "Uh, sorry. Maybe I shouldn't have been so blunt. Tell me more about your mom."

After chewing his pizza, he swallowed it down with some soda. He sat for a moment, gazing at his plate. What was there to tell, really? "She uh, was really involved in the church."

"Really? And yet she drank alcohol? Isn't that forbidden?" Collin's gaze searched his face.

Nodding slowly, Tristan tensed his brows. "She hid it from people and didn't drink too much before church. She always had mints and gum in her purse." What was Collin driving at? It was just how it was. He picked his pizza back up and took another bite.

"It didn't really hide it, though, did it? I mean, you still must have smelled it on her." Collin stuffed more mashed potatoes into his mouth.

Tristan shrugged. "No, it didn't really, but I guess she thought it did and no one seemed to question her about it." And if they did, boy would they get an earful.

Collin pursed his lips and gazed at his plate for a moment. "So, when was the first time you jerked off when another boy was around?"

He stopped with his mouth hovering over the next bite of pizza as heat swept up his neck. He pulled the pizza from his mouth untouched, then whispered, "I was ten."

Collin nodded and continued eating. "And how old were you when your mother caught you doing it?"

Dropping his pizza to his plate, Tristan covered his face with his hands. "I don't want to talk about this here." Could anyone hear them?

Collin set his fork down and rested his hand on Tristan's forearm. "Hey, I didn't mean to upset you. We'll talk about it back at the room, okay?"

Memories flooded his mind. His mother's shrill voice pushed through. *You a fucking little faggot, Tristan? Huh? Is that what you are? You should've never been born! Boys like you go to Hell. To Hell!* His eyes stung and a lump formed in his throat. He snuck his lip between his teeth and sniffed, holding the tears back. When he dropped his hands, Collin was fixated on him with his forehead creased.

"You okay? You look like you're going to cry." Leaning over, Collin wrapped an arm around his shoulders and planted a quick kiss on Tristan's cheek, then stayed close. "It must have been really bad, huh?"

Tristan shut his eyes and lifted his hand to the pocket opposite Collin. He rimmed the edge of the pocket. Collin couldn't see, could he? No. "Yeah." His cock swelled in his jeans, beckoning him. He slipped his fingers inside and let them run quick circles over the head of his erection, letting the delicious sensation drive away the pain. As his fingers rubbed down over his shaft, he sat back and picked up his pizza with his free hand. Pleasure enveloped his body. He ate the remainder of his dinner as if famished.

Keeping his attention fixed on Tristan, Collin sat back in his chair, furrowing his brows, and tapping his finger on his lips. After a moment, he resumed eating.

"Hey, Collin." A blonde woman strolled to the table. Her long hair fell in waves down her back and over a v-neck shirt, exposing an ample bosom. As her large, brown eyes fluttered at Collin, a wide smile played on her pretty face.

Collin twisted in his seat and looked up at her. "Oh, Jessica, hi."

"Did you figure out what subject to use for your paper?" She glanced at Tristan.

He lifted his head to gaze up at her. It was the woman he saw walking with Collin into sociology class today. He wrinkled his nose as his chest tightened. What the hell did she want?

Collin stood, grabbed her arm and led her away from the table, taking a quick peek at him. "About that..."

Tristan caressed his cock in long, hard strokes, easing the ache in his chest. Why didn't Collin introduce him? What was Collin talking about that he couldn't say it in front of him?

Collin let out an easy laugh from across the room and rested his hand on Jessica's arm.

She returned the laugh, her attention focused on Collin's face, and set her hand over his, then gave it a quick squeeze and let go.

With a nod, Collin headed back to his table, a wide smile stretching his face.

Tristan sunk low in his seat. Collin wouldn't see his hand position this way. "What was that all about?"

Collin waved it away. "Oh, that was just Jessica. She's my advisor for my psych thesis. She's really smart, working on her Ph.D. already."

"So, did you come up with a subject?" He let his finger's swirl over his erection, heightening his need, soothing his nerves.

Collin shrugged. "Uh, yeah."

"So, what did you choose?" A pulse shivered from his cock up to his spine. *I should stop before Collin sees something...Just a little more.*

"Oh, it's a really boring subject. Something I'm sure you've never heard of anyways." Collin studied him. "You ready to go back to the room?"

Tristan frowned. "Yeah." Did he think he was an idiot?

———

AFTER HEADING BACK to their room, the hand Tristan normally used in his pocket hung at his side and fisted as Collin unlocked and opened their door. Keeping it out of his pocket all the way up to their room had been unbearable.

Collin stepped inside the room, walked to his bed, and took a seat at the edge.

After stepping into the room, Tristan shut the door behind him. As he walked toward Collin, an ache deepened in his groin. How he longed to touch himself. He rested his fingers on the edge of his pocket.

"Can we talk some more?" Collin's focus drew to Tristan's hand, fingering the pocket.

Tristan pursed his lips. "I have some studying to do." All this talking was making him anxious.

"Just come here, then." Collin held out his arms.

Tristan walked into his arms and dropped to his knees between Collin's legs.

Collin surrounded him in a loose hug. "You seemed so upset at dinner I just wanted to make sure you're all right." He pressed a quick kiss on his lips. "So, are you alright?"

"Yeah, I'm fine." Tristan's pulse hammered and the ache in his groin grew. He cut his gaze to the far wall. He needed to find a way to be alone.

"Look at me." Collin leaned to the side, putting himself in Tristan's view.

Tristan's gaze drew to his face. "I'm fine." He kept his face slack. "I uh, need to go to the bathroom." That would be his way out of this.

"Oh, okay." Smiling, Collin lifted his arms.

Tristan stood and took careful steps toward the restroom, the itch inside him mounting.

Standing up, Collin walked to his desk. "I'll just be studying."

Tristan let himself into the bathroom and locked the door, then turned and rested his back on it. All his senses focused on the purring need in his groin. He shoved his hand in his pocket and slid his fingers under his sac and up over the tip of his hard cock. He thrust his hips and a soft moan left his parted lips. If only he could savor it, draw it out like he was used to. He let his fingers play and tease, sending rippling pulses through his body, then released a sharp gasp and brought his hand down low, under his sac.

He pushed at his entrance. What would it feel like to have Collin put his cock there? A delicious shiver raced up his spine. What would it feel like to have something inside him? He scanned the bathroom. He'd need lube. What could he use?

He bumped off the door and opened the medicine cabinet, perusing the glass shelves of bottles. His gaze stopped on a small, plastic bottle of lotion. Would that work? Maybe. A smirk crept over his face as he plucked the lotion out and set it on the counter.

Quickly, he unfastened his belt and jeans and dropped them to his feet, then stepped out of them and grabbed the lotion as he took a seat on the shag rug covering the floor. Resting his back against the wall, he spread his legs out wide and lifted his shirt up under his neck, holding it with his chin.

He opened the cap on the lotion and squirted an ample amount into his fingers. Rubbing the fingers together, he snuck his hand down between his legs and fingered his entrance, probing and testing to see what felt good.

After circling his fingers around his hole, he slipped the top of his index finger inside. A strange sensation of pressure filled him. His cock jerked. A devious thought came to mind. *Use both hands.* He stopped and poured lotion onto the fingers of both hands and slathered up his cock and sac.

Putting one hand at his entrance, he wrapped the other around his seeping cock. He wetted his lips, slid his palm over his erection and snuck a finger inside. Momentary burning lit up inside him, but quickly subsided as he relaxed into it. He stroked his hole, probing for the internal spot he'd heard of. His need tingled to a raw edge, and he stopped the stroking on his cock. It wouldn't take much more.

Sliding a second finger into his passage, he pumped. A delicious jolt raced through his body and a loud gasp erupted from him. *Oh God, that felt good.* He pumped his fingers in and out, hitting the internal spot over and over.

He rocked his hips, his body shaking, release coiling inside him. His breath came in quick pants and his cock twitched and dribbled onto his stomach. He grabbed hold of his erection with his free hand and jerked up and down, spreading pre-cum over his shaft. With his fingers pumping inside him and his palm jacking his cock, his climax screamed forward.

Sharp rapping cut through the room. "Tristan, are you okay?"

"Shit." Cum shot over his chest. Intense waves of pleasure pinched inside him to mix with the brutal tingling in his cock as each spasm hit. He gritted his teeth and curled his toes, letting only sharp breaths out of his mouth.

"Tristan?" The doorknob jiggled. "Why did you lock the door?"

As he calmed, he dropped his hands to his sides and panted, in a daze.

"Tristan! Open the door, damn it. This isn't funny." Collin growled.

CHRISTIE GORDON

Jolting out of his daze, Tristan sat up and darted his gaze around the room. "Oh, shit, oh, shit, oh, shit." He snatched a towel from the floor and wiped himself off. What had he done?

A thud reverberated in the room. "Let me in or I'll break the damn door down."

"I'm coming, Collin. Just give me a minute." He rose and hurried to dress and wash his hands. Looking in the mirror, he assessed himself and primped his hair.

"Tristan!"

"I said I'm coming!" He stepped to the door, unlocked it, and yanked it open, slamming it against the wall.

"What the fuck, Tristan?" Collin glared at him with his hands on his hips, his chest heaving with deep breaths.

Tristan dropped his gaze to the floor, his brows wrinkling. What the hell could he tell him? Not the truth.

"What were you doing in here for so long?" Collin glared at him.

"I-I don't know. I had to—to take a shit." Tristan stole a peek at him.

Collin sucked in a deep inhale. "No, you didn't. Either that or you've got the most stealthy shit on the fucking planet."

"What?" Tristan dropped his mouth open.

Collin grasped him by the elbow and hauled him out to the center of their room. "Your shit doesn't smell like shit, Tristan. It smells like fucking cum."

Trembling, he crept his gaze to meet with Collin's, then flinched. He was so pissed off right now. Why? "I-I don't know what you're talking about."

"Why would you do that? Why would you prefer to jerk off in the bathroom when I'm sitting right here? You know I want to be with you. You know I'd have sex with you." Collin shifted his stance. "I'm waiting for a fucking answer, Tristan." He gave him a harsh nudge in the shoulder.

Wincing, Tristan rubbed his shoulder and focused on the floor. His mother's voice came screaming up inside him. *Freak!*

You're nothing, Tristan, nothing but a freak! He flickered his gaze over the floor as his heart thundered in his ears. His vision blurred and in a cracked voice, he whispered, "No, I'm not. Collin even said so. He said I'm just messed up."

"What?" Collin's stance relaxed and his brows knitted. He draped his arms around Tristan's shoulders and drew him into his chest. "Tell me what just happened to you. Who were you talking to?"

Where am I? What just happened? His gaze searched the room as if it held all the answers, keeping his arms straight at his sides. "M-mother. She said I was, I was a freak. B-but I told her what you said. I told her you said I'm not. B-but she won't listen."

"Oh, shit..." Collin tightened his embrace and kissed the side of his head. "I'm sorry. I'm so sorry. I never should have yelled at you like that." He rubbed soft, slow circles over Tristan's back. "It's okay if you want to do that. There's nothing wrong with jerking off, okay? Whenever you need to do that, you just go right ahead."

Tristan shut his eyes tight, his breath hitching and a sob building in his chest. Tears filled his eyes and tumbled, one after another, down his cheeks. How had it come to this? What was wrong with him? "No, it's not right, Collin. What I've been doing is, is messed up, just like you said. I-I touch myself all the time. I can't do anything without it. The more upset, or, or, anxious or scared I get, the more I have to do it. Even now, even after I just came, I feel like doing it. I need help." He lifted his arms to wrap tightly around Collin's waist and plunged his face into Collin's neck, letting himself weep softly in Collin's protective hold.

"Shh...We'll get to the bottom of it. I'll help you, I promise." Collin placed another soft kiss on his cheek and swayed him in his arms.

After a few minutes, Tristan calmed, all the emotion spent. God, he was a mess. As he freed a ragged sigh, he released Collin.

Collin dropped his arms to hang his hands loosely on Tristan's waist. Hunching his shoulders, he peered up under his blond hair and into his face. "You okay?"

With a nod, Tristan sniffled. His gaze rose from Collin's chest to his eyes. "How can I stop? Can you really help me?" What it would be like to be free of this, to be normal?

"Yes, trust me." Collin leaned in and pressed a soft kiss on his lips. "Just trust me."

With wide eyes, Tristan slowly nodded his head.

"Do you want to talk some more, or do you need to study?" Collin twisted his lips.

"I think I need to study." Tristan sighed and raked a hand through his long bangs.

"Yeah, well, I think you've been through enough today." Collin released him and headed to his desk. When he reached it, he placed his hand on the back of his chair and looked at Tristan. "If you need anything, to talk, or maybe just, I don't know, a hug or something, no matter how silly it might sound, let me know."

"Okay." Tristan ambled to the refrigerator between their desks and grabbed a can of soda. After popping it open, he stepped to the chair at his desk, slid it out and sunk into it. He stared at his computer for a long moment. A strange numbness permeated his whole being as if his emotions had completely dissolved into nothingness. "Collin?"

Collin, seated in his chair and typing at his laptop computer, glanced at him. "What?"

"I don't feel anything." Frowning, he furrowed his brows and took a swig of soda. He'd never not felt *anything*.

Collin twisted in his seat and rested his arm on the back of it. "Like, nothing at all? Not even like you want to touch yourself?"

Keeping his gaze affixed to the blank screen of his computer, Tristan said, "Yeah."

"Well, maybe that's a good sign? You got some stuff out and now you're getting some relief from your compulsion." Collin roamed his gaze over him.

"It's a compulsion?" Tristan shifted to focus on him.

"Yeah, and it's a common one. Sort of a sexual addiction, I suppose." Collin lifted his brows.

"I'm a sex addict?" Tristan widened his eyes and set the can of soda on his desk.

"Probably, but the only one who can really say if you're an addict is you. You fit the profile for it, obviously. In any case, the first step and probably the hardest step to getting better is admitting it." Collin peered at him.

Tristan stared at the floor, mulling over Collin's words. "So, there are other people who do what I do?" If this was a known thing, then maybe it could be cured?

Collin relaxed his shoulders and softened his gaze. "Sure, having a masturbation compulsion is probably one of the most common sexual addictions there is. And lots of people have sexual addictions." Collin bent forward, planting his elbows on his knees. "Listen, you were traumatized by your mother. She didn't accept your sexual preferences and emotionally abused you about it. And you were part of a very strict church that forbids just about everything. No wonder you became compulsive about touching yourself. So, see? You're not a freak after all. Just a normal guy who was put through some heavy shit and found an unhealthy, but absolutely common way to deal with it."

He locked his gaze on Collin's as a heavy weight lifted from his chest. "I-I'm normal?"

"Yes, Tristan, you're normal." A faint grin played on his lips.

"Oh." Tristan nodded and turned to face his computer. He hit the enter button and logged in. *Normal.* His chest bloomed with warmth and his mouth quirked to a smile. He bit his lip to keep from laughing out loud. Peeking over at Collin, he let his eyes trail over Collin's long fingers, typing at the keyboard, the muscular arms, the stunning face, now so focused on his studies. An ache filled his chest. *God, how I love him.* He shifted his attention back to his own computer and pulled up a paper he needed to write for his art history class.

CHAPTER SEVEN

Tristan sat in the chair at his desk and glanced out the window at the darkness. It was already getting late. He and Collin had both been focused on their studies, referring to various books on the shelves over their desks and typing on their laptops. He leaned back in his seat and raised his arms over his head for a long stretch, glancing at Collin.

Collin typed furiously on his computer with a pen clenched in his teeth as if no one else in the world existed.

Dropping his arms, Tristan leaned to the side toward Collin. What the hell was so interesting?

With a determined click, Collin switched the screen on the computer to a web page.

"What were you writing about?" Tristan let a soft grin play on his lips. He was still feeling good about their discussions. Collin *liked* him.

"Nothing of interest." Collin clicked a few more times, pulling up page after page on the internet.

"Oh, come on. Something sure seemed fascinating. You were typing like a mad man for awhile." He let his grin widen to a full-on smile, picked up an empty soda can from his desk and tossed it into a mesh trashcan beside his chair.

Collin faced him. "No, it was just my boring thesis."

"What is it about?" Collin sounded off. Tristan's pulse quickened. Why?

"I told you, it's boring and you probably wouldn't understand it anyways." Collin scrubbed his face and clicked the screen saver on, then rose from his chair and climbed onto his bed to lie on his back.

Sighing, Tristan narrowed his eyes at him. "I'm not stupid, you know. I think you'd be surprised at what I'd understand. And besides, you've got me interested in psychology now, too."

Collin raised an arm over his head and tucked a hand under an ivory pillow. "It's boring, believe me." He tilted his head to gaze at Tristan. "Why don't you come over here and lay down with me?"

Heat rushed his cheeks, and he dropped his gaze to the floor. "Why?" A smile tugged at the corner of his mouth.

A quick smirk ran across Collin's lips. "Because I want you to."

Tristan jumped from the chair, then strolled to Collin's bedside and climbed onto his bed.

Collin shifted to make room while Tristan lay on his side, facing him.

As Collin wrapped an arm around Tristan, he rested his head on Collin's chest, his hand toying with the thin fabric of Collin's t-shirt over his stomach. What would they do tonight?

"How are you feeling?" Collin gave him a quick squeeze.

"Um, I don't know. Okay, I guess." Tristan snuggled his head into Collin's shoulder.

"No urges right now?" Collin placed a soft kiss on his head.

He furrowed his brows. Of course, he had urges. He always had urges, didn't he? He'd been fighting them off all day and losing the battle most of the time. His cock swelled.

"Well?" Collin ran his hand down Tristan's side, over his hip and down, between his legs. He cupped Tristan's burgeoning erection.

Gasping, Tristan pushed off him and jerked his hips back. "What're you doing?"

"Getting an answer to my question. Judging by how hard you are, I'd say the answer is yes." A slow grin crept over Collin's face.

With his cheeks heating, Tristan glared at the wall. "Well, what did you expect?" Especially if Collin was going to touch him like that.

Collin's grin waned and he placed his fingers on Tristan's chin, directing his gaze back. "How often do you normally, uh, make yourself come?" He studied him.

A sharp gasp escaped Tristan and his jaw dropped. "None of your business."

"But if I'm going to help you, I need to know all of it." Collin's gaze roamed his face. "So how often?"

Tristan focused on Collin's chest and shrugged. "I don't know. That depends, I guess."

"On?"

His gaze met with Collin's, the ache in his groin heightening. What were they doing here? He played with the edge of his pocket, his hand twitching. "On what's going on. How much time I have." He focused on Collin's lips.

"You want to do it now, don't you?" Collin's breath quickened.

Tristan nodded. *Always.*

"But you never answered my question. How often?" Collin raked his teeth over his lower lip.

Tristan wrinkled his brows and wetted his lips. "Uh, I usually only come once in a day. Well, before you and I got together."

A soft smirk ran across Collin's lips. "Oh, come on." He gave Tristan's shoulder a playful nudge.

Tristan chewed the side of his mouth. "Really. I um..." How could he confess to him exactly what he did?

"You what?" Collin watched him, his pupils growing wide.

Tristan shifted his gaze to the far wall. How he craved the feel of his hand in his pocket. Only sheer will kept him from plunging it in and surrendering to the itch demanding to be scratched. "I like to uh, just, I don't know, tease myself. All day." His cheeks warmed and he rolled forward, dropping his forehead against Collin's chest. *What does he think of me now?*

"What do you mean?" Collin stared at him a moment, his gaze darting over his face. "You play with yourself all day and don't come?"

Tristan clenched his eyes shut. In a small voice, he said, "Yes."

Collin dropped his jaw open. "How long can you stay hard?"

"A couple hours, I guess." Tristan cringed.

"A couple hours? Holy shit, dude. That's unbelievable self-control." Collin pushed him up by the shoulders to look into his face.

Tristan kept his eyes shut and twisted his head away from Collin. *Don't make me look at you right now.* Not after admitting that.

"Look at me, Tristan."

Slowly, with a long exhale, Tristan turned his head and opened his eyes. "What?"

"Why do you do that? Tell me, exactly, what you like about that." Collin's gaze searched his face.

"Do I have to tell you?" Tristan's cheeks heated once again, and his pulse quickened. "Maybe I'm not just like anyone else who has this problem. Maybe I'm not as normal as you say I am?"

"Oh, Tristan." Collin drew him into his chest and wrapped him up with his arms. "It's just a variation on a theme, don't you see? For whatever reason, you feel the compulsion to do it, but you don't feel worthy and so you deny yourself satisfaction. You only allow it once a day and I bet when you do, it's sort of a big thing, huh?"

Tristan nodded his head. "When I touch myself, it takes away everything else." How was Collin able to explain it all like this?

"Like what?" Collin caressed up and down Tristan's back. "Like the pain at remembering what your mother did to you?"

He widened his eyes. "Yeah, that's exactly right." Collin knew, he understood, and it was all making sense now. Why didn't he ever see this before? "When I feel anything at all, anxious, scared, whatever, I just touch myself and it all seems to disappear."

"Just like I thought. It's a soothing mechanism." Collin sighed.

Lifting his head, Tristan gazed into Collin's brown eyes. "So how do I stop?" Could he do this? Maybe.

Collin shrugged. "Do you really want to stop? Because, you have to be ready to quit or you won't be able to."

He thought a moment, pressing his lips together. What would his life be like if he didn't have to hide this thing all the time? Maybe he'd actually have friends. Maybe he'd actually feel good about himself for a change. He met Collin's gaze. "Yes, I'm ready. Tell me how."

Collin shifted on the bed. "Okay. I read that we need to basically break the habit first, go cold turkey. That means abstinence, from that anyways."

"Abstinence?" Trembling started up in his body and his chest squeezed. He fisted his hands. He wouldn't let fear stop him. "How?"

"Tell me something first. Does the type of underwear you wear have anything to do with your compulsion?" Collin studied his face.

"Um..." Tristan glanced at the wall. "I suppose so. This is really embarrassing, Collin."

Collin brushed up and down Tristan's arm. "It's okay. I'm not judging you for it. I just want to understand so I can help."

Nodding once, Tristan said, "It makes it feel good when I rub the inside of my pocket against it." Warmth flooded his cheeks, and he dropped his gaze to Collin's chest. "Jesus, I can't believe I'm telling you this."

Leaning forward, Collin placed a tender kiss on his forehead. "It's okay. Now I have a good idea of what we should do."

Tristan's cock ached. His need heightened in rebellion against the idea of stopping. "I hope I can do this."

Collin pulled him against his chest. "You can. I know you can. Listen, do whatever you have to tonight to prepare yourself mentally, okay? Then tomorrow, I'm going to give you some of my boxers to wear. Then you won't be able to do what you normally do. I know it'll be hard, but just try to get through the morning without touching yourself, okay?"

Wrapping his arms around Collin, Tristan squeezed him. "Just the morning?"

"Yeah, we can meet up after and talk about how you did and I, um, well I want to show you how it is to be with someone." Collin placed his palm on the back of Tristan's head and gave him another soft kiss.

His heart jolted and he plunged his hand into his pocket, stroking hard over his erection. Pleasure blanketed him, calming him. He let out a soft moan and rocked his hips into Collin's thigh. "Do you want to be with me now?"

Collin claimed Tristan's mouth in a passionate kiss. "God, Tristan, I always want to be with you." He roamed his hands over Tristan's body, pulling him closer, caressing and massaging the muscles beneath his t-shirt.

Parting his lips, Tristan snuck his tongue inside Collin's mouth, tasting him fully, deepening the kiss. He rubbed his palm over his aching cock. A sharp gasp escaped him. His sensitivity heightened. His sac grew tight for release.

Collin placed his hand over Tristan's on his jeans. "Stop, Tristan, leave it for me." He rocked his hips, pressing his hard cock against Tristan's thigh.

Slowly, Tristan slipped his hand from his pocket. His body trembled and an urgent need swallowed him. "Collin, please, do it now."

Collin sucked and nipped a trail down his jaw to his neck. He dropped his hands to Tristan's stomach, then unfastened Tristan's belt and opened his jeans.

A shudder of desire rippled through Tristan's body, and a low moan rose from his chest.

Collin tugged at Tristan's jeans. "Lift up so I can take these off."

Staring at him, Tristan said, "Y-you mean you want me to be naked?"

A soft grin crept over Collin's lips. "Of course. I want to see you this time. I want to feel your bare skin against mine."

Tristan looked him up and down. "I-I don't know." Could he do this?

Brushing Tristan's cheek, Collin said, "Don't be afraid. I'll be naked, too."

"No one's ever seen me naked." Tristan huffed.

"That's too bad, because I'm sure you're beautiful under all those clothes. Besides, I did see you in just your underwear." Collin freed a soft snort.

Tristan's cheeks heated. "I thought you were sleeping." God, it seemed like a lifetime ago.

Collin nodded once. "Come on, lift up." He tugged at the open waistband of Tristan's jeans.

Biting his lips, Tristan lifted up.

Collin sat up and skimmed Tristan's jeans and silk briefs down and off his legs, then removed his socks and focused on his face. "Sit up so I can take off your shirt."

Rising off the bed, Tristan lifted his arms.

Collin grasped the hem of Tristan's shirt and lifted, tugging it over his head, then threw it to the floor.

Tristan's necklaces fell back down, just under his neck, and he shivered. *I'm naked.* He crossed his arms on his chest and gazed at his curved erection, jutting up between his thighs. He couldn't look at Collin.

"See? You are beautiful." Collin brushed his long fingers over Tristan's lean shoulders, his arms, his thighs, and dipped in to rub his finger pads up Tristan's thick shaft.

Tristan sucked in a breath and closed his eyes, his cock pulsing with the soft touch, pleasure flashing through him.

Collin's breath quickened. "God damn it, Tristan, you have

no idea how much you turn me on." His voice was husky and ragged. He ran the heel of his palm over the hard bulge in his own jeans. "I want you to do this to me."

He lifted his gaze and watched Collin stroke himself through his jeans with lust flaring inside his body. His cock twitched. "Take off your clothes, Collin."

Collin's gaze locked on Tristan's. A slow smirk quirked his lips as he shucked his t-shirt over his head and unfastened his jeans. He lifted his hips for a moment, skimming them down and off with his boxers. "There, now we're both naked."

Tristan's breath caught as his gaze roamed down Collin's muscular chest, the ripples of his abdomen, the V at his hips and his thick cock, rising up to almost touch his navel. He flicked his tongue over his lips.

With his gaze affixed to Tristan, Collin laid on his back. Raising his arms up, he gestured for Tristan to come to him.

As a shy smile spread over Tristan's lips, he tucked himself into Collin's arms, on his side. He lifted his head and Collin's mouth descended over his in heated kisses.

Collin groped Tristan's body, tugging their skin flush, and raced his fingers along the hollows and curves as if he couldn't get enough. Soft gasps left him between frantic kisses and urgent licks over Tristan's neck, his collarbone, and down to a nipple.

With his back arching, sensation filled all of Tristan's senses. He rocked his hips and his stiff cock rutted against Collin's. Pleasure sparked over him, into him, through him. He thrust harder and roamed his hands over Collin's muscular back and down to cup his perfect ass. As his need heightened to an exquisite hunger, a carnal moan ripped from his throat.

Collin rocked his hips in time with Tristan's and lapped at his chest, then grasped both their cocks in one hand and thrust, making each shaft stroke the other.

Release hurtled forward and Tristan cried out. Intense tingling built to a raw edge in his erection and spilled over. His body shuddered and hot cum erupted out of him to slick both their writhing stomachs again and again.

Panting, Collin dropped his forehead to Tristan's chest and gave a deep moan. He tightened his grip around their seeping cocks and with a violent shudder, his cum spurted out between them to mix with Tristan's. He shivered against Tristan and his hips slowed to a stop.

Tristan laid in sheer ecstasy for a few minutes in Collin's arms with Collin resting on his chest. If only this moment never ended. A heaviness weighed on his heart and emotion threatened to overwhelm him. This had been his first time. No one had ever cared to be with him like this. He'd never been wanted before. He'd never been worthy of it. He took a deep breath and let out a ragged exhale.

Collin tightened his hold. "That was unbelievable, Tristan."

Nodding, Tristan shut his eyes, then peeked at Collin and looked away.

Collin lifted his head. "Are you okay?" His gaze searched Tristan's face.

In a whisper, Tristan said, "Yeah." The corners of his eyes stung.

"Look at me then." Collin tugged at his chin, turning his head.

Tristan's attention drew to him. What could he see there? Could Collin ever feel the same thing he felt? *Could Collin possibly love me?*

"Tristan, sweetheart, don't cry." Collin placed a tender kiss on his lips.

Flicking his gaze to the wall, his chest and face heated. "I'm not crying. Stop saying stuff like that." Collin didn't need to point everything out, did he? It was overwhelming enough.

A grin ghosted over Collin's mouth. "What do you want me to say when your eyes are all watery?"

He grimaced and focused on Collin. "They are not." Collin

was going to think he was a baby on top of everything else. Besides, crying wasn't allowed.

"Tristan—"

"They are not." Glaring at Collin, Tristan pushed him away.

Collin lifted his arm off him and dropped it between them. "Okay, okay, fine. They aren't then. I don't know what you're getting all worked up about. I thought it was sweet that you get all emotional when you're with me."

"I'm not emotional." He rolled to his back and swiped his eyes with the back of his hand, then glanced at Collin. He really had to get control of himself. It was bad enough he had this sexual condition.

Collin lifted his brows and gave a slow shake of his head.

"I'm not. Just, got something in my eye." Tristan huffed.

"Fine, I won't point it out again, okay?" The corners of Collin's lips twitched.

"There's nothing to point out." Tristan fisted his hands and made to get up.

Seizing him by the shoulders, Collin pinned him down, hovering over him.

"Don't get mad at me. Not now." Collin creased his brows, gazing deeply into his eyes.

Tristan's gaze darted between his eyes, the tightness in his chest relaxing. *Should I trust him?* "Just don't do that," he said in a low voice.

With his gaze softening, Collin said, "I want you to be comfortable with me. I want you to feel safe with me. I know it's hard for you. I understand you haven't had much practice letting anyone in. But I want to be let in, Tristan."

Tristan's chest pinched and his heart pounded. Why was he still so scared of him? Collin had done nothing but be good to him. Could he let Collin in? "I'm afraid."

"Of what?" Collin held Tristan's gaze.

"Of everything. I'm telling you stuff, secrets I've had most of my life and on top of that, I'm having, um, sexual experiences with you that I've never had before. How am I supposed to feel?" Tristan's eyes prickled and a lump climbed up his throat.

"I want you to trust me. I'm not judging you. I would never, ever judge you. You fascinate me in a way no one's ever done before. Can't you see that?" Collin brushed his knuckles over Tristan's cheek.

Tristan looked at the ceiling beyond Collin. "I-I guess so." He frowned and his vision blurred, an ache building in his chest. Why did this hurt so much? It was everything he'd ever wanted.

Collin cupped his cheek. "Why does that make you sad?"

With a blink, a hot tear tumbled down the side of Tristan's face. He swatted it away and squirmed under him. This couldn't be real, could it? "Why the hell did you pick me? Huh? Why?" His breath hitched. "God damn it, let me up."

"I won't." Collin pinned him to the bed again, their arms raised above them.

"Let me up! I'm all fucking sticky and gross and you already know what a freak I am. You don't have to know what a fucking baby I am, too, okay?" Tristan halted his motions and stared at him. Oh shit, not again. Why did he have to say that?

Collin hung his mouth open, then shut it. "First of all, why you? I think I already answered that question. Do I have to say it again?" He huffed. "I like you. I think you're hot. I find you, I don't know, interesting to say the least and for some fucked up reason I want to help you." His gaze and voice softened. "I don't care if you're a baby, as you call yourself." He furrowed his brows and glared at him. "And you are not—I repeat not—a fucking freak."

Pain sliced through his chest, and he scrunched his face. Why was this so hard? It's what he wanted, wasn't it? As a sob built in his chest, he choked it back.

Collin dropped down and held him tight. "It's okay, Tristan. Just relax. I don't want us to be mad at each other, okay? Let's just forget this, clean up, and get some sleep. Sound good?"

Tristan nodded against Collin's shoulder, the warmth and pressure of Collin's hold soothing him.

"Do you want to sleep with me tonight?" Collin lifted his head to gaze down at him.

"With you? You mean, in the same bed?" Tristan's heart warmed.

A soft smile played on Collin's face. "Well, yeah." He glanced at Tristan's bed. "Maybe we should both sleep in your bed, since mine's kind of a mess right now."

What would it be like, sleeping with him? "Have you ever spent the night with someone?" Tristan studied Collin's face.

Collin chuckled. "Sure."

Heat pierced Tristan's chest and he darted his glare at the wall. "Maybe I shouldn't have asked." He surely shouldn't have asked. Of course, Collin had done that.

"Tristan..." Collin placed a tender kiss on his lips. "Think about it this way, all those other people I've been with, things didn't work out. You're the one I'm with now and you're the one I want to be with."

Tristan chanced a peek into Collin's eyes. Could he really believe him? Why did it hurt so much to hear what Collin did or didn't do before him? Why was it so hard to believe someone would want him?

"What are you thinking about?" Collin traced his index finger over Tristan's nose.

"I just have...doubts." Tristan sighed. "I don't want to be one of those people, someone it didn't work out with." Especially with *Collin.*

"With this sort of thing there are no guarantees. I won't lie to you about that. But it's worth the risk." Collin kissed his cheek.

The ache rose up inside Tristan's heart and he swept his gaze over Collin's face. "Maybe that's why I'm so scared. I really, uh, like you, Collin. I really—" Taking a quick inhale, he bit his lip and focused back on the wall. *Shut up, you almost said the* love *word, damn it.*

"I know. Let's just let it be, okay? And don't be scared of me. I'm not going anywhere." Collin pressed a gentle kiss on his forehead and smiled.

Tristan gazed deeply into his eyes. He had to trust him. There was no other choice. His feelings were too far gone already.

"Let's get cleaned up." Collin pushed away from him and climbed off the bed, then glanced back at him. "Coming?"

Tristan nodded, sat up and dropped his legs to the side of the bed. "Don't you want to go first?"

Collin walked back to him and grasped his hand, then tugged. "I'm going to clean you up."

As his checks warmed, Tristan stood up and stepped toward him. "You're not my mother, you know."

"Oh, shut up and let me take care of you." Collin huffed out a laugh.

CHAPTER EIGHT

THURSDAY, NOVEMBER 6

Tristan, lying on his bed, snuggled his back closer into Collin's chest as the first rays of morning sun slid between their computer desks and crept over the carpeted floor of their dorm room. A soft pressure lay across his side and warm fingers entwined in his. He stirred and fluttered his eyes open. A faint grin curled his lips. Collin was sleeping behind him. He and Collin were together. *Shit, I promised to stop touching myself today. How the hell am I going to get through the morning?* His chest pinched and his heart raced as his body stiffened.

Collin lifted his head to peek over his shoulder. "You okay?" he asked in a husky voice.

Tristan trembled. "Y-yeah."

Propping himself on an elbow, Collin said, "No, you're not. You're white as a ghost and shaking like a leaf." He squeezed Tristan's hand. "It's our plan, isn't it? The abstinence is upsetting you."

"N-no, it's fine, really. I just, um, have a—a test to take today. I forgot about it until now." Tristan hid his face in the pillow.

How the hell could he admit how scared he was? What if he couldn't do it?

"You're a terrible liar." A smirk tugged the corner Collin's lips. "Listen, it's completely normal to be upset or afraid, or whatever, about changing your behavior, okay?"

Tristan nodded into the pillow, then lifted his face out of it. "I don't know if I can do it, Collin." An ache filled his already stiff cock. Just the thought of stopping made him want to touch himself.

Collin let go of his hand and brushed his fingers over Tristan's hair. "You can do it. I know you can. These will probably be the hardest hours of your life, but just remember, if you get through them, it'll get easier."

He squeezed his eyes shut. "I can't." His cock pulsed with need. His freed fingers twitched and readied to dive into the sheets and between his thighs.

Collin shifted back on the bed and reached under the covers, then grasped Tristan's wrists and hauled his arms up over his head.

"What're you doing?" Tristan furrowed his brows, studying Collin. Did he know somehow?

"Just making sure you're not already doing it." Collin gave him a warm smile. "I'm going to shower with you, too. Then I'll know you aren't pulling a fast one in the bathroom again." He chuckled. "Literally."

Tristan swiveled his head to look at the far wall and frowned. "I can't shower with you. That would be really unbearable, seeing you all naked right in front of me."

A chuckle choked out of Collin. "Yeah, maybe you're right. I'd have a hard time keeping my hands off you and we probably shouldn't do anything. It wouldn't be much of an accomplishment if you started off your day, uh, satiated, so to speak." His smile waned and he looked at Tristan a moment. "Okay then, I'll just watch you shower and be with you in the bathroom while you get ready. Sound like a plan?"

Tristan drew a deep inhale. "Yeah, sure." He climbed out of bed and picked up his jeans from the floor. As he straightened to slide the jeans up his legs, necklaces swung on his chest and bracelets jangled. Sighing, he raked his hand through his disheveled hair and glanced at Collin.

Collin watched him from the bed with a faint smirk on his face.

"So? You coming or what?" He dropped his hand to his side.

Collin's smirk widened. "Yeah, I was just enjoying watching your ass when you bent over to pick up your jeans."

Tristan's cheeks warmed. "You're more of a pervert than I am." He crossed his arms on his chest and fought off a smile.

"Maybe so." With a soft snort, Collin threw the covers down, climbed out of bed, and pulled his gray sweatpants up his legs. He stepped to Tristan and wrapped his arms around his waist from behind.

Tristan let his head fall against Collin's.

Taking a deep inhale, Collin said, "I can't help what you do to me."

Tristan closed his eyes, relishing in his soothing embrace. *God, the things he says to me.* He should pinch himself to be sure it was real. "Can I really do this, stop um, touching myself?"

"Yes, you can. Let's get in the shower." Collin freed him and slapped him on the ass.

Gasping, Tristan's hips jerked forward, and his cheeks warmed a second time. He turned and threw Collin a glare. "Stop that."

Collin chuckled and grasped Tristan's hand, then towed him into the bathroom, opened the glass shower door and started the shower. "Here, you go first." The patter of rushing water hitting tiles filled the room.

Standing in front of the shower door, Tristan asked, "What, and you'll just watch?"

"Yes." Collin released his hand and gestured toward the shower.

Pursing his lips, Tristan dropped his jeans to the floor and kicked them off, then stepped into a cascade of water. Warmth flooded down his body, cleansing the remnants of sweat and love-making off his skin. He turned and opened his eyes.

Collin sat on the closed lid of the toilet seat with a soft smile floating over his lips. "You're beautiful, Tristan." His gaze darkened and raked over Tristan's wet, naked body.

Heat flared over Tristan's skin and his cock swelled. He grabbed the soap off a small shelf in the corner and clenched his eyes shut, then turned to face the wall while running the soap over his arms and chest. Collin didn't need to see him getting hard just from a look.

Tristan glided the soap down behind him and over his ass cheeks, his legs, his groin. His stiff cock pulsed under the soap, sending a ripple of pleasure through his body. *Oh God, it feels good.* He rubbed slick fingers over his sac and up his shaft, then stopped at the head and gave it a quick squeeze. A soft gasp worked out of his throat as sensation flooded his body. *Damn it, I can't stop.* It was too good. He needed this. The creak of the shower door sounded, and a firm hand grasped his arm.

"Tristan." Collin's voice was stern.

Sneaking his lip between his teeth, Tristan faced him, his gaze darting over the tiles on the shower floor while slowly stroking his shaft.

Collin tugged Tristan's arm, yanking his hand free from his cock. "Tristan, you have to stop."

Fisting his hands, Tristan shut his eyes. "I'm sorry, Collin." His chest tightened while tension coiled in his gut and his dick ached.

Collin gave him a gentle push into the cascading water. "It's okay. Just wash your hair and get out." He stepped back and closed the shower door.

Need filled every fiber of Tristan's body. He fought against it while he washed his hair. How the hell was he going to last all morning? He couldn't, not now, not since he'd already started. *Fuck, I can't do this.* He turned off the shower and stepped out.

Collin handed him a towel. "Good thing I was here, huh?"

He glanced up into Collin's face as he wiped off his body and wrapped the towel around his waist and his still hard cock. "I can't do this, Collin, I just can't." His voice wavered.

Collin drew him into his arms. "Shh, I don't want to hear any more talk like that. You can do it and you will."

Resting his cheek against Collin's shoulder, Tristan said, "How can you be so sure? If you weren't here to stop me, I'd have, well, you know." Thank God, Collin had been here. Otherwise, he'd have lost himself to it.

"Because we're breaking the cycle. You'll see, as soon as you wear some different underwear, it'll be better." Collin sighed. "It probably didn't help having me watch you. I have to admit, it took every bit of self-control to not take you in the shower." He freed a soft chuckle.

Lifting his head, Tristan gazed into his eyes. "Why? What do you see in me?" How could Collin possibly want someone as wretched as him?

Collin brushed a wet lock of long hair from Tristan's face. "Tristan..." He wrinkled his brows. "You are worth having. You are...driving me crazy standing here with only a towel on. I can feel your hard-on, you know." He smiled.

With heat rushing up his neck, Tristan stepped back and roamed his gaze down to Collin's groin. Was he hard, too?

A clear erection jutted out from underneath Collin's sweatpants. "Yeah, you gave me a boner, too."

Tristan smirked. "Oh." He raked his hand through his wet hair. "Guess I'll get dressed now." He turned Collin on, *he* did.

"Yeah, and I'll get you some boxers before I shower. Don't do anything." Collin wagged a finger at him. "You know I'll have my eye on you." Collin left the room for a moment. When he returned, a pair of dark boxers dangled in his hand. "Here, put these on."

As Tristan dropped the towel from his waist, he pursed his lips and grabbed the boxers from Collin, then stepped into them and slid them up his legs. "I don't think I've ever worn anything like these. They look like old man underwear." He snickered and peeked at Collin.

Collin planted his hands on his hips. "Old man underwear? You're lucky I like you so much or I'd slug you right now." He shook his head. "Maybe I will." He gave Tristan's shoulder a light punch.

"Ow." With a grin, Tristan rubbed his shoulder and peered at him.

Collin ticked his chin at him. "Get dressed."

"Fine." Tristan brushed by him and padded to his closet, then pulled a white shirt off a hanger and slid it over his head and arms. He rifled through his collection of jeans and found a pair his mother had gotten him for Christmas one year. He held them out and looked them over. They were much tighter than his normal jeans and he'd only worn them once, to please her. His mother's voice rose up in his mind. *Here you go, Tristan. You'll look so much better in these. Who knows, maybe a girl will even notice you?* He frowned. She knew damned well he didn't care about girls. His chest clenched. With a huff, he yanked the pants of the hanger, making it fling up and fall to the floor.

"Hey, hey, easy now." Collin stepped up behind him and placed a soft kiss on the back of his shoulder. "You okay?"

Trembling, Tristan twisted around to face him, clutching the jeans. "Why do parents do things like that?"

"Like what?" Collin raised his brows.

"Like go on and on about getting a girl when they fucking know you like guys?" Tristan studied him. What would Collin have to say about that? It had sounded like he'd never been through it.

Collin's gaze softened and he clamped his hand on Tristan's shoulder. "It's just a hard thing for them to understand. Underneath it all, they all want one thing. For their kids to grow up healthy and happy. Being gay just isn't in that equation for them.

So, they deny what's right in front of their noses, or worse, in your case."

Blowing out a long exhale, Tristan slumped his shoulders. "Yeah, worse is an understatement." Collin had a decent explanation for pretty much everything. At least an explanation he could live with.

Collin ducked his head to peer into Tristan's face. "Hey, let's just get through the next few hours and see how it goes. Don't think about everything or you'll get overwhelmed, believe me."

With a nod, Tristan said, "You're right." He bent over, slid the jeans up his legs and fastened them, then threw a glance at Collin. "You ever going to shower?"

Collin shrugged. "Just making sure you're okay." His gaze roamed down Tristan's lean body to the snug jeans and a coy smile swept over his lips. "Wow, you look really good in those."

As his cheeks warmed, and Tristan twisted around. "Stop it. I already feel weird enough." *But Collin thinks I look good in these?* He glanced at him.

Collin tongued his lips and cupped Tristan's ass. "I can't help it. You *really* look good in those." He snickered.

Tristan's cock swelled under his zipper. Whirling around, he slapped Collin's hand away. "You're not making this easy on me." He looked down at the bulge in his jeans. "Great." It was like any little thing was going to set him off today.

Covering his mouth with his hand, Collin held in faint snickers. "There is no way you're going to be able to do anything today."

Tossing him a glare, Tristan said, "Oh yeah? What if I just go into the bathroom, huh? What then?" Why was this making him so angry? Was his addiction so strong that it was fighting him like a living, breathing monster inside him?

"You won't. It's not the same. In any case, it'd still be breaking the cycle, wouldn't it?" Collin hooked his arms around Tristan's shoulders and drew him near. "You'll be just fine, you'll see."

Tristan closed his eyes and returned the embrace, breathing

through the boiling emotion inside him. Collin was here. *He won't let me fail.*

———

After eating breakfast with Collin, Tristan hurried off to his art history class. He walked through the front door of a modern, brick building, passed angular abstract statues in metal sitting in a haphazard pattern in the foyer and down a hallway to a classroom.

Once inside, he took a seat at a desk toward the back of the room. He dropped his backpack to the floor beside him, unzipped it and sorted through it for his pen and notebook. He came back up with his things clutched between his fingers and steadied himself.

The class filled and a professor took the podium to begin the lecture.

His fingers itched to reach into his pocket and his cock strained against the inside of the tight jeans. This was so uncomfortable. He shifted in his seat. The jeans were too tight. How the hell did guys wear this stuff?

He toyed with his small, hoop earrings in an attempt to distract himself and forced himself to listen to the lecture and take notes. His cock ached. His mind flooded with memories of Collin and the feel of fingers racing along his shaft. If only he could touch himself. He dropped his pen beside his notebook and rested his cheek in his hand, his elbow perched on the desk. He crept his other hand down to the edge of his pocket and stopped. *Don't do it.*

He toyed with the edge of his pocket, testing and teasing. *Don't do it.* He rested his fingers on the fabric of his jeans, on his erection, warming it. He pressed on the head of his cock, sending a pulse of pleasure rippling through him. He shut his eyes and parted his lips, his breath quickening. *Shit, don't do it.*

Opening his eyes, he shifted in his seat and brought his hand back to the edge of his pocket. Would his hand even fit in there with him sitting like this? Clearing his throat, he slid down in his seat and stretched his legs out in front of him. *Don't, do, it... Damn it!* He squeezed his fingers inside his pocket and wriggled his hips to get them positioned over his aching cock.

Tingling surged in his shaft and lit up his desire. He pressed down, over and over, unable to do anything else. His breath quickened to a soft pant, and he licked his lips. His gaze raced across the room.

A girl seated next to him, and one row up, turned around and glared at him.

He ceased all motion. Shit, did she see? What sort of a freak would she think he was if she did? Slowly, he tugged his fingers out of his pocket and rested his hand on his desk, then gazed at the professor.

The professor had his back to the class and wrote on a whiteboard with a black marker.

What was he going on about now? He raked his teeth over his lower lip and focused on the lecture. His dick ached and he squirmed in his seat. The tight fabric of his jeans teased his erection with pressure. How the hell would he ever get through this?

His chest squeezed. This was too much. He couldn't do it. An ache wrapped around his heart. *I'm not good enough.* His eyes pricked and his throat tightened. He listened hard to the lecture, blinking the tears away and swallowing the lump in his throat. His muscles itched to flee.

He glanced at the clock. Only fifteen minutes to go. He could run to the bathroom. Maybe if he came it would be easier. Yes. He spread a smirk over his lips. Just once, that's all he'd need to get through his other classes. His cock pulsed in his jeans. He slipped down and rocked his hips, letting the pressure of the tight fabric taunt him.

He rolled and swayed his hips every so often through the remainder of the class, writing notes and watching the professor. His need heightened inside him, begged him for more.

"So, the paper is due next Thursday, if you have any questions on it, be sure to see me." The professor set his marker down on the shelf at the white board.

All around him, students packed their things and rose to leave.

Bending down, he dropped his things into his backpack. After zipping it up, he stood facing the wall and looked down. Damn it, he was still hard, and it showed. He stretched his t-shirt out, pulled it over the bulge in his jeans and stuffed a hand into his pocket. There, now it wasn't so noticeable.

He picked up his backpack and held it front of him as he exited the class. Time to get into the bathroom. He had fifteen minutes before his next class started, plenty of time to do what he needed. He strolled out of class, through the hallway and out the foyer into bright, morning sun, then squinted.

"Hey, Tristan." Collin bound up to his side from an expanse of grass. A dark shirt exposed a patch of tanned skin just under his neck and his jeans fit snug on his hips.

"Collin? What are you doing here?" Tristan froze, keeping his backpack over his front.

Collin smiled. "Just making sure you're all right." He took him in from head to toe. "So how are you doing?"

Furrowing his brows, he hung his head to focus on the cement walkway. "I'm fine." Could he tell?

"Look at me." Collin grasped Tristan's arm holding his backpack.

Tristan turned his head. "I said I'm fine." He frowned. *I have to get rid of him.*

Collin pushed on Tristan's arm, dropping the pack down to his side. "No, you're not."

Gasping, Tristan whipped the backpack up and glared at him. "Stop it."

"Tristan, I'm trying to help you. Get your hand out of your damned pocket." Collin pinched his brows together.

"Just leave me alone." Tristan's chest tightened and his gut clenched.

Collin seized his other arm and yanked his hand out of his pocket. "You have to be strong. I know it's hard."

Heat surged in Tristan's chest. "No, you don't. You have no fucking idea what I'm going through. Who the hell do you think you are, telling me what I can and cannot do with my own body? Huh? Who?" He gritted his jaw. Collin didn't deserve this but fuck if he could stop himself.

A few students passing by stopped and stared at them.

Collin held his palm out. "Keep your voice down." He clutched Tristan's arm, his fingers digging into Tristan's bicep, and guided him down the walkway, past a few palm trees.

Tristan yanked his arm, trying to free it, but Collin's fingers tightened. "Let me go," he hissed.

"I will not. You're coming with me." Collin hauled him through the grass and behind the wall of a brick building.

"Damn it, I have another class. What the fuck do you think you're doing?" He scowled.

Collin shoved him up against the cold bricks of the building. A thud filled the air as Tristan's back hit. He put himself directly in Tristan's face and pinned Tristan's arms at his sides. The backpack still dangling from Tristan's hand. He glared into Tristan's eyes. "I'm keeping you here until your next class. I won't let you fail."

Panting, he lowered his brows. His cock strained against the tight jeans. He ached to thrust against Collin. He whined, "I can't do this, Collin. I just can't." His breath hitched.

Collin ducked his head to peek under Tristan's blond hair. "Yes, you can." His hold on Tristan's arms tightened even more.

With pain eating away at his heart, he said, "Why is this so hard?"

"Because it just is. Take a deep breath and relax." Collin wrinkled his forehead and gazed deeply into his eyes, then leaned in and placed a soft kiss over his lips. "Relax...please. You got this."

Tristan blew out a long exhale, then pinched his lips. "How much longer do I have?"

Collin freed him and stepped back, glancing at his watch. "Only another two hours." His gaze snapped back to him. "You're used to jerking off in class, aren't you?"

Tristan twisted his head to look off across the campus. "Yeah." *So?*

With a shrug, Collin said, "Maybe you shouldn't go to your next class. Maybe you should just go for a walk or something."

A walk? "But I have to go to my anatomy class. It's important." His pulse kicked. How would he get through a two-hour class? He shifted his stance. Maybe Collin was right.

Collin pressed his lips together and watched him, tapping his fingers on his chin. "Well, is it more important than you getting better?"

With a slow shake of his head, Tristan murmured, "No." He nudged a small patch of dirt with his booted foot.

"Seems to me if you put yourself in a place where you don't usually do it, you might be able to control yourself better." Collin's gaze trailed up Tristan's body and rested on his eyes, then he patted him on the shoulder. "Take a walk. Let's meet for lunch at noon in the cafeteria, okay?"

Tristan let a smirk play over his lips. "How do you know I won't just go off and do something I shouldn't?" But would he now, after Collin had put up with all his bullshit and still tried to help him?

"I don't. But I'm trusting you." Collin sighed. "The only one you'd be hurting, really, is yourself."

Tristan dropped his smirk. "I do want to get better." The impulses that had been raging in him were numbed for the moment. Collin had stopped it.

"I know." Collin pressed a tender kiss to his lips. "And you will."

———

A FEW MINUTES LATER, Tristan trudged up the main street of the college campus. Modern buildings mixed with the arches and domes of traditional, mission-style architecture. His blond hair rippled in a light breeze and the sun warmed the top of his head and shoulders. A few cars rumbled by him while he walked past a blending of scrubby oaks and palm trees. As he came to the edge of campus, he stopped and looked both ways before crossing a wide street into two-story buildings made of creamy stucco and red roof tiles.

The ache inside him dissipated the more he walked. Maybe Collin was right? Maybe it was sitting in the classroom that almost caused his failure? His gaze rose and he took in the anti-quated buildings surrounding the campus. He let his gaze run over ornate, pre-cast framing surrounding mullioned glass windows.

Stopping his progression up the street, he let his fingers run over the smooth, mortar surface. The honk of a car horn startled him, and a man in a gray suit nudged his backpack as he walked by, heavily engrossed in a cell phone conversation.

His surroundings became heavy with sound and light. The cars, trees and buildings took on vibrant hues.

People walking by took notice of him. An Asian woman smiled as she passed and nodded her black head.

He grinned back and dropped his hands to his sides. Where was that art supply store he'd heard so much about? He widened his grin to a broad smile and held his head up high, strolling up the street, looking at the plastic signs over all the small shops lining the street.

After walking a few blocks, the art supply store came into view. A small window held an assortment of art books and canvases painted with local artwork.

He tugged open a glass door and stepped inside. The scent of paint and thinner and leather wafted over him. Rows of metal shelving held neatly stacked and sorted supplies of every variety.

Walking into the charcoal section, he widened his eyes. Maybe he could draw Collin naked? He let out a soft chuckle and covered his mouth with his hand.

"Can I help you?" A girl with black hair and a shock of purple in her bangs stood at the end of the isle. She rested her hands on her hips. A white smock covered her black clothes.

"Uh, maybe." He let his grin fade and dropped his gaze to her booted feet.

"Tristan?"

His gaze cut to her brown eyes. Thick eyeliner rimmed the top lid. "Uh, yeah?"

She smiled and stepped toward him. "I thought that was you. Why aren't you in class or drawing somewhere or something?"

"In class? Drawing?" He stepped back, his heart pounding. Who was this girl? Why did she know his name?

She stopped right in front of him with a smirk planted on her lips. "I've never seen you off campus. Guess I figured you were some kind of super-student or something."

Furrowing his brows, he asked, "S-super student?" He raised his hand to the seam of his pocket, ready to plunge if the moment required it.

She glanced down at his raised hand and shifted her stance. "Yeah, too good to even talk to anyone else in art class."

"What?" He strummed the edge of his pocket with his fingers. Could he even get them inside if he wanted to?

She gave his shoulder a playful pat, knocking his fingers from his pocket. "Oh, come on now. Everyone knows you're the best damned artist at this stupid college. Way better than anyone I've ever seen."

Dropping his mouth open, his chest warmed, then he smiled. "Really? You think I'm, I'm good?"

"Hell, yeah." Her voice rose in pitch. "Best damned portraits of naked guys I've ever seen. Hot naked guys, I should add." She lifted the edge of her mouth.

His cheeks heated and he dropped his gaze to the floor. "Oh...

you've seen those." He'd always embellished a little, okay maybe a lot, in his life drawing classes.

Her eyes twinkled at him, and she swayed her body. "I'd give just about anything to get one for my apartment." Her grin faded. "Why don't you make prints and sell those things, anyways?"

Tristan let out a soft chuckle. "Oh, come on, no one would want one of those." Was she serious?

"I, for one, would. I know lots of girls who'd want one. A Tristan Tolken original."

He stared at her, his chest tightening. "How do you know my full name?"

She touched his forearm. "Come on, you're practically a celebrity in the art classes."

Did I hear her right? A celebrity? "I-I don't know what you're talking about." He glanced around the store. Surely, she was pulling his leg.

"Maybe if you'd look up once in a while and let yourself out of that little bubble you keep yourself in, you'd see it." She shook her head. "Really, you act like no one else in the world exists. Uh, I'm Ally, by the way."

"Ally." He sucked a quick inhale. "Nice to meet you, Ally." He held his hand out to her.

She gave his hand a quick shake. "I could sell your work here, you know, in the shop."

"You could?" He dropped his hand to his side. How was this conversation even happening?

"Sure. I'm in good with the owner and he appreciates my taste in art." She nodded slowly.

He looked her up and down, his pulse quickening. Sell his art? His art of nude men? Well, maybe the non-sexual poses could be sold. He spread a smile over his lips. "So how do I do that?"

She dug in the pocket of her smock, fished out a business card and held it out to him. "Here, take my card and give me a call. We'll set up an appointment to bring in some of your pieces and go over them with the owner. Then, we'll get them framed and hang them up in the window."

He took the card from her and stuffed it into his pocket.

As a small squeal of excitement escaped her, she hugged her arms to her chest. "Oh my God, I know a bunch of my friends are going to freak when they hear about this."

He laughed. "Why?"

"Because they'll be breaking the door down to get one of your pictures, dummy." She bit her lip and held still as if waiting for something.

"Uh..." He twisted and perused the contents of the store. What should he say now? He focused on her for a heartbeat. "Okay, so, I um, should get going." He ticked his head toward the door.

She dropped her arms. "Aren't you going to buy something?"

"Oh..." He peeked at the charcoals on the shelf next to him and snatched up a box of thin, pencil-styled sticks. "Okay, I'll take these." He'd needed more of those anyways.

———

TRISTAN STRODE across the college campus with a light bounce in his step. He was a celebrity. People actually liked his art. They *liked* it. And best of all, he'd done it. He went all morning without touching himself. Well, pretty much all morning. There was that nasty incident in Art History class. Collin would be proud of him. Hell, more than proud. He stopped at the glass doors to his dorm building and pulled one open.

A female student in shorts waited on the other side, looking him over.

"Oh, hello. After you." He stepped aside and held the door for her while she passed through.

"Thanks." With a smile, she walked past him and off into the campus.

As he entered the building and headed to the cafeteria, he kept up a light step and passed through double metal doors.

Collin sat at a round table in the corner in deep conversation with Jessica, seated next to him. He leaned into her and pointed down at a book, resting between them on the table. As the conversation stopped, he flinched and took a deep breath.

Twisting her head toward Tristan, her gaze met his. A white t-shirt drew tight across her ample chest. Her lips curled in a smirk, and she tapped Collin on the shoulder.

Collin turned in his chair, then slapped the book shut. The corners of his lips twitched into a grin, and he shoved the book toward her.

Grasping the book, she tucked it away in her backpack.

Tristan trudged to the table, staring at the gray carpet with his pulse quickening. He didn't like that girl, not at all.

Collin rose from the table as Tristan approached. "Hey."

Tristan chanced a quick glance at Jessica, who gave him the once over, then fixated on Collin. He shoved his hands into his front pockets and spread a faint smile over his lips. "Hey, Collin."

"Um, this is Jessica." Collin held his palm out to her. "I don't think I introduced you before."

"No, you didn't." Tristan's gaze slowly drew to her.

She gave him a short wave. "Hello, Tristan." Her gaze ran down his chest and rested on his crotch for a second.

With heat flaring up his neck, he ripped his hands from his front pockets and covered his groin, fingers entwined. What the hell was she looking at? He wasn't hard right now, thank God. "Hello, um, Jessica."

A smirk raced over her lips, and she flicked her gaze to his face, dropping her hand into her lap. "It's nice to finally meet you." She glanced at Collin. "I've heard a lot about you."

Collin's eyes grew wide. "Yeah, lots of good things, right, Jess?" A stuttered chuckle sprang from him.

Tristan knitted his brows. What the hell was going on here?

Something didn't seem quite right. He shifted his stance. Or was his messed-up head seeing things that weren't there?

Turning in her seat, she rose from the table. "Well, I suppose I should be going." She bent over, picked up her backpack and faced Tristan. "Nice jeans."

What? Heat swarmed his chest. No way would Collin have told her about the jeans, right? Collin had said they looked good on him, so maybe she was trying to be nice?

She stepped toward the door, then stopped. "See you later, Collin." She strolled toward the door.

"Yeah." As a chuckle sprang from Collin's throat, he brushed his hand down the back of his head.

Tristan stared at Collin. "What's going on, Collin? Why would she make a comment about my jeans?" There had to a good explanation, right?

A thin-lipped grin spread over Collin's lips. "Nothing's going on. She probably just thinks you look good in those jeans, same as me. Relax." Collin leaned forward and planted a quick kiss on his cheek.

Recoiling, Tristan swiped his cheek with his fingers. Was he making more out of this than there was? "Does she know about us? I mean, did you tell her we were—"

"Of course, I did. She's cool with it. I wouldn't hang out with someone who wasn't." Collin eyed him.

Tristan pursed his lips. "What was that book you two were looking at?" And why had he closed it so suddenly?

With a sigh, Collin relaxed his shoulders. "Come on, Tristan, it was just a psychology book. I told you she's helping me with my thesis. She brought a book to help with my research."

Tristan dropped his gaze to the floor and examined the carpet. "What is it you're doing your thesis on again?" Would he tell him this time?

"It's not important. Actually, I'm not positive I've picked a subject yet. I might change it." Collin blew out a breath, then grasped Tristan's arm. "What *is* important is how your walk went."

God, I'm being such an ass to him. All he cares about is me. As the memory of his discussion with Ally filled his head, he puffed out his chest and let a broad grin play on his face. "It went really well, actually." He beamed. "I did it. I really did it."

A wide smile swept over Collin's face. "No problems since your first class?"

"No, that walk did the trick. And you know what?" Tristan lifted his chin.

Collin cocked his head. "What?"

"It seems I'm some kind of celebrity in the art department." A smug tone dripped from his voice.

"Really?" Collin shifted his stance and dropped Tristan's arm. The smile on his mouth grew. "And what exactly do you mean by that?"

Tristan smirked and straightened his spine. "My drawings are so good, this girl told me I should start selling them."

Collin blinked a few times. "Wow, that's great, Tristan. It sounds like you've had quite the day. How about we get some lunch, and you can tell me all about it?"

"Sure." Tristan sighed.

CHAPTER NINE

Tristan looked down at his hamburger, resting among a couple dozen fries on a plastic plate.

Collin, sitting next to him at the table, grabbed a fry from Tristan's plate and shoved it into his mouth. "So where did you go?"

Tristan sipped his soda, then swallowed it down. "I just went into town and spent some time at the art supply store. That's where I met this girl in my art classes."

"You met a girl?" Collin straightened in his chair.

Tristan shrugged. "Yeah. She's the one who told me my artwork was good enough to sell." As he sat forward, his face lit up. "In fact, she wants a piece for her apartment, and she said all her friends would be breaking the door down trying to get some of my drawings."

With a smirk, Collin said, "Breaking the door down?" He let out a soft chuckle. "Come on. I thought you just drew portraits or something. These must be some amazing portraits."

With his gaze falling to the table, heat flushed Tristan's face. "Well..." Should he tell him? He'd find out anyways.

Collin dropped his head and peeked up under Tristan's long bangs. "Well, what?"

Giving Collin a mischievous grin, Tristan focused on him. "Actually, I draw men. Nude men. And sometimes, they're in sexual positions."

A belly laugh erupted out of Collin. "You what? Oh my God, that's classic." He slapped his hand on the table. "No wonder the chicks will be banging the door down to get at those."

Tristan sat back and frowned.

"How the hell are they going to let you sell gay porn in the art supply store?" A new round of chuckling sprang from Collin's throat. He wiped a napkin over his lips.

Tristan's chest heated and he leaned forward, glaring at Colin. "It's not porn, Collin. It's art. And I'm good at it, really good."

With his grin fading, Collin cleared his throat.

Tristan furrowed his brows and focused on the table between them. His voice grew soft. "Besides, I'm only going to give them the nudes to sell, not the ones in the sexual poses."

Leaning forward, Collin placed his hand on Tristan's arm. "Listen, I'm sure you're good at it and I'm sure your art is amazing. I'm sorry I laughed. I was just imagining...Well, it doesn't matter. Maybe you could draw me sometime." He waggled his brows.

Tristan's gaze cut to Collin, his heart lifting. "Yeah? I was sort of hoping to."

Giving him a wide smile, Collin said, "Sure, I'll even let you draw me naked." He arched a brow.

His mind filled with the image of Collin lying naked on a bed, hard and ready for him. His cock woke and swelled. Wetting his lips, he shifted in his seat and adjusted his jeans.

Collin sniggered and ticked his head at him. "You like that idea, don't you?"

Warmth flooded Tristan's cheeks. "Stop it."

Collin lifted a soupspoon to his lips and blew over the lumps and broth of beef stew. "Hey, this must be the longest time you've gone without jerking off, huh?"

Holding up his burger, Tristan took a large bite, then tensed his brows and swallowed his food. "Yeah, I suppose." Need flared inside him. Talking about it made him itch for it even more. He coughed into his hand and shifted in his seat.

"Well, when was the last time you didn't do it for a whole day?" Collin ate more stew.

"Do we have to talk about it *now*?" Tristan pressed his lips together. A whole day? Did that mean Collin wanted him to continue like this?

Collin leaned toward him. "Why not? It's not like anyone can hear us."

Tristan fixed his gaze on his plate. "Because it makes me uncomfortable." He adjusted himself again, his erection pulsing in the tight jeans. He let his hand linger for a moment and pressed on the head of his cock. Pleasure rippled through him. He shouldn't be doing this.

"Tristan..."

His gaze met Collin's.

Taking a quick glance toward Tristan's arms, Collin nodded once. "Did you get hard talking about it?"

Tristan's breath quickened. Why was this so difficult? "Let's not talk about it here."

Collin pursed his lips. "Well, did you?"

Glaring at Collin, Tristan said, "I said, let's not talk about it." He clenched his jaw. Why couldn't he leave it alone for now?

Collin sat back. "Okay, okay, I'm sorry." He mumbled, "Guess I got my answer anyways." His focus returned to his stew, stirring it with his spoon. "I don't mean to push, Tristan. I'm just trying to figure this out with you."

Resting a hand over his now aching cock, Tristan enjoyed the soothing heat and faint pressure. "Let's just eat and get out of here." He had to tame this monster inside him and quit getting so angry all the time.

"Yeah." Collin squirmed in his seat and fixated on Tristan's arm.

Tristan picked up the hamburger and shoved it into his mouth.

———

A half hour later, Tristan followed Collin down the hallway to their room with his hands in his front pockets, hiding the obvious arousal still taunting him. No way could he keep this up, not today. Collin had said he only had to do it for the morning, right?

Collin pushed a key in the lock on their door and opened it. After stepping inside, he held the door for him.

Tristan walked into the room to the far end and dropped his backpack on his desk. As he turned, he let out a heavy sigh.

After shutting the door, Collin strolled to him, then stopped to stand before him. "You okay?" He let his backpack slide off his muscled arm and hit the floor, his gaze searching Tristan's face.

Tristan peeked at him and focused on his lips, his body aching. Should he kiss him? "Collin?"

"Yeah?" Collin brushed his long fingers up Tristan's arm.

"I uh...well, I want to um..." Why couldn't he just say it? His throat tightened and he furrowed his brows.

"You what?" A soft smirk played on Collin's mouth

His touch became a sensual caress on Tristan's arm. His gaze drew back to Collin's stunning face, the dark eyes, the tongue now licking a circle and wetting his full lips. His breathing quickened and his breath caught. "I uh—"

"Go ahead, Tristan, it's okay to want something from me." Collin skimmed his fingers lower to brush over Tristan's hips, back and forth, going lower and lower. As he brushed over Tristan's erection, need hummed inside him and a tickle twitched his hard cock inside his jeans. He closed his eyes and snuck his tongue out to wet his lips, breathing heavily. "Oh, God, I want you, Collin, right now." He swayed his hips into Collin's touch.

"You sure?" Collin's pupils grew wide, and he leaned in,

placing a passionate kiss on his mouth while moving teasing fingers over the head of Tristan's erection.

Collin rubbed up and down Tristan's shaft, increasing the pressure and speed.

Parting his lips, Tristan let Collin penetrate him, probe inside him with his tongue. Searing pleasure rushed through his body. Moaning, he thrust into Collin's hand. Sensitivity rocketed to a sweet, dangerous level. He was too close. "Shit." He ripped away and stepped back, panting.

"What's the matter?" Collin reached out for him.

Tristan took another step back. "I, uh, just need a minute." He turned around to face his desk, warmth rising in his cheeks. *Why can't I control myself with him?*

Collin grasped his arm, just under the shoulder and gently tugged him back around. "It's okay. Let's just go slow."

"We were, weren't we?" Tristan focused the floor. He couldn't look at him. It was all too embarrassing.

"Well, obviously not slow enough." Collin wrapped an arm around Tristan's shoulders and guided him to his bed. "What do you think would be better, keeping your clothes on or off?"

Tristan lifted his gaze from Collin's tennis shoes, to the bulge in his jeans and up to his face. What did he see there?

Collins darkened eyes watched him, studied him.

"What do you want to do?" Tristan asked in almost a whisper. He could trust Collin, right?

A soft chuckle escaped Collin and he leaned forward, brushing his lips over the shell of Tristan's ear. In a husky voice, he said, "First, I want to lay you down beside me. Then, I want to undress you, slowly, and lick every part of you."

Collin's breath tickled Tristan's ear and a shiver raced down his spine. His breath quickened and his cock ached.

"After I've done that..." Collin cupped Tristan's balls. "I want to take you in my mouth."

A soft gasp rippled from Tristan, and he took a hard swallow.

"And suck on you, deeply and slowly." Collin straightened and looked Tristan in the eye, a coy grin playing over his lips.

Tristan trembled as need flooded all his senses. "Th-that doesn't sound s-slow." But he definitely wanted all of it.

Bringing his mouth close to Tristan's, Collin said, "Oh, but it will be. I'll make sure of it." He brushed his lips over Tristan's in a barely there kiss.

A shudder raced through Tristan's body, and he lifted his hand to toy with the edge of his pocket, waiting to dive inside. His groin hummed.

Grasping Tristan's hand, Collin led it away from the pocket and pressed it to his own jean-covered erection. "Touch me, Tristan." He rocked into Tristan's palm, releasing a sharp gasp.

Collin's hard shaft jerked in Tristan's palm. He closed his eyes and a low moan crept from his throat. Could he do this? Could he control himself long enough to give Collin what he wanted? He wrinkled his brows.

Collin crushed his lips to Tristan's, kissing him hungrily. He pressed his body against him, and their hips met as he hooked his arms around Tristan's waist, then rubbed his cock from side to side against Tristan's.

Clawing at him, Tristan grasped for any and every part of him. Sweet friction drove his need higher, and he struggled to keep it in check. "C-Collin, maybe slow wasn't such a good idea." He craved the feel of Collin's velvet skin against his own.

Collin sucked and nipped a slow trail down Tristan's chin and onto his neck.

A violent shudder rocked Tristan, rippling pleasure from his swollen cock to his neck.

"No, this will be better." Collin caressed up Tristan's stomach to his chest and gave Tristan's nipple a light pinch.

With a gasp, Tristan rutted against Collin, his cock hardening further, his sac tightening. He whined, "P-please."

"Please what?" Collin continued the assault on Tristan's body, licking and sucking over the sensitive skin of his neck and behind his ear.

"Please just do it already." Heat burned over every inch of Tristan's skin.

"No." Collin pulled away from him and placed a palm on Tristan's cheek. Gazing into Tristan's eyes, Collin's pupils flared, and his eyelids hooded. "It's going to last this time."

Tristan's gaze darted between Collin's eyes. Could he do it? He nodded his head, fixating on Collin.

A faint grin grew on Collin's lips. "Come on, let's get on the bed." He climbed onto the bed, sat to one side, and patted the empty space next to him.

With his body shaking with need, Tristan mounted the bed and lay on his back beside Collin, then flicked his tongue over his lower lip.

Collin rolled on top of him, propping up on his elbows on either side of Tristan's head. "How are you doing? Are you close?"

Tristan rolled his hips into Collin's, unable to stop himself. Delicious pressure ground on his cock. He ached to keep thrusting, to bring on release right now. "No, but I could be in a second."

Brushing his knuckles over Tristan's cheek, Collin asked, "Why is it you can play with yourself all day and not get off and then when you're with me you're like a pressure cooker ready to explode?"

With a scoff, Tristan twisted his head to look at the wall, his cheeks warming. "I don't know. Why do you have to ask me things like that?"

"I'm just trying to figure you out, that's all." Collin brushed a lock of blond hair from Tristan's forehead. "Are you still scared of me?"

Tristan shifted his attention to Collin's dark eyes. "No. I just—"

"Because why else would you have such control over yourself

normally, when you're alone, but not when you're with me?" Collin narrowed his eyes.

Tristan tensed his brows. "I don't know. I'm not scared, not anymore."

"Then how do you feel about me?" Collin's neck dipped with a hard swallow.

Tristan's heart jolted. "What?" He stared at him.

A soft smile ghosted over Collin's lips. "Relax, I just asked you how you felt about me."

I love you...don't say it out loud. "Isn't that obvious? Haven't we already been over this?" Tristan's muscles stiffened. What answer was Collin looking for? Did he want to hear those words? No way could he say that.

Collin placed a lingering kiss over his mouth. "Well, maybe it's because of your feelings for me that you're having such a hard time. How long did you jerk off and think of me?"

Gasping, Tristan clenched his eyes shut. "Stop it, Collin."

"Open your eyes and look at me and answer my question." A firm gentleness filled Collin's voice.

Tristan opened his eyes and heat rushed his cheeks. "Ever since I first saw you in class." Hadn't he already told him that? But maybe not exactly that.

"Since the beginning of the school year?" Collin's face tensed as if in deep thought. "So, it started on the first day?"

He nodded. "Yes."

"Every day?" Collin lifted his brows.

"Yes." Tristan winced.

"All day?" Collin's brows rose even higher.

"Yes." Images of his fantasies with Collin flooded his mind, of Collin fondling him, of Collin sucking him under his desk, of Collin telling him how much he loved him.

"Are they happening now? I mean, is what we do like what your fantasies were about?" Collin dropped his brows and tensed a corner of his mouth.

"What do you think?" Tristan chanced a peek at him. Why was Collin asking all this? Would it really help him in some way?

"Tell me what you used to fantasize about," Collin said in soft and husky voice. He pressed his firm cock into Tristan's through their jeans and nuzzled into his neck, kissing and nipping at the soft flesh.

"I, uh, used to..." His breath caught as pleasure knotted in his gut. He gasped and ground his dick on Collin's, sweet pressure and friction heightening his sensitivity.

"Go ahead, tell me. Did I do this?" Collin pushed lower on Tristan's body and raised Tristan's shirt, exposing his stomach, then licked into the hollows of his abdomen and thrust his tongue into his navel.

Tristan let out a sharp moan. "Y-yes."

Collin dipped his tongue lower, under Tristan's belt and the band of his boxers, licking and teasing him. "Did I do this?"

"Yes," Tristan growled, clutching at the back of Collin's hair, attempting to push him lower.

Swiftly, Collin unfastened Tristan's belt and zipper and opened Tristan's jeans, then dove downward, sucking and nibbling at Tristan's cock through the thin fabric of his boxers.

"Oh, God." As pleasure rushed through Tristan, he arched his back.

"Did I suck on you, Tristan?" Collin tongued through the slit in Tristan's boxers and licked up his shaft.

"Yes!" His voice rang out in the small room. He clenched his teeth and his toes curled. Release surged forward to the raw edge. "Do it now, please!" He tugged on Collin's head.

In a flash, Collin shucked Tristan's boxers down, baring his erection, then devoured his cock, pumping over it while his free hand groped at his own stiff flesh still under his jeans.

Tristan bucked and cried out while Collin's tongue raced up his shaft and circled the head, again and again. Sensitivity heightened to a sweet peak and his climax flashed inside him. Delicious contractions spurted cum into Collin's hungry mouth. As it slowed, his chest heaved with deep breaths. "Oh, shit." He panted. "Oh, shit."

Tipping his head up, Collin gazed at him with darkened eyes. "Like that?"

Tristan struggled to find words, his voice, anything coherent. "Uh...um...shit...shut up."

Climbing up, Collin laid beside him. "Cause it's my turn." He unbuckled his belt, popped open the button of his jeans and lowered the zipper. Then, he lifted his hips, slid his jeans down to his ankles and kicked them off with his shoes and socks. "Ready." Twisting his head to Tristan, he smirked.

Tristan smiled. This was more like it. How it should be. He climbed on top of Collin and crouched down between his legs. How many times had he thought about this very thing? And now here he was, about to take Collin's dick into his mouth.

Licking up Collin's shaft, Tristan tasted the bead of pre-cum gathered at the head. Collin's urgent moan swept over his ears. He took in Collin's perfect erection, thick and curved and hard, just for him, then cupped Collin's sac and sucked him into his mouth.

Collin's seeping cock pulsed. "Jesus, that feels good." He rocked his hips.

Tristan drove his mouth down and came up slow, savoring Collin's taste, the feel of slickened, silky skin over rock hard flesh. Fondling Collin's sac, he pumped up and down over him, pressing his tongue to the underside of his shaft. Collin's cock grew harder and twitched in his mouth. More pre-cum dribbled from the tip and he took it all in, swirling his tongue over the head.

Collin bucked and groaned, a satisfied, sensual groan. "That's it. Go faster." He thrust quicker into Tristan's mouth.

Sucking Collin's thick cock, Tristan's cheeks hollowed, and he pumped faster. Heat filled his groin and his cock swelled again. He moaned over Collin's pulsing dick.

Collin grew rigid beneath him, and he gave one hard thrust

into Tristan's mouth, slapping his hands to the back of Tristan's head. "Oh, shit...I'm coming, Tristan, I'm com—" He gasped.

Collin's cum filled Tristan's mouth. He kept on him, pumping him with his lips, stroking his sac, swallowing it all down his throat. *I'm doing to this to Collin, making him come undone. Me.*

As Collin released into his mouth, Collin's hips jerked and his body writhed.

Tristan's erection ached. As he lapped at Collin, he squeezed his thighs tight, trapping his erection between them. The pressure and friction drove pleasure through him. Pulling his mouth off Collin's spent cock, he gave a low, deep moan, thrusting into his thighs, then dropped his forehead onto Collin's navel and clutched the sheets on either side of Collin's hips. Tension coiled to a delicious peak and a second climax erupted out of him, sweet spasms slickening his thighs and sharp gasps ripping from his throat. It slowed and warm hands grasped his shoulders to nudge him up.

"Come on, Tristan."

Breathing heavily, Tristan willed his body to move and his mind to clear. What just happened? He looked down at Collin's stunning, naked body below him and laid beside him.

Wrapping an arm around Tristan's shoulders, Collin held him to his chest. "You okay?"

Tristan nodded, his mind in a daze.

"Good, 'cause that was fucking hot." Collin kissed his head.

Tristan let his gaze wander up to Collin's grinning face. "What?"

A soft chuckle rumbled Collin's chest. "I said that was hot."

Darting his gaze to the wall, heat flushed Tristan's cheeks. "Really?"

"Fuck yeah. I don't think I've ever seen someone get so worked up over a blow job." Collin released a soft snicker.

"Stop it." Tristan buried his face in Collin's chest.

"No, really. I never knew you could make yourself come with

your thighs like that. It was a real turn-on. See?" Collin pointed down to his groin.

His gaze fell to Collin's cock. It lay erect against his stomach. "Oh."

"Oh? I don't even think it had time to get soft before it got hard again and all you can say is *oh*?" Collin gave him a playful squeeze. "You're really something, you know that?"

Tristan shook his head. He wasn't used to any of this.

"You are. I've never met anyone like you. You're such a sexual being when you let it out." Collin raked his free hand through his hair and sighed. "Maybe I shouldn't be trying to change you."

He lifted his head to peer into Collin's gorgeous face. "What? But I thought what I was doing was wrong?"

Collin chuckled. "It is, but that doesn't mean it's not hot." He pressed a gentle kiss on Tristan's lips.

A slow smirk curled Tristan's mouth. "Do you want me to um, give you another blow job, right now?"

Collin looked up at the ceiling for a moment. "I'm afraid if you do that we'll never stop." He chuckled again. "I mean, I'd come, and you'd get turned on, then you'd come, and I'd get turned on and well, it could be a never-ending cycle. We have to start coming together, I think." His eyes twinkled.

"Right." With a quick nod, Tristan grinned. He'd never thought he could ever be this happy.

Collin peered at Tristan's thighs. "You're a mess. Let me get you a washcloth." He untangled himself from Tristan and climbed off the bed. As he stepped toward the bathroom, he stopped and glanced at him, wagging his brows. "One word, Tristan, *hot*." With a quick laugh, he walked to the bathroom.

He lay on his back in Collin's bed and gazed up at the ceiling. *Collin thinks I'm hot.* A smile spread over his lips and a short chuckle escaped him. Never in a million years did he ever think Collin would feel that way about him. Warmth bloomed in his chest.

Collin returned from the restroom with a wet washcloth in

his hand. Propping a leg on the bed, he leaned down and wiped Tristan's thighs.

Warm, wet heat brushed over Tristan's legs with Collin's caring touch. He smiled at him.

"What?" Collin skimmed the washcloth over Tristan's leg.

"You." Tristan widened his smile.

Collin's face lit up. "Me what?" He straightened and held the washcloth at his side.

"You just..." Tristan sighed and glanced at the ceiling. "You make me feel good about myself."

Collin tossed the washcloth to the floor and plopped down on the bed to lie on his back beside Tristan. "Well, that's a good thing, isn't it?"

Nodding once, Tristan said, "I'm not all that used to it." He shifted to his side and gazed at Collin. "In fact, I don't remember ever feeling good about myself."

"Even when you were little?" Collin twisted his head to face him.

Tristan knitted his brows. How did he feel when he was little? He struggled to form memories from elementary school. His head filled with a sad little boy, standing in the corner of a playground alone. He shut his eyes against the vision. "No, I was always different."

Collin turned to his side and placed a hand on Tristan's shoulder. "How do you mean?"

"I never really had many friends. I remember always being by myself." Tristan gazed deeply into his eyes.

"Always? Why?" Collin bit the corner of his lower lip.

Tristan shrugged. "I don't know. I suppose I always knew I was attracted to the same sex, and I knew it was a terrible sin. Other boys talked about girls. I only thought about boys. I knew there was something not right inside me." He sighed. "Plus, I never wanted to bring anyone around my house. My mom always embarrassed me."

Collin leaned forward and gave Tristan a lingering kiss on his forehead. "Did she embarrass you because she was always drunk?"

Blinking hard, Tristan's vision blurred as his chest squeezed. He opened his mouth, then pursed his lips. It was too difficult to talk about, even now.

"Tristan, please talk to me. I want to know about you. You trust me, right?" Collin skimmed his hand down Tristan's side.

Tristan focused on him. "Trust you?"

"Yeah, you know I'd never do anything to hurt you, right?" Collin pulled him close again.

Tristan rested his head on Collin's chest with his arm bent up between them, snug in his embrace. "Yeah, I know."

"Do you? Really?"

Tristan nodded. "Yes."

"Then talk to me. Tell me everything." Collin's hold on him tightened.

Pressing his lips together, Tristan drew a deep inhale. "She was always drunk. I learned early on not to bring friends home because she'd be stumbling around the house saying nasty things to me and whoever I was with. When I did have a friend or two, I'd start out going to their house a lot, but you know how moms always want the other mom to reciprocate. When their mom started complaining that we never went to my house, I'd sort of disappear."

"Disappear?" Collin asked.

Tristan traced a small circle on Collin's muscled chest. "I just wouldn't be friends with them anymore. Then they'd never have to come to my house." He pursed his lips. That was how it had to be. He'd never had a friend for more than a few months.

"When was this going on?" Collin shifted and placed a kiss on Tristan's head.

"Uh, pretty much all through grade school." Tristan sighed. "And then there was this disastrous time I actually kissed a guy in high school."

"You did what?" Collin shifted to focus on him.

Tristan sucked in a deep breath. "Yeah, my only real kiss, actually, well, before I met you." His cheeks warmed.

"You're kidding?" Collin rested his head onto his pillow and gazed at the ceiling. "You kiss pretty good for someone who's only kissed once."

Tristan shrugged. "Thanks. I've certainly thought about it a lot."

Collin's attention drew back to him. "Tell me what happened, when you kissed that guy in high school."

Rolling to his back, Tristan said, "His name was Sean, and we were both seniors. We were friends for almost two years at the time. His parents were divorced, and his mom worked nights at the hospital. She was a nurse. Anyways, you can see how this worked in my favor. We never spent any time at my house."

"And so, you kissed him one night at his house when his mother was away?" A faint smirk formed on Collin's lips.

"No, worse."

Collin shifted to his side and rested his head on his hand, propped up by an elbow. "Worse how?"

Giving him a quick glance, Tristan said, "He had other friends at school and we got invited to a senior party at this big house. Of course, there was drinking involved. Well, I sort of caught him outside the bathroom in a hallway and just planted a big, ole kiss on him." He frowned.

Colin caressed Tristan's shoulder. "Did you have feelings for him?"

How did he feel about Sean? Did he love him? *No, not the way I love Collin.* He turned his head to look deeply into Collin's eyes. "No." His heart ached with emotion. "Definitely not."

A soft smirk crept over Collin's lips. "Then why did you kiss him?"

"I don't know. I was drunk." Tristan let out a soft snort.

"Good answer..." Collin gave him a playful nudge in the side. "So, what the hell happened after that? Did he kiss you back? Did you two make out?"

"God, no. He took a swing at me and missed. He was more drunk than I was." He pursed his lips. "The asshole went and told everyone at the party I was a fag and that I kissed him." His gut tightened.

"Oh." Collin's voice was soft, and his grin faded. "And so, I guess you left."

"Yeah, right after a few of the guys from the football team beat the shit out of me. Fucking tore me up." Visions of snarling faces and menacing threats filled his memory. Heat pierced his chest, and he clenched his teeth for a moment. "Those fuckers always hated me anyways. They made fun of me all the time in school, made me drop my books and fucked with my locker so the combination wouldn't work."

"Jesus," Collin said under his breath, wrinkling his brows. "No wonder you don't like bullies."

His gaze roamed the stunning features of Collin's face, and his body relaxed. Why was looking at Collin so soothing to him? *I really can talk to Collin. It's okay.* "But you know what's even worse?"

"No, what?" Collin stopped the caress of Tristan's arm.

"A few days later, my mom heard about it."

"And?"

"And she hit me with a bottle of vodka." Tristan shut his eyes against the memory, his chest squeezing. She was never there for him. She was as bad as the rest of them.

"Holy shit, dude. Where, on the head again?" Collin shifted on the bed.

Tristan shook his head. Sudden pain swelled up inside him, ravaged him. His eyes stung. "No, she just...she just kept hitting me over the back with it and, and..." A hot tear tumbled down the side of his face. He sniffled and bit his lip.

"Damn it." Collin yanked him into a tight embrace. "Tristan, why—"

"She always screamed at me, told me I was a freak and a faggot and, and..." Tristan's breath hitched. The pain heightened, became unbearable. "Going to Hell and I'm not worth anything, just like my father." A sob broke from him.

"Shh, settle down now." Collin tightened his hold on him. "None of that's true, you know that. You better know that now."

Holding his breath, Tristan fought to gain control of his emotions, taking deep breaths.

"You know none of that's true, right?" Collin gave him a slight shake.

"I-I don't know. Am I really worth anything?" Tristan's voice cracked.

"Shit, Tristan, you're worth a lot to me." Collin pressed a hard kiss on the side of his head.

"Really?" He pushed off Collin to gaze into his face.

"Fuck yeah. I uh, well, I..." Collin tensed his brows and dropped his gaze.

"You what?" Tristan grabbed Collin's chin and pulled, making Collin face him. Would he finally hear what he wanted to hear? *Does Collin love me?* Collin flicked his gaze away. "Well, I said I liked you, right?"

Tristan's heart dropped. In a soft voice, he said, "Yeah, you did."

Collin looked at him. "So, when was the last time you spoke with your mother?"

Blinking a few times, Tristan lifted his brows. "Um, I actually talk to her every Sunday." But what was Collin going to *say*?

"Really? I would have thought you didn't talk to her much." Collin eyed him.

"No, I talk to her every week." Tristan sighed. "If I don't, I get in trouble." He pressed his lips together. He was lucky if she was sober when he talked to her, too.

"I think you'd get in trouble no matter what you do." Collin let out a soft chuckle. "Hey, what are you doing for Thanksgiving?"

"Thanksgiving?" Tristan released his hold on Collin and rolled to his back, raking a hand through the long locks of his blond hair. "Nothing, why?" He usually tried to find a reason to stay on campus, even if that meant eating alone.

Collin tapped his finger on his chin. "Because I don't have to go home, and I'd like to meet your mother."

"Why the hell would you want to do that?" Tristan let out a ragged exhale.

"Because I think it would be helpful for me to meet her. Then I could really see the dynamic between you two and it would help me to help you. Maybe it's time she saw that being gay isn't so bad." Collin gave him a smug smile.

Tristan's pulse quickened. Would Collin be able to deal with his mother? Maybe it would be different this time. Maybe Collin's grasp of psychology and his knowledge of the situation would make it okay for once. Maybe. "I-I don't know."

Nudging him, Collin let a soft smirk quirk his lips. "Oh, come on. What have you got to lose? I already know what she's like, so I know what to expect. And besides, I'll be there for you if anything happens. Maybe what she needs to see is someone who's okay with their sexuality and that someone digs her son. I don't know, hell, I'm just thinking out loud."

He mulled over Collin's words. "Do you really think you could make a difference in how she treats me?"

A wide, confident smile swept over Collin's mouth. "Sure. I could really talk you up. But on the other hand, Tristan, it's time you spoke up for yourself."

"What do you mean by that?" A shudder rolled through his body. He couldn't do that. Was Collin insane? Had he not heard anything he'd said?

"You need to stand up to her. I'll bet you never have, have you?" Collin cupped Tristan's cheek and looked deeply into his eyes.

Tristan mumbled, "No." Thoughts jumbled through his mind of screaming and hitting, rage and hurtful words hurling at him, stinging him, breaking him. He trembled. "I don't think I can do that."

"What do you mean? You were strong enough to stop touching yourself today. You can do this. I'll be right by your side, remember that." Collin pressed a deep kiss on his lips. "You can do it. I know you can. Besides, you're a celebrity, remember?"

Warmth swelled Tristan's chest. *That's right. I'm the best artist on the campus.* He focused on Collin's dark eyes. "Maybe I can."

"Good, so now that that's settled, I've got some studying to do. Let's clean up." Collin shimmied to the edge of the bed and stood, then held his hand out to Tristan.

He looked up at Collin as a shudder worked down his spine. Could he really confront his mother? "Collin, I—"

"No more discussion, we're going. I'll book the flights. I'm sure you have the money?" Collin grasped Tristan's arm and hauled him up.

He nodded. Thankfully, the college fund left to him by his grandparents had been very generous. And his mother couldn't touch any of it.

CHAPTER TEN

Tristan sat back in his chair at his desk, sighing, and gazed out the open window between their desks. The sunset poured orange and blue hues across the sky like some sort of abstract painting. His stomach grumbled and he glanced at Collin's screen. Was he at a place where they could stop and get dinner?

Collin ticked over the keyboard of his laptop at a furious pace, focused wholly on the screen.

Quietly, Tristan leaned over and squinted. What did it say? It looked like it could be Collin's psychology thesis again. His gaze ran over the psychology books scattered on the floor, then focused back on the screen. A word flashed out at him, clear as day. "Masturbation?" He gasped and sat back.

Clicking his mouse, Collin's screen flipped to his email. "What?" He turned to face him.

Tristan pointed at the screen. "I clearly saw the word *masturbation* on your paper. What are you writing about, Collin?" There had to be an explanation, right?

Collin widened his eyes and rubbed his forehead, glancing at the screen, then faced him. "No way, Tristan. You must have been seeing things." He pressed his lips together.

"No, I wasn't. I saw it very clearly." His chest pinched. Had he really seen that? "Just tell me what your thesis is about." He peered at Collin, watching him.

Collin stood and stepped toward him, then dropped his hands over Tristan's shoulders and opened his mouth as if to speak.

Swatting Collin's hands away, Tristan stood and paced to the center of the room, raking his hand through his long bangs. He had a right to know if something was going on here, didn't he? "What are you writing about?"

Collin huffed. "Oh, come on, Tris—"

Rapping filled the room.

Glancing at the door, Tristan said, "Who is it?"

Collin strode by him and stopped at the door. "It's Jessica." Grasping the knob, he turned it and swung the door open.

"Well, hello, Collin." A smug smile hung on Jessica's face. Her tight jeans hugged long legs over high heels and a knit shirt dropped low, baring the tops of her breasts. She strolled past Collin and into the room. "Hello, Tristan."

Tristan dropped his gaze to the gray carpet covering their floor, then mumbled, "Hello." Now he'd never figure out what he saw.

"Hey, Jess. Thanks for stopping by on such short notice." Collin jogged to his chair and slid it out for her to sit on.

She dropped into the chair and set her hands in her lap. Her gaze swept from Collin to Tristan and back again. "So?"

Wringing his hands in front of him, Collin stepped toward Tristan, the edges of his lips twitching. "Hey, uh, Tristan, would it be okay if Jessica and I had some time alone to go over some research for my paper?"

Tristan lowered his brows, his gut clenching. Was he being kicked out of his own room? "What?" He planted his hands on his hips and shifted his stance.

Collin let out a stuttered chuckle. "I got a little stuck, so I texted her to come over."

"You didn't look stuck to me." He snuck a peek at Jessica, watching them with a smirk on her face, then he wrinkled his nose. He didn't like the looks of this.

"Oh, come on, aren't you hungry? You could get some dinner and bring me back some. I'm sure we'll only be maybe forty-five minutes, right, Jess?" Collin turned to glance at her.

She raised her brows and gave a nod of her head while crossing her arms over her chest.

"Why do you have to be alone? Why can't I be around while you do your research?" He glanced from Collin to Jessica. He didn't trust her for one second. What would she try to pull when he left?

She stood up and strolled to Tristan. "Because we need to concentrate, and I don't think Collin can really concentrate with you here." She freed a soft snicker as her pointed fingernail brushed down Tristan's arm, giving it a light tickle.

Tristan jerked his arm away and rubbed it, focusing on Collin. "That sounds like a load of crap."

"Tris—"

Placing her index finger over Collin's mouth, she shushed him and stepped between the young men, facing Tristan. "It's not a load of crap. It's the truth. I think you could be courteous enough to give us a little privacy, don't you?"

With pursed lips, he stared at the floor. *What a bitch.* He fisted his hands. She was giving him no choice and making him look bad if he stayed.

"Well?" She sighed. "You might as well pick up some dinner for me, too."

Tristan glared at her. "Really, and what would you like, Your Highness?"

"Tristan!" Collin stepped out from behind her and grabbed Tristan's arm.

He yanked his arm away from Collin and took a step back. He was being an ass, but he couldn't help himself with her smug attitude. What sort of hold did she have on Collin anyways?

She held her arms out, separating the young men again. "Listen, Tristan, I'm not the enemy here. I'm just trying to help your, uh, friend with a very complicated thesis. You could be a little more understanding."

He dropped his jaw open. "What? Who the hell are you to tell me I'm anything? You don't even know me."

She held up her hands, showing her palms. "Relax, there's no reason to get so defensive."

Blowing a long exhale, he turned his back on her, focusing on the wall, staring at nothing. What the hell was he so upset about anyways? All she was doing was making him look like more of an ass. *I am hungry...*

"Tristan?" Collin placed a hand on Tristan's forearm and tugged him gently back around.

Tristan gazed into his dark eyes.

Collin whispered, "Please, just let us do what we need to do. I don't understand why you're getting so upset about this." He caressed up and down Tristan's arm.

Leaning over, he glanced at Jessica. In a low voice, he said, "I don't like her."

"Shh...don't let her hear that. What's the matter with you?" Collin lowered his brows.

Tristan's cheeks heated and he dropped his gaze to the dark fabric covering Collin's chest. "I-I don't know. I'm sorry." He had to learn how to control his emotions better. Problem was, he wasn't used to dealing with emotions at all. Not without...

Collin sighed softly. "Please just go get some food and let her help me, okay?"

Tristan's gaze drifted to Collin's stunning face, then fixated on his plump lips. Desire flamed through his body. *He's so close.* He exhaled a soft breath. "Whatever. Okay, what do you want?"

"Huh?" Collin raised his brows.

"To eat. What do you want to eat?" A memory flashed through Tristan's mind of how Collin's delicious cock had tasted in his mouth. He blinked the memory away and swallowed hard. He had to stop thinking about that.

"I'll have a salad. They have a great chicken Caesar down at the cafeteria." Jessica stepped to stand beside Collin, studying Tristan.

Glancing at her, Tristan ticked his head before turning his focus back on Collin.

"Just get me whatever the special is. I'm sure it'll be good." Collin turned to Jessica. "So? Let's get some work done."

Jessica stepped to Collin's bed and took a seat on its edge. "I'm ready."

Brushing by Collin, Tristan snatched his backpack and trudged to the door.

"See you in a little while," Collin called out to him.

"Uh-huh." He opened the door and stepped into the hallway. It didn't feel right to leave them alone, but what else could he do?

———

TRISTAN SAT at a table by a tall window in the cafeteria, eating a large slice of pepperoni pizza. He let his gaze wander out a window and over the manicured lawn and rows of roses lit up by landscape lighting just outside. He had to get his mind off Collin's thesis. And what about Jessica? Why did she bother him so much?

He shifted in his seat and bit into his pizza. Because she was beautiful and smart and all the things he wasn't. Wasn't Collin attracted to her? He must be or he was blind.

With a frown, he sipped his soda from a straw sticking out of a plastic glass. They were alone, she and Collin. His pulse quickened. He flicked his fingers to the pocket of his jeans, then squirmed them inside to fondle his cock. He could barely move his fingers in the tight jeans, and the fabric of the boxers didn't feel right. Damn it. With a scowl, his chest squeezed and he dug his fingers in deeper. *What are they doing up there?*

He probed and pressed on the head of his swelling cock, but pleasure evaded him. Adjusting his position, he tried again. A pulse rocketed through him, and he let out a soft gasp. Shit, what was he doing? He had to stop. He tugged his hand out of his pocket and sat up straight, looking around the room. No one noticed him. They'd notice Jessica if she were sitting here.

He furrowed his brows and leaned back in his chair, his heart heavy. He should study. Bending to the side, he unzipped his backpack and fumbled through it for his art history book, his bracelets clinking over his wrist. His gaze caught on Ally's business card inside the backpack. He dropped further and fished it out. As he examined it, he straightened in his chair. He should call her. Maybe that'd take his mind off Collin and Jessica for a little while.

He dove back into his backpack and searched for his cell phone, finding a hard, flat object and pulled it out. Glancing at the card in one hand, he dialed her number with the thumb of the other, then set the card on the table and pressed the cell phone to his ear.

The phone rang a few times, then clicked. "Hello?"

"Um, is this Ally?" Tristan rubbed his forehead.

"Yes, who's this?" she asked.

He fingered the edge of the card on the table. "It's, um, it's Tristan."

"Oh, hey there, Tristan. What's up?" Cheer resonated in her voice.

"Well, I wanted to see if I could maybe come by tomorrow and bring some of my artwork, uh, if you're working and—"

"Yeah, sure, tomorrow's great."

"Really? Will you be there around ten-thirty?" He tapped the edge of the card on the table.

"Let me think a minute...Uh, yeah, I can."

"Okay, I'll um, see you then."

"Yep."

He furrowed his brows and examined the card again.

"Tristan?"

"Yeah?"

"Was there something else you wanted?"

He worried his lip. Could he talk to her about Collin? "Um, no, I guess not. I'll just see you tomorrow."

"O-kay..."

"Bye." He pressed the red button on his cell phone, ending the call. "Shit." That call took no time at all. Now what was he supposed to do? He dropped the phone into his backpack and took a large bite of pizza. While he chewed, he fought the urge to run back up to the room. *Just eat, get their food, and go back up.* It would be okay.

———

AFTER TRISTAN FINISHED his pizza and soda, he bought food in to-go containers—one filled with Caesar salad and the other with meatloaf and mashed potatoes, then rode the elevator and ambled down the hallway to his dorm room with his backpack slung over one shoulder, holding the containers out in front of him. When he reached the door, he stopped.

The high pitch of female laughter snaked out from behind the door followed by laughter of a lower pitch, Collin's.

He transferred the containers to one hand and fisted his other hand to knock on the door.

"Yeah, can you believe it? It really worked." Collin's voice rang out from behind the door.

"You're a stud, Collin." A second round of laughter erupted from her.

Placing his hand on the doorknob, he twisted. They'd left it unlocked. Heat swarmed his chest. He opened the door and stomped into the room.

Collin laid on his bed, shirtless, on his back next to the wall, smiling up at the ceiling.

Jessica sat next to him, cross-legged, with her open hand on his stomach, looking down on him.

"What the fuck?" Tristan yelled, his chest heaving. He threw the food containers onto his own bed and dropped his backpack to the floor.

"Jesus." Collin lurched up to sitting and stared at him.

Gasping, she twisted around and looked up at Tristan with wide eyes and an open mouth.

"What are you doing back so early?" Collin clamored to the edge of the bed, making Jessica bounce.

"Some fucking studying, Collin." Trembling, his nerves frayed. It sure didn't look like studying to him. No, it looked like way more was going on here. Was that why they'd asked him to leave?

She held out her hands in a soothing gesture. "Calm down, Tristan. There's nothing to be upset about."

"Nothing?" He paced the room, from his desk to the closet, fisting and opening his hands. "So, I should have no problem with you two lying on a bed together. I should be fucking happy to hear you calling him a stud?" He gritted his teeth.

"What? We weren't lying on the bed together. She was just sitting next to me." Knitting his brows, Collin rose from the edge of the bed, glanced at her, then focused on Tristan. "When did you come in? How long were you standing there listening?"

He stomped to Collin, glaring at him. "Long enough. What's going on between you two?"

She dropped her bare feet to the floor. "Noth—"

"Shut the hell up!" He glared beyond Collin to her.

Collin snatched his arm in a firm hold. "That's enough."

Pain raced through Tristan's arm and lodged in his shoulder. He yanked his arm, but Collin's hold tightened. "Let go." Emotions swirled inside him. What was happening to him? His vision blurred.

"No." Collin hauled him into the hallway, then shoved him up against the far wall.

Tristan's back hit with a thud and he clenched his teeth.

"What's the matter with you? Huh? I thought you trusted me? What the hell was that all about?" A mere inch separated Collin's face from his.

Tristan stared down the hallway, tears threatening to spill down his cheeks. Pain curled up inside him, gnawed at his insides. He held his breath.

"Look at me!" Collin grabbed Tristan's cheeks between his thumb and fingers, twisted his head to face him and let go.

Tristan's breath hitched and his lower lip trembled. With a blink, a tear tumbled down his cheek. "I-I'm sorry." His voice wavered. Where had this anger come from? A sob built in his chest.

"Tristan..." Collin's voice and gaze softened. "Sweetheart, don't cry." He wrapped his arms around Tristan's shoulders and pulled him into his chest.

Tristan fell into the embrace, plunged his face into Collin's neck and draped his arms around his waist. "I'm so sorry, C-Collin. I thought, I thought—"

"Shh, it's okay. I know what you thought. It must have looked pretty bad, but it wasn't, really. Please believe me." Collin squeezed him tighter.

"Collin?" Jessica stood in the doorway with high-heels arching her feet and a food container in her hand.

"Just leave us, okay? I'll talk to you tomorrow." Collin's voice was firm.

She dipped her head and strutted down the hallway toward the elevator.

"Come on." Collin kept an arm wrapped around Tristan and led him back into their room, kicking the door shut after they walked through.

Sniffling, Tristan rested his head on Collin's shoulder. What an idiot. How did he let himself get so out of control again? What was it about Collin that messed with his head so much? Another hot tear journeyed a wet trail down his cheek.

Collin brought him to Tristan's bed, moved the food container to the end of it and sat down, pulling Tristan with him. He brushed the blond bangs out of Tristan's face and placed a tender kiss on his cheek. "It's okay." He tangled his fingers in Tristan's and dropped their entwined hands into Tristan's lap, then wound his arm around Tristan's shoulders. "I guess you're pretty insecure with all this, huh?" He pulled him close.

In a soft voice, Tristan said, "You could say that."

"For the record, there's absolutely nothing going on between me and Jessica. She's just my advisor, that's all." Collin peeked at him.

Tristan gave a slight nod of his head and sniffled again. It felt so good in Collin's arms, so soothing after all that. How could he have thought something had been going on between them? He leaned further into him. "Collin?"

Collin drew a deep inhale. "What?"

"What is your thesis about? Tristan swiped his nose.

With a shake of his head, Collin chuckled softly. "God, you just can't give it up, can you?"

Tristan shifted in his hold. "But I don't understand why you won't just tell me." He focused on the hands in his lap.

Collin released him and straightened his spine. "Let's just say it has to do with a mixture of cognitive behavioral therapy and classical conditioning."

Pinching his brows together, he looked at Collin. "What?"

A soft smile spread over Collin's lips. "See? I told you, you wouldn't understand."

He dropped his gaze to his lap again. "Tell me what it means in normal terms." There had to be a way he'd understand it. He wasn't stupid.

Collin grabbed both his hands. "It's hard to explain without a lot of psycho-babble." He leaned forward and gave him a lingering kiss on the lips. "Besides, we have much more interesting things to talk about."

Tristan gave a single nod of his head. His conversation with Ally popped into his mind and his attention shifted to Collin. "Yeah, I'm meeting Ally tomorrow with a bunch of my drawings."

"Really? Tomorrow already?" Collin patted him on the back. "That's really cool."

Leaning over, Tristan took a quick glance behind Collin at the foot of the bed. "Uh, aren't you hungry?"

Collin twisted and looked at the haphazard food container. "As a matter of fact, I am." He grabbed the container, popped it open and took a deep sniff. "Still smells pretty good."

"I, uh, brought you some silverware, too." Tristan rose up from the bed, walked to his backpack and leaned down to unzip it. After rummaging around for a second, he brought a silver knife and fork out, then stepped back to Collin and handed them to him. "I'm really sorry." He plopped down next to Collin and rested his elbows on his knees.

"It's okay, you don't have to say it again to me. Maybe you should tell Jessica next time you see her, though." Collin slid a bite of meatloaf into his mouth.

Tristan pursed his lips. How could he ever face her again? "How did you meet Jessica?"

Collin swallowed his food down. "She was suggested to me by my psychology professor." He filled his fork with mashed potato and shoveled it into his mouth. "Why?"

With a shrug, he gazed at Collin's stunning face, framed perfectly by auburn hair. "I don't know, I guess it seems like you two have known each other for a long time. Longer than just a few months anyways."

Collin huffed out a chuckle. "Why would you say that?"

"I don't know. You're just so...comfortable with each other." Hanging his head, Tristan blew out a long exhale.

Collin sat sideways on the bed. "Really, Tristan, you don't have to worry." He stood up from the bed, stepped to his desk and placed his almost empty food container on it. "I don't have any interest in her." He knelt down before the refrigerator and opened it.

"But you like girls, right?" Tristan wrung his hands in his lap. Why couldn't he leave this alone?

Collin pulled out a soda from the refrigerator and shut the door. Snapping the soda can open, he twisted on his heels to face him. "Look at you, all upset about this again." He looked him up and down. "And you know what?"

"What?" He tensed his brows as his chest tightened.

"Your hands. Look at them." Collin ticked his head at Tristan's lap.

Tristan looked down at his hands, wrestling with one another. "So?" He refocused on Collin.

Taking a sip of soda, Collin stood and stepped to Tristan. "What're they doing?"

With his brows crinkling, he watched his hands. "Nothing, just sort of...I don't know." Sighing, he lifted one hand and raked through his hair, making his bracelets jangle. What was he going on about?

Collin dropped to sit on tucked legs in front of him, cupped Tristan's cheek and gazed at him with a smirk curling the edge of his mouth. "They're nowhere near your pocket."

Lifting both hands to his face, he gazed at his palms and gaped.

"How do you feel?" Collin beamed at him.

"I don't know. Anxious, I suppose." Tristan flicked his gaze to Collin's dark eyes.

"But do you feel like touching yourself?" Collin lifted his brows.

A rush of desire flooded his body. "I didn't, not until you mentioned it." He squirmed in his seat.

"Oops, maybe I shouldn't mention it, huh?" Rising up on his knees, Collin placed a kiss on his mouth. "But I wanted you to see how quickly you're getting better. You should be proud of yourself."

He dropped his hand to his sides and grinned. "Yeah, I should, huh?"

"In fact, I think we should celebrate, as long as you keep this up all through tomorrow. Don't you think?" Lifting the can to his lips, Collin gulped his soda.

"All through tomorrow? You mean all day?" His heart sped up. Could he really do it?

"Yes. If you can contain yourself all day tomorrow, I'll take you out to the clubs tomorrow night." Collin gave him a smug grin. "How's that?"

"The clubs? You mean nightclubs?" He stuffed his hands under his ass and glanced out the window. "I don't know if I like nightclubs all that much." He'd never even been to one.

Collin traced a circle on Tristan's thigh. "Oh, well, how about just a bar then?"

A vision of he and Collin flooded his mind, of talking with beers set on a table in front of them, laughing, enjoying each other's company. "Yeah, you know? That would be fun."

"Great, I know a gay bar down by the piers we could go to." Collin sat down on his tucked legs and sipped more soda.

"A gay bar? You've got to be kidding me." A wide grin spread over his lips. Damn Collin...

"Why not? You're gay, aren't you?" A laugh tumbled out of Collin.

"Yeah, but, aren't those places sort of well, gay?" Tristan choked out a chuckle.

Collin shrugged and tossed his now empty can of soda into the trash next to Tristan's desk. "So? I think it'd be good for you get out among your people, so to speak, and not feel the need to hide yourself."

He stared at the poster-filled wall over Collin's bed. What would it be like to be with other guys who liked guys? For that matter, what would it be like to be openly *with* Collin in public, in a place where they wouldn't stick out?

"Well? What do you think?" Collin tapped Tristan's thigh.

Startling, Tristan cut his focus to Collin, then smiled. "I think I'd really like that."

Collin shifted to sit cross-legged and leaned back on outstretched arms. "So, there's only one catch."

"A catch?" Raising his brows, he leaned forward. "What's that?"

"You have to control yourself until tomorrow night. Think of it as a reward for good behavior." Collin lifted his chin.

"Are you really telling me that you won't take me there if I mess up?" Tristan eyed him and a smirk quirked his lips. Surely, a little slip up wouldn't stop them from going.

"Yes, I am." Collin dropped his smile.

A sharp pain tugged at his heart. "Come on—"

"I mean it, Tristan. I want you to get better." Collin crept forward and placed his hands on Tristan's knees. "I want you to earn this, to learn that feeling your emotions is okay, not something to be covered up by stimulating yourself."

His breath snagged in his throat and he stared at the pillow resting at the head of the bed. If he messed this up, would he lose Collin, too?

Collin lifted onto his knees between Tristan's legs. "You understand, don't you?" He wrinkled his forehead.

Giving Collin a single, slow nod, Tristan fixated on his pillow. He had to do this now. He just had to.

Collin leaned in the direction of Tristan's gaze. "Look at me."

Tristan whispered, "What'll happen if I mess up?" His eyes stung.

"What?" Collin asked.

Twisting his head, Tristan locked his gaze to Collin's. "I said, what'll happen if I mess up?" He bit his lower lip.

Collin puffed out an exhale. "Um, I guess we won't go to the gay bar." His gaze studied Tristan's face. "You won't mess up."

Tristan's gut pinched and his heart thumped in his ears. "But what if I do? What if I can't stop, just like that?" He huffed. How could he be expected to stop so suddenly?

Collin crept closer and placed his hands on Tristan's shoulders. "You'll do it. I'll make sure of it."

Straightening, Tristan sucked in a deep inhale. "It's not up to you." He clenched his jaw. "It's up to me and I'll be damned if I'll let myself start that up again." He could do this. He had a reason to stop, and he would. He had Collin now.

A grin widened Collin's lips. "That's it, Tristan. You're over the worst part of it anyways, remember? You got through the first day."

Smiling, he placed his palms on Collin's cheeks and gazed deeply into his eyes. "And I have you to thank for it, all of it." He placed a lingering kiss on Collin's lips.

Collin parted his lips to let his tongue dance inside Tristan's mouth.

Letting out a soft moan, Tristan glided his tongue over Collin's, then bit at his lower lip and slanted his mouth over Collin's, kissing with renewed hunger. Heat rushed his groin, hardening his cock. He broke the kisses and pressed his forehead against Collin's. "Thank you, Collin." His voice was breathy and soft. His cheeks warmed and desire set his body on fire. "God, I want you, again, now."

Collin jumped up from the floor, shoving Tristan backward and sideways onto the bed. "All you have to do is ask." As he took a second to look down on Tristan, a mischievous grin quirked his lips. He pounced, landing on top of Tristan, grinding his swelling shaft against Tristan's through their jeans, kissing and nipping the soft skin of his neck and shoulder.

Tristan thrust his hips, groping and kneading flesh and muscle through the fabric of Collin's thin shirt. He gasped and moaned. An urgent need built inside him, and pleasure threaded from his aching cock up his spine. *More, I need more.* He bucked his hips and shoved Collin against the wall.

Gasping, Collin's back and arm smacked against the wall.

In a flash, Tristan scrambled on top of Collin, and dove his hand down between them and into Collin's jeans, between skin and velvet curls. Righting Collin's erection, he curled his fingers around the thick cock and pumped. "Oh, God." He rocked against Collin's thigh while placing frantic kisses on his lips, cheeks, neck, anyplace he found skin.

Collin bucked his hips, panting and squirming under Tristan, fighting for any control over him. "Hey—"

Covering Collin's mouth with a heated kiss, Tristan groaned in pure pleasure. Sensitivity heightened to a delicious tease in his shaft, but didn't spill over. He slid his hand free from Collin's jeans, unfastened them with trembling fingers and plunged his hand back down, placing quick jerks over Collin's freed cock.

"Holy shit, Tristan." Collin clenched his teeth, and his body stiffened. "S-stop it or I'm going to—"

Tristan jerked faster, tighter, milking Collin for everything he could and bit into Collin's neck.

Crying out, Collin tipped his hips back and shoved Tristan off him.

Tristan shifted to lay opposite Collin, on his side, and dove his head down. He slipped his slick mouth over Collin's cock and sucked hard, pumping down and up, his cheeks hollowing. Cupping Collin's sac with one hand, he shimmied the other into his pocket to fondle his neglected dick.

Crying out a second time, Collin bucked and slapped his hands to the back of Tristan's head. "Shit!" His cock pulsed and grew harder between Tristan's lips.

As hot cum spurted down Tristan's throat, he moaned and swallowed it down, writhing, sliding his fingers hard and fast over his own cock through pocket lining and boxers.

As his release slowed, Collin panted, then clutched Tristan's belt buckle, unfastened it, and plunged the zipper down on his jeans. In one quick movement, he exposed Tristan's seeping cock and slipped it into his mouth.

A loud gasp ripped from Tristan's throat. He freed Collin's spent dick and clenched his eyes shut. Wet pressure flicked over the head of his erection and licked up the shaft while hot lips pumped him. His climax rushed to the surface and teetered to an urgent humming. As his peak hit full force, his toes curled, and he groped at fabric, tightening around Collin's shirt and tugging. Contractions racked his body, spilling cum into Collin's lapping mouth, one after another, until he was totally drained.

With heavy breathing, Collin freed him and laid against the wall. "Holy shit, Tristan, what was that?"

"I don't know…" A soft chuckle rumbled Tristan's chest. "I-I think I was possessed or something." The chuckle became louder and turned into laughter. He twisted his face into Collin's legs.

Soft laughter trickled from Collin and grew to match Tristan's. "Dude, you're an animal when you want to be."

Tristan rose up and looked down into Collin's smiling face. "Yeah?"

"Yeah. I always knew you had it in you. Just had to let it be unleashed." Collin raked a hand through his clumps of damp hair. "Whew."

"I guess that'll last me until tomorrow night." Warmth swelled inside his chest and he lifted his gaze to the ceiling. Another round of laughter built and escaped from him.

Collin propped himself up by the elbows. "What's so damn funny?"

Tristan's laughter slowed. "I don't know. Maybe I'm just happy for once."

"Happy or nuts? Maybe all the blood drained permanently from your brain so it could fill that enormous dick of yours."

With a smirk, Tristan peered at him. "Good thing your mouth's even bigger so it'll fit inside."

"You…" Grasping the pillow under his head, Collin flung it at Tristan's face.

Tristan batted the pillow away and jumped off the bed. Tucking his cock into his jeans and fastening them, he said, "So a pillow fight, is it?" He lurched forward and snatched the pillow from Collin's bed.

"Wha—"

Tristan launched a pillow and hit Collin square in the head.

"Bastard." Quickly, Collin tucked his cock back into his jeans and fastened them. As he rose up from the bed, Tristan swatted him with another pillow in the chest. His auburn hair danced on his head.

Wicked chuckling sprang from Tristan's chest. "Got you."

"Yeah?" Snatching a free pillow from the bed, Collin jumped off it and slapped the pillow on Tristan's side.

Tristan stepped sideways with the force of the blow, his bracelets rattling. "Fucker..." As he went to hit him, Collin blocked him with his own pillow and slapped it down on the top of Tristan's head. Tristan swung his pillow in a wide arc and swatted Collin's side.

Whirling around, Collin wrapped his arms around Tristan's waist in a firm embrace. "Got you."

Squirming in Collin's hold, Tristan let out soft pants. "No, you don't."

"Yes, I do." Collin tightened the hold.

Collin's heavy breath whispered over Tristan's ear. He locked his gaze to Collin's, his heart blooming with emotion. He opened his mouth. "I lo—"

"Shh, don't say a word." Collin pressed his mouth to Tristan's, smooth, silky, and sweet.

Tristan closed his eyes, surrendering to all it had to offer and fell hopelessly, aimlessly.

Breaking the kiss, Collin gazed into his face. "Told you I had you."

Tristan opened his eyes and fixed his gaze on Collin, still holding him. "More than you know." He swallowed hard. *Should I finish my sentence? Tell him I love him?*

Clearing his throat, Collin released him and turned around, rubbing his forehead. "Yeah, um, you want to get ready for bed?"

Tristan blinked a few times. *Stupid, Tristan, he doesn't want to hear that.* His heart ached and he stared down at the carpet. "Uh, sure. It's late anyways."

CHAPTER ELEVEN

FRIDAY, NOVEMBER 7

Tristan stood in the bathroom with a towel around his waist. As he shaved, he watched the smooth strokes of his razor skim the surface of his cheek, taking away the last remnant of shaving foam. He'd slept in Collin's arms again all night and even though the bed was small, he'd slept like a baby.

Rapping filled the bathroom. "Hurry up in there."

Tristan stopped shaving and glanced at the door. "Just come in, it's not locked."

The knob twisted, the door opened, and Collin padded into the bathroom, his hair a disheveled mop and gray boxers hugging his slim hips. Smiling, he peered at Tristan and held out a pair of boxers. "I think it's time you got yourself your own old man underwear."

Tristan chuckled. "Yeah, guess so. Never thought I'd see the day when I'd be subjected to wearing those." He placed his razor into the water pooling in the sink and dropped the towel to the floor.

Tilting his head, Collin's gaze roamed Tristan's bare body. "Nice."

"Shut up." Tristan snatched the boxers from him and bent down to step into them. As the boxers slipped up his legs, his cock swelled and hardened. "Damn it, look at what you did now." Frowning, he pulled the elastic band over his erection and watched the fabric tent out in front of him.

Collin stepped to him and slid his fingers down the shaft of Tristan's erection through the thin fabric, then nipped at his neck.

Pleasure shivered down Tristan's spine and lodged in his balls. He tilted his hips back. "Stop it, Collin. We don't have time for this." Why was Collin starting something when he had to control himself today?

Collin wrapped his arms around him, pulled him close and kissed the side of Tristan's head, then whispered into his ear, "I sure wish we did."

Closing his eyes for a moment, Tristan let the embrace soothe him. How would he get through the day? Now he was on edge. It'd taken all his willpower not to touch himself in the shower and now this.

"You okay?" Collin lifted his head and loosened his embrace.

"Yeah." Tristan nodded his head. As he stepped back, he kept his gaze on the floor.

Collin cupped Tristan's chin. "Look at me."

Tristan resisted the tug of Collin's fingers. "No." Collin didn't need to see how anxious he was about today.

"Please, Tristan." Collin tugged harder on his chin.

With a loud exhale, Tristan twisted his head out of Collin's grasp and turned around, then swept a hand through his wet hair. Why did one touch, one suggestive comment from Collin make such a mess of him?

"What's wrong?" Collin stepped toward him and tapped his shoulder. "Are you nervous about today? Do you really think you won't make it?"

Tristan gnawed at his lower lip, then whirled around to face Collin, looking directly into his eyes. "What do you think? You're not exactly helping me any."

"Hey, that's not true. I'm here for you. You know that." Collin planted his hands on his hips.

Tristan pursed his lips and glanced around the bathroom. "Yeah, I know. I'm just not in the best of moods today, sorry." He needed to cool it and not get so upset about every little thing.

Collin pecked his cheek. "It's okay." He grasped Tristan's hand. "You know, I can be with you as long as you want today. I'll even go to your art class this afternoon if you want. I'll help you bring your drawings to the art supply store." A faint smile floated over his lips.

Gazing into Collin's stunning face, Tristan asked, "Really?"

Collin shrugged. "Sure, why not? We should stop by the store and get you your own underwear, too." A chuckle rose from his chest. "And maybe some more of those tight jeans."

With a lift of the edge of his mouth, Tristan said, "You just like how my ass looks in those jeans." His heart warmed. Collin had said he was hot.

"Damn right." Collin raked his darkened gaze over Tristan.

———

AN HOUR OR SO LATER, Collin followed Tristan into the sociology class and took a seat at a desk right beside him.

Tristan looked over and admired the way Collin's black t-shirt hugged his strong shoulders, the way the fabric of his dark jeans hugged the muscles of his thighs. How did he get so lucky?

Collin leaned toward him. "What?"

With heat creeping up his neck, Tristan fixed his gaze on his desk. "Nothing."

"Are you okay?" Collin wrinkled his brows.

With a nod, Tristan gazed into his eyes. "Yeah." With Collin here, he'd make it.

Sitting back in his seat, Collin let out a soft sigh. "Okay, I'm a little nervous about you wearing your baggy jeans again."

"I didn't have anything else. It's all in the wash." Tristan fingered the edge of his desk.

The professor entered the room and took the podium. All around the room, students hushed and focused on the front. "Good morning, class."

Tristan mumbled, "Shit." He leaned down to the side, unzipped his backpack and fished out a pen and notebook. As he straightened over his desk, he watched Collin doing the same.

With a smug grin, Collin placed his things on his desk and glanced at Tristan.

The morning's lecture started, and Tristan focused on the topic at hand, taking quick glances at Collin sitting beside him, all studious and sexy at the same time. Taking up his pen, he began a sketch of Collin in the top corner of his notebook. Halfway through the class, his concentration waned. He stifled a yawn, dropped his pen, and absently placed his fingers at the edge of his pocket, then snuck them partially inside to rub the head of his cock. Desire flooded his body and he hardened. His gaze left the professor, writing on a white board with blue marker, and fixed on Collin.

Leaning forward in his desk, Collin wrote notes with a black pen, darting his gaze between the professor and his notebook.

Tristan shifted in his seat. Just a little couldn't hurt. He ran a finger up and down his shaft and his vision dazed as pleasure tickled up from his groin. His breath quickened.

Collin quit writing and did a double take of Tristan, then snapped his brows together. Leaning to the side, he poked Tristan in the shoulder.

With a blink, Tristan fixated on him, holding his fingers still over his erection, teasing him with heat and pressure.

Collin pursed his lips and his gaze hardened. He whispered through his teeth, "I know what you're doing over there. Stop it."

Sitting up straight, Tristan tugged his fingers out of his pocket. "No, I'm not." No way could Collin see what was going on. Could he?

Collin leaned over toward him. "Yes, you are. Now stop."

Holding up the hand opposite Collin, Tristan splayed his fingers. "I'm not, see?"

Collin glared at him. "Don't think I won't pull you out of here."

"Is there a problem, gentlemen?" The professor stood close to the first row of desks, slapping a marker into his palm. All the students turned to face them.

Collin's cheeks flushed. "Um, no, no problem, sorry."

Tristan stared at the desk and the half page of notes he'd taken along with a sketch of Collin. Shit, the whole class was noticing them. As the professor began his lecture once more, he glanced at Collin.

Collin eyed him and gave him a slow shake of his head.

Tristan's gut knotted. Why couldn't he stop? Were they still going to the bar tonight or did he just ruin his chances? He fixated on his notebook, picked up his pen and drew absent circles at the bottom of the paper, his still-hard cock aching. How he wanted to continue to pleasure himself to the edge of release, like he was used to. But he had to be strong. It was time to stop all that.

––––––––

WHEN THE CLASS ENDED, he picked up his things, then bent over and placed them in his backpack. As he stood, he slung the backpack over his shoulder and watched Collin. What would Collin have to say about what happened?

Collin stood up with his green backpack in his hand and placed it on the desk. Frowning, he dropped his things into the pack and brought it up over one shoulder, then freed a long exhale and combed his fingers through his auburn hair.

"Collin?" Tristan pressed his lips together.

"What?" For a second, Collin stiffened, then another male student passed by, nudging him, and drawing his attention.

Tristan wrung his hands over his stomach. "Um, are you

mad?" It hadn't been a big deal, had it? He'd only touched himself for a few minutes.

"Let's go outside and talk. You have a few hours now, don't you?" Collin snuck a peek at him.

"Yes, but I have to get over to the art supply store. I'm supposed to meet Ally at ten-thirty." Tristan studied him. Collin seemed upset. Had he let him down?

"Oh." Collin trudged down the aisle and to the door.

Tristan followed Collin close behind with his pulse quickening and chest growing tight, as if waiting for a prison sentence.

When they reached the sunlit morning outside the building, Collin stopped and faced him. "Listen, Tristan, I don't care so much what you were doing in there, but what I do care about is you lying to me about it."

Birds chirped in oak trees overhead and students spilled out onto cement sidewalks from buildings all around them. Tristan studied the graceful curves of a Spanish archway in a building behind Collin. What could he say to that? He did it. He lied. "I'm sorry. I didn't mean to."

Collin shifted his stance. "How can you not mean to lie to someone? You either do it or you don't." He took hold of Tristan's wrist and tugged, bringing their faces close. "Don't lie to me. Ever."

Collin's glare bore into him, and he snuck his lower lip between his teeth, his chest aching. "I'm sorry, Collin. I just did it for a second. I just wanted to...shit, I don't know." He dropped his gaze to the sidewalk, a heavy weight falling on his heart. "I suppose we can't go out tonight. I failed. I'm a failure."

Collin released his wrist, hooked an arm around his waist and drew him into his chest. "Shh...you're not a failure. Don't look at it like that. You might have had a few minutes of recurrence, but you stopped. You didn't keep it up and that's a good sign. I don't expect you to be perfect. We'll still go out tonight."

Tristan's body relaxed and he grinned at Collin. "Really? I didn't fuck it up?"

Collin chuckled. "No, not yet. Now if you'd kept it up or run to the bathroom for a quick rub, then yes, you'd have fucked up." He loosened his hold on Tristan.

"Did you still want to go with me to bring my artwork to Ally?" Tristan lifted his brows, his gaze searching Collin's face. Now he was determined. It wouldn't happen again.

"Sure, let's get going." Collin took a step back and grasped Tristan's hand, entwining their fingers together.

———

AN HOUR OR SO LATER, Collin chanced a peek into the window of the art supply store before following Tristan through the glass door.

Tristan held the door for Collin with one hand and his leather portfolio with the other. Butterflies fluttered in his stomach. Would any of these drawings really sell? Maybe Ally would decide she didn't like them so much after all.

Strolling past Tristan and into the store, Collin looked around as if lost.

"Over here." Tristan waved his hand at him and started up the paint and brush isle toward a long counter with a cash register on it.

An older man with a balding head in a white smock stood behind the register, eying a package of pastels.

Collin got to the counter first, stopped and stuffed both his hands in his back pockets.

The older man looked up at Collin. "Yes? Can I help you?"

"Um..." Collin glanced at Tristan.

Tristan stepped to the counter. "Uh, hi, um, is Ally here?" He hadn't seen her when they'd come in.

"She's running a little late, but she should be here in just a minute. Are you Tristan?" The older man lifted his brows.

With his pulse kicking up, Tristan glanced at Collin for a second, then focused on the older man. "Yes, I am."

The man's warm smile wrinkled around his eyes, and he held his hand out to Tristan. "Oh, hello. I'm Dave Pinter. I own the store."

Tristan shook his hand. "Uh, this is my friend, Collin." He gestured to Collin.

Collin stepped closer to the counter and held out his hand. "Pleased to meet you, sir."

Dave shook Collin's hand and released it, then focused on Tristan. "Well, let's see your work."

Oh, shit. Where the hell was Ally? What if this guy didn't like what he saw? "Um, now?" Tristan shifted his stance and fumbled with his portfolio.

"Go ahead, Tristan, pull out your stuff." Collin wrinkled his brows, studying Tristan.

"S-sure." Tristan set the portfolio down, unzipped it and carefully slid a few sheets of drawings out. This could be bad...

"Set them down right here." Dave stood back and pointed at the counter.

Tristan laid the drawings across the counter and took a deep inhale, his insides humming with tension.

Dave looked over the top drawing, a charcoal of a naked man lying down on pillows from his life drawing class, but done with Tristan's style—thin, penciled strokes and smudgy, smooth shading, making the man much more beautiful than possible, giving him the look of a Greek God.

"Holy shit, Tristan. You really drew that?" Collin hung his mouth open.

Frowning, Tristan's gaze snapped from Dave to Collin and back again.

Holding up the drawing, Dave touched it lightly with his fingertips. "You've sealed this already, I assume." He perused the paper from top to bottom, then on to the drawing underneath, then he set it back down on the counter.

Tristan held his breath.

Picking up a few more drawings, Dave peered at the ones

below them, then smiled broadly and looked at Tristan. "These are beautiful. You truly are as talented as Ally said."

Ally burst through the door and stopped in her tracks. "Damn it."

Collin and Tristan turned to look at the young woman. Her black dress of straps and lace fell to her knees over green and black striped leggings and surfer tennis shoes. She jogged through an isle to join them at the counter. "I'm so sorry, Tristan. I really wanted to be here." She touched his arm. Thin, silver, and black bracelets dangled over her wrist.

"It's okay." A soft grin curled Tristan's lips, and his attention drew to Dave. He liked his work, but would he want to sell it?

Tilting her head, Ally examined the drawings on the counter. "See? Is he good or what?" She slapped a hand on the counter. Her gaze flicked to Collin. "Oh, hello." She smiled at him.

Collin stepped out from behind Tristan and offered her a coy grin. "Hi. I'm Collin, a friend of Tristan's."

She looked him up and down. "A friend, huh?"

Tristan coughed into his fist. "So, Dave, do you want to sell my work here?"

"Of course, he does. I can tell just by looking at him. He's got that gleam in his eye." She let out a soft laugh.

With a smirk, Dave glanced at Ally and leaned toward Tristan, resting his forearm on the counter. "I'd love to sell your work here. I think we could get upwards of two-hundred dollars for the originals and then I can put you in contact with a good print shop if you want to try and sell prints. Of course, we can frame a few of them, at your expense, and then the price would be a little more for those. Oh, and the shop takes twenty percent."

"Twenty percent?" Tristan glanced at his drawings. Was that a good rate? A good price? He had no idea.

Collin grasped Tristan's arm and tugged him close. "Dude, twenty percent's nothing. My Mom used to work in a gallery in Scottsdale and I think the gallery took like fifty percent there."

Cutting his gaze to Collin, Tristan said, "Really?"

Collin nodded

Fingering the edge of the top drawing, Tristan knitted his brows. Even if he only sold a few, he'd still be getting some decent money. "Um, okay. Let's do it."

"Cool. Oh my God, I can't wait to tell my friends." Ally clapped her hands together in front of her chest.

Tristan faced her. "Are they really going to buy them for two-hundred dollars, though?"

"Are you kidding? They all have rich parents and trust funds. I'm sure they can afford it. If not, they'll just have to wait for the prints. I can get some pre-ordered, you know." Ally beamed at him.

"Oh." Numbness filtered through Tristan. Was this really happening? What if no one bought them? His chest clenched.

Collin grabbed his hand. "Tristan, aren't you happy?"

With a hard swallow, Tristan said, "Um, yeah, I'm happy."

A phone rang from somewhere behind Dave.

Dave cleared his throat. "Listen, I'm going to take that in the office. I'll leave you with Ally to work out the details."

"Oh, thanks." Tristan gave him a quick grin and a nod.

With a wave of his hand, Dave strode to the side of the store and opened a door. "You're welcome." He darted behind the door and closed it.

Collin took a step toward Ally. "So how many of these do you need?"

"I'll take them all if he'll let me." She gathered up the drawings.

"No, wait." He planted his hands on Ally's forearms, stopping her. "I-I don't know if I want to sell all the originals." How could he part with all of his work? Each piece meant something to him. He hadn't thought of that.

"What?" Collin stared at him.

Tristan chanced a peek at Collin, then focused on his drawings. "Some of those are, um, special to me. I need to go through which ones I want to sell, and which ones can be just prints."

Ally's gaze softened. "Sure, Tristan, no problem. Let's go over them one by one and we'll figure this all out, okay?"

Collin peered at the drawings and shifted his stance. "What's so special about some of them?"

With a shrug, Tristan said, "I don't know, they just are."

Ally smirked at Collin. "Guess you're not an artist, huh?" She gathered the drawings up once again, organizing them.

"No, I'm a psych major, actually." Collin turned back to Tristan. "What, did you like some of those guys or something?"

Tristan widened his eyes and dropped his mouth open. "Collin..."

Ally straightened, her gaze cutting from Collin to Tristan. "It figures." She planted her hands on her hips.

"What do you mean, it figures?" Collin's attention drew back to her.

"You two are together, aren't you?" She shrugged. "It's always the hot guys that're gay." She shook her head and went back to the drawings.

"Uh, thanks, I think." Collin choked out a laugh.

Tristan stared from Ally to Collin. What was he supposed to say to that? Did everyone know he was gay?

"Come on, Tristan, let's go through these and figure out which ones we'll sell, which ones we'll frame and which we'll just have as prints." She brushed her fingers over the drawings and gazed at them as if admiring the lines and curves of Tristan's charcoal strokes.

———

As they headed across a plaza in front of a coffee bar on the college campus, Collin grabbed Tristan's arm and stopped him. "Who are those guys you drew?"

Blinking a few times, Tristan faced him. "I told you, just some guys. I don't know who they are, exactly."

"Then why are their drawings so important to you?" Collin huffed.

Tristan yanked his arm free. "Why do you care so much? They're just drawings, they aren't real." What the hell?

"Just tell me who they are." Glaring at him, Collin crossed his arms over his chest.

"Stop it, Collin. It doesn't matter." Tristan sighed. "I'm hungry, can't we just get something to eat?"

"Fine." Collin pressed his lips together.

"I don't understand why you're making such a big deal about it. What are you so mad about?" He held his palm out, studying Collin.

"I'm not mad." Collin shook his head and took a step, then stopped. "Let's eat, then. You said you were hungry."

"Collin, please. You want me to be straight with you and here you're lying to *me*." Tristan blew out a breath.

"Okay, fine. I am mad. I'm mad because once again, you're holding something back." Collin scrubbed his face. "I'm getting tired of always having to grill you for information. Why can't you just be open with me from the start?"

Tristan dropped his gaze to a patch of clover straining through a crack in the cement, then to his tennis shoes. He opened his mouth and shut it again with a frown. "That's not fair." What could he say to that? Was Collin right? But he wasn't used to telling people things. Telling people things always ended badly for him. Besides, he couldn't tell Collin the real reason why he'd kept those drawings. "Maybe I just need to keep some things inside."

"That's bullshit, Tristan." Collin puffed out an exhale,

Tristan's chest heated and he glared at him. "You don't necessarily tell me everything either, now, do you?" He set his free hand on his hip. "What about your thesis, huh? Why is that such a big mystery?"

"Uh..." Collin took a step back, gaping, his gaze darting over a neat row of rose bushes bordering the plaza. "I did too, tell you about it. You just don't understand it, that's all." He lifted his chin.

A few female students passing by stopped and stared at them a moment.

Tristan hung his head, slumping his shoulders. He might as well just tell him. "I kept those drawings because those are my fantasy guys." He let out a long sigh.

"Your what? Fantasy guys? You mean—"

"Shh! Can't you ever keep your mouth shut?" Glaring at Collin again, he yanked him close and whispered in his ear, "Those are just drawings of guys I made up. Guys I, um, fantasized about being with."

A slow smile crept over Collin's lips. "Really...have you got a drawing of me in there somewhere that I haven't seen yet?"

Tristan smirked. "No, you're real. Those guys were purely fantasy." Was Collin jealous of his fantasy guys?

With Collin's smile fading, he pulled away from Tristan. "Okay, but real guys are better, right?"

Tristan sniggered. "I suppose. Depends on the guy." Touché.

"Bastard." With a smile, Collin batted him on the arm. "Let's get something to eat."

AFTER LUNCH, Tristan strolled next to Collin as they wound their way down a walkway between two old campus buildings and tall palm trees. "You sure you want to come to my drawing class?"

"I said I did and I am." Collin's backpack bounced on his black t-shirt as he walked.

"How many classes did you miss because of me today?" Tristan's gaze roamed Collin's muscular chest and shoulders. God, he was gorgeous.

"Not many. I have three classes on Fridays, and we were both at sociology this morning." Collin stuffed a hand in his front pocket.

Tristan stopped and looked up at the clean lines of the art

building. "Hey, here it is." He walked to the front doors and opened one for Collin.

Collin strolled in and looked over the metal sculptures in the foyer. "Very artsy." He lifted the edge of his mouth.

With a soft smile, Tristan tapped his arm. "Come on, it's this way." He led Collin down a hallway and into a large classroom. A few students sat on metal stools in front of easels with tall drawing pads perched on them. Stainless sinks and dark cabinets lined one wall of the room. He went to his usual corner, opposite the sinks, set the portfolio down and took out his drawing pad.

Collin scanned the classroom. "So, are you drawing naked guys again today?"

A male student sitting across from them stopped drawing on his pad and frowned, peering at Collin.

"No. We're working on still life today. See those set-ups over there?" He pointed to a series of three carts in the center of the room. Various flowers in pots and plastic fruit in bowls sat amidst wrinkled sheets in an attempt to appear as noble and yet antiquated as a Dutch master's painting.

"Yeah?" Collin narrowed his eyes.

"Well, we're supposed to draw those." Tristan took out his new charcoals. Collin had no idea what was going on.

"That looks pretty boring." Collin sighed softly.

"It is, but it's good practice for shadowing and shape." Tristan continued setting up.

"Whatever. I thought there were going to be naked guys in here." Collin slumped his shoulders and looked across the room.

"Dude, why don't you strip for us?" The male student across the room smirked while the other students chuckled in a mocking chorus.

Collin took a step toward the student. "Maybe I will." He waggled his brows.

"Collin, stop it." His mind flashed with a clear vision of Collin naked and sprawled across the floor for them to draw. His cock swelled and he shut his eyes for a moment as lust shivered up his spine.

Collin turned to Tristan. "What—"

A rush of students, including Ally, entered the room like ants piling out of a wet mound, set up and took their seats. Ally smiled at them and mouthed, *hi*.

Smiling, Tristan ticked his head at her, then focused on Collin. "Sit down and don't cause any more problems." This was his domain, and he was in charge for once. With a smirk, he started on a drawing of the closest set-up.

The rustle of students pulling out drawing supplies and whispering to each other filled the room.

An older man with a bald head and gentle eyes entered through the doorway and took a quick inventory of the students. "Okay people, today's focus is on contrast and shadow, so let's get started." His plaid shirt hung un-tucked over a pair of corduroy trousers. He stepped passed a student and walked up to Tristan and Collin, focusing on Collin. "Hello, are you a new student or just an observer?"

Collin's gaze drew from Tristan's paper to the professor. "Uh, just an observer."

"Well, you certainly picked a wonderful artist to observe." The professor gave Tristan a nod and a warm smile.

Tristan smiled back at his teacher. "Thanks, Mr. Murphy." He'd heard this before from him, but this was the first time he actually believed him.

"Did you know Tristan's going to start selling his stuff?" Collin dropped his backpack to the floor.

Mr. Murphy glanced at Tristan, then focused on Collin. "You don't say..."

With heat creeping up Tristan's neck, he hung his head and dropped his hand into his lap. Collin *had* to tell him. What if none of it sold?

"Yeah, the art supply store is selling it for him." Collin flashed Tristan a wide grin.

"Well, I must say I'm not surprised. I told him a long time ago to start soliciting the local galleries in town." Mr. Murphy nudged Tristan's arm.

"You did?" Collin focused on Tristan. "Why didn't you ever do that?"

Tristan gazed at his knees. "I-I don't know. I just never really thought I was that good." Not until today.

"You see, that's the problem with him. Humble to a fault." Mr. Murphy let out a soft laugh.

"Yeah..." Collin wrinkled his brows, then patted Tristan's shoulder.

The professor planted a hand on his hip and directed a look at Collin. "And so, who might you be?"

My lover. A warm feeling like a summer breeze swept over Tristan and he snuck a peek at Collin. What would he say?

"Uh, I'm his roommate." Collin raked a hand through his bangs.

"Oh, I didn't know he had a roommate." The professor gave Tristan another warm smile.

"Um, he just moved in recently." What more should he let on to his professor? Tristan squirmed in his seat as if it'd suddenly become hot.

"I see. And you're an art enthusiast mister..." The professor lifted his thick brows.

"Collin, sir, Collin Stanley and yes, I'm beginning to be quite the art enthusiast." Collin gave Tristan a knowing grin and arched a brow.

"Well, Mr. Stanley, enjoy the class." The professor gave Collin and Tristan a quick nod and walked off to the next student.

Tristan whispered, "Sit down, Collin, and quit embarrassing me."

Collin grabbed a stool and raked it across the floor. A high-pitched, sharp scraping noise filled the class. All the students looked up from their work at Collin.

Ally covered her face and giggled.

Tristan spoke through his teeth, "Collin..."

"Oh, sorry." Collin set the stool next to Tristan and dropped onto it. Sighing, he bent down, unzipped his backpack, and pulled out a textbook. When he straightened himself, he glanced at Tristan.

"What's that?" Tristan gestured to the book in his lap.

Collin shrugged a shoulder. "Just a book from my philosophy class."

Tristan narrowed his eyes and peered at the book. Collin only wanted to come here for the naked men.

"What?" Collin lifted his brows.

Shaking his head once, Tristan focused on drawing. "Nothing. Go ahead and read. I figured this class might get too boring for you."

Collin cocked his head. "I can read and watch at the same time. I'm good like that." With a soft smirk creeping over his lips, he leaned over and whispered, "Don't think I'm not watching you like a hawk. So don't get any funny ideas. I'm going to make sure we both make it to the gay bar tonight."

He rounded his eyes, his heart shuddering. "Shh, shut up about that for now, okay?" Could anyone hear that?

Collin sat back in his stool, a smug grin widening his lips. "As long as you heard me, that's what counts."

With a huff and a contented smile, Tristan puffed his chest a little and drew. Here he was in his element, no matter what Collin did or said.

CHAPTER TWELVE

C ollin held the dorm room door open for Tristan. "Those new jeans are going to be so hot on you tonight."

With shopping bags and portfolio in hand, Tristan sauntered into the room and dropped the bags, portfolio, and backpack to the floor. "Shit, that was heavy." He sighed and plopped down on his bed, lying on his back.

Collin closed the door and walked up to Tristan's bedside with a mischievous grin on his lips. He placed his hands on the bottom hem of his shirt and slowly, sensually, lifted.

Tristan tipped his head, his gaze roaming over the taut abdomen peeking out from under Collin's t-shirt. "What are you doing?"

Collin flicked his tongue over his lips, glanced at Tristan's groin and focused on his face. "Trying to decide what the best position would be for you to draw me."

Tristan lurched up to sitting on his bed. "What?"

Giving a quick tilt of his head, Collin yanked the shirt up and off, then threw it to the floor. "You heard me. Naked, partially clothed, or maybe just some sheets wrapped around me?" He unfastened his belt and jeans and dropped the jeans to the floor.

His cock stood hard and ready under the thin cotton of his boxers.

His breathing grew shallow, and his own cock swelled at the site of Collin's erection. "Um, um..."

"Naked, yeah." In one quick movement, Collin stepped out of his tennis shoes and jeans and brought the boxers down and off with his socks. He straightened with a smirk running across his lips, then cupped his sac. "How's this?"

"Uh..." Tristan's hardened cock ached in his jeans, and he adjusted himself, squeezing the head of his erection. It twitched as a wave of pleasure washed over him.

Affixing his gaze on Tristan's eyes, Collin backed up to his bed and lay across it, placed one arm up, bent, and behind his head like a pin up in a magazine. He rested his free hand over his dick, giving it one long, slow stroke, then hissed, closing his eyes and rolling his hips. "Just like this, Tristan. Capture me touching myself, thinking of you. Thinking of your mouth on my dick. Do it." He slid his hand up and down his shaft in an agonizingly slow motion. His brows tensed and his mouth opened in obvious pleasure.

Tristan's body shook with need and his cock grew painful, aching for release as he watched Collin. "O-kay, um, let me get my things." His voice wavered. Swallowing hard, he crouched down and retrieved the charcoals and drawing pad from the portfolio, then sat up on his bed and set the pad in his lap to draw. He looked at Collin.

Pre-cum glistened at the tip of Collin's shaft. He ran his fist over it and swirled over the head. With a quick thrust of his hips, a throaty groan released from his mouth.

Tristan's balls tightened and became full. Even the slightest movement might send him over the edge. "Oh shit, Collin. I-I don't think I can do this."

In a husky voice, Collin said, "Yes you can. I want my picture to be the only one you need. The only one you can't sell or even show to anyone because it means so much to you." He slipped his fingers down his shaft and ran circles over his sac. Gasping, he shuddered.

Holding his breath, Tristan forced himself to focus on the perfect curves and lines of Collin's body, the contours of muscle and tendon, the beautiful arc of his thick cock and rounded buttocks. Desire jolted through him, and he grew raw with need, shutting his eyes tightly. *Shit, focus, Tristan.* Opening his eyes, he blew out a breath and drew with an artist's eye, seeing shapes and shadow and light.

Lifting his hips again, Collin stroked hard over his erection and circled the top, letting out one soft moan after another. "Lick me, Tristan. Just once."

Tristan stopped his hand over the drawing, his cock twitching in his jeans. "Uh, just once?"

"Yeah, come on. Just once." Collin stroked his swollen cock down and up with his thumb and index finger. "Hurry, I'm close."

Tristan set the drawing pad and charcoal stick on the bed, stepped to Collin and leaned over his waist, resting on his elbows. Collin's erection was a mere inch from his lips. His mouth watered.

"Come on, Tristan. But just once. I don't want to come yet." Collin released the hold on his cock.

Tristan took a deep breath and opened his mouth, then ran his slick tongue just under Collin's balls, licked slowly up to the base, the shaft, the head and swirled over the tip. A deep moan rippled from his chest.

"Oh, God..." Shuddering, Collin's hips jerked.

Overcome, Tristan engulfed Collin's cock and sucked hard.

Shoving Tristan away, Collin tilted his hips back. "Stop!"

Tristan sat on the floor against his bed, staring at him and aching with need. "I'm s-sorry." But he couldn't help himself. Collin had tasted so good.

Propping up on his elbows, Collin said, "You don't want me to come yet, do you?"

"I guess not." Tristan's groin pulsed, distracting him. He pressed on his erection, straining for relief and he shut his eyes as tension coiled inside him.

"Hey, don't touch yourself. Finish the drawing." Collin huffed.

"It's not fair. You're touching yourself." Tristan dropped his hand to the floor.

"Okay, take your cock out and come over here." Collin offered a coy grin.

"What?" He raised his brows.

Collin dropped back to the bed. "You heard me."

Standing up, Tristan unfastened his belt and jeans, rustled in his boxers to free his erection and stepped toward Collin. What would Collin do?

Collin sat up and with hooded eyelids and wide pupils, he placed his fist around the base of Tristan's cock, squeezed, then devoured it with his mouth.

Gasping, Tristan fought for breath, for control over his body. Delicious sensation ravaged him, threatened to drive him over the edge. He clenched his teeth and slapped his hands to Collin's hair, then clutched auburn locks.

Collin released Tristan's erection and gave his hips a slight push. "Okay. Draw."

Panting, Tristan nodded and stepped to his bed. How would he ever get through this? He'd been so close. He pulled the pad onto his lap and picked up the charcoal with shaking fingers. His exposed erection pulsed again. Struggling to concentrate, he put the stick to the paper and attempted to draw. The lines squiggled. "Shit, I don't think I can draw now."

Collin lay back in his original position with his fingers curled around his cock, giving it lazy strokes. "Didn't you ever sit and jerk off while you were drawing in class?"

He snapped his brows together. "Yeah, so?"

Collin shrugged. "So do it now."

Peering at Collin, he said, "But I thought I couldn't do that anymore?"

"What you can't do anymore is just sit and masturbate in class all by yourself. I'm talking about doing it with me, in the privacy of our dorm room, while you draw me. It's not the same." Collin slowly stroked himself.

Tristan lowered his gaze to his engorged cock. Was it really all right? If Collin said so..."So can I, um, put my old underwear on?"

Collin stopped the stroking of his erection, then lifted his head. "No, absolutely not."

Pursing his lips, Tristan's chest stiffened. This didn't seem fair somehow. He wrinkled his brows and peered at him. "Why not?"

A long exhale tore from Collin's chest. "Because, that would be too much like what you're trying to stop."

Tristan twisted his lips, then curled his fingers around his still-solid cock and gave it a tentative stroke. Delicious pleasure raced through his body. Gasping, he stroked harder, faster.

"Hey, cool it. You're supposed to be drawing me, not just beating off." Collin smirked, his head tilting, then he dropped back to the bed while resuming lazy strokes over his shaft.

As Tristan stilled his hand, closed his eyes for a moment and snuck his lip between his teeth. When he reopened his eyes, he gazed at him with determination. "Okay." With his left hand, he put the charcoal stick to paper and outlined the curves and gentle slopes of Collin's body. Working fast, he placed absent strokes on the head of his erection, just enough to tease and fill him with calming sensation. His breathing, shallow and quick, kept pace with the movement of his hand.

As Collin watched Tristan draw, his darkened gaze became softer, as if he were admiring Tristan. He kept a slow, rhythmic pace on his weeping cock.

Tristan drew Collin's face, fighting to capture the expression perfectly. His gaze met Collin's and for a moment, an intense craving, longing, and love bloomed in his heart. He stopped his hand over the drawing. "Collin, I..."

Collin stilled his fist over his erection. "What? What is it, Tristan?"

Dropping his gaze to the drawing, Tristan said, "Nothing." *Don't ruin everything by telling him how you feel.* He focused on the drawing and completed Collin's face, the look he'd seen in his eyes, maybe projecting the love from his own heart into the charcoal eyes, maybe making in them a reflection of his love for Collin. When he finished, he sat back to examine his work. His gaze flicked from the drawing to Collin's naked body and back again.

Collin resumed his lazy stroking over his stiff cock. "Hurry up. I don't think I can wait much longer." He swiped his thumb over the tip of his erection and swirled pre-cum over the surface in quick circles. "Shit, Tristan, what's taking so long?" His eyes shut and he let out a long groan of pleasure.

Biting his lip, Tristan said, "Just a minute." Using the finger pads of his right hand, he smudged the black lines in a few places until the shadows depicted the image in front of him. "There." His attention drew back to Collin.

Collin squeezed his cock as if struggling to hold back release.

"Collin?" Tristan lifted his brows.

"Get over here. Now." Collin gasped.

Tossing the drawing pad to the end of the bed, he darted across the room, snatched the hand holding Collin's erection and whipped it up over his head as his body fell over of Collin's and their cocks crushed together.

"What are you doing?" Collin gave him a coy smile.

"Making you wait for me." Tristan claimed Collin's mouth, thrusting his tongue deep inside, tasting the sweet wetness he'd wanted draped over his aching cock.

Collin met his kiss with equal intensity, sucking at his tongue, nipping at his lips. He bucked his hips, sliding friction and pressure over their dicks.

The soft skin of Collin's slick cock rubbed against Tristan's, sending a shudder of desire, of intense arousal to sear through him. "More, Collin, I want more." He ground on Collin, taking all he could from him.

"Fuck, Tristan, I'm close." In an instant, Collin stopped and held Tristan impossibly close and still with a firm embrace. He whispered softly, yet firmly, "Don't move." He pressed his forehead against Tristan's.

Tristan held as still as possible with urgent need coursing through every cell of his body. He knew this feeling and knew it well. It was the one he'd tried so desperately to hold onto every day of his life before Collin became such an immense part of it. His ragged breathing slowed.

Gradually, Collin moved his hips, resuming a light sliding of their shafts against one another. "Take your clothes all the way off. I want to feel every part of you."

Hell yes. Tristan stood up and disrobed, throwing his t-shirt to the floor, kicking off his tennis shoes, socks, and jeans. When he stood naked and exposed before him, Collin widened his arms and he fell down into the promise of all he'd ever hoped for, his Collin, his lover.

Collin rained down on Tristan with heated kisses and sensual nips to his neck, his shoulder, the hollow of his collarbone.

Rocking his hips, Tristan struggled to find the lovely sensation of a few moments ago. His cock seeped and grew harder as it rutted against Collin's. Pleasure threaded over him to cloak him in impossible heat. His balls tightened and filled for release.

Collin slapped his hands on Tristan's ass and gripped tightly, digging his fingers into the globes of muscle.

Piercing, aching pain mixed with pleasure as Tristan writhed against Collin in a snakelike, horizontal dance over messy bedcovers. He grasped any part of Collin he could find, their stomachs, hips and cocks slickened with pre-cum and slithering over and across each other.

Collin grunted and his body went rigid. He bucked his hips into Tristan, pushing his erection hard against Tristan's cock, then bit the flesh of Tristan's shoulder and with a shudder, his hot, slick cum spurted out between them.

The raw edge of climax jolted through Tristan, and he rutted as the peak of sensation blazed through him. With another thrust, sweet waves of pleasure rolled inside him, mixing his cum with Collin's. Sharp gasps rippled out of him until it all slowed to heavy breaths.

Collin lay still beneath him with his eyes closed, his face slack. "Wow, Tristan. That's all I can say is...wow." He lolled his head to the side with a soft snicker.

With his breathing slowed to a natural rhythm, Tristan curled his fingers around a lock of auburn hair. Contentment spread through him like a warm fog, creeping its way over tense muscles to relax and soothe. A lazy smile quirked his lips and dimpled his cheeks. A dull ache pulsed a memory of teeth biting into flesh on his shoulder. He gasped. "You bit me." He tipped his head and looked at the indents of half crescents and beginnings of a bruise on his shoulder.

Collin chuckled and peeked at Tristan's shoulder. "So, I did." He placed a gentle kiss on it. "Sorry." Sighing, he loosened his hold on Tristan's torso. "I couldn't help myself. If I could have eaten you and gotten away with it, I think I would have." A deep chuckle rumbled in his ribs.

Tristan lifted himself onto his elbows and peered into Collin's face. "Why do you find that funny? I'm going to have a mark now." He smiled though he did his best to sound irritated.

"Good. Just another thing to remember me by." Collin brushed his hand down the back of Tristan's head.

Scoffing, Tristan climbed off the bed to stand on the floor. Gazing down at the sticky mess on his stomach and groin, he ran an absent finger through it, snuck it into his mouth and sucked.

"Ew, gross, Tristan." Collin sniggered.

Cutting his stare to meet with Collin's eyes, Tristan's mouth filled with the salt and bitter taste of their lust. He pulled his finger from his lips with a plop. "What?"

Collin sat up on the bed. "You're eating your own, well, and my cum."

"So?" Tristan cocked his head. Was it really so weird?

"So? You didn't blow me." Collin wrinkled his nose.

Tristan focused on the glistening finger. "I always, uh, eat it."

After letting out a sharp laugh, Collin said, "You're kidding me. I've heard of that, but never thought I'd be with someone who did it."

Tristan's chest heated. "Fine. Just add that to your list of fucked up shit I do." With a curt turn, he stomped into the bathroom, shut the door, and locked it. His chest heaved and he shut his eyes tightly, still facing the door. *Why did I have to say that? Why can't I just let things go?* A dull pain wrapped around his heart.

The doorknob clinked and hard pounding filled the room. Collin's muffled voice snaked through. "Open the damned door, Tristan."

Tristan glared at the door like it was Collin. "No."

The door shook as if Collin jerked the knob from the other side. "I said open it! We agreed you wouldn't do this anymore, remember?"

"I don't remember that." Tristan sighed. He'd only needed a moment alone.

A heavy sigh came from the other side. "Please, Tristan. I didn't mean to hurt you."

"You didn't..." Tristan unlocked the door. "Hurt me."

The door ripped open.

Tristan caught the door just before it thumped him in the forehead. "Shit, Collin, watch it." He stepped back.

Collin trudged into the room, his forehead wrinkled, and examined him. "Oh God, I'm sorry." He grabbed hold of Tristan's shoulders, tugged him close and kissed his cheek. "Are you all right?"

"I'm fine." Tristan thought a minute and a slow, mischievous grin crept over his lips, then waned. He could fuck with Collin over this. "Or maybe not." He looked into Collin's eyes.

Collin's gaze searched his face. "I'm sorry, Tristan. I didn't mean to upset you. I didn't mean anything by that comment. It's common, really, to do that."

Bending at the knees and dropping his head, he licked Collin's stomach from his navel up to his chest.

Collin gasped and his muscles tensed.

"Mmm, guess I'm the one who wants to eat you now." Focusing on Collin, Tristan smirked and brushed his tongue over his lips.

"You're sick." Collin let out a belly laugh and planted a kiss on Tristan's lips, pushing his tongue inside to lap up the taste of them both from Tristan's mouth. "Let's get ready for our night out, shall we?"

———

A FEW HOURS LATER, Collin asked, "So you ready for your first gay bar experience?" Collin jogged out over the sidewalk to the curb with the late evening wind rustling his hair. The indigo sky hugged the waves off the shoreline of the beach like a long-lost lover. A faint mist hung in the air, filled with the scent of the Pacific Ocean.

Nodding, a wide smile spread Tristan's lips as the heavy breeze blew long bangs over his eyes. He swiped them away, following Collin to the curb.

"Thanks for dinner, Collin. I can't remember the last time I ate such good food or was so far off campus." Tristan rubbed his full belly.

"You're welcome." Collin stopped his older red Maxima and opened the passenger door.

Ducking his head, Tristan threw a windbreaker into the back seat and slid into the front. His snug jeans groaned over black leather seats and he adjusted a black t-shirt underneath the buttons of his dress shirt. He'd wanted to look nice for Collin tonight.

Collin shut the door and strode to the other side of the car. His black, V-neck sweater billowed in the breeze and tight jeans hugged his hips.

Tristan rubbed his hands together. His first gay bar. With Collin.

Climbing into the driver's seat, Collin glanced at Tristan with a mischievous smile. After turning the key in the ignition, the engine rumbled, sending little tremors through the car's black interior. The stereo came to life and alternative rock music surrounded them. "Hey, now that you've been in it a few times, what do you think about my car?"

"Um..." Tristan roamed his gaze over the deep red hood in front of him, then peered out the darkened windows. "It's nice."

"Nice? I put some decent cash into those chrome rims and this stereo puts out 400 watts." Collin ticked his brows.

"Really?" Tristan nodded. He should be impressed, but cars never were his thing.

"Yes, really, and the guy I bought it from did some engine work that increased the horsepower by 30 percent." Collin gave him a wide smile.

"Oh." Tristan giggled.

"What's so funny?" Collin put the car in gear and headed onto the road.

"I'm not much into cars, Collin. Like I said when we left, I don't even own one."

Collin shook his head. "I have no idea how you've gotten around all these years without a car."

"I took buses and walked." He pursed his lips. But really, he'd had nowhere to go but to his room or class.

"Well, I guess now you have me to drive you around." Collin playfully slapped Tristan's thigh.

"Guess so." As Collin drove the car down the street, Tristan looked out over the ocean. Whitecaps speckled the dark water and the twinkling lights from restaurants and shops danced out on the piers above it. His body relaxed. It felt right, being with Collin.

After ten minutes of listening to Collin's off-pitch voice singing with the radio, an old warehouse came into view. Bricks peeked out of cracked stucco and windows with square mullions gave a faint amber glow. A large metal overhang hung from one side of the building and numerous tables with men sipping beverages littered the patio underneath it, overlooking the water on the side of the pier.

Collin pulled the car into an open parking spot and turned off the engine. After the car went quiet, he turned to Tristan. "Here we are." He roamed his gaze over Tristan. "You look good tonight."

Tristan's cheeks warmed. "Yeah?"

"Yeah. Good enough to eat." Collin sniggered.

Tristan slapped at Collin's shoulder. "Quit teasing me about that."

Collin chuckled. "Okay, let's go. It looks like there still might be some room on the patio."

"Better take my jacket then." Tristan climbed out, grabbed his jacket from the back seat, then stood and slid into it before slamming the car door shut.

"Come on, Tristan. I don't want to have to sit inside." Collin waved at Tristan.

"Okay, okay." As he paced toward Collin, he fumbled with the zipper on his jacket.

Just as they reached the door, Collin snatched Tristan's hand.

Tristan scanned around them. Would anyone notice they were together and say something nasty? As they walked through the threshold, he watched other young men, not much different than he and Collin, holding hands, giving flirtatious smiles, and knowing touches while standing at the bar and sitting at tables. A wide smile quirked his lips and dimpled his cheeks. They were all like Collin and him. No one would care.

Collin towed him to the patio, past the bar made of wood

scavenged from an old barge and craftsman-style tables with chairs made of ash. Rustic lamps hung down from the ceiling in a dome of golden light. His black boots clapped over rust-colored cement as they walked.

A few patrons threw appreciative looks at Collin.

When they'd navigated their way through open sliding-glass doors, Collin took Tristan to a vacant four-top table in the center of the patio, and they dropped into chairs next to each other. Water lapped at the columns and beams of the pier below them.

"Well?" Collin leaned toward Tristan.

"Well, it seems, uh, nice." He darted his gaze around the patio, taking everything in. The faint scent of stale beer and fried food wafted on the shimmer of a breeze. A warm pressure enveloped his arm, resting on the table. He looked down. Collin's hand grasped his arm.

"Look at me, Tristan," Collin said.

His gaze drew to Collin's face.

"Why do you look so scared?" Studying him, Collin gave Tristan's arm a brief squeeze.

Tristan stared at the table. "I'm not." He frowned. Maybe he'd been a little anxious when they'd come in.

"Then look at me." Collin released Tristan's arm.

Taking a deep inhale, Tristan's gaze met his.

A waiter with dark hair in short spikes strolled up to their table and eyed Collin for a moment before clearing his throat. He held a round tray to his chest. "What can I get you, gentlemen?" He swayed his hips.

"I'll have a mojito." Collin glanced up at the waiter and gave him his signature flirtatious smile.

"What's that?" His chest tightened. Maybe he didn't really belong here after all.

Collin's gaze met Tristan's. "Get him a mojito, too." He placed his hand over Tristan's on the table. "You'll like it."

"Sure thing." The waiter tipped his head as he jogged off inside the building.

Collin focused on Tristan and squeezed his hand. "What's wrong?"

Pursing his lips, Tristan said, "Nothing's wrong." Collin had been so happy to come here. He shouldn't ruin it with his problems.

"I thought you'd like this place." Collin's face grew slack.

Sighing, Tristan hung his head. "I do, Collin. It's just really different for me. You have to understand that this week's been, well, amazing but also very stressful for me. A lot's happened, you know?"

"Yeah, I know." Collin wrapped his hand around the back of Tristan's head and gave his cheek a lingering kiss. "Hard to believe that having my roommates kick me out of that old dingy apartment would lead to me finding you."

Tristan studied his face. What exactly had happened between him and his roommates? He'd never found out.

Collin focused on him. "I can't believe how quickly the two of us hooked up. Well, maybe I can." Shifting in his seat, he glanced away, then came back. A sly smile quirked his mouth. "I'm not one to wait around for something I want. And with us living together, I'm surprised I waited as long as I did."

"Y-you wanted me? Right away?" Warmth flooded up from Tristan's toes to flood his body. Collin had wanted him.

With his cheeks reddening in the low light, Collin dropped his gaze to the table. "Uh..."

Tristan leaned toward him and squeezed Collin's hand. "What? Tell me."

Giving a slow shake of his head, Collin said, "No, I can't."

"Yes, you can. You always make me tell you everything." Tristan jiggled his foot on the floor. Would Collin say what he wanted to hear?

"No, I..." Collin cut his gaze to Tristan's. "Okay, I really like you, Tristan. A lot. More than I think I know what to do with." He leaned back and looked around him, his lips parting and closing. "Um, in fact when I first saw you in that dorm room, lying in bed, it took just about all my will power not to jump in bed with you right then."

"Really?" Tristan smiled broadly, his heart warming with emotion, then he jumped up and across the table to give Collin a fierce hug and a kiss.

"Okay, get a room you two." Setting their drinks down on the table, the waiter shook his head. "Tsk, tsk. What kind of a place do you think this is? A gay bar?" Smug sarcasm rang out in his voice.

Tristan freed Collin and sank into his seat, beaming, his heart almost bursting. He smiled up at the waiter. "What? It isn't a brothel?" He let out a hearty chuckle and Collin joined him.

Smiling, the waiter shook his finger at Tristan and went to the next table.

CHAPTER THIRTEEN

After an hour or so of talking and drinking, Collin rose up from his chair. "Be right back, have to take a piss."

"Oh, okay." Tristan leaned back in his chair and glanced around at the men chatting at tables all around him. He was alone. Alone and in a gay bar. His heartbeat quickened and he gripped his glass tighter, staring at his drink, drawing deep breaths. A few minutes passed.

"Hey." An older man, maybe in his thirties, dropped into the chair across from him and set a glass filled with dark beer on the table. "How are you?"

"Um, good." Tristan lifted his gaze to the man's face.

The man's large, brown eyes gazed back at him. Mussed, black hair, parted in the middle, framed the angles of the man's brow and jaw-line. His smile was warm and inviting. "Just good, huh?" The man pulled the lapel of his black blazer toward the center of his chest, then held out his hand. "I'm Robert."

Wow, this guy's handsome. Tristan gave the man's hand a tentative shake. "I'm Tristan." *Shit, what if Collin comes back?* He flicked his gaze toward the direction Collin walked off to.

"Something wrong?" Robert took a deep swig of beer.

"Um, well, I'm uh, here with someone." Tristan pressed his lips together, then sipped his drink.

"So?" Robert gave him an easy smile. "So am I. You."

"No, I mean I'm really here with someone. I came with someone." Tristan shifted in his seat. What was he supposed to do in this situation? Surely this guy saw Collin's drink still sitting on the table?

"Hmm, maybe you'll be coming with *me* later." Robert arched his brow.

A slight tremble shook Tristan's insides, and he glanced at the doorway. When would Collin come back? What was taking him so long? "I-I don't think so."

"Relax, it was just a joke." Reaching up from under the table, Robert rested his hand over Tristan's on his glass. "Can I buy you another drink? That one looks about done."

Tristan snuck a peek at his almost-empty glass. "Uh, I don't know."

"What's the matter? Am I really that scary?" Frowning, Robert withdrew his hand.

"No, I just..." Think of something to say to make him leave. "It's just that my boyfriend is sort of uh, jealous. You know, he gets really pissed off if guys hit on me. And he's big, really big, plays um, football." He chanced a look at Robert. Would he leave him alone now?

Robert sat back in his chair. "Really now." A smirk rose on his lips. "And where is this boyfriend of yours? Seems he's left you all alone. Maybe he's taking his time with some other guy in the bathroom? I know I'd never do that to someone as gorgeous as you."

"What?" Dropping his mouth open, Tristan straightened in his seat. "Collin wouldn't do that." He wrinkled his nose.

"So where is he?" Robert tapped his index finger on his beer glass.

Tristan took another peek at the doorway.

Leaning up against an antiqued wall, Collin stood just beyond the doorway, talking with a tall young man with dark hair who could've passed for a movie star. Collin smiled, dipping his head.

Heat prickled inside Tristan's chest. *No, don't do this to me.* He stared out across the water, letting pain eat away at him.

"So?" Robert twisted in his chair, then came back. "Isn't that him? The guy talking to Christian, against the wall?"

"Yes, I suppose." Tristan gritted his teeth and jerked his head around. "What? You saw me sitting with him earlier? You already knew I was with him?"

Robert snickered and twisted his drink on the table. "Sure, but lots of guys come in here with someone and leave with someone else. Happens all the time." His gaze met Tristan's.

"Not me." Tristan gritted his teeth. And neither would Collin. He'd be sure of that.

"Oh, you love that guy, huh." Robert nodded slowly.

Tristan furrowed his brows as his eyes stung. "Maybe." He'd never admit that to some stranger. He gulped down the remainder of his drink, rum and mint mixing with sugar to slide down his throat. "Okay, go ahead and buy me that drink."

A smug smile spread over Robert's full lips. "Sure." He raised his hand, and the waiter was there in an instant. "Get my friend here another mojito and make it a double this time." He glanced at Tristan. "Another beer, too, please, Timmy."

With a wave of his hand, Timmy jogged off again.

Robert looked behind him as if assessing the situation between Collin and Christian. "Looks like your boyfriend did well. Christian's quite a guy." His attention drew to Tristan.

"Yeah, whatever." Pain focused inside him like the stab of a knife, grinding round and round into his heart. He stared at the wood grains in the table surface, struggling to think. Why hadn't Collin just come back to their table? Nausea coiled in his gut.

"And here's your drink, sir." Sarcasm dripped from Timmy's voice as he set Tristan's drink on the table in front of him. He ticked his head at Robert. "Add it to your tab?"

Robert gave Timmy a smirk. "Yep."

Timmy waited a moment tapping his finger on his chin. "Does the guy you came in here with want another drink?"

As he glared at his own drink, Tristan frowned. "I don't know. Why don't you go and ask him?"

Robert leaned toward Tristan. "I'll get him one. Was he drinking the same thing as you?"

Tristan fixed his glare on Robert. "No. Don't get him anything."

Sitting back, Robert shrugged at Timmy. "Well, you heard him."

Timmy clucked his tongue and touched Tristan's shoulder.

Tristan jerked back from his touch. Maybe he should find a way to go home. There must be busses out here, right?

"Oh, jealous, huh? I tell you, boyfriends are hard to come by, but even harder to keep. Don't worry, Robert here will take care of you." With a knowing glance, Timmy walked off into the sea of tables.

"I'm a nice guy, Tristan, really," Robert said.

Throwing a glance at Robert, Tristan grabbed his drink and downed a few gulps. Burning tightened his throat and he coughed.

Robert placed a hand on Tristan's shoulder. "Take it easy."

The pain in Tristan's chest grew and tears threatened to surface. He took another gulp of his drink. The hand on his shoulder tightened.

"Hey, babe, don't drink it too fast. I don't want you to uh, well you know, not be able to perform later." Robert released a soft snicker.

"Oh really." Tristan glanced at Collin, now laughing, and standing closer to Christian, then he glared at Robert and downed the rest of the drink. "Thanks for the drink, but I think I'll be going home alone tonight."

With his mouth hanging open, Robert stared at him.

Tristan popped up to standing, shoved his chair back and stomped toward Collin.

Collin landed his hand on Christian's arm and drew him near, bringing his lips close to Christian's ear.

Tristan glared at Collin, his chest heaving. As he reached him, he swung out and slapped him in the chest, throwing him against the wall.

"What the fuck?" Collin stared, wide-eyed at him. "God damn it, Tristan, what's the matter with you?" He shoved Tristan away from him.

Tristan stumbled back. "What're you doing, Collin? Picking up on this guy? Did you just fuck him in the bathroom?"

Christian held his palms up to them. "Hey, man, Collin and I were just talking."

"What?" Tristan stepped further away from Collin.

"Jesus, Tristan. Where the fuck did you get that idea?" Collin glared at him.

"W-well, um..." Tristan's gaze flicked between Collin and Christian. Had he been wrong?

Collin clenched his teeth and turned to Christian. "Sorry, man. This is my...sometimes overly jealous boyfriend I was telling you about." Collin glanced at the floor, then focused on Tristan. "You remember those roommates I told you about?" He pressed his lips together.

"Yes?" Frowning, Tristan stared at Christian, giving him a smug look.

Christian held out his hand. "I'm Christian, one of Collin's old roommates."

"Um..." Tristan gave his hand a brief shake. "S-sorry."

Collin stepped forward and threw his arm around Tristan's shoulders. Leaning in to Tristan's ear, he said firmly, "You really need to start trusting me."

Warmth climbed up Tristan's neck. *Fuck, I'm so stupid.* "I'm sorry." He focused on Christian. "It's just that this guy was picking up on me and—"

"This guy what?" Collin dropped his mouth open, then cut his gaze to the patio, his brows lowering.

Tristan shifted his focus to Collin. "This guy, Robert? He bought me a drink and—"

"He bought you a drink? You let him?" Collin glared at Tristan.

Tristan's heart beat a frantic rhythm in his chest. "Uh, well..." He wrung his hands together. Collin looked pissed. Really pissed.

Collin's gaze searched the patio. "That guy at our table?" He pointed to their table.

"Yes." Tristan hung his head.

"Well, let's go and have a talk with him." Looking at Christian, Collin ticked his head toward the patio. "Come on, Christian."

Christian snatched Collin's arm and twisted him around. "Dude, just leave him alone. You know how this place is."

"What, are you being a pussy now?" Collin stared down his friend.

Christian shifted his stance and glanced away for a moment. "Don't fucking call me that. You're always starting shit, Collin. You can't just leave shit alone. You always have to start something even when it's not needed." Raking a hand through his dark hair, he sighed. "Just leave it alone this time. There wasn't any harm done."

Collin's gaze drew to Tristan.

Tristan shrugged. No way did he want to go back and face Robert. The whole thing was just embarrassing now.

Christian threw an arm toward the bar. "Come on, I'll buy us all a shot. Whatever you want."

Collin drew a deep inhale. "Yeah, okay."

The three of them headed to the bar and sat at barstools with Tristan between Collin and his friend.

"So, what do you want?" Christian smiled at Tristan.

"I don't know." Tristan's head was still reeling from the whole confrontation. What sort of shit had Collin started when they were roommates?

"Let's just do a shot of tequila. A good one." Collin slipped his hand to the small of Tristan's back.

A balding man turned and smiled at the three of them. "What can I get you?"

"Tequila—whatever your best is." Christian fished into his front pocket.

The bartender bent down, pulled out shot glasses and poured tequila into them. "Need training wheels?"

"What?" Furrowing his brows, Tristan peeked at Collin.

"Do you want lime and salt with your shot?" Collin spread a smirk over his mouth.

"Yes. There's no way I could do a shot of that stuff without it." Tristan's gaze roamed Collin's face and rested on his lips.

"Wuss..." With a smirk, Collin faced the bartender. "I'll take mine without. He needs the wheels."

Tristan's chest heated. "Don't call me a wuss. What's up with you tonight?" He glared at Collin. They were supposed to be having fun. This wasn't fun anymore.

"Ah, you two never went drinking before? Collin turns into an ass when he drinks." Christian leaned forward to glance at Collin.

The bartender set their drinks in front of them.

"Shut up. Just 'cause you never got in my ass doesn't mean you have to talk smack about me." Collin grabbed his drink and held it up. "Come on, Tristan, hold up your drink."

Tristan poured salt on his hand, licked it and held up his drink to Collin's and Christian's, then they clinked the glasses together and he downed his shot. Warmth slid down his throat. He bit on the lime. The sour taste mellowed the flavor of the tequila. His mind dulled almost immediately, and he looked at Christian. "So, tell me more about Collin."

With a small shrug, Christian gave Tristan a wide smile. "What do you want to know?"

"Anything." Tristan looked him over.

Christian huffed out a laugh. "Has he tried to fix you yet?"

Tristan's heart plummeted. "What?"

"Fuck off, Christian." Collin tugged Tristan back and stepped between him and his friend. "Don't fill his head with that crap. It's not my fault Steven broke it off with you, okay?"

Christian stepped toward Collin. "I'm sure your little mind games helped."

"Listen, I left. Isn't that enough? Do you have to go over this shit every time I see you?"

Christian's gaze turned hard. "Whatever, man. I'm out of here." He focused on Tristan. "Dude, be careful with this one."

Tristan's chest clenched. Maybe he shouldn't be trusting Collin after all. But hadn't he helped him this week? "What did he mean by that, Collin?"

Looking at the floor, Collin's face tensed. "I don't know. Don't listen to him." When his gaze found Tristan's, he tongued his lower lip. "You want to go home now? I think it's time we celebrated your accomplishment in a different way." He gave Tristan a charming grin.

Tristan's heart melted. "Sure." Maybe Collin had done something bad with Christian, but he'd been nothing but good to him.

A few hours later, Tristan ambled into the dark dorm room and Collin closed and locked the door behind him. When Tristan came to the center of the room, Collin's warm arms surrounded him from behind and his soft lips tickled his ear.

"You know what I want to do to you tonight?" Collin's breath whispered over Tristan's ear.

Heat rushed Tristan's groin, hardening his cock. "No, what?"

Collin rocked his hips, driving his erection into Tristan's ass through their jeans. "I want to fuck you."

Tristan's breath caught in his throat. How long had he wanted that? "Y-you mean—"

"Yes." Collin thrust his stiff cock harder into Tristan's ass.

Tristan's hips jerked forward, and his jeans grew tight. "O-okay. B-but you know I've never—"

"I know." Collin pressed hard kisses to the back of his neck.

Shivers ran up and down Tristan's spine and his cock ached. He let out a soft groan and made to turn around.

Collin grasped his arms just under the shoulders and held him in place. "No, you just stand there and let me do, well, whatever I want. Okay?"

Tristan whispered, "Okay."

Collin unzipped Tristan's jacket and with one quick movement the jacket was tossed aside. As he unbuttoned Tristan's shirt, he devoured the back of Tristan's neck with hungry kisses, the side, and the top of his shoulder.

As desire and heat built within Tristan, he tilted his head, to the side, exposing his skin, and a soft moan rippled from his chest. He tilted his hips forward in expectation. The shirt was thrown to the floor and Collin lifted the t-shirt over his head.

Trailing his hand in circles over Tristan's chest, Collin stopped to give his nipple a light pinch.

Tristan's breath caught and his cock jerked in his jeans. The ache in his groin grew unbearable. "Please, Collin..."

"You going to beg me, huh?" Collin nipped and sucked a trail down Tristan's spine, stopping every so often for a harder bite.

"If that's what you want." Tristan lost himself to sensation, anticipation, and pure lust. His breath came in deep draws. "I'll, I'll do anything you want, Collin. Anything." He shut his eyes and slipped his lower lip between his teeth.

Collin stopped, crouched down with his hands sliding to the front of Tristan's jeans and his mouth on his lower back. "Anything?"

"Yes." Tristan groaned.

"So, you trust me now?" Collin nipped at his skin.

"Yes." Tristan breathed deeply.

"Completely?"

"Yes."

"Good." Collin reached around and dropped his hands to Tristan's inner thighs, rubbing and caressing the sensitive muscle under the thick fabric. "Because I only want you, Tristan. You have to know that." Collin brushed over Tristan's balls and the swollen tip of his erection, giving them a light tickle.

Tristan gasped. "Yes." Rocking his hips involuntarily, the fabric pulled tightly across his hard cock. He moved his hand to his groin and Collin slapped it away.

"Nope, none of that anymore." Collin placed a soft bite on Tristan's ass cheek. "We're not touching that at all tonight."

Tristan popped his eyes open. "What?" How would that work?

A soft chuckle rumbled in Collin's chest. "Well, maybe a little. You'll see."

Slowly, he closed his eyes again, overcome with the sensation of Collin caressing his thighs.

Collin unfastened Tristan's belt and his jeans and opened them up. As he lowered the fabric, he kissed and nipped a trail down the back of Tristan's legs, then crept around to the front. "Step out."

Tristan toed out of his shoes and then his jeans. He peeked down. His hard cock tented out his boxers.

With a smirk, Collin glanced up, then plunged his face between Tristan's thighs. Licking and sucking, he taunted the flesh all around his erection, but never quite on it.

A loud moan freed from Tristan, and he thrust his hips. "Come on, Collin. Touch me, please."

"I am." Collin plunged Tristan's boxers down and ravaged the naked skin in the crevice between his legs and groin.

Tristan gasped and slapped his hands to the back of Collin's head in a desperate attempt to guide his mouth to his aching cock. "Oh, please."

Collin pulled away and stood up.

In a daze, Tristan took in the stunning beauty of Collin, while his chest heaved with deep breaths. "Why did you stop?"

Smirking, Collin lifted his sweater over his head and tossed it to the floor, then unfastened his pants, lowered them with his boxers and kicked them of with his shoes. He grasped Tristan's hand. "Over here." He led Tristan to his bed. "Bend over."

"What?" Tristan twisted to peek at Collin's face. Collin wasn't going to do it right here, was he?

Still grinning, Collin gestured to the bed. "You heard me."

He stared at Collin. "But, I-I don't know why—"

"You don't need to know. You have to trust me, remember?" Collin threw a glance at the bed.

Tristan swallowed hard and focused on the bed. Trust him. Tentatively, he bent at the waist.

Collin guided his hands to rest on the bed with his arms straight. "Perfect."

"P-perfect?" Tristan's pulse kicked.

"Yep. Be right back." Collin paced into the bathroom.

Tristan watched for Collin to return. What the hell was going on? This wasn't at all how he pictured it should be.

Jogging back, Collin stood behind Tristan's ass. "This'll be a little cold." Slick coolness brushed up between his butt cheeks from Collin's fingers.

"What are you doing?" Tristan swiveled his head to peer behind him.

Collin bent over Tristan's back, his lips brushing the shell of Tristan's ear. "Preparing you." His voice was soft and husky.

"What?" Tristan's gaze darted over the bed. What did that mean?

"Relax." Collin circled his slick fingers over Tristan's hole while pressing soft kisses to his neck, shoulder and back

Shivers ran up and down Tristan's spine and his cock jerked. "Ah..."

"Feel good so far?" Collin teased Tristan's entrance and rubbed his stiff cock against the globe of his ass. "You want this, right?"

"Y-yes." He pushed back into Collin's teasing fingers. Pleasure crept up from his entrance to his balls and into his seeping cock.

His brows tensed. What would it feel like to have Collin inside him?

Collin slipped a finger passed the rings of muscle and stroked Tristan's passage while his free hand caressed and soothed and his lips continued soft kisses on Tristan's back.

Burning lit up inside Tristan, then he relaxed. Letting out a low groan, Tristan rocked with the rhythm of Collin's finger, pressure and friction filling him. "More, Collin."

"More?" Collin plunged his finger deeper, stroking quicker.

Pleasure jolted up Tristan's spine, and pre-cum seeped out of his hard cock. "Oh, God." He needed more of that.

Collin slipped a second finger inside Tristan and cupped his balls with the other hand, kneading and teasing. "How's that?"

"Good, really good." Panting, sensitivity built deep inside Tristan, and he thrust in time with Collin's fingers and palm.

After rolling a condom on and applying more lube, Collin nudged the head of his erection into Tristan's entrance. "You ready?" With his cockhead tucked into the crevice of Tristan's ass, he released a sharp gasp.

Need filled every fiber of Tristan's body. "Yes." He pushed his ass into Collin's hot dick. "Come on. What're you waiting for?"

"You like that, huh?" Collin slid the head of his cock into Tristan's hole. "Shit, you're so tight."

"Keep going. You're driving me crazy with all this stopping, damn it." He pushed from the bed, thrusting his hips backward and driving Collin's cock all the way into him. Burning and fullness rippled inside him. "Oh, God." It was bad, but in a good way.

"You okay?" Collin's voice was ragged. He dropped his chest to lie against Tristan's back.

Tristan panted and relaxed his body. "Yes, please, just do it already." Somehow, he needed more, needed Collin to move.

Collin nibbled on his back. "No problems there." He pulled out and slowly drove back inside with a slow groan.

Tristan hummed with pleasure as Collin's thick cock

massaged his insides, sliding over his internal bundle of nerves, throwing little sparks up his spine. "Harder, Collin, go harder."

Collin bit at the back of Tristan's neck and thrust his hips, driving his thick cock into and out of Tristan's slickened entrance. Sharp moans, one after the other tore from his throat. "Oh, shit, Tristan."

Exquisite need built to a crescendo inside Tristan. Pleasure swept up his balls to the tip of his cock, making it ache and seep for attention. He dropped his head between his straight arms, his blond hair hanging in clumps in his face. A sheen of sweat broke out on his skin. Oh, how he wanted to touch himself, to relieve the ache in his dick.

Collin reached around Tristan's sides, groping, and fondling any flesh he could find. He pinched at Tristan's nipples.

Crying out, Tristan rocked harder in time with Collin, impaling himself on his thick shaft. His insides heightened with sensitivity. Panting, his balls tightened for release and his cock pulsed over and over with each pass of Collin's hard dick pegging his prostate. "Come on, Collin, please. I can't take much more. Let me come. Jerk me off."

"You want to come, Tristan?" Collin kneaded Tristan's nipples into hard nubs.

"Yes, damn it." Tristan writhed in his hold, desperate to feel himself topple over the edge.

Collin's hot breath swept over Tristan's back. Droplets of sweat fell onto Tristan's shoulders to mix with his own. Still, he drove into Tristan. He snuck his hands between Tristan's legs and kneaded his sac and inner thighs, always taunting and teasing.

"Fuck, Collin, stop it." Growling, Tristan twisted and peered at Collin.

Collin ceased all motion. "Stop? Did you say stop?"

"You know damn well what I mean." Tristan sucked in heavy breaths. "Stop teasing me. Let me come."

Driving into Tristan, Collin held it. His eyelids hooded and his brows tensed. "Damn, Tristan, you're so fucking hot right now. I don't want it to end."

"Please, Collin." Tristan turned back around and hung his head. "I need to come."

Collin pulled out and drove in again, returning to his previous rhythm, then wrapped his hand around Tristan's aching cock and gave it a brief squeeze.

Gasping, Tristan rocked into his hand. Sweet release taunted him, sensitivity skyrocketing to a harsh edge.

Collin relaxed his hand and stroked over him with a light touch.

"Quit teasing me." Tristan pushed back onto Collin's hard cock and drove forward into a soft palm and fingers.

"You want it, Tristan?" Collin asked in a gruff voice.

"Fuck, yeah." Tristan groaned.

Trembling over Tristan's back, Collin's breath caught. He drove in and held tight to Tristan's hips. As his body shuddered, he buried his cock deeper into Tristan. Between clenched teeth, he cried out. His cock pulsated inside Tristan's hole.

Collin is coming without me. Tristan rutted into Collin's limp fingers, aching to join him.

Collin pulled out and drove in, one long, slow motion. He tightened his fist around Tristan's seeping erection and pumped, over and over.

Intense pleasure seared from Tristan's cock to his balls and pinched his insides. Clutching the covers of Collin's bed, his release tore out of him, the force of his climax painting ribbons of cum on the wall behind the bed and over the covers. Again and again, fierce contractions raged on. As it slowed, Collin fell down over his back and Tristan's arms almost crumpled. He drew heaving breaths into and out of his mouth.

"You like that?" Collin gave Tristan's back a lingering kiss and rose upright behind him, sliding his spent cock from Tristan's hole.

With a lazy grin, Tristan fell sideways onto the bed and looked up at Collin. "Holy shit, that was great. I didn't think it was ever going to stop." It was probably the best orgasm he'd ever had.

After discarding the condom, Collin sat on the edge of the bed and slapped Tristan's leg. "Told you to trust me." His gaze roamed the covers on his bed. "Damn, look what you did to my bedspread."

Propping up on one elbow, Tristan peered at the mess of wet blobs on the bed, then huffed out a chuckle. "Sorry. It was your idea, you know."

A quick laugh erupted out of Collin. "Yeah, it was worth a few stains."

Tristan jumped off the bed and started toward the bathroom. "I'll clean it up." He hadn't understood what Collin had been doing in the moment, but it sure turned out good. The best.

"Okay. Hey, let's sleep in your bed tonight." Collin sighed.

CHAPTER FOURTEEN

SUNDAY, NOVEMBER 8

Collin stood at Tristan's desk and held out Tristan's cell phone. "Go on, call her."

Sighing, he twisted in the chair at his desk. "But I really needed to get some more studying done." They'd pretty much spent their Saturday studying, but it seemed there was always more to do to prepare for Monday's classes.

"You said you called her every Sunday and it's almost dinnertime. I just want to make sure it's all set up for us to see her over Thanksgiving before I get the tickets." Collin shook the phone, gesturing for Tristan to take it.

Tristan roamed his gaze up Collin's tall frame, taking in the tight jeans, and black t-shirt pulled over his broad chest. "Fuck. Okay. But I need some privacy."

"Privacy? You've got to be kidding. I want to see how you talk to your mom." Collin shifted his stance and planted a hand on his hip, his brows furrowing. "It's important, Tristan."

"B-but, I...Oh, all right." He snatched the phone from Collin's hand, found the number for his mother and hit the green call button, then tapped on his desk with his free hand. It rang a few times, then clicked.

"Hello?"

"Mom?" Tristan tossed a glance at Collin.

"Oh, hello, Tristan. How are you?"

"Good. Listen I—"

"Doing well at school?"

Tristan crossed his jean-clad legs at his desk. "Yes, I—"

"Still in all those art classes?" A condescending tone rang out in her voice.

"Yes, you know I am." Tristan lowered his brows.

"Honestly, I don't know what you think you're going to do when you get out of school."

"Mom, you know I can get a job as an illustrator or a graphic designer. We've been over this. I'm good at art. It's what I want to do." Tristan gripped the phone tighter, his chest stiffening.

Collin dropped down to his knees in front of him. "Tell her about the art store selling your stuff."

"But why can't you study something else, just in case? I don't like you putting all your eggs in one basket." Her voice became firm.

With a peek at Collin, he swiveled in his chair and rested his elbow on the desk. "I know, but Mom, the art store—"

"Art store, are you working at the art store now?"

"No, I'm not. I need to talk to you about—"

"Because I'd rather you found a job somewhere else. Maybe at a burger joint? Get you away from all those strange artistic types."

"Mom...please, listen to me." Tristan clenched his jaw. As usual, this was not going well. "I'm not working at the art store. They're selling some of my work."

Collin placed his hand on his thigh and gave it a tender squeeze. "Tell her about Thanksgiving."

Placing his hand over the phone, he said, "I will. Give me a minute."

"Tristan, honey, is someone there with you? Do you have a

friend? Because it's about time you found a friend. You've been alone too long."

"Yes, I have a friend with me. His name is Collin." He looked at Collin, watching his every move.

"Collin? No girlfriend, huh?" She huffed.

"Girlfriend? No—"

"When are you going to find a girlfriend?"

"Mom, please..." Pain stabbed at Tristan's heart. Not this again.

"Don't whine at me, Tristan."

"Tell her, Tristan. You have to stand up to her. Just tell her you're bringing a friend for Thanksgiving." Collin looked directly into Tristan's eyes.

Tristan nodded his head. "Mom. Listen to me. I'm bringing my friend, Collin, home for Thanksgiving." He grimaced.

"What? Oh no!"

Clanking filled the phone. "Mom? Mom?"

His mother's voice sounded far away. "No, kitty, that was bad. Very bad."

"Shit." Tristan sighed. This was impossible. She never paid any attention to him.

"What happened?" Collin came close as if straining to hear the phone pressed against Tristan's head.

"The cat did something and she's dealing with it. I don't know if she heard me." Tristan brought the phone down and glared at it.

"Well don't hang up on her. Make sure she heard you. Take charge, Tristan." Collin pressed his lips together.

"I am. Just let me handle it." Tristan placed the phone against his ear once again. "Mom?"

"Oh, yes, Tristan. I'm sorry, but the cat knocked one of my plants onto the floor. I've gotta go."

"But did you hear me?" Tristan gripped the phone so tight, his knuckles turned white.

"Hear what?"

"That I'm bringing my friend, Collin, home for Thanksgiving?" His voice was louder than intended. He pinched the bridge of his nose and exhaled.

"What friend?"

"My friend, Collin. He's my new roommate at college." He gritted his teeth. She hadn't listened to a thing he'd said.

"So, you have a boy to bring home. Great." Her words were sharp.

Tristan's chest squeezed and he lowered his brows. "What's that supposed to mean?"

"Nothing. It's fine, Tristan, just fine. At least you finally have a friend." She coughed away from the phone.

What does she mean by that? Better to play dumb. "Yes, Mom, I finally have a friend. So, I guess it's not a problem if he comes with me for Thanksgiving?"

"No, of course not. He's not an art student, too, or some theater type, is he?" She huffed a laugh.

"No." Tristan gazed at Collin's stunning face. "He's a psychology major."

"Oh. Well, I look forward to meeting him then."

Tristan pursed his lips. So, if Collin was another art student, she wouldn't welcome him into her home? What was that supposed to mean? "Yeah, okay, Mom. I'll let you go now."

"Okay. Bye and talk to you next Sunday. Try not to call so late next week."

He balled his hand into a fist. "Yes, of course, Mother." He took a deep breath. "Good—"

The phone went dead.

"That bitch." His eyes stung and he rubbed them with his index finger and thumb.

Collin grabbed both of his wrists and held them to Tristan's chest, his gaze darting between his eyes. "Hey, are you all right?"

A light sniffle escaped him. "Yeah." His gaze locked onto Collin's. "She hung up on me and didn't even say goodbye."

Collin freed Tristan's wrists and dropped his hands into his lap. "Does she always do that to you?"

"No." Tristan huffed. "She's just so preoccupied with everything else, anything else but me. It's like I don't matter to her at all." His vision blurred, and he clenched his teeth.

Collin kissed his forehead. "It's okay, Tristan. We'll get to the bottom of it when we go home for Thanksgiving. And anyways, I care about you. You have to know that." A light smile rested on Collin's lips. He caressed Tristan's upper arms and shoulders.

He gazed deeply into Collin's eyes. Was he telling the truth? Just how much did he mean to Collin? How he'd wanted to ask, how he'd wanted to hear a certain three words come out of his mouth. But he couldn't ask, not yet.

"Hey, let's get some dinner and get to bed early tonight. I have to meet with Jessica before sociology class in the morning." He popped up to stand in front of Tristan.

Tilting his head back, Tristan's gaze chased him. "Really? Before class?"

"Yep, I know it's sort of a drag." Collin grabbed Tristan's phone, placed it on the desk, then grasped his hands in his and pulled him up out of his chair. "But I'll be there in time for class to start."

CHAPTER FIFTEEN

MONDAY, NOVEMBER 9

S tepping into the sociology class, Tristan scanned the room of
mulling students and hushed voices for Collin. He played
with the hem of his green t-shirt as his gaze took in row after row
of desks. Where was he? Still with Jessica? But class was about to
begin.

Out of the corner of his eye, the professor appeared from the
doorway with his usual papers in files and books pressed to his
chest.

Tristan hurried to two empty desks in the back of the room,
took one of the chairs and sat down while the other students
scrambled to their own desks. Reaching over, he unzipped his
backpack and took out his notebook and pen. His attention drew
to the professor, setting his things on the podium.

"Good morning, class. I'm sure you all had a good weekend."
The professor's wiry, gray hair puffed out at the sides of his head
and a v-neck sweater vest rested over a white oxford shirt.

Furrowing his brows, he focused on the door and let the
professor's words wash over his ears. *Where the hell is Collin?* It
wasn't like him to be late to anything, let alone this class.

Absently, he brought his hand up to his pocket and let his fingers toy with edge of it on his snug jeans.

He tried to focus on the words now pouring out of the instructor's mouth, but he found it more and more difficult with each passing minute. Did something happen to Collin? Could he be hurt? *Collin's with Jessica.* As his heart raced, he took a deep inhale and wriggled his hand into his front pocket.

His gaze flicked to the clock on the wall just behind the professor. *Collin's already ten minutes late.* Should he look for him? He passed his fingers over the head of his cock. This was the old way he'd handled such feelings. He shouldn't. He was over this now, wasn't he?

He pressed on the head of his swelling cock, letting sensation ripple through him. It'll be all right. Collin was fine, just late was all. And he was alone. Alone to do as he wished for once. No one to stop him. A smug grin grew on his lips as he crept lower in his chair. He ran his fingers down his shaft to his sac, giving him the familiar tease of pleasure as they went, then glanced at the door.

The door swung open and Collin rushed in from the hallway. Auburn hair poked up from the sides of his head and his red polo shirt, tucked in earlier that morning, wrinkled around his waist in un-tucked spurts. He stopped just inside the door and looked around the room for a moment, sweat trickling down the sides of his face.

Shit! Tristan ripped his hand out of his pocket and sat upright. His pulse quickened. What had happened to Collin? Why did he look so messed up? He held his hand up partway, attempting to get Collin's attention. The seat next to him was still empty.

Collin's gaze met his for a split second and he hung his head, striding for an open desk in the front row.

Tristan's heart sank. Something was going on. He just knew it. Why didn't Collin sit by him? *Oh no, could he have possibly seen what I was doing? No...* His gut clenched and he stared at the top of the desk, then focused on Collin, sitting far ahead of him, swiping at his head, combing his hair with his fingers.

He watched Collin. What could have happened? Did he do something with Jessica? Pain crept up into his heart. *No, don't think like that. You have to trust him, remember?*

"And so the answer to the question is, Mr. Stanley?" The professor walked out from behind the podium and approached Collin.

Tristan sat up straight in his chair, holding his breath.

Fumbling with his notebook, Collin shifted in his seat. "Uh, what was the question again?"

"It was very simple, really. I asked you what time this class started." The professor raised his brows and slapped his market to his palm.

"Oh, um, nine, nine o'clock." Collin shrugged. "Sorry I was late. I had a..." He sucked a deep inhale. "Got caught up in something."

"I see. Let's not make it a habit." The professor turned to his whiteboard.

"Of course, sir." Collin dipped his head.

Sinking back in his seat, Tristan freed a held breath, then focused on the professor, now continuing on with the lecture. He couldn't wait for class to be over and find out what happened to Collin.

———

"THAT'S ALL FOR TODAY." The professor closed a book with a thud and all the students stood up and packed their things.

Tristan shoved his notebook into his pack, threw it over his back and raced down to meet up with Collin. He stopped in front of him just as he stood up. "Hey."

"Hey." Collin let out a puff of air, blowing a lock of auburn bangs out of his eyes, then walked toward the door.

"So?" Tristan stayed on him, following close by his side.

Collin hung his head, staring at the ground. "So, what?"

Snatching Collin's arm, he tugged him to a stop. "What happened? Where were you?"

Collin jerked his arm out of Tristan's clutch and started toward the door again. "Nothing. Just with Jessica, like I told you."

"B-but..." He followed Collin out the doors and into the sunlit morning among stucco buildings, red tiles and rose bushes. Birds chirped a loud chorus in oak trees above them. The tightness in his chest grew with every step Collin took away from him. He jogged up and regained his hold on Collin's arm. "Stop, Collin, and tell me what happened."

Collin whirled around and faced him. His eyes shimmered in the sunlight. "I told you it was nothing!"

Dropping his mouth, Tristan took a step back. Was he about to cry? "C-Collin?" He grabbed onto Collin's arms and attempted to embrace him, but Collin reared back.

"Don't, Tristan. Not here." He swiped at his eyes with the back of his hands.

With a sturdy grasp of Collin's hand, Tristan hauled him across campus, over grass and pathways, past bougainvillea-surrounded arches and tall palm trees, through meandering students with curious glances, all the way to their dorm and up to their room. Once safely inside, he placed his backpack on the floor and set his attention on Collin.

Collin stood by their desks, gazing out the window into the campus below.

Stepping to him, Tristan slid his backpack down his arm and placed it on the floor. "So tell me what happened." He needed to be there for Collin, especially after all the times he'd been there for him.

"I don't know I...I got into a little argument with Jessica." Collin sighed and stared out the window.

"What was the argument about?" A knot formed in Tristan's

gut. That couldn't be good. He'd never seen Collin like this, and he didn't like it.

Collin stood there, gazing out the window.

The knot in Tristan's gut grew. What could have happened? Oh no..."Did she come on to you? Is that what happened?" Grabbing Collin by the arm, he swung him around. "Did you let her?" He eyed him from head to toe.

Collin winced. "No." He focused on the wall behind Tristan.

"Oh really, then why can't you look at me?" Wrinkling his nose, trembling started up in his body. "What did she do to you, Collin? Why were you so messed up when you came to class? Did you fuck her? Huh?" His voice rose in pitch with every word. His eyes pricked. Why did he always have to go there? Was he still so insecure of what he had with Collin?

Sneaking his lip between his teeth, Collin's gaze drew to Tristan's. "God no, it wasn't like that. Stop accusing me of stuff like that. She just...shit." He paced away from Tristan and sat down on the edge of his bed, planting his elbows on his knees and his face in his hands. "She thinks I'm a fucking asshole. Maybe I am." His voice cracked.

"What?" He rushed to the bed and dropped in beside Collin, draping an arm around his shoulders. "I don't understand."

"I don't want to talk about it. Okay?" Collin's voice wavered. He sniffled and wiped his eyes, then as his head came up, his gaze met Tristan's for a moment before looking away. "I, um, I've helped you. Haven't I?" He focused back on Tristan with wet, dark eyes.

Tristan sat back, keeping his gaze locked on Collin's. "Sure, you've helped me a lot. Why would you ask me something like that?" This made no sense. Of course, Collin had helped him. He'd been able to quit his self-soothing, at least for now.

With a shrug, Collin gave a quick shake of his head. "I don't know. It seems I'm always fucking things up."

"Why don't you just tell me what happened? Because right now you're not making a whole lot of sense." He edged closer to

Collin and tightened his hold around his shoulders. "Talk to me. You'd never let me get away with this."

Collin exhaled a rush of air and lowered his head to Tristan's shoulder.

Closing his eyes, Tristan trailed a slow circle over Collin's back, then whispered, "Come on, talk to me." He could be here for Collin the same way Collin had been there for him.

"Well, things I've done for you, they worked, didn't they?" Collin tipped his head to peer into Tristan's face.

Tristan tensed his brows. "Yeah, I told you it helped."

"I mean, you're not touching yourself anymore and you seem a lot more, uh, confident in yourself than when I met you. And it's only been what, a little over a week?" Collin rested his hand on Tristan's thigh.

"Yes, I feel a lot better about myself." Tristan kissed the top of his head.

"And my idea to meet your mother's a good one. Isn't it? Don't you think that'll solve a lot of old issues for you? If you can get your mother to accept you for who you really are?" Collin sniffled and straightened, squeezing Tristan's thigh.

"Yes, but what does this all have to do with your fight with Jessica?" Tristan furrowed his brows. He really wasn't making any sense.

Collin twisted to face Tristan and placed his free hand on Tristan's other thigh. "So, what I'm doing here is working. I'm doing the right thing by you because, because I—" His gaze darted between Tristan's eyes.

"You what, Collin?" Tristan's heart ached for Collin's next words. Please let them finally be what he wanted to hear.

"I don't want to do the wrong thing here. I don't want to—to make a mess of you." Collin's throat dipped with a hard swallow.

Tristan's heart sank and a lump formed in his throat. "Oh."

"Because I really care about you, really care." Collin slid closer to him and smiled. "That bitch let me fall into the damned bushes."

Tristan blinked a few times. "She what?"

"You heard me. Why do you think I looked like such a slob when I got to class? She actually shoved me at the café, and I fell backward into some bushes." Collin let out a soft snort.

Tristan widened his eyes. "Why is that so funny? Why would she shove you?" He couldn't imagine her doing something like that. Slap him in the face, maybe, but not shoving.

Collin straightened and placed his hands in his lap. "It wasn't supposed to be a hard shove. I just lost my balance and went down. But the bitch didn't even try to help me. And then she told me I deserved it. I must have looked like a real idiot." His smile waned.

"Why would you deserve it?" He eyed Collin up and down. There was something he wasn't telling him. "Would you just tell me exactly what happened?"

Collin waved his hand at Tristan. "Oh, it doesn't matter now. It was just a disagreement and it's over." He looked at the watch on his wrist. "I have to go meet with my thesis instructor in a few minutes. I'll have to catch up with you later." Bending over, he snatched his backpack and flung the strap over his shoulder as he stood up. After giving Tristan a quick smile, he jogged out of the room.

———

AN HOUR LATER, Tristan walked through campus in afternoon sunlight. His gaze traveled far out over the distant mountains to catch a few fluffy clouds floating in a sea of deep blue sky. The scent of distant flowers wafted on a warm breeze. After losing himself in his drawing class, contentment flooded his body as it always did.

"See you later," A woman's voice called out.

*Jessica...*His gaze darted around the university grounds until he saw her blond head and perfect figure, always draped in something tight and revealing.

She turned and her gaze locked on him. Immediately, her head hung, and she coughed into her hand.

"Jessica!" He took off at a jog toward her with one hand waving.

She twisted around and started off in the opposite direction.

"Jessica, hey, wait!" He picked up speed.

She made an abrupt stop, her back still to him.

He caught up to her and tapped her shoulder. "Hey, I want to talk to you for a second."

She cleared her throat and faced him, her normal, smug smile widening her plump lips. "Oh, hey, I didn't see you there. What did you want to talk about?"

Didn't see me? But she looked right at me. "I, uh, wanted to know what you and Collin fought about this morning." He studied her, gauging her expression.

"So, he didn't tell you?" With a huff, her brows furrowed, and she looked at the ground.

"Tell me what?" He shifted his stance.

Wrinkling her brows, her attention drew to him. "Um, n-nothing. I need to go. I have a class to get to." She started off.

Snatching her arm, he stopped her and dragged her toward him.

"Stop it, Tristan. Let go of me." She glared at him, her lips in a thin line.

He released her arm. "Please, just tell me what happened. I can't put my finger on it, but it seems like Collin's hiding something from me and you know what that is, don't you?"

She took a deep breath and her gaze softened. "Listen, Collin is developing some deep feelings for you. He needs to come to terms with some of his behavior and it's not my place to tell you about it. He needs to do it. And I don't want to betray his confidence. That's it."

With a few quick blinks, he took a step back, his heart fluttering. *Is Collin falling in love with me? Is that what the argument was about? But why would that start an argument?* "But—"

"I have to go." Grasping her backpack tight to her shoulder, Jessica hurried down a cement pathway covered by a scrubby oak tree.

He hung his mouth open. *He loves me, doesn't he? Collin's just too afraid to admit it and maybe Jessica pressed him on the issue. Maybe Jessica tried to get him to confess his feelings and he got mad at her? He loves me...*

He spread a wide smile over his lips and the air around him sweetened, then walked toward the dorm with his heart and step lightening. *It's going to be all right now.*

CHAPTER SIXTEEN

Salt Lake City, Uta

TUESDAY, NOVEMBER 25

Tristan sat in a seat on a plane, looking out over the tarmac through a tiny window as they taxied up the runway to the terminal. Small bits of snow laid in absent piles among the scurrying baggage carriers and the whole scene was made dull by a heavy layer of clouds. His mind went over Jessica's words again, as it had over and over during the last few weeks. *Collin is developing some deep feelings for you.* A flood of calm eased the churning emotions in his gut. He'd have to see his mother soon. And soon, she'd meet Collin. He squeezed Collin's warm hand, lying under his own on the armrest between his seat and Collin's and shifted his gaze to the stunning features of his sleeping face. He leaned in toward his ear. "How the hell can you sleep while the plane is landing?"

"Mmm, we're here?" Collin twisted his head to face Tristan and his dark eyes fluttered open.

"Yes." Tristan squeezed his hand.

A ding sounded and the captain announced the plane's arrival. Clicks and excited voices filtered through the cabin as passengers all around them unhooked their safety belts and stood up to retrieve baggage from overhead bins.

Tristan unhooked his seatbelt from over his snug jeans and stood as best he could in the cramped space next to the window, his silver necklaces swaying over his chest. "Wake up. We have to get going." He nudged Collin's shoulder.

A dark sweater covered Collin's chest and ran down the length of his arms. Looking up at Tristan, a slow grin quirked his lips. "That anxious to see your mother?"

Tristan dropped his brows as his chest pinched, then he worried his lower lip.

Resting his warm hand on the thick fabric of Tristan's black sweatshirt over his forearm, Collin said, "It'll be all right. We've been over this. She can't hurt you now. Not with me around." A grin ghosted over his lips as he lifted his chin.

"I know, but I still can't help worrying about her reaction." Tristan clenched his teeth and bent down to whisper in Collin's ear, "Did you know the Mormon Church actually uses shock treatment to try and make gay guys heterosexual?"

Collin sat back and scoffed. "Oh, come on. That's fucking archaic."

"Archaic, but true. And my mother believes in this crap. She thinks they can just shock the gay right out of me." Tristan spat out the words and fisted his hands, his chest squeezing further still. How the hell was Collin going to combat all of this?

"Okay, well at least you can tell her how great your art's been selling. You're in a gallery now, dude. You're someone." Collin squeezed Tristan's arm.

Tristan looked at Collin's beaming face and gave him a wide, dimpled smile right back. "Yeah, I had no idea how big the gay culture was in California. And to think there's a gay gallery right in downtown Santa Barbara? I don't know why I never even considered that."

Chuckling, Collin shook his head. "I'm glad we went back to

that waterfront bar, and you talked to Robert again, even if he flirts way too much with you."

"Who'd have thought he owned an art gallery?" And thanks to Ally and her friends, he'd been happy to have his work there. Tristan looked up at the line of people filling up the aisle. They'd finally started moving. "Hey, get up and let's get this over with. Then maybe I can relax."

With a heavy sigh, Collin rose up from his seat, straightened his brown cargo pants and moved into the aisle.

———

A LITTLE WHILE LATER, Tristan walked to the curb with Collin close behind him, then shifted his black suitcase to his other hand and rubbed the sweat from his palm on his thigh. An inner trembling threatened to overtake him. Would his mother be drunk already? Would she be ready with her normal insults? He'd come so far. Would it throw him right back to where he'd been? But he had Collin now.

Collin stepped up to his side as cars drove slowly by on the road in front of them, splattering melting snow and water under their tires. "You okay?"

With a glance at Collin, Tristan gazed off in the distance at the tall Wasatch mountains. Patches of white topped the barren peaks like marshmallow topping on a chocolate ice cream sundae. "Yeah, for now." He shifted his focus to Collin. "I just don't know what to expect, you know? Sometimes she's just fine, pleasant even, but most the time she's just mean."

Collin grabbed Tristan's hand. "That's the alcoholism. It makes people moody. It has nothing to do with you."

Clenching his jaw, Tristan said, "Okay." As he looked up, his mother's silver Chevy Malibu rolled up to the curb. "Oh, shit, here we go."

His mother, a woman with piercing blue eyes and a ruddy complexion, opened the door and stepped out of the car. A large coat bundled around her down to her knees and a long skirt billowed out from underneath. A single string of pearls hung from her neck. "Tristan?" She rushed to the curb with her arms outstretched.

Tristan dropped his suitcase to the sidewalk and let himself be engulfed by her embrace. The smell of liquor and mint rushed at him. "Hi, Mom."

"Oh, Tristan, I missed you so much." She gave him a tight squeeze and let him go. When she stepped back, she gave him a brief inspection, straightened her coat and cropped hair, then focused on Collin. "Hello, are you that friend Tristan was bringing home?"

Collin stepped forward with his hand out. "Yes, I am. My name's Collin."

She took his hand for a brief shake. "Collin, huh." She eyed him. "You aren't another art student, are you? Cause you don't look like one. You look like a nice boy." She smiled at him. "Handsome..."

Collin's face flushed and he glanced at Tristan.

Tristan furrowed his brows. "No, Mom, I told you he was a psychology major, remember?" She hadn't listened to him, but what else was new?

She brought a sloppy hand to her mouth in mock surprise. "Oh, yeah." She let out a soft giggle. "Good thing, a little psychology is probably just what Tristan needs."

"What do you mean by that?" Heat swarmed Tristan's chest. She was up to her little tricks again, making insensitive comments about him.

"Oh, Tristan, don't get so upset already. Can't you ever be happy? At least you have a friend for once and they don't look like some pervert." She stepped to the trunk and opened it with her key fob. "Drop your luggage in here." Grinning, she strutted to the car and got inside.

Collin grabbed Tristan's arm and pulled him aside.

Tristan glared at him. "Did you hear that? She's already on my case. What the hell am I supposed to say to that? And she's drunk already. If I stand up to her, she'll get even worse."

"I know, Tristan. When someone's drunk it's not the time to engage them. Wait until morning and then address the issue." Collin took Tristan's hand and gave it a gentle squeeze.

"How am I supposed to address it?" Tristan scowled. Maybe this was a bad idea.

"Let's talk about that later. Right now, we need to address the fact that she thinks she's going to drive us home in that condition." Collin grabbed his and Tristan's suitcases, walked to the trunk and threw them inside. With a deep sigh and a hardened gaze, he strolled over to Tristan's mother's side of the car and rapped on the window.

She rolled the window down. "Yes?"

"Um, Miss Tolken, I'd like for Tristan to drive, if you don't mind." He gave her his best smile.

Tristan waited at the curb, shifting from one booted foot to the next. No way was this going to work. Collin was about to get the wrath of his mother and they hadn't even gotten home yet.

She eyed Collin. "Oh, and why is that?" Her words were sharp.

"Uh, well, because Tristan promised to show me some of his favorite places on the way to your house and I think it'd just be easier. In fact, why don't you just sit in the back seat and relax on the way home?" An easy grin crept over his lips.

"Well, I *am* tired." She sighed. "Okay."

Collin opened the doors for her, and she stepped out of the car and climbed into the back seat. After closing the back door, he waved at Tristan and jogged around to the front passenger seat.

Tristan came around the front of the car and slid into the driver's seat. As he buckled his seatbelt, he took a quick glance at Collin and mouthed, *thank you.*

—————

A HALF HOUR LATER, Tristan turned into a tract home neighborhood on the outskirts of Salt Lake City with small, bungalow houses and large yards, hailing back from the 1970s. A park centered the development with old, rusted playground equipment sitting atop sand enclosed in railroad ties. A prominent metal spaceship structure with a long slide loomed over swings and monkey bars. Tristan looked out over the park. "See that playground?" He pointed out Collin's window.

Shifting his focus toward the park, Collin said, "Yeah."

Tristan snuck a peek behind him. His mother was passed out in the back seat. Good. "That's where I always went when things got too rough at home."

"Really?" Collin studied the structures of the park. "Sort of let off steam there?"

"Yeah, that big slide has some good places to hide in it." He focused back on the road and pulled up into the driveway of his childhood home, just a few blocks from the park, and turned the car lights and engine off, then glanced in the rear-view mirror at his sleeping mother. "We're home, or something close to it."

Collin peered out at the single-story, white house, sitting at the end of the driveway in the middle of huge yard. Two large ash trees swayed their branches over shake shingles. A set of two plastic chairs surrounded a round table and rested on a small front porch. "Wow, the house is tiny."

"Yep, only two bedrooms and two bathrooms. Just enough for me and my mother." He opened the car door, climbed out and opened the back door. Leaning in, he gave her shoulder a gentle shake. "Mom, we're home."

Her dazed eyes flitted open. In a moment, they focused on him. "Already? My, I must have dozed off." She sat upright.

"Yes, you did." Tristan helped her out of the car.

After climbing out, Collin stood at the trunk.

Tristan helped his mother stand and walked to the trunk, pressing the button on key fob to open it for Collin.

As the lid of the trunk opened, Collin reached inside and hauled both suitcases out.

"Hey, I'll take that." Tristan gestured to his suitcase.

"No, I'll get them both. Why don't you help your mom get in the house?" Collin glanced at Tristan's mother and ticked his head at her.

Tristan clenched his jaw and gave Collin a single nod before striding over to her, still standing beside the car. "Come on, Mom." He took her by the elbow and made to guide her into the house.

She jerked her arm away. "I can walk to the house by myself." She ambled away from him and stopped at the front door of the house.

With his gut clenching, he followed close behind her while Collin took up the back.

When Tristan stopped at the door, he slid the key in the lock, twisted it and swung it open. A rush of decaying food and stale liquor assaulted his nose. "Jesus, Mom, when's the last time you took the trash out?" He stepped aside to let his mother enter first.

"Honestly, Tristan, I don't know what you're talking about." She ambled into the house, flipped a light switch just inside the door and two ceramic lamps perched on cheap end tables lit up at both ends of a couch, sitting against the far wall. An orange floral pattern covered the couch and matching throw pillows rested in the corners.

Tristan entered the house, walked across a beige shag carpet to the kitchen and peeked inside the top of a plastic garbage can sitting at the end of the counter. "Fuck." Tiny white larva the size of rice squirmed over a melee of discarded food, soda cans and glass liquor bottles. "Mom, it looks like you have maggots."

Collin came up behind Tristan and peered over his shoulder into the garbage. "Yep. Let me take care of that." He scooped up the trash can and headed toward the door. "Where're the cans located? And I'll need a hose."

"Oh, what a dear. The cans are on the driveway-side of the

house and the hose is in front. But it might be frozen." Watching Collin, his mother shrugged off her coat, tossed it over the couch and dropped into the center of it.

With a quick nod, Collin hauled the stinking garbage outside and shut the door behind him.

Tristan stepped back into the main room and, with a soft exhale, took a look around. His and Collin's suitcases rested in front of a cabinet housing an old television backed up to the wall across from the couch. A picture window with dusty curtains filled the space over the television and a dingy reclining chair sat haphazard in the corner of the room with a reading lamp and table beside it. Piles of old newspaper covered the top of a weathered coffee table.

"Well?" His mother's voice broke through the inspection of the house.

"Well, what?" He frowned. The house wasn't much different than the last time he'd been home.

"See anything else that needs to be cleaned up?" She pinched her lips and crossed her arms over her chest.

With his brows knitting, he stared at the carpet, then mumbled, "No." He wasn't about to give her a reason to go after him even more.

She sat forward. "Are you sure? Seems there might be a bit of dust over there on the TV or maybe some cat hair on the couch here." She ran her hand over the cushion beside her.

"Come on, Mom. Don't be like that." Tristan gritted his teeth. He already wanted to leave.

"Like what? At least your friend had the decency to just take care of it instead of whining about it." Huffing, she sunk into the couch, re-crossing her arms over her chest.

Tristan pursed his lips. "So where did you want us to sleep?" Hopefully that wasn't a loaded question.

She swiveled her head toward him. "I suppose one of you can take your bedroom and one of you can take the sleeper here in the couch." She studied him for a moment. "Don't think for a second

I'm going to let you two sleep together." She glared at him. "Mark my words, Tristan. There will be no perverted antics going on here in my house."

Parting his lips, he stared at her. "No, I—"

Collin burst through the front door holding up the garbage can. "All clean. Where are the garbage bags?"

Tristan's gaze flicked to him. Saved..."U-under the sink, in the kitchen."

"Oh." Collin nodded once and strode to the kitchen.

His mother's glare bore into Tristan. He dared a peek at her, then looked toward the kitchen. *What does she want from me?* "I'm uh, going to help Collin." He raced toward the kitchen.

In the faint glow from the front room, Collin was bent over at the far end of a beige counter in the shape of a long *U*, pillaging in a dark wood cabinet under a stainless-steel sink. A small window perched over the sink looked out into a dark back yard. The back of the kitchen housed a white stove and oven with an equally white refrigerator. The front counter held cabinets underneath and bar seating toward a small breakfast nook with two metal chairs propped up to the counter.

"Need a hand?" Tristan stepped toward him.

Collin straightened with a plastic garbage bag in his grasp and a smug smile stretching his lips. "Nope, I got it."

With a frown, Tristan wrung his hands. He didn't want to face his mother. Why didn't she just go to bed already and leave them alone? A click and the sound of television voices snaked out from the main room into the kitchen. As Collin finished with the garbage, Tristan took a few tentative steps toward him, Tristan's forehead wrinkling. In a low voice, he said, "Collin, I-I don't know what to do."

Collin peered at him. "What do you mean?"

"Well, I asked my mom where we should sleep and she's already on my ass about doing something perverted with you." Tristan studied his reaction to his words. *Don't make me confront her already.*

"Listen, let's just do whatever it takes to make her happy tonight. Okay? I'm tired anyways and I don't think that Mexican food at the airport sat so well with me." He winced. "It's okay. Don't let her get to you." Winding his arms around Tristan's shoulders, he pulled him in for a gentle embrace.

As if a warm blanket had been draped around him, Tristan closed his eyes and relaxed into his hold. "Thanks, Collin." Collin would make it all right.

Collin gave his head a light kiss. "For what?"

"Being there." Tristan hooked his arms around Collin's waist.

CHAPTER SEVENTEEN

WEDNESDAY, NOVEMBER 26

Tristan's eyes fluttered open to slits of sunlight travelling in through a set of wood blinds covering the window over his bed. With a light groan, he moved his limbs and rolled from his side to his back, then looked up at the popcorn surface in the ceiling in his bedroom. Collin was here, in this house. A faint smile quirked his lips. How he'd missed having him in bed with him. But Collin was right. It was better to do what his mother had wanted last night.

What would happen today? His heart squeezed. Would Collin tell his mother what was really going on between them? Would he make him face her? He clutched at thin white sheets and pursed his lips. *It'll be all right. As long as Collin's here, she can't hurt me.*

Throwing a midnight blue comforter and the sheets off to the side, he climbed out of his plain oak bed and stood in his boxers. He pressed his lips together as he scanned the dingy old room he used to live in. There was never much in here except his drafting desk and art supplies, which still sat against the far wall. His gaze travelled to an oak nightstand sitting next to his bed and then back to his desk, where a digital clock recorded the time —ten AM.

As he wiped sleep from his eyes, he padded to the end of the bed and over to the wall, where his suitcase lay open in front of the sliding doors of his closet. He bent down, rummaged in it, and pulled out a pair of jeans and a dark, flannel shirt. After dressing he strolled down a small hallway, passing childhood portraits of himself and into the main room, perusing the sleeper sofa for Collin, but found it empty. He must be up already.

His mother's voice snaked out from the kitchen, behind a wall on his left. "Yes, it has been hard for him. I know that." A clink sounded, like metal hitting ceramic.

"He's really come a long way." Collin's voice rang out from the area of the kitchen.

Startling, Tristan stopped in his tracks and strained to hear the conversation.

"Do you have any idea how talented your son really is?" The timbre of Collin's voice rose as if trying to gain his mother's confidence.

She sighed. "I know. But those people are so...well, you know."

"No, I don't. They're so what?" Collin asked.

Her voice became harsh. "They're mostly homosexuals and perverts. God knows I've tried to protect him from that sort of thing. And the behavior he engaged in as a teenager," she said. "Well, he just isn't right. Just like his—" The groan of a chair sliding across linoleum filled the air.

"Just like who?" Collin's voice became louder.

"Never mind. It's none of your business." The click of women's heels rippled out from behind the wall.

Tristan widened his eyes. *Who is she talking about?* He took a step forward, breathing in deeply, readying himself to face Collin and his mother.

"They're not freaks, you know." Collin's voice was low.

Tristan stopped and stood still again, his chest clenching. Frowning, he strained to hear.

"You listen here, young man. You may be all high and mighty with your college education in psychology, but homosexuality is a perversion. It's not right and I won't have my son engaging with those sorts of people. Period."

Collin let out a heavy sigh. "I'm sorry if I upset you, Miss Tolken."

"Apology accepted." The sound of running water rushed from the kitchen area. "My, what a lovely day it is out there."

Tristan sucked in a deep inhale and padded out from behind the wall and into the kitchen. "Hey, Collin."

His mother turned around from the sink. Her white blouse, buttoned all the way up her neck, tucked into tan slacks. "About time you got up. I suppose none of those art classes you take start before noon."

Tristan creased his brows. "What?"

With her head shaking and a tsk, she turned back to the sink to wash dishes. "Nothing..."

Tristan's gaze flicked to Collin, sitting at the counter with a tall glass of orange juice before him.

"Tired, huh?" Collin shrugged.

"Yeah, guess so." Tristan padded toward the back of the kitchen, grabbed a glass from a cabinet and poured himself some orange juice from a pitcher sitting on the counter. "Sure could use some coffee right about now."

Still washing dishes at the sink, his mother said, "Now, Tristan, you know you're not supposed to drink that. It's in the Word of Wisdom."

Tristan frowned and glanced at Collin. "No caffeine and no hot drinks."

With a nod, Collin said, "I heard already."

His mother faced them. "Listen, I have some errands to run today for the church. I trust you two will be okay without the car for a few hours?"

"Yeah, fine." Tristan grabbed his orange juice and walked over to sit on a stool next to Collin.

She looked Tristan up and down as if assessing him and twisted back to the sink. The sound of rushing water and clanking dishes rang out in the room.

Collin bumped him with his shoulder.

Tristan whispered, "What?" He glanced at his mother. Collin surely didn't want him to confront her now.

In a soft voice, Collin said, "Tell her." He ticked his head at her.

"Tell her what?" Tristan's pulse thrummed.

"Tell her about how she hurt your feelings last night. Tell her about how your art is in a gallery now. It's time to start talking to her and standing up for yourself." Raising his brows, Collin nodded his head.

Tristan's heart jolted. "Now?" But Collin had already pissed her off this morning.

"Yes. Go on. I'm going to go get showered. Do it." Collin rose from his seat.

Tristan's gaze chased him. "B-but—"

"Do it." Collin poked Tristan's shoulder and walked from the room.

Tristan blew out a heavy exhale and squirmed in his seat. He so didn't want to do this. Why did Collin have to get on him already? He'd just woken up. At least Collin could let him wake up a bit more first.

His mother shut off the water to the sink and set the last of the dishes to dry on a towel on the counter.

"M-mom?" Focusing on his juice, he rimmed the glass with his index finger.

She turned and stepped to him. "What is it?"

"I, um, I—" He furrowed his brows and his heart beat a frantic rhythm in his ears. He couldn't do this.

"For God's sakes, Tristan, what is it?" She planted her hands on her hips.

"I need to talk to you about s-something." He shifted his gaze to hears, then refocused on his glass.

"I'm listening." She huffed.

He inhaled deeply. "S-sometimes you, I mean, I feel like, like you don't quite, that you sort of—"

"Out with it, already." Slapping her hands on the counter surface, she leaned toward him.

His chest heated. That was enough. He glared at her and rose from his seat. "See? You always treat me like I'm some imbecile. Like I'm not even a real person with real feelings. But I am, Mom, I do have feelings and some of the things you say to me are down-right mean. I am an artist and a damned good one."

Dropping her jaw, she took a step back.

"In fact, I'm so good that my drawings are selling at an art gallery in Santa Barbara. I'm a—practically a celebrity in the art department because I'm so good." He slammed his fist on the counter. "And there is nothing wrong with being an artist." Pant-ing, his heart pounded. He peered at her, taking her all in. What would she say to that?

She shook her index finger at him. "Stop this, right now, Tris-tan. I won't have you talking to me this way. It's disrespectful. You should never have left the church. Is that what they teach you over at that university? How to be disrespectful?" Glaring at him, she took a step toward him.

Startling, he dropped his gaze to his glass, then set his hands on the counter and gnawed his lower lip. Could he keep going? Should he? "I, no they don't. But I need you to hear me on this. You do say mean things to me sometimes, hurtful things." His vision blurred. Oh no, not now. He blinked a few times.

She sighed and her shoulders relaxed. "I know."

With his breath catching, he glanced at her. "You know?"

Striding around the counter, she placed her hand on his back. "Yes."

He stiffened. She rarely touched him, not since he was very little. "Then why do you do it?"

Dropping her hand, she said, "Listen, I know I'm not the mother of the year, but I'm doing my best to meet my obligation to God for you." She smoothed his hair down and her gaze softened. "I do love you, Tristan. You're my son, my only child. It's just very hard to for me, to live the life I was given. Your father abandoned me and left me to raise you all alone, and well, it isn't the natural way a family should be. The only help, the only salvation from it all has always been the church. They took me in and gave me work, everything."

"Oh yeah, the church." He pressed his lips together.

She slapped her hand on her hip. "That's right, the church. The very thing you ran from and are determined to sin against. Let's face it, Tristan, you and I both know about your evil, perverted tendencies. You and I both know—"

"That's enough." Raising his head and straightening his spine, he fixated on her. "I won't have you making me feel bad about that anymore. It is what it is, and it's done. Over."

Her eyes rounded for a heartbeat, then narrowed and she pursed her lips. "Well I—"

"Over. No more." He locked his gaze to hers. He wasn't going to hear this shit from her anymore. Collin was right. He *could* stand up to her.

She gaped a moment, then huffed and stomped into the main room, snatched her purse and coat from the couch and left, slamming the door behind her.

Tristan freed a long exhale and slumped over the counter. "Holy shit." His heart slowed.

Collin jogged down the hallway, bare-chested, his damp hair swaying on his head and low-slung jeans on his hips. "What happened?" His brows wrinkled.

Tristan propped his elbows on the counter, then placed his face in his hands. "I don't know."

"What do you mean?" Collin rested his hand on Tristan's shoulder.

"Well, she seemed to listen to me for once and then she just went off on me again about, about..." His voice cracked. Pain sliced through his heart and his breath hitched, his eyes stinging. He clenched his eyes shut against the tears. "She's just so fucking hell bent on telling me I'm a pervert and evil."

Collin wrapped his arms around Tristan's shoulders and rested his cheek against his back. "But you know you're not, right?"

He shut his eyes tighter.

"Right? Tell me. I want to hear you say it." Collin placed a soft kiss on Tristan's back.

"I'm not evil or a fucking pervert." The words spit off his tongue. He raised himself upright with Collin still holding onto him. Turning in Collin's embrace, he gazed into his dark eyes. "I'm okay, Collin."

"Really?" Collin looked him over.

"Yeah, really." Tristan huffed out a breath.

A tiny smile quirked one side of Collin's lips. "This is only the beginning, and it sounds like you at least broke through. You can't expect her to all of a sudden change into a different person. I'll bet from now on, she'll think twice before she treats you badly."

"I hope so." Slumping his shoulders, Tristan sighed.

"She will." Collin freed Tristan and looked around the room for a moment. "So, what did you want to do today?"

"Let's get out of here and have a few drinks when my mom gets back. I'm going to need it." Tristan forced a smile. He didn't want to be around when she came back.

"Sure. You know of a place? I mean I didn't think they really had bars out here." Collin raked his hand through his bangs.

"Sure, they do. They're just called clubs, but it's easy enough to get a membership." He leaned back in his stool and his stomach grumbled.

"You need a membership to get a drink?" Collin chuckled, side-eyeing him.

"Yeah, I know it sounds weird. Just another way the Mormon

Church tries to control everything out here. There's actually a place we can go to that's not far." Tristan's body relaxed. There'd be no more confronting his mother today.

———

A FEW HOURS LATER, Tristan stood by the front window of the house, his gaze snagging on his mother's silver car making its way through mud and puddles up the driveway in late afternoon sun. "I see her coming up the drive."

Collin bound up behind him and peered out the window. "Yup. You sure she won't mind us going out for the night?"

Tristan faced him. "I'm sure. She'll probably be relieved to have the house to herself." Same as he'd be relieved to leave it. He returned to the window.

His mother had the rear door to the car open and bent over the seats to pluck plastic grocery bags out of it.

"Oh, looks like she's got groceries for tomorrow. We better go help her." Tristan started for the front door.

"Right." Collin came up behind him and followed him out the door and to his mother's car.

Squinting, Tristan walked out into the late afternoon sunlight and cool air and stopped beside his mother. "Mom, you need some help?"

She straightened with a few bags in her hand. "Yes, you can get the rest of the bags and the turkey."

An overpowering scent of alcohol hit Tristan in the face. *She's already at it?* "Okay." He creased his brows as he stepped aside to let her pass, then snuck Collin a quick glance and bowed into the car to grab some bags.

Collin ducked down beside Tristan. "Drinking again?"

"Yeah. Let's hurry up and get out of here." He picked up the bags. Things could only get worse.

———

AFTER MAKING it to the club for a drink, Tristan followed Collin up to the main entrance of a brick-and-mortar building. Collin, all dressed up in brown cargo pants and a rich, thick sweater of dark silk, opened the glass front door and waited.

With a faint grin, Tristan brushed by Collin and entered the building. His snug jeans hugged his hips and his sweatshirt hood peeked out from over the collar of a blazer-style leather jacket, an outfit Collin had dressed him in. He stopped in the foyer and looked around. A contemporary wooden bar filled the wall on the left and a white screen divided the bar area from the dining area of the bar and grill. A television hung on the wall behind a bartender, washing glasses in front of brass beer taps. A few men sat at one end in casual conversation. "Want to just sit at the bar?"

Collin nodded and grasped Tristan's elbow, then lead him to the bar. They climbed onto barstools in front of the TV playing highlights from last week's football game.

A middle-aged man with a balding head and wire-rimmed glasses looked up at them from the stainless-steel sink behind the bar. "Good afternoon. Are you members here?"

Collin looked to Tristan.

"No, we're from out of town. Can you sponsor us for a guest pass? We'd like a few drinks and maybe a bite to eat." Tristan gave the man a casual smile. Being in bars was feeling more and more comfortable all the time.

"Sure. They're fifteen dollars each and are good for the week." The bartender reached under the register and produced some small cards. "What's your name?"

"Tristan Tolken." He shifted on the padded barstool.

"And your friend there?" The man wrote on the cards.

"Uh, my name is Collin Stanley." Collin placed his elbows on the bar and crossed his forearms while watching the bartender.

The man behind the bar finished writing on the cards and handed one to Tristan and one to Collin. "There you go."

Tristan stuffed the card into his front pocket.

Collin eyed his card before adding it to an assortment of credit cards lining the inside of his leather wallet.

The bartender placed his hands on the bar. "So, what'll it be?" Tristan glanced at Collin. "Uh, how about a rum and Coke?"

"Can you make a mojito?" Collin faced the bartender.

"Sure. One rum and Coke and one mojito coming up." The bartender made the drinks and set them down in front of Tristan and Collin.

Collin took a sip of his drink from the edge of the glass. "I can't believe your mother was already drunk when she came back from shopping."

Tristan frowned. "I know. I wonder where she got it from?"

"Does she go to bars?" Collin lifted his brows.

Looking at Collin, Tristan said, "No way. She'd be mortified if anyone from her church saw her having a drink. More than likely, she's hiding bottles in her car or has those little airline bottles in her purse."

Collin shook his head and gave a light chuckle. "It's odd to think of her sitting in some parking lot slamming little airline bottles of vodka or something."

Taking a sip of his drink from a black straw, Tristan sputtered and burst into a fit of giggles. "Oh my God, that's too funny. She's probably drinking straight Jack Daniels, throwing it back like a sailor."

As Collin laughed, he squeezed Tristan's arm. "Hey, maybe she just does shots of tequila."

A muffled chime sounded from a side pocket in Collin's cargo pants. He fished out his cell phone and pressed a button, lighting up the display. A smile spread on his lips, and he typed on the screen.

"Who're you texting?" Tristan drank his drink.

"Oh, no one in particular." Collin kept typing.

Tristan nudged him in the shoulder and Collin glanced at him. "Oh, come on, tell me."

With a huff, Collin pressed his lips together. "Don't worry

about it. Just let me finish." His fingers flew over the keyboard, making ticking noises.

Tristan thought on it a moment. He should let it rest. They were having a good time for once.

———

As the afternoon went on, the two shared a few more drinks and some appetizers, sitting at the bar and chatting well into the evening. Various patrons came and left, with hardly a notice from either one of them.

All at once, Collin's laughter slowed, and his face went slack. "Tristan, I wanted to ask you something."

"What?" He leaned back in his chair and gazed at Collin. He wasn't sure he liked the tone of Collin's voice and the alcohol in his veins was messing with his head.

Collin knitted his brows. "So, your mother really never told you how your dad died?"

"What? No." Tristan's gaze flicked to his drink, and he took a quick sip, then focused on Collin. "Why would you bring that up?"

Collin rimmed his glass with his long fingers. "Well, don't you find it sort of...odd?"

"Odd how?" An ache wound through his heart. Where was Collin going with this? He studied him.

"I'd think that'd be something you ought to know. I mean, it's a pretty important thing. Don't you think?" Collin shifted in his seat.

Tristan opened his mouth to speak. *What the hell can I say to that?* He shut his mouth.

"Are there any pictures of him around the house? Have you even seen what he looks like?" Collin leaned forward and gulped his drink, narrowing his eyes.

"N-no. I..." Tristan thought a moment. "I guess it was always such a sore subject, I never felt comfortable enough with my mother to ask about it." And at some point, he'd just stopped wondering. He'd had bigger things to deal with, like his mother's drinking.

"Well, what did she say about him? Do you know how they met, where they got married, anything?" Collin's focus on Tristan grew intense.

"N-no. I know she didn't like him much. She always said he was good for nothing and a, a freak, like me." Somewhere, deep inside him, a realization floundered and fought to be freed. He stuffed it deep inside. "I don't like talking about this." He twisted to face the television and pretended to be interested in a sports talk show.

Collin placed his hand on Tristan's forearm, resting on the bar, then cleared his throat and removed his hand. He leaned in close to Tristan's ear and spoke in a low voice. "Why? What is it, Tristan? What happened to him?"

Scowling, Tristan glared at him. "I told you. I don't know what happened to him. Why do you have to keep asking about it? He's gone. Dead. That's as much as I know or, or even care to know." And opening old wounds wasn't something he wanted to do right now.

"I don't believe that for a second." With a smug grin, Collin leaned back in his seat. "Do you ever think that maybe she's not telling the truth?"

"No, I don't." Tristan pursed his lips, then sipped his drink.

"But why not? Why wouldn't she have any pictures of him? Why would she be so damned spiteful if he just died? It seems to me like something happened between them. Something terrible enough for her to despise him after all these years and force her to keep you from him."

He widened his eyes and a feeling inside him screamed to be let up into his consciousness. He swallowed hard and focused on Collin. "I-I don't think—" He glanced at the door for a moment. What could he say to get Collin off this topic?

Two young men in leather jackets and jeans entered the establishment and headed for the bar. One had a crew-cut of jet-black hair and the other had brown hair, cut equally short.

Tristan's breath snagged in his throat. *I know him.* "Shit, it's Sean," he said under his breath. His heart pricked and quickened. He downed his drink and held up his glass to the bartender.

The bartender nodded and got him another.

"What did you say?" Collin leaned in close again.

Tristan shifted in his seat and fought to steady his nerves. "Don't get so close to me."

"Why?" Collin focused on the two young men, taking barstools a few seats away from them. "Are you that pissed at me for asking about your dad?"

Tristan cut his gaze from Sean to his new drink and gulped half of it down. He needed to settle his nerves. Maybe Sean wouldn't notice him.

"Jesus, Tristan, take it easy. What's up?" Collin swayed and studied the young men, now ordering beers and taking noticeable looks at him and Tristan. "Do you know them?"

Between his teeth, Tristan said, "Yes." He took another generous gulp of his drink and hissed.

"Who is it?" Collin leaned on the bar on one elbow.

Tristan whispered, "It's my high school friend, Sean."

"Oh shit, dude, really?" A chuckle rumbled in Collin's chest.

Tristan's gaze snapped to Collin. "It's not funny." Collin knew what had happened.

Collin's grin faded. "Sorry. Think he recognizes you?"

"I don't know." He peeked at Sean from under his long blond bangs.

Sean watched Tristan, leaned over to his friend, and spoke to him in a voice too low for him to hear. His friend looked at Tristan and smirked.

"Yeah, I'd say he recognizes me." Tristan clenched a fist under the bar and pursed his lips.

"Well, why not go over and say hello? How about you introduce me to the first guy you kissed?" Collin gave Tristan a playful bump on the shoulder.

Turning his back on Sean, Tristan glared at Collin. "I told you it's not funny. This isn't a game, you know. He probably still hates me. You have no idea how shitty gay people can be treated around here."

Collin stared at him a moment, sinking back into his chair, then he straightened his shoulders and pressed his lips into a grim line. "Let him just try to start something with me. He'll be sorely mistaken. Maybe it's time he was paid back for getting you beat up in high school."

Widening his eyes, Tristan hissed, "No, don't you dare try anything." Collin had been drinking. Hadn't he been warned about that from Christian all those weeks ago? Shit.

Collin focused on Sean, sizing him up.

"Did you hear me?" Tristan tapped on Collin's shoulder

Collin drew his gaze back to him. "Yes, I heard you."

"I just want to forget any of that ever happened." Tristan toyed with the edge of the square paper napkin under his drink.

Collin leaned close to Tristan's ear and in a low voice, said, "I don't think you'll be able to."

"What?" Tristan looked up, his gaze catching on Sean and his friend walking up behind Collin. "Oh, shit."

"Hello, Tristan." Sean looked from Collin to Tristan.

"Uh, hi, Sean." Tristan focused on the white t-shirt under Sean's leather jacket.

"Long time, no see." Sean shifted his weight onto one foot.

Collin twisted in his barstool to face Sean and his friend. "So, you must be an old friend of Tristan's."

Sean's attention drew to Collin. "Yeah, who are you?"

Collin held out his hand. "I'm Collin, pleased to meet you." He shook Sean's hand. "I've heard a lot about you, actually."

A wicked smirk swept across Sean's mouth. "Really? Like what's he told you? Did he tell you what good friends we were in high school?" He glanced at Tristan. "Or did he tell you what a fucking faggot he is?"

Heat swarmed in Tristan's chest. He glared at his old friend and through gritted teeth, he said, "Fuck you, Sean."

"No, fuck you, Tristan. What the hell are you doing around here anyways? Don't you know they aren't supposed to serve your kind? I'd thought your mother would've had the church fix you by now." Sean snatched Tristan's necklaces and yanked him forward. "But I see she hasn't. You're as fucking flaming as ever."

Jumping off his barstool, Collin flung his hand over Sean's fingers, gripping Tristan's chains, and squeezed until his knuckles went white. "Keep your fucking hands off my boyfriend, asshole."

Sean dropped his mouth open, tensing his brows, and his friend stepped up close behind him to glare at Collin. Sean freed Tristan's necklaces.

Tristan leaned back, releasing a loud exhale, his heart thrumming in his chest. That was close.

The bartender jogged over to the group. "Hey, I'll have none of that here. Cool yourselves, gentlemen."

Sean eyed Collin. "Did you hear the man, faggot? How about we go outside so I can whip your pussy ass?"

Cracking his knuckles, a sly grin spread over Collin's mouth. "Anytime, cocksucker."

"Oh, I think that's your department," Sean's friend piped in.

Collin's focus cut to Sean's friend, and he took him in. Collin stood at least a few inches taller than the young man. "Yep. Cocks, they're my favorite." He smirked with a glint in his eye.

Wrinkling his brows, Tristan grabbed Sean's arm with one hand and Collin's with the other, then peered at them both. "Come on, guys. Listen to the bartender. Let's stop this." He focused on Sean. "Just leave us alone, okay?"

"Fuck, no, Tristan." Collin glanced from Sean to Tristan. "It's time to stand up for yourself. Isn't this the bastard who made sure you got the shit kicked out of you? A guy you trusted, someone who was supposed to be your friend?" He stepped closer to Sean and came within inches of his face. "What a shitty friend you are. Can't keep a secret and so scared of your own faggot tendencies that you had to be sure Tristan was punished for his, for liking a moron like you." He puffed his chest, his gaze growing darker, harder.

Sean threw a punch at Collin. Ducking down, Collin snatched Sean's arm and held it centered on Sean's back in a fraction of a second.

"Fuck!" Sean bent forward, but Collin held him back with one arm.

"Gotcha now." Collin pushed up on the arm he held at Sean's back.

Stepping forward, Sean's friend gave two quick punches to Collin's kidneys. With a groan, Collin dropped Sean and bent forward, planting his hands on his knees.

Only slightly aware of the others in the bar standing to watch, Tristan jumped off his barstool, snatched the smaller man by the back of his jacket and tossed him away.

Sean's friend flew sideways and hit his face on the edge of a nearby table.

Blood poured out of his nose onto his shirt. "Fuck, you broke my nose!"

Out of nowhere, the bartender grabbed Collin from behind in a full-nelson. "You're done."

As Tristan straightened, he was grabbed by a man with heavily muscled arms around his shoulders and neck in the same hold. A deep voice growled in his ear. "Get the fuck out of my bar."

"I'm going. I'm going." Tristan stepped to the door with the man's firm hold on him.

"What the fuck did we do? They attacked us." Collin staggered beside Tristan with the bartender still guiding him.

With a loud cackle, Sean straightened. "I told you they don't serve faggots!"

At the doors, the bartender and the man holding Tristan released them.

With his shoulders slumping, Tristan looked to Collin.

After dropping his arms, Collin twirled around to face the bartender. "So let me get this straight. You let assholes like that come into your bar and you kick out out-of-towners that are just minding their own business?"

The bartender shook his head. "It's like he said. We don't serve faggots."

Collin's eyes widened. "What?"

Glaring at Collin, the man pointed at Tristan. "I had a feeling about him as soon as you walked in. But I let it slide because *you* at least, looked decent enough."

Pursing his lips, Tristan could only glare back.

The other bar worker stepped up to Tristan. "Pay your fucking bill and get out of here. I don't even want to look at you anymore. You make me sick."

Collin put his hands on his hips. "Fine, let's get the fuck out of here. These people are obviously a bunch of backwards fucking hicks." He focused on the bartender while digging his wallet out of his pocket. "Too bad we didn't know this sooner. I'd rather not have spent any money in this pit you call a bar."

The bartender showed Collin the bill and Collin paid him in cash.

"Thanks, I'll just keep the change for the trouble." Turning toward the bar, the bartender headed back with the other man.

Frowning, Tristan shoved the glass doors open and stomped through them into the cold parking lot and to the driver's side of his mother's silver car.

A heavy weight fell over Tristan's heart. What had he ever seen in Sean? Little clouds of breath puffed out of his mouth.

Collin jogged up behind him and wrapped his arms around Tristan's shoulders. "It's okay. It's not our fault. All these people around here are just fucked up."

With a huff, Tristan glanced at the building. "Why do some people hate gay people so much?"

"They're just scared, is all. Scared we're going to hit on them and they might just like it. Scared of something they don't understand. Scared of anything that's different from what their limited little world has shown them already. It makes them feel better about themselves to belittle people like us. I even think some of them are jealous, jealous that we can be happy and they, in their fucked up heteronormative world, will always be miserable, married to some person who'll never understand them, never truly know them, never truly love them."

Tristan twisted in his embrace and looked deeply into his dark eyes. "Where did all that come from?"

Dropping his arms and taking a step back, Collin shrugged. "Hell if I know. Just seems my parents were sort of like that until they split." He placed both hands on Tristan's shoulders. "I do know this. It's so much easier being with a guy. We can understand each other. There's none of those cat and mouse games chicks like to play. It's just plain and real and..." He leaned in and gave Tristan a passionate kiss. "Good, like that." Pressing Tristan up against the car, he claimed Tristan's mouth and roamed his hands up and down Tristan's back.

An immediate fire lit up Tristan's groin. Pressure ground on his swelling cock. As Collin placed heated kisses on his mouth, nipped at his lips and neck, a low moan escaped him. Pleasure ignited all through his body. "Collin, let's go home."

Collin released him with a mischievous grin. "Don't have to tell me twice."

CHAPTER EIGHTEEN

Laughing, Tristan stumbled in through the front door of his house. His gaze caught on his mother, sleeping on the couch with the television droning on and he covered his mouth, stifling the laughter. The delicious scent of Thanksgiving turkey cooking in the oven filled the air around him.

Collin stepped up behind him just inside the doorway. "Oh, is she sleeping?"

Tristan whispered, "Yeah, get in so I can shut the door."

Sniffing at the air, Collin came inside. "Damn, does that smell good."

"I know." Tristan closed the door, then shimmied out of his sweatshirt and leather jacket, pulled them apart and set them over the top of the television cabinet.

"So, you guys cook the turkey all night and it doesn't get dried out?" Collin stepped further into the house.

"Yep. It's a recipe passed down from my grandfather. We put the bird on a higher temp for an hour or so and then turn it way down and let it cook over night." Eyeing his mother, Tristan walked toward her and the couch. When he was close to her, he peered at her sleeping face, tilted upward on the back cushion of the couch as if looking at the ceiling. Her mouth hung open and her breath was drenched with the scent of alcohol and heavy with sleep.

"Dude, she's passed out, isn't she?" Collin stood just behind Tristan.

"Think so." With a smirk, Tristan lifted her arm up by the wrist and let it drop. Her arm fell down to her side to bounce just a bit, but she didn't move otherwise. Her breathing kept its slow and deep rhythm.

Twisting his head, Tristan gave Collin a knowing grin. "Well?" They could do whatever they wanted now.

Collin snatched Tristan's hand and pulled him down the hallway to his bedroom. Once inside, he shut the door and locked it.

Grabbing Collin from behind, Tristan placed heated kisses on the back of his neck and ran his hands up and under his smooth sweater to pinch Collin's nipples.

Letting his head fall back, Collin let out a soft groan. "God, it's about time."

Tristan smirked and bit into the velvet skin of Collin's neck.

"Oh shit, do that again." Collin twisted his hips in Tristan's hold.

Biting Collin's neck a second time, he pinched both nipples, all at once.

"Fuck." Collin thrust his hips into nothing. "That's good, Tristan."

Rolling Collin's nipples between his thumbs and index fingers, Tristan continued the soft bites, hot licks and nips on Collin's neck. As his cock hardened, he rocked against Collin's ass, shoving him against the door, aching pleasure sparking through him.

Collin squirmed and tried to free himself from Tristan's hold. "What are you doing?"

Groaning, he held tight to Collin, rolling his now hard cock against Collin's ass through the fabric of their jeans. With each thrust of his hips, delicious friction teased his erection. "Trying something new. Maybe I should fuck you tonight?" He rubbed the hard flesh beneath Collin's zipper.

"Very funny, Tristan. You know I only top." Collin moved his hips in time with the rhythm of Tristan's palm on his cock.

Desperation enveloped Tristan. He needed more and he needed it now. Unwrapping himself from around Collin, he took a step back. His chest heaved with each breath.

Raking a hand through his hair, Collin twisted and leaned his back on the door, his gaze roaming down Tristan's body to rest on his groin. "That's what I like to see."

Tristan gave him a shy smile. "Yeah?"

Collin came at Tristan, pushing him toward the bed. "Yeah. And what was this about you fucking me?" He shoved, making Tristan fall back on the bed.

"Oh, shit." Letting out a soft chuckle, Tristan braced himself as Collin dropped down over him.

Propping up on his elbows, Collin looked down on him, rutting and rubbing their stiff cocks together through their jeans. "You're so beautiful, Tristan. Do you know that?"

Heat flushed his cheeks and he looked at the wall. "Yeah, yeah."

Collin wrapped his long fingers around Tristan's chin and drew him back.

"No, really. You are." A smirk raced over his lips. "And hot... but so not going to fuck me—" He pressed his lips hard over Tristan's and snuck his tongue inside to tangle with Tristan's.

Tristan thrust into Collin, taking sweet friction from him, then cupped Collin's ass, tightening their hips, the sensation in his cock growing. He slanted his mouth over Collin's, claiming him again and again, letting out a deep groan.

Collin skimmed his hands all over Tristan, devouring him with nimble fingers and teasing palms. "Do something for me, Tristan," he said against Tristan's lips.

Tilting his head, Tristan gave him access to his neck. Tingling pleasure raced from his neck down his spine as Collin gave him nips and sucking kisses. "What do you want me to do?" His breath came in deep draws.

"Touch yourself. Like you used to." Collin bit at his neck.

"What?" Shoving Collin to the side, he stared at him. He hadn't done that in weeks now.

Licking his lips, Collin righted himself to lie on his side next to him, the edges of his mouth twitching, then caressed Tristan's arm. "Come on, Tristan. It was really hot when you used to do it. I just want to see it this once. It won't hurt anything, really."

"I-I don't know." A knot wound in his stomach. Why would Collin ask for something like that after they'd worked so hard to stop it? If he did it, would it make him want to do it more?

"Come on..." Collin snaked his hand to the front of Tristan's jeans, then brushed his fingers over the head of Tristan's erection in circles. "Isn't this sort of what you used to do?"

Tristan's eyelids hooded with pleasure. *Yes, it felt just like that.* He jerked his hips in time with Collin's finger.

Collin pressed harder, making faster circles and worked his thumb up and down Tristan's shaft, then locked his gaze onto Tristan's face.

Shutting his eyes, Tristan lost himself in the heightening sensitivity in his cock, the old sensation ripping him back into the craving he'd fought so hard to keep buried.

Collin halted his fingers.

Opening his eyes, Tristan gazed at him.

With a tilted head, Collin rubbed the bulge in his own jeans the same way he'd rubbed Tristan. "Wow, you know that does feel pretty good." He rubbed harder and rocked his hips.

An intense desire rushed over Tristan's body. An ache he hadn't felt in weeks welled up in his groin. Shoving a hand into his pocket, he joined Collin, watching and touching himself the same as Collin.

"Tell me when you get close." Collin's voice was husky. "I don't want you to come like this." He rocked his hips faster, his fingers and palm moving rougher and harder over his erection.

Although it was difficult in the snug jeans and boxers, Tristan pushed his hand in deep and found the perfect friction. Pleasure teased and rippled from his groin. A jolt of familiar sensation rocked through his body. With a deep moan, he kept his thoughts and gaze on Collin, on watching Collin, on feeling everything that Collin felt, and connected in a way he never thought he could. They moved together, but apart. Both linked in lust and pleasure. Sensation peaked to a dangerous level. "Oh—" He shuddered and gasped.

"Tristan." Collin grabbed his wrist.

Squeezing the head of his cock, Tristan staved off the inevitable. "Shit."

Collin tightened his hold on his wrist. "Did you come?"

"Um, no, I don't think so. I mean, I didn't." He panted and carefully relaxed the hold on his erection.

"You sure?" Collin eyed him.

"Yes, I'm sure, shit." Tristan rolled to his back and gazed up at the ceiling, then rested his palm on his forehead.

Collin leaned over, his stunning face coming into view and hovering over him. "You okay? That was all right to do, wasn't it?" He winced.

Frowning, Tristan peeked at Collin. Was it? Maybe, maybe not.

"I mean, it's not like it was just the same, so I guess technically it's all right. Sort of like being an alcoholic and getting stoned instead of drunk." Collin focused on him for a moment. "Right?"

"How the hell should I know? I'm not the psychology prodigy, remember? In fact, you seem to think I'm too ignorant to know much of anything about psychology if I—"

Collin dropped his hand over Tristan's mouth, then gave him a coy smile. "Shut up and get naked."

He grinned under Collin's hand.

Collin hopped off the bed, then rushed to Tristan's suitcase by the wall and fumbled through it until he found their lube and a condom.

Tristan shimmied his shirt off over his head, toed off his shoes and shoved his jeans and socks off in one quick sweep. A delicious memory of how Collin had felt inside him filled his mind. His thick cock twitched on his belly, eager for it to start.

After undressing, Collin climbed onto the bed on his knees. He opened the cap to the lube and squeezed some into his hand. "Come on, turn over."

With a frown, Tristan sighed and turned to his side, ready to get onto his knees and lift his ass in the air. Why did Collin always have to do it this way? "Hey, Collin?"

Collin brought his hips close to Tristan's ass. "What?" He slathered lube on Tristan's hole, circling it.

Shivering as the slick cold gel touched him, Tristan leaned forward, out of reach. "Let's do it some other way, okay?"

"Like what?" Collin arched brow.

"Well, like some way where we can kiss or where I can at least see your face when you come." He rested his forehead on his hands underneath him.

"What, like have missionary sex like if you were a girl?" Collin erupted in a sharp chuckle. "Got news for you. You're not a girl."

With a huff, he fell to his side and glared up at Collin. "I know I'm not a girl and I know that guys can do it like that. You think I've never looked at gay porn?"

Collin dropped to sit on his tucked legs, lube still in one hand, cock jutting up between his thighs. With a heavy sigh, he hung his head. "All right."

Tristan raised his brows. *All right?* He placed his hand on Collin's thigh. "What's wrong?"

Sneaking a peek at him, Collin said, "I thought you liked it the way we were doing it, that's all. If you didn't, you should have said something before."

Tristan dropped his jaw open. "But I—" He *had* said something, more than a few times, but Collin never listened. Now was not the time to figure this out. He caressed Collin's thigh. "I do like it the way we've been doing it. I just want something different." He shrugged. "I want you close. Is that so bad?"

Collin worried his lower lip and tossed a glance at Tristan. "Okay, well then turn on your back."

He shifted to his back and spread his legs around Collin, knees up, then place lazy strokes over his softened cock.

Collin squeezed lube into his palm and rubbed it over his own flaccid cock, making it harden again.

"Hey Collin, give me some of that stuff, will you?" An evil thought entered his mind. He'd get what he wanted tonight, even if he still couldn't fuck Collin.

Leaning over, Collin squeezed lube onto Tristan's palm.

Tristan kept his hand out. "More."

Collin snapped a brow up. "More?"

"Yeah." Tristan lifted the edge of his mouth.

Collin gave him more, put the cap on the tube and set it on the bed. As he rubbed his hand over his hard cock, he watched Tristan's every move.

Working his hand over his erection, Tristan skimmed the finger of his other hand down between his legs and circled his entrance. Pure pleasure seared into his groin and he thrust his hips, tightening his ass cheeks. A low moan ripped from his throat.

Collin's breath came in pants while he jerked his fist over his erection. pre-cum beaded at the tip, and he swiped it away with his thumb.

Tristan pushed a finger deep inside him and pumped while continuing to stroke his cock. A sensation of raw need surged inside him. There was no going back this time.

Collin's eyelids hooded as his eyes darkened. "Fuck, that's great, Tristan." He rolled the condom over his dick, then added more lube.

Tristan slowed his motions. "Come down here and kiss me."

Collin dropped over Tristan onto an elbow, and claimed his mouth, kissing with a flurry of passion Tristan had never felt from him. Collin wrapped his hands around Tristan's head as if never wanting to let him go. He flicked his tongue against Tristan's and sucked at his lips.

Tristan took it all in, savoring the closeness. Lifting his hips and reaching down between them, he guided Collin's thick cock to his hole, wrapped his legs around Collins hips and squeezed. As the head of Collin's cock entered him, heat seared inside his body.

Collin let out a sharp gasp and lifted his head.

Pulling him back down, he gave Collin a fierce kiss, then wrapped his arms around Collin's back and neck, not letting him go.

Needy little noises erupted out of Collin as he rocked his hips, thrusting his hard cock fully into Tristan, pumping him in an urgent rhythm.

Tristan kissed Collin's mouth, his cheek, his neck and bit just at the start of Collin's shoulder, goosebumps working their way up Collin's skin.

Shudders of pleasure erupted inside Tristan, each one more delicious than the last. Wrapping his legs higher around Collin's hips, he squeezed him tighter, so their bodies were completely flush. His slick cock glided against Collin's taut stomach and his climax built to a raw edge.

Collin buried his face into Tristan's shoulder, his body trembling and his thrusts becoming shaky.

"Collin, look at me." Tristan tried to force Collin up, but he resisted. "Collin...look at me." He pushed on Collin again. He was so close, but he wanted to see it this time, wanted to see Collin coming with him, for him.

Collin lifted his head and gazed deeply into his eyes, his brows tensing, his lips parting. He brushed his fingers over Tristan's cheek.

"Collin?" Tristan's heart burst with emotion.

Pressing his forehead against Tristan's, Collin's body went rigid, and he thrust deep inside Tristan. "Oh, God." He cried out.

With sharp gasps, Tristan's climax plummeted over the edge

in sweet pulses of pleasure. He thrust equally hard, Collin's cock filling him again and again, his own cock rubbing over and over. His cum spurted between them as he yielded to sweet contractions.

As it slowed, he embraced Collin with all he had. The pure emotion he'd seen in his eyes at that moment, the moment when all is stripped away and the truth revealed, told him all he'd ever need to know. Collin loved him. And he was saved.

After it all calmed, Collin cleared his throat and lifted off Tristan, then stepped off the bed. He stood and rubbed his eyes. "I'll get something to clean up with."

With a smug smile, Tristan ran his finger up his stomach, sliding it over the blobs of cum, and popped it in his mouth. "There's tissue on the desk over there and you won't need much."

"Yeah." Collin discarded the condom in a trash can in the corner of the room and hung his head while snapping a few tissues out of the box. When he came back to Tristan, he handed them out. "Here."

"What, not into cleaning me off tonight?" Tristan rolled sideways and snatched the tissue from Collin.

Collin dropped onto the edge of the bed. "No, not tonight." Leaning over, he rested his elbows on his thighs.

After cleaning up, Tristan threw the tissues on the floor, his heart quickening. "Hey, something wrong?" Collin never acted this way after sex. He laid a hand on Collin's back.

Collin shook his head. "No, maybe I'm just tired. It's been a long night, you know?"

Pushing up on his arms, he tugged Collin's shoulders and pulled him down on the bed to lie beside him. "Then just stay here with me awhile."

"Let's get under the covers, huh?" Collin snuggled into his chest.

"Yeah." As he and Collin shifted on the bed, Tristan shimmied the dark blue covers down and then back over them both, edging his chest to Collin's back. Placing an arm around Collin's chest, he pulled Collin in closer. How he loved lying with him like this. And especially now. Now that he saw that wonderful look in Collin's eyes, on his face. "Collin?"

"What?" Collin asked.

Tristan kissed Collin's back and took in the sweet scent of Collin's hair. His heart was heavy with adoration, with love. "I- I've never said this to—"

"Hey, do you have an alarm in here?"

"What?" Tristan pressed his lips together. Why would he ask about that?

"I'm really sleepy, Tristan. How about we save the talking for the morning, okay?" He pulled Tristan's arm tighter around him.

"Oh, okay." Tristan shut his eyes tightly. *Idiot, now is not the time to tell him how you feel.*

"So, where's the clock? I'll set it to like 5 AM or something before your mom gets up, okay?" Collin chuckled. "Probably wouldn't be a good idea if she found us in here together like this."

Tristan opened his eyes. Oh..."Yeah. It's on the desk."

"The desk?" Collin rolled back a little.

"Yeah. I used to sleep through it, so my mom made me keep it on the desk, so I'd have to get up to turn it off." Tristan sighed. Collin was thinking about logistics and how to keep them out of trouble.

"Figures." With a light chuckle, Collin rose from the bed, padded to the desk, and set the alarm. After climbing back into bed, he pulled Tristan's arm tightly around him once more and kissed Tristan's knuckles.

CHAPTER NINETEEN

THANKSGIVING DAY

A house-shaking slam startled Tristan awake. Sucking a deep inhale, his gaze darted around the already bright ceiling. "Oh, shit."

Collin rolled to his back and covered his eyes with his forearm. "What the fuck was that?"

*Morning...*As a jolt cracked through his heart, he snapped up to sitting and flicked his gaze to the open doorway, the door still swinging on its hinges.

Glaring at the two of them, red faced, Tristan's mother stood in the doorway with one hand on her robed hip and the other holding up a skeleton key.

"Oh, my God." Tristan stared at her, his nerves fraying, his whole body shaking.

Collin sat up, glanced at Tristan, then flung his gaze toward her. "Shit, the alarm...it never went off."

His mother held up a shaky index finger to the two of them. Her face tensed up, her fiery gaze boring into them. "Perversion! The two of you are nothing but a demonic perversion!"

"Mom—"

"Get out! Get out of my house! Now!" She shrieked.

"But, Mom—"

"You heard me!" She stabbed her finger at them.

"Miss Tolken, please." Collin held his palms up to her.

She stomped toward them with her fists in the air, then through her teeth, said, "Don't you Miss Tolken me. You're just bad as he is, just as much a freak as all the rest of them."

As she stopped at the bed, Tristan cringed. His eyes flooded with tears, and he bit his lip trying to hold them back. The iron-filled taste of blood covered his tongue.

Collin flicked his gaze around him, patting at the covers and yanking them over his naked body.

Looking at the ceiling, she held her hands up in prayer. "Oh, Heavenly Father, although I thank you for giving me a son, please have mercy on his perversions. Yea, Oh Lord, I beseech thee, please help these wretches remove the demonic forces within them." She peered down on them, spread her arms in an arc over them and said, "Yea, that thou may conquer Satan, and that thou may escape the hands of the servants of Satan that do uphold his work. In the name of Jesus Christ, amen."

Tristan lifted his knees and wrapped his arms around them, then buried his face in his arms and rocked. His breath hitched and brutal trembling shook his body.

Wrapping his arms around Tristan's shoulders, Collin pressed up against his side. "Shh, Tristan." He glared at Tristan's mother, staring, her mouth slack. "Stop this! Can't you see what you're doing to your son?"

Her gaze snapped to Collin. "What I'm doing? What have you done to him?" She sneered at him and growled, dropping her fists to her sides.

"I've done nothing but give your son exactly what he deserves —kindness, love, understanding, affection. All the things he was missing his whole life, all the things he never got from you." Collin hardened his glare.

Love? Tristan snuck a peek at Collin through his disheveled hair. The tears spilled over to run down his cheek and drip onto the sheets covering his knees and thighs. No way could he stop them.

"That's not true. I-I gave him all those things." Her voice softened and her eyes dazed over for a moment. As she refocused on Collin, her gaze hardened. "Don't you for a minute try to tell me I didn't do everything I could for that little freak of nature. He should have never been born!"

Tristan burst out in sobs.

"Never. Been. Born," she spat.

Collin tightened his hold on Tristan and became calm and collected. "I understand. It must have been terribly hard for you."

"You listen…" She eyed him and her face went slack. "Yes."

"I mean, having a son who clearly demonstrated a liking for the same sex, it goes against everything, doesn't it? It's not the natural order of things." Collin peered at her.

Her shoulders relaxed and she took a step back. "No, it doesn't. It's wrong, wrong and perverted."

Tristan's sobs slowed to a stop, and he stared, wide-eyed at Collin. *I can't believe my ears.* Collin can't believe that, can he? He watched Collin.

"And I'm sure when you saw these things in him, it dashed all the hopes and dreams you had for your son." Collin fixated on her.

"Yes…" Her brows and the corners of her mouth twitched as she took another step back. She smirked. "When he was a baby, I dreamed he would play football. I dreamed he would be tall and strong and that he'd maybe be a lawyer or a doctor and marry a nice girl and make me a grandma." With her eyes shimmering, she leaned against the wall.

Tristan's gaze met his mother's. *Is she really that disappointed in me? I'm not any of those things.* An ache rose up in his chest, squeezing his heart. Fresh tears journeyed a wet trail on his cheek.

"But that'll never be, now, will it?" she said.

"And where was his father when he was a baby? Where was *he* in all your dreams?" Collin asked.

Her face scrunched up, her lips curling. "He was dead."

"Oh, fuck." Sudden nausea wrenched Tristan's stomach. He leapt from the bed, still naked, snatched his clothes and shoes from a pile off the floor and ran into the bathroom.

After slamming the door shut, he leaned over the toilet and vomited in one quick lurch. As swiftly as he could, he dressed and stuck his face into the sink to lap water from the faucet. Lifting his head, he swiped at his face, not daring to look at himself in the mirror. When he opened the door, he dashed out into the main room, snatched up his sweatshirt and ran out into the crisp morning.

"Tristan! Hey, wait. Don't go." Collin called out.

"You come back here this instant." His mother screamed.

Tristan ran down the wet street, hardly taking notice of the heavy gray clouds overhead or the occasional snowflake meandering down to kiss his cheek. He ran past tiny houses all shuttered and trees naked and ready for winter. Potholes littered the road, reminding him of the last time he took flight like this.

The park with its ominous spaceship slide came into view behind a large spruce tree. He slowed to a fast walk and slid his sweatshirt on over his cold shoulders. His breath came out in ragged huffs, sending tiny clouds of white bursting out of his mouth.

He walked onto the hard ground littered with patches of brown grass and green weeds and made his way to the sand of the playground. After stepping onto a railroad tie along the edge, he let his tennis shoes sink into the sand, making his own divots in a sea of tiny hills.

As he climbed onto the circular steps of the slide, his numb mind filled with images, replaying the horrid scene of his mother in the doorway, the prayer for his sins against nature and the terrible disappointment in her face. *Never been born...* The words haunted him, clear as the second she'd said them. His father was dead, and his mother never wanted him. The pain crept up to cripple him as he stepped on a landing. He buckled and went down on an outstretched arm. "No..."

He wrapped his arms around his waist and shimmied back against the cold metal wall, trying in desperation to hide himself in the crevice between the landing floor and the wall. He needed to disappear.

Tonguing his lower lip, the faint taste of blood stunned him for a moment. Did he really bite his lip that hard? He pondered the question, letting his mind hover for a second on something that didn't hurt, didn't try to drown him in misery. And what of his father? What really happened to him?

Never been born... He tensed his face as tears blurred his vision and his breath hitched. Pulling his knees in tightly to his chest and covering his face with his hands, he screamed, "No!" His soft weeping mingled with the gentle fall of the snow.

"Tristan?" Collin's voice rang out over the playground.

Tristan lifted his head and peeked out from behind his long bangs.

How long had he been here? He didn't know. Long enough for his ass to be numb and his legs to be cramped. A shiver coursed through his body.

"Tristan, where are you?" Collin appeared at the bottom of the slide steps and looked up. "Tristan?"

He shifted. He should answer, but he couldn't. He wasn't ready.

Collin took a few steps up the stairs, making clanking noises as he went and wrapping a black pea coat tighter around him. He stopped and peered up, squinting. "Tristan?"

His gaze caught Collin's.

"Oh, shit." Collin scrambled to the landing where Tristan sat and crouched down beside him. "Come here." Wrapping his arms around Tristan's shoulders, Collin yanked him into his chest and sat with his legs out. He kissed the top of Tristan's head. "Are you okay?"

Tristan mumbled, "Yes...no."

"You look like you've had one hell of a cry." Collins squeezed his shoulders.

Tristan twisted his face into Collin's shoulder.

"I don't blame you. What she said in front of you was absolutely uncalled for." Collin held him tighter. "Now I know how you got so messed up in the first place. None of this is your fault, Tristan. Not one bit."

Tristan nodded his head against Collin's shoulder.

Pushing Tristan out to see his face, Collin asked, "Did you really hear me?"

"What?" Tristan chanced a peek at him.

"I said it's not your fault. You've done nothing wrong." Collin's gaze searched his face.

"Except be her son." Tristan dropped back into the comfort of Collin's chest and sighed. A fresh wave of melancholy washed over him.

"No, she loves you, Tristan. She really does. She just doesn't know how to show it. Apparently, her parents weren't exactly great, either." Collin gave Tristan another squeeze. "But it doesn't make it right, what she said and how she's treated you."

Heaviness weighed on his heart. All his life it had seemed he'd tried to understand his mother, tried to make her proud of him in some way. But it had never worked. "I don't care anymore."

"Don't care?" Collin placed light kiss on his hair. "Oh, but I know you do. She's your mother, your own flesh and blood. You will always care about her, no matter what. And that's okay, that's healthy. What you need to do is detach."

"How the hell do I do that?" Tristan's chest pinched. It seemed an impossible feat. Hadn't she ruled his every waking hour? Hadn't her criticisms of him always hung over his head?

"There are ways. We'll work on them when we get back."

Collin brushed his hand up and down Tristan's back. "For now, just know that I'm here with you and whatever happens, whatever she says or does to you or to me, I'm strong enough to take it on. I'll be here for you." He kissed Tristan's head again. "I won't let her hurt you, not anymore."

Intense emotion bloomed in Tristan's heart. Collin did make it better. He made him feel safe, even after all that had happened. A pleasant ache, a longing started in his chest and words hung on the tip of his tongue. "I love you, Collin, so much." He snuggled in deeper to Collin's embrace.

Silence.

Collin coughed, then loosened his hold on Tristan. "Um, well, you might be surprised to know that I think I talked her down anyways."

His heart skipped, then pounded in his ears. *I said it, finally, those three words. Why didn't Collin say it back to me?* As he hid himself against Collin, he tightened the hold around his own waist. Should he push Collin on it? Should he flat out ask Collin how he felt? Did he have the nerve? No, especially not now.

"Did you hear me? I said I talked her down. I think it'll be okay if we go back now." Collin patted Tristan's shoulder, releasing a faint chuckle.

Tristan stared at him. Collin was behaving as if it was all better, just like that. He should probably pretend nothing happened, too. Pretend he'd never said those three words. "Yes, I heard you." He thought a moment on his mother and Collin's handling of the situation. "How the hell did you do that?"

A smug smile swept over Collin's mouth. "I have my ways."

"Don't fuck with me, Collin. I know my mother and I know there is no way you or I can ever go back in that house again...or, at least not for a day or so." He raked his gaze over Collin's face. How many times had he slept on this very slide?

"No, really. She's calm now and I think she may even be civil for the day." Collin lifted his brows.

"No fucking way. What the hell did you say to her?" Tristan

straightened. Could he really believe what Collin said? Could he even get through the rest of this day?

"Lots of things. But first and foremost, I just listened. You'd be surprised how much better people behave and how much they'll open up when you listen and really try to understand their point of view." Collin unwrapped himself from around Tristan.

So much for listening to me... As his heart faltered, he breathed in deeply. He needed to get through this day and not look like a lunatic. He'd been through enough already, hadn't he? It was the only way to deal with Collin *and* his mother until Saturday, when he could go back to their dorm room, and all this would be over.

Collin stood up and held a hand out to Tristan. "Come on, let's get back. That turkey was smelling really good."

Tristan took his hand and stood with a groan as his aching muscles stretched after sitting for too long. He focused on Collin. "So how am I supposed to act when we get back? I mean, it's not like nothing happened."

Stuffing his hands in the back pockets of his jeans, Collin shifted his stance. "Yeah, but I think it's better to pretend nothing did happen. Her way of dealing with things is to look the other way, so to speak. Really, that's what she's done with you all along. She doesn't like to face what's really happening and the alcohol helps her do that. She just drinks it all away and sees the world through rosy glasses." Collin gave him an uneasy grin, then patted Tristan's shoulder. "It'll be okay, just wait and see. She'll be drunk and back to her normal self when we get back."

Tristan took a deep inhale. It didn't feel right. Was it Collin, his mother, or both that seemed off? "I'll believe it when I see it." He attempted a smile.

As they walked back to the house, the sun tried to peek through gray clouds and a few inches of powdery snow lay on the ground, crunching under their shoes. They came up the drive and through the front door.

The lovely scent of turkey and sage dressing floated through the house.

Tristan's mother hummed in the kitchen, clanking pots and pans around the stove. On the television, the Macy's Thanksgiving Day Parade chimed out marching band music while enormous cartoon character balloons bounced along between the buildings of New York City.

Tristan's pulse kicked up a notch. He glanced at Collin. Was this really happening, or was he walking into a trap?

Collin shut the door behind them and gestured to the kitchen. "Go on in and just have a seat. Let her speak first."

With a nod, Tristan shuffled into the kitchen and took a seat at the counter in a metal chair.

His mother grabbed a blue plastic glass and took a sip of its contents before turning around to Tristan. "Oh, hello, son. Looks like it's going to be a wonderful Thanksgiving, doesn't it?"

He widened his eyes. "Yeah, it does." *Is this real?*

She twisted back to the stove and stirred a pan full of bubbling gravy. The turkey rested on a cutting board on the counter to her right. "I guess I owe you an apology for what I said earlier. You know I didn't mean it, right, dear?"

"Yeah." Tristan clutched at the sweatshirt over his chest.

"It all just took me by such a surprise. I didn't know what was going on."

Frowning, Tristan shifted in his seat. "About that, Mom, we need to talk—"

"Oh no, honey, let's just leave it as it is, okay?" She reached out for her cup and took a gulp. "I mean, you're a full-grown man now and I did do my best..."

Kitting his brows, Tristan stood, stepped up beside her and looked down into the plastic glass, still in her hand. A red mixture of what looked like tomato juice swirled inside it. He pointed at the cup. "What is that?"

She smiled at him. "Oh, just a little something to celebrate the holiday."

He sniffed at her, smelling vodka. "I see, a Bloody Mary to get you in the holiday spirit?"

Turning around to him, she scoffed. "Tristan Thomas Tolken, it's only V-8 with a hint of vodka. God knows I should be able to bend the rules just a little bit."

"Yeah, sure, Mom." He walked away from her and into the main room, where Collin sat on the couch, watching the parade on the TV. Plopping down next to Collin, he sighed.

"So?" Collin kept his focus on the television.

"So, you were right. She's pretending like it never happened." Tristan huffed a chuckle. "She even apologized." Putting his leg up on the couch, he turned to Collin. "I don't understand. She found us in bed together, naked. She used to beat the shit out of me for just *hearing* about me liking guys."

"Uh-huh." All Collin's attention was on the parade.

"Did you somehow make her believe we didn't do anything? Did you make her think there's nothing going on between us?" He watched Collin, then nudged his arm, saying, "Are you listening to me?"

Collin looked at him. "What?"

"Did you hear what I said?" Tristan furrowed his brows.

"Yeah, yeah, I heard you. I love this parade, watched it since I was a kid." With a grin, he pointed at the TV.

Tristan glanced at the television for a second.

"So, I told you what happened, I just listened." Collin peeked at him.

"But does she think nothing's going on between us?" Tristan pressed his lips together. *Why won't he answer me?*

Collin faced Tristan and grabbed his hand. "Listen, I think she doesn't want to know what's going on. She didn't even ask me. She just spilled her story to me and that was pretty much it. I think she's had a lot bottled up for a long time." He freed Tristan's hand and leaned sideways, bringing his mouth close to Tristan's ear. "I think she might have a personality disorder. I'm even thinking she has Borderline Personality Disorder." He sat back. "Although, she could be histrionic, too."

"What the hell are those?" Tristan arched a brow.

Collin's attention drew back to the TV. "Well, they're actually pretty serious illnesses. They both result in a lot of the behavior your mom exhibits—severe and quick mood swings, the alcoholism and being very, well, upset about your father abandoning her, even if he died. I mean, it's not like he could help it, but she's really got a lot of anger around that whole issue, and I think she somehow equates you with him."

"Yeah, I can see that." Tristan pursed his lips, his gaze falling to his lap.

Collin let out a soft chuckle and focused on Tristan. "But with histrionics you see a lot of inappropriate sexual behavior."

"Like what?" Tristan inched closer to him.

"Well, like flirting all the time in situations where, clearly, it's not right." Collin grinned at Tristan. "But I don't see her being all that flirtatious, so the more I think about it, the more I think it's Borderline."

"So, the mood swings, that's how she flies off the handle in a second like this morning and now she's all calm and fine like nothing happened?" Tristan inhaled in a deep breath.

"Yep, that and the alcohol. She's self-medicating." Collin's attention drew back to the parade.

Tristan reclined on the couch. "When we get back, I want to do some reading on this Borderline Personality thing, okay?"

"Sure, I know of some good material I can get you." Collin glanced toward the kitchen, where his mother continued her humming and preparing of the Thanksgiving meal. "For now, maybe the one thing that can help, is for you to know that all those hurtful things she says and does are really just a symptom of her illness, not because she really means it and certainly not because they're true."

Tristan glanced at the kitchen, then eyed Collin. "An illness?"

"Yes. Most psychologists believe that alcoholism itself is a disease and Borderline may be caused from a chemical imbalance in her brain. I've heard it can run in families." Collin patted

Tristan on the hand. "Okay, that's enough mumbo-jumbo for now. Let's watch the parade before it's all over."

"Okay." Tristan let his gaze wander to the television, staring at it. Holy shit, maybe Collin really did know his stuff. He'd have to learn more when they got home.

———

"DINNER'S READY," Tristan's mother called out from the kitchen.

Collin nudged Tristan, dozing next to him on the couch, his head on a pillow on the armrest. A football game blared from the television. "Hey, time to eat."

Tristan fluttered his eyes open and sat up, rubbing his eyes. "I must have fallen asleep."

Collin chuckled. "Yep, I'd say so. I think you were snoring at some point."

Furrowing his brows, Tristan said, "Was not."

"Was too." Collin hurled a couch pillow at Tristan, hitting his side and making his white shirt puff.

Tristan wore uncharacteristic black slacks, which was the Mormon missionary uniform, but his mother had insisted. "Stop it." He threw the pillow back at Collin and it landed in Collin's lap, over beige slacks. "Just because you had to watch that boring game."

"Boring?" Collin raised his brows.

"Did you hear me?" His mother stood at the couch in her best blue silk dress and steadied herself on the armrest.

Tristan looked up at her.

She hiccupped and clapped a hand over her mouth. "Oh, excuse me." She let out a soft giggle as she sauntered back into the kitchen.

"Great." Tristan stood and glanced at Collin, also rising from the couch, admiring the way his thin V-neck sweater showed off his broad shoulders.

Collin shrugged. "Don't worry about it."

"I'm not. How about I put a little of her vodka in our eggnog?" Tristan smirked. That would be one way to get through this.

Collin grinned at him. "Sounds fantastic."

After making his and Collin's eggnog drinks, Tristan walked to the table, set with white china and a tablecloth, silver utensils and serving dishes filled with food, and sat down beside Collin. "Here you go." He set Collin's drink in front of him and his own at the top of his plate.

His mother sat at the head of the table, studying him, as if assessing him.

He glanced at her. "What?"

"If you're quite done, I'll give the Thanksgiving prayer." She folder her hands in front of her, bowed her head and closed her eyes.

Tristan and Collin did the same.

"Oh, Father in Heaven, thank thee for the blessed food ye hath given unto us and thank thee for the blessed time thee hath given me with my only son. In the name of Jesus Christ, amen."

With his brows lowering, Tristan murmured, "Amen."

"Amen." Looking around the table, Collin dug into the dressing, placing a heaping mound on his plate, then passed the dish to Tristan's mother and dug into the turkey.

Passing food to each other, the three of them filled their plates. As they started up a seemingly normal family banter, they ate and drank their fill.

———

AFTER DINNER, Tristan finished washing the last plate and set it on a towel on the counter to dry. Leaning over, he grabbed his glass and downed the rest of his sixth spiked eggnog. A pleasant heat washed through him. Peeking toward the main room, he let out a soft giggle. Collin was in there waiting for him and with any luck, his mother would be passed out drunk. His cock swelled. He'd be taking Collin to bed tonight.

He strolled into the main room and found Collin sitting at the end of the flowered couch, his mother asleep in the reclining chair in the corner and yet another football game on the television. The front yard was dark beyond the window, but the thin covering of snow shimmered in the moonlight.

Collin sat with his elbow on the armrest of the couch and his cheek in his hand, his eyelids drooping occasionally.

Tristan stepped to Collin, leaned down and took his free hand. "Come on."

Looking up at Tristan, Collin frowned. "What? I'm watching the game." He pulled his hand out of Tristan's.

Sneaking his lower lip between his teeth, Tristan dropped down next to Collin and leaned over to whisper in his ear, "She's passed out again. Don't you want to go do..." He cupped Collin's balls through his slacks. "This?"

Collin batted his hand away and glared at him for a second. "Stop it. I'm tired."

Dropping his mouth open, Tristan sat back against the couch cushions. No way. "Tired? Too tired for—"

"Yes." Collin's gaze softened. "It's been a long day for both of us, all right? Let's just give it a rest."

With a frown, he drew his legs onto the couch. This didn't sound like Collin, not at all, and he sure as hell didn't like it. He scanned the room. How could he talk to Collin without making him more aggravated? "Well, so it was a pretty good dinner, anyways, wasn't it?"

Collin peered at him. "Yeah, it was. Pleasant even."

Toying with a fold in his shirt, Tristan said, "My mom was even nice, wasn't she?"

"Yeah. Everything worked out really well." Collin nodded.

Tristan thought for a moment. "Is that why you don't want to do anything? Because you're afraid of getting caught again?"

Collin turned to face Tristan, bringing a knee up on the couch between them. "I do think it'd be a good idea to just let things chill for the rest of our trip here. It's only another two days anyways." He took a deep inhale. "Besides, I think she'll get used to it a lot easier if it's not shoved in her face, so to speak. Don't you?"

Tristan thought on it a minute. "Yeah, guess you're right." Turning to the TV, his chest tightened. *Maybe Collin doesn't want to be with me anymore? Maybe this was too much? Or maybe I totally messed up by telling him how I feel about him?* "Collin?"

Watching the game again, Collin scowled, then twisted to look at Tristan. "What now?"

"This isn't, um, there isn't something else going on here, is there? I mean if there were something bad between us, you'd tell me. Wouldn't you?" Tristan wrinkled his brows and pressed his lips together.

Leaning toward him, Collin grasped Tristan's hands and held them. "No, there is nothing bad between us."

"Well, so everything that's happened, it hasn't made you not want to be with me anymore, has it?" He winced. What a fool he sounded like.

"God, no. I told you I'd stick through this with you and do whatever I could to help, and I meant it." He wrinkled his forehead, squeezing Tristan's hands.

"Okay." He studied Collin. He'd sounded sincere. He should take Collin at his word.

Collin shook their hands. "I'm not going anywhere. I've told you that a thousand times. Haven't I?"

Tristan nodded and attempted to smile.

Squeezing Tristan's hands and shaking them again, Collin said, "I'm not going anywhere." He gave Tristan a pointed look.

CHAPTER TWENTY

Santa Barbara, California

SATURDAY, NOVEMBER 29

C ollin freed a long exhale as he walked into their dorm room with his black suitcase in his hand, wearing low-slung jeans and a gray sweatshirt. "Wow, that took forever."

Tristan shut the door and followed Collin in, his bracelets jangling on his wrist under the sleeve of a red and gray striped, crew-neck sweater. "Yeah, it did. We got to the airport at what, ten this morning? And it's already time for dinner."

Collin threw his suitcase on his bed, unzipped it, and unpacked his things. "Dinner sounds pretty good, right about now." He turned to Tristan and wagged his brows. "And then, dessert."

As Tristan unpacked, he twisted around with a shirt in his hand. "Dessert?"

Collin stepped to Tristan and wrapped his arms around his waist. Swaying them both and smirking, he said, "It's been almost three days. In my book, that's way too long to go without sex."

Tristan gazed deeply into his eyes. Finally, Collin seemed to be back to normal. "You were the one who decided we couldn't do anything at my mom's." He enjoyed the hold Collin had on him and dropped his head to Collin's shoulder. It had been forever since Collin had given him any real affection, probably not since the slide.

Collin kissed the top of Tristan's head. "I didn't want to take a chance of there being anymore drama happening. I figured you'd been through enough on that first day."

Tristan lifted his head to gaze at him. "Oh really? That's a new one."

"A new what?" Collin snapped his brows together.

"A new reason. You had me thinking there was something wrong between us. That maybe the whole incident with my mom totally turned you off or something." He frowned. He'd been so plagued with insecurity and fear the rest of the trip.

Collin gave him a squeeze. "But I told you there wasn't. You should know better than that by now." He pressed his swelling cock against Tristan's hip. "So did you have any little indiscretions over the last few days?" He smirked.

"What do you mean?" His gaze searched Collin's face.

"You know, did you jerk off?" Collin trailed light kisses over Tristan's jaw and neck.

"Did *you*?" Tristan huffed. Why did everything have to revert back to this? He stiffened his body.

Collin pulled away and looked at Tristan, his eyes twinkling. "Of course, I did."

"What? When?" With wide eyes, he scanned Collin up and down, focusing in on the hard cock beneath his jeans, imagining the pleasant sight of Collin touching himself.

Freeing him, Collin stepped back to the open suitcase lying on his bed. "In the shower, where else? If you didn't, I think it'd be a record, wouldn't it?"

Heat flushed Tristan's face and he stared at the gray carpeted floor. "Yeah, I did. So what?"

Collin faced him. "You didn't go back to your old ways, though, right? You did what normal guys do?"

With a shrug, he met Collin's gaze. "Yeah, I guess so." He

spread a smile over his lips. "*I*, at least, had the privacy of a bedroom."

Collin stepped to him and grabbed him by the hips, rubbing his erection against Tristan's through their jeans. "Did you think of me while you did it?" He placed a heated kiss on Tristan's lips.

With warmth flooding his cheeks, Tristan lifted the edge of his mouth. "Yes." Cupping Collin's ass, he ground his hard cock onto Collin's. Pleasure rippled through him. "Are you sure you want to wait until after dinner?"

With a sigh, Collin let go of Tristan and stepped away, combing his fingers through his auburn hair. "Yeah, I'm famished actually, and I told Jessica I'd meet her later, so I better eat."

"You have to meet Jessica? Did she have to come home a day early for cheap airline tickets, too?" His chest tightened and he clenched his teeth. Why did Jessica have to get caught between them already?

Collin hooked a brow at him. "No, her family lives here. They have a house just off campus on the corner of Main and 3rd."

"Well, so when are you supposed to meet her?" He fisted his hands. He probably shouldn't be getting so worked up about this, especially after what Collin had just been through for him.

"Just...later. She texted me this morning and I told her I'd let her know when we could get together." Collin studied Tristan and stepped toward him. "What are you so upset about?"

Walking away from Collin and toward the window, he puffed out a sharp exhale. "I don't know." He glanced at Collin, still eyeing him. "It's just that I figured we'd finally have a night to ourselves, you know? Especially since you were all coming on to me just a minute ago." He thought a second. "Wait, why was she texting you anyways? Have you been texting her all weekend?"

Collin shook his head and raised his hands. "Settle down. We always text each other. So yeah, I guess you could say we were texting all weekend."

He glared at Collin. "Why do you have to see her?" He gritted his teeth. Why was he getting so upset? Could it be the uneasy feeling he'd had since he'd confessed?

"Jesus, Tristan, she's got some information for me that I need for my thesis. You need to stop getting so worked up about her." He strode to Tristan and wrapped his arms around Tristan's shoulders. "It's no big deal. It'll probably only take a half hour or so."

Tristan relaxed in his arms.

"Let's eat, I'll meet with Jessica and then we'll have the rest of the night together. Okay?" Collin pecked a kiss on his cheek.

He locked his gaze on Collin's. Was Collin being straight with him? He looked like he was. "Okay."

WHILE SITTING at his desk perusing the internet on his laptop, Tristan checked the time in the corner of his screen. "Shit, nine already." He frowned. Where the hell was Collin? He said he'd only be a half hour and an hour and a half had already passed. His heart flickered and he pursed his lips, then slapped his hand on his desk. "Damn it." Something was up.

He jumped out of the chair and scanned the room for his jacket. He was going to find Collin and figure out exactly what was going on, once and for all. He was sick of all this crap between him and Jessica. He was sick of this uneasy feeling he had whenever they were together.

He eyed a zippered sweatshirt peeking out from the floor of his closet and bound toward it, then grabbed it and slipped it over his sweater. With a huff, he strode to the door and grabbed the handle.

The knob twisted in his hand and the door flung open to hit his knee with a loud crack. Sharp pain rocketed through his leg, radiating from his kneecap. "Ouch, shit!" Bending over, he snatched his knee and hopped on his other leg.

Collin stood in the doorway with his backpack slung over one shoulder. "Oh my God, Tristan, I'm sorry." With wide eyes, he rushed at Tristan and steadied him. "Are you all right?"

Tears sprung into Tristan's eyes with the intense pain in his leg. He blinked them back, taking deep breaths. "I-I don't know."

Holding onto Tristan's waist, Collin guided him to his bed and sat him down. As he dropped in beside Tristan, his backpack fell to the floor, the contents spilling out over the carpet through an open zipper, papers floating and books sliding. "Here, let me see."

"No, it hurts. Just give me a minute, okay?" Tristan winced and hissed. The pain subsided into a sharp ache.

"Get your pants off." Collin unfastened Tristan's jeans and pulled at the waist band, trying to get them down.

"Wait, Collin." Tristan lifted his hips and Collin tugged his jeans down over his thighs, exposing his knee.

"Can you extend your leg?" Collin gently prodded Tristan's injured knee.

"I don't know." Tristan flinched.

Collin skimmed his finger pads over Tristan's kneecap.

Reflexively, he jerked his leg into his stomach, further bending the joint. The ache remained the same. As his breath caught, he steadied himself. He must be okay. Nothing seemed broken.

Collin gently poked around Tristan's kneecap. "This hurt?"

With a shake of his head, Tristan said, "No."

Supporting Tristan's leg, Collin extended it and poked deeper. "This?"

"No." Tristan freed a long breath.

"How about this?" Collin pushed Tristan's kneecap to the side and up and down.

Tristan winced. The pain was lessening, not getting worse. "Uh, no. It, it must be okay."

Collin placed a soft kiss on Tristan's knee. "I'm so sorry."

"It's okay, I know it was an accident." Tristan set his feet on the the floor with his jeans hanging around his calves.

Collin came close, his face hovering over him. "Where were you going anyways?"

"To find you." His gaze roamed Collin's face. *He was so worried about me.*

"Why?" Collin wrinkled his forehead.

He pressed his lips together. "Because you were supposed to be back an hour ago." His chest heated. "Where were you?"

Collin puffed out a breath. "I told you, I was with Jessica. It just took longer than I thought, that's all."

He twisted to face him. "You could pick up a phone, you know."

Collin sighed and lay down on the bed, bringing his arm up to rest across his forehead. "I know. I'm sorry, okay?"

With a knot forming in his gut, Tristan clenched his jaw. Something didn't feel right since the day he spilled his feelings. How many times had he wanted to talk about it? Could he now? No...another time. "I'm going to get in the shower. I feel gross after travelling all day." He stood from the bed and bent over, taking his shoes and jeans off. The papers on the floor caught his attention. "What the fuck is this?" He dropped to the floor on his knees.

"What?" Collin sat up.

Tristan rifled through the papers. "Printouts of birth records?" He stopped at one, confusion tangling his mind. "What's all this shit from this ancestry website?"

Dropping to the floor, Collin snatched the papers from Tristan and hurried to gather up the remainder of his things from the carpet. "I can explain."

Tristan sat up, his legs tucked beneath him, still in his boxers and sweater. "I'm sure you can." He studied Collin.

Stopping his motions, Collin glared at him for a heartbeat, then his gaze went soft. "I just, I-I was trying to um, trying to figure something out, that's all."

"Figure what out?" He eyed Collin. "Does this have something to do with our trip?" Collin couldn't be trying to see what happened to his father still, could he?

Collin scoffed. "No, of course not. It's information for my thesis."

Huffing, Tristan glanced at the floor, then focused on Collin. "Of course, your thesis. The big black hole you never want to talk about. Although I can't imagine how that stuff could be useful."

Collin dropped his mouth open and glared at Tristan. "What's with the attitude? For your information, there are these things called trials and getting someone's...history is useful."

Creasing his brows and worrying his lip, Tristan thought for a moment. "Are you doing real experiments on people?"

Collin's eyes grew wide. "What? N-no, well, sort of. I suppose you could call it that. But it's not like dangerous in any way or anything." He stuffed the papers and books into his backpack. "I thought you were going to get in the shower?"

He scanned the area around him, then stood up. "Yeah." After peering at the top of Collin's head, he padded into the bathroom, finished undressing and turned the shower on. The patter of water hitting tile filled the room and soon, steam poured over the top of the glass door. He opened it and stepped inside. Soothing heat cascaded down his body in a wet blanket. He stood in the spray for a minute, letting it wash away the tension in his neck and back.

The shower door opened beside him with a whoosh.

Tristan looked out of the water.

Collin entered the shower, a coy grin playing on his lips. "Thought I'd join you." Dropping lube and a condom to a shelf in the corner, he came at Tristan with heated kisses and prowling hands and pushed Tristan up against the back wall.

The cold hard surface slapped against his back, and he sucked in a quick breath.

Collin ground his erection against Tristan's belly and a low moan escaped his lips.

Tristan's cock hardened in an instant and he kissed Collin

back with equal intensity. How he'd longed for this over the last few days. Their solid cocks brushed against each other and he thrust his hips, craving more.

"Oh, God, Tristan, I missed you." Collin licked and kissed down Tristan's neck to his chest and bit at his nipple.

Tristan groaned, his cock jerking. He wanted that mouth on his dick. "I missed you, too."

Collin teased Tristan's other nipple with his fingers and worked his mouth down Tristan's stomach, stopping to lick his navel.

Pleasure raced up from Tristan's stomach and down into his groin, tightening his balls. Desire thrummed inside him, made his cock ache. "Please, Collin." He thrust his hips, nudging his erection into Collin's mouth.

Licking and nipping his way around Tristan's groin, Collin brushed his cheek against Tristan's shaft.

As Tristan's cock pulsed, pre-cum seeped from the tip. He fisted Collin's hair and pushed Collin's head where he needed him. "Come on."

With a smirk, Collin stopped and tipped his head to peek up at Tristan. "You're pretty fucking hard, Tristan."

"What do you expect?" Rocking his hips, Tristan brushed his cockhead against Collin's lips. "Suck on it."

A broad smile spread over Collin's face, and he took Tristan's erection in his mouth.

Wet heat enveloped Tristan's cock. Collin's slick tongue worked up and down his shaft and ran circles over the sensitive spot under the lip of Tristan's erection. Letting out a sharp moan, Tristan's knees buckled. "Oh, God. Keep going." Pleasure engulfed him. Delicious shudders rolled through his body as Collin's tongue found the sensitive spot over and over again. He peeked down at Collin.

Collin cradled Tristan's balls with one of his hands while the other stroked his own erection with quick jerks.

Watching, entranced in Collin's movement, Tristan imagined

what Collin would look like in the shower he grew up in back in Salt Lake. A sudden burst of sensitivity shook through his body. "Oh..."

Collin halted everything and stood up. Pressing his cock against Tristan's, he whispered, "You close?"

"Uh." Tristan swallowed hard. "Yeah."

Collin feathered his lips over the shell of Tristan's ear. "Turn around."

Glancing at Collin, Tristan asked, "What? Why?"

"I didn't bring the lube and a condom in here for nothing." Collin chuckled and guided Tristan around to face the shower tiles.

While Collin fumbled with the condom, then the lube, Tristan tilted his hips, jetting his ass out. Sweet anticipation ached through his body.

Collin's heated body pressed up behind him and his slick fingers worked their way between the crevice of his ass, circling his entrance.

Burning, then waves of pleasure washed over Tristan, and he released a ragged moan, dipping his forehead to the cool tile.

Collin rubbed his cock on Tristan's inner thigh while he worked his fingers inside Tristan, stretching him. "God, you feel tight." As he placed hungry kisses and soft bites on Tristan's shoulder, he kneaded the flesh on Tristan's chest and stomach with his free hand.

With Collin's fingers stroking his insides, need heightened inside Tristan, and he groaned. "Hurry, Collin." As Collin plunged his fingers over his internal bundle of nerves, a jolt of pleasure rocketed through him. "Oh, shit." His hips bucked.

Pulling his fingers out, Collin rolled on the condom, added more lube, then nudged his dick into Tristan's hole.

Tristan rocked his hips forward and attempted to turn around. How he wanted to face Collin, to see him come undone in front of him.

With a firm grip on Tristan's hips, Collin kept him facing the wall. "What are you doing?"

Tristan tilted his head against Collin's. "I just wanted to turn around. I want to see you."

With a soft snort, Collin gave Tristan a playful pinch on his ass cheek. "And make me miss watching this beautiful ass? No way."

Tristan pinched his lips. "But—"

"Oh, come on, Tristan. Let's do it my way tonight, okay?" Collin bit at Tristan's shoulder, then freed a low growl.

Tristan dropped his forehead on the tile and exhaled. What should he do? Force Collin to face him? But was that fair to Collin?

Rubbing the head of his cock against Tristan's entrance, he caressed Tristan's hips, then skimmed his fingers around to Tristan's groin and stroked his shaft, placing passionate, soothing kisses on Tristan's back. "I just love to see you this way, that's all. You're so nice to look at, so fucking hot." He thrust and the tip of his cock entered Tristan. "That's okay, isn't it?"

"Yeah." Delicious pressure and heat lit up Tristan's insides and he groaned, biting his lip, tensing his brows. Arousal overtook him and he shoved backward, fucking himself on Collin's thick cock. If Collin wanted him this way, enjoyed him this way, then he'd take what he could.

A gasp ripped from Collin's throat, and he thrust his hips, driving into and out of Tristan in a quick rhythm. He planted heated kisses and bites on Tristan's neck, back and shoulder while pumping Tristan's weeping cock with his palm. "Come for me, Tristan."

With a loud cry, Tristan's sensitivity drove over the edge. A sweet climax rippled through him from head to toe, his cum spurting over Collin's hand, painting the shower wall.

Collin grew rigid behind him, his fingers digging into Tristan's hips. Then he wrapped his arm around Tristan's chest and pressed his cheek against Tristan's back. With one deep thrust, he let out a sharp gasp and filled Tristan. He shuddered once more and finally, he relaxed.

Rolling his hips forward, Tristan released Collin's softening cock from his body, then turned around in Collin's loose embrace. "Collin?

Collin gazed into Tristan's eyes. "What?"

"How come you never want to face me when we do it?" Studying him, Tristan pursed his lips. Should he be pressing this point right now?

"What?" Collin stepped back, removing the condom and tying it off, then letting the steady stream of water cascade down his chest. He dropped the used condom to the floor.

Tristan hung his head. "Well, I mean, you—"

"Can't we talk about this after we wash? The hot water's going to run out." Collin picked up the soap, lathered it in his hand and ran soapy fingers over Tristan's torso, spreading tiny bubbles over his chest. He placed a quick kiss on Tristan's lips. "Here, let me wash you."

Closing his eyes, Tristan stepped toward Collin and let his touch soothe him. Collin obviously cared for him. Why would he wash him otherwise? *I'm being stupid and should stop questioning him.*

AFTER THE SHOWER, Collin laid on his side and flung his bed covers down in front of him, making an opening for Tristan.

Tristan crawled into Collin's bed, wearing only his boxers, then lay on his back next to Collin and sighed.

Collin propped himself up on his elbow, his cheek resting in the palm of his hand. "What's up?"

"Um..." Was this a good time to have that talk? He pinched his brows and gripped the covers under his chin. "Well, I was just wondering something."

"What?" Collin studied Tristan's face.

With a shrug, Tristan cleared his throat. "It seems sort of strange to me that you, that you, um, never want to have sex facing me." As his chest squeezed, he tightened his fists over the covers.

"Where did that come from?" A grin threatened to curl Collin's lips. He gave Tristan a playful jiggle. "We had sex facing each other, at your mom's house, remember?"

"Yeah, but it was only once." He met Collin's gaze. *Collin needs to take me seriously this time, damn it.*

"Uh, I uh, really, Tristan, I don't know what you're getting all worked up about. If you have a thing for the missionary position, then we'll do it like that more often. Okay?" Rolling to his back, Collin huffed.

"Collin, how do you feel about me?" Oh shit...The words had just tumbled out. His pulse pounded inside him, and he yanked the covers over his mouth.

"You know how I feel about you." Collin turned to his side again and peered down at Tristan. "What's this all about? I don't understand how a sexual position could have anything to do with my feelings for you."

Swallowing hard, he pushed the covers down to his chest. "It just seems like you don't want to look at me when we, uh, have sex and it seems like if you really, um, had f-feelings for me, then you would want to look at me." God, he sounded pathetic. *What's wrong with me?* "Just—just forget it. It doesn't matter." He rolled over, turning his back on Collin. How the hell could he bring the real topic up? How could he ask Collin if he loved him?

"After all I've done for you, supporting you with your addiction, your mother, your artwork, everything, you're still so messed up you don't think I have feelings for you because I happen to like fucking you from behind?" Collin slapped his hand on the wall. "Jesus, Tristan, what do I have to do? Declare my total and undying love to you?"

Tristan widened his eyes and rolled to face him. "C-Collin, do you—"

"I'm not that guy, Tristan. Okay?" He scowled. "You need to trust in me. Is it that hard?"

"N-no." Tristan pursed his lips. Now was his chance, he wouldn't blow it. "But it would be nice to hear it from you, just once."

Collin rolled on top of him and pressed his lips to Tristan's, letting the kiss linger, then deepened it with his tongue, gliding it along Tristan's, the kiss gentle, and firm at the same time. He lifted his head and gazed deeply into Tristan's eyes, stroking Tristan's cheeks with his thumbs.

Tristan's gaze flicked between his eyes, his heart fluttering. Would he finally hear what he longed for?

"I'm sorry." Collin held his gaze. "I'll look at you next time, I promise. I love looking at you. You're so beautiful..." He kissed Tristan again, slowly, deliberately.

Tristan's heart almost burst with emotion. Was it enough? Maybe. He broke the kiss and looked deeply into Collin's eyes again.

"Let's get some sleep. I have a lot of work I want to get done tomorrow." Collin gave him a faint grin.

Tristan nodded, turned to his side, and snuggled into Collins chest with Collin's arm wrapped around him. For now, it was enough.

CHAPTER TWENTY-ONE

SUNDAY, NOVEMBER 30

Tristan sat at his desk, wearing sweatpants and a plaid wool shirt with the early afternoon sunlight streaming in through the window blinds and his cell phone pressed against his ear. "Hi, Mom."

"Hello, son. How was your trip home?"

"Good." Glancing at Collin, sitting on his bed with books all around him in a long sleeve t-shirt and jeans, he drew a circle on his desk with his index finger.

"That's it? Just good?" The sound of clinking like ice in a glass came through the phone.

She's drinking already. Tristan frowned. "Yeah, that's about it. We were pretty tired when we got home, but there weren't any delays or anything."

"Well, Tristan, I went to church today and..."

Collin hopped off the bed and, bending over the chair at his desk, logged onto his laptop computer. He typed, his fingers flying over the keyboard, then he clicked at something with his mouse.

Tristan lost track of his mother's voice, too focused on Collin. "Uh-huh."

A rock song sounded from Collin's cell phone, lying beside his computer on the desk, and Collin picked it up. "Hello?" He studied the computer screen and made a few more clicks with the mouse.

Tristan pretended to listen while his mother droned on about her work at church. "Uh-huh."

Yeah, be right there." Collin ended the call and slipped his phone into his back pocket, then gestured to Tristan. "Be right back."

With a nod, Tristan said, "Uh-huh."

Collin left the room and shut the door with a thud.

"...and so, Mrs. Johnson wanted to see me about..."

Scanning over the room, Tristan's gaze snagged on all of Collin's papers sprawled on the bed and his computer screen still showed a web page. An idea crashed down on him. "Mom, hey listen, I have to go." He jumped from his chair.

"Now?"

"Yeah, right now. I'll talk to you next week. Okay?"

"Well, okay."

"Bye."

"Bye."

He ended the call with his chest squeezing and his heart pumping in his ears. Did he really want to do this? Gnawing his lower lip, he stalked toward the bed, taking a closer inspection of Collin's things. Yes, something wasn't right. He needed to know.

He rushed to the door, locked it, then came back to Collin's computer. Bending over the keyboard and mouse, his fingers trembled as he clicked on icons and scroll bars. He clicked on Documents and then Thesis. A rash of Microsoft Word Documents came up on the screen. He clicked on a document called, *Thesis-Rough Draft.*

The document opened and the title rushed at Tristan, making

265

his pulse quicken, *Masturbation Addiction and Therapies in a 21-Year-Old College Student—Rough Draft.*

"Oh my God." With a jolt to his heart, Tristan's chest pinched. He fought to breathe, and his body shook. He dropped his gaze further down the page.

Abstract: The subject is a 21-year-old college student afflicted with a clinical masturbation addiction stemming from physical and emotional abuse from both a parent and the Mormon Church. The subject is also homosexual and much of the abuse was a direct result of his sexual preference. Therapies undergone include a behavioral-cognitive approach along with coping mechanisms for dealing with stressors and the development of a support network.

With his skin prickling, he flicked his gaze over the document, taking in bits and pieces.

Introduction: The subject, 21-year-old Tristan Tolken, is enrolled in his senior year at University of...

...grew up in Salt Lake City in the absence of a father or father figure and was raised by a mother with Borderline Personality Disorder...

...the subject became obsessed with the use of specific types of clothing, mainly silk brief underwear and loose-fitting jeans, in order to masturbate in public...

....withheld orgasm for hours at a time...

...the addiction is believed to be a self-soothing mechanism...

...The subject has had little or no prior history with romantic relationships...

...self-confidence being extremely low, a system of reward

was established to mainstream the subject into normal homosexual society...

A knock sounded at the door.

He startled and clicked the document shut, then swallowed a lump climbing up his throat.

"Tristan? Are you still in there? The door's locked." Collin's voice snaked in from the hallway.

Hesitating, he darted his gaze around the room and raked a shaky hand through his hair. Electric shocks sparked through his whole body, leaving him numb.

"Tristan? Are you there?" The door jiggled with hard pounding. "Tristan?"

"Uh, yeah, I-I'm here." He drew deep breaths, then stepped to the door and placed his hand on the knob. What should he do? Say something? Keep his mouth shut? What? He opened the door.

Collin stomped into the room with a stiff Fedex envelope in his hand. "What the fuck? Why did you lock the door on me?"

Staring at him, Tristan asked, "Wh-what?"

Collin planted his hands on his hips. "You locked the door. Why?"

With his emotions boiling over and heat burning inside him, Tristan shouted, "What the fuck's going on, Collin? Huh?" He stomped toward Collin to stand chest to chest with him, glaring into his eyes.

Collin took a step back. "What?"

Tristan jabbed at Collin's chest. "How about you tell me about your fucking thesis." He seethed.

"What do you mean, my thesis? What's wrong with you?" Collin's eyes grew wide.

Gritting his teeth and fisting his hands, Tristan stomped to Collin's computer and reached for the mouse.

"Hey!" Collin swiped for Tristan's arm.

Tristan clicked and the thesis appeared on the screen.

"Fuck." Collin poked at the laptop's power button.

Tristan swatted Collin's hand away. "Tell me about this, Collin. Tell me about this test subject, 21-year-old college student with a fucking masturbation addiction," he spat, turning to face Collin.

"Uh, Tristan, I uh—you went through my stuff?" Collin dropped his mouth open, staring at him.

Tristan glared at him. There was no explanation for this, none.

Stepping back, Collin sucked in a deep breath, rubbed his forehead, then focused on Tristan. "Listen, Tristan, you got it all wrong."

"Fuck you!" He lunged at Collin, shoving him down on Collin's bed. Jumping on top of him, Tristan punched at him again and again, hitting his chest, his arms, his cheek. "You fucker! You motherfucker! You used me all this time. You never cared about me. You fucking used me."

"Tristan, stop! Stop this, I can explain!" Holding up his arms, Collin tried to deflect Tristan's blows.

"I bet you fucking can." Tristan punched Collin's ribs, his shoulder, then back at his face, hitting Collin's arms instead. "You never loved me!" Sharp pain pummeled his heart. "You never loved me." The punches slowed. The pain overtook him, and his breath hitched, tears flooding his eyes. He dropped his arms to his side. "You never loved me...Oh, God." He fell backward, crumbling to the floor in a heap.

"Tristan." Collin leapt from the bed and crouched down next to Tristan, curled up in a ball, face down. He placed a tentative hand on his side.

Tristan slapped the hand away. "Don't touch me."

Sitting on tucked legs, Collin said, "I'm sorry, Tristan. I-I don't know what I was thinking. This whole thing, it sort of snowballed on me and I couldn't...I couldn't tell you, I—"

"How many people know about my problem?" His voice cracked and he clenched his teeth.

"Um, no one, just—"

Lifting his head, he glared at Collin. "How many?"

Collin's eyes rounded. "Uh, well, there's, there's me and my, my instructor and, and—"

"Jessica? Does she know?" Tristan sniffled.

"Well, yeah." Collin hung his head. "And maybe a few others..."

"Others? Are you fucking kidding me?" As heat swarmed his chest, Tristan fisted his hands.

Collin held up his palms. "They don't *all* know your name." He winced. "Look, don't hit me again, okay? Let's just talk this thing through."

Leering at Collin, Tristan said, "Talk? About what? How you betrayed me? How you fucking told the whole goddamned school what a freak I am?"

"Tristan, you're not a—"

"Shut up!" Tristan's chest heaved. "You used me for a God damned psychology experiment. You made me think you cared about me when all I wanted...all I ever fucking wanted was for you to love me." He bit back a new round of tears and swallowed hard.

"Tristan, I-I do love you." Collin wrinkled his forehead, his lips bowed down, his eyes shimmering.

"I don't believe you. It's too late, Collin." Tristan stared at the floor. He couldn't look at Collin. A wave of nausea rolled over him. "It's too late."

"Wh-what are you saying?" Collin reached out for him. "Come here, don't say that."

Tristan hopped up and looked down at Collin. Numbness worked over him. "No, it's done. You need to leave." It was over. There was no going back.

A tear rolled down Collin's cheek. "B-but, I told you I loved you. I-I—"

"Leave. Get what you need for now and leave. I can't stand to even look at you." Tristan's gaze travelled over Collin's bed. A memory pricked at his heart, of he and Collin sleeping in that very bed only hours ago, bodies entwined.

"You can't be serious." Collin's voice cracked. "Where am I going to go?" He stood up. "You love me, too, don't you? You said so at the playground." Tears tumbled down his cheeks.

Tristan glanced at him. How broken and pathetic he seemed. "That was a million years ago. When you were my hero. When I trusted you." He freed a shaky exhale. "And you couldn't even say it back. So much for trust. So much for love." He gritted his teeth, tears clouding his vision.

Reaching for him, Collin said, "Come on, you can't really kick me out. It's my dorm room, too."

Tristan glared at him. "Get the fuck out of my room. Now, right now. I don't give a shit where you go!" Lunging forward, he shoved Collin in the chest.

Collin stumbled back. "B-but what about my things?"

"Just take what you need for now. You can get the rest later." He chanced a peek at Collin. Pain crept into his chest. *Don't look.*

Taking a step forward, Collin swiped at his eyes. "Tristan, come on. Let's talk about this. Look, I wanted to tell you, I did. But—"

"It's fucking over, Collin. Over. Done. Finished. Get your shit and leave before I throw you out. And I will throw you out." With his lips pinched, Tristan shot him a glare, fisting his hands. "Get the fuck out!" he shouted.

"Shit, okay, okay," Collin mumbled. He stomped around the room, collecting his duffle bag, clothes, books, lap top computer and backpack. When he was packed up, he stood in the doorway and turned to face Tristan. "Are you sure about this?" Tears hovered on his eyelashes.

"Yes. Never been so sure of anything in my entire life." Tristan pursed his lips. A lump climbed up his throat. He only had to be strong for another minute more.

"Okay." Collin glanced at the floor. "I'm sorry, Tristan, really sorry. I really do love you." He opened the door and left.

Tristan watched the door shut with a soft click and threw himself on his bed, head down. Snatching his pillow, he yanked it to his face. The pain returned, an agonizing, heartbreaking pain. He let out a wretched sigh and was overcome with heavy sobs.

CHAPTER TWENTY-TWO

TUESDAY, DECEMBER 2

Tristan lay curled up in his bed and opened his eyes. The late afternoon sun lit up the back of the shut blinds at the window. What time was it? He leaned over the side of the bed, grabbed his cell phone, resting on the floor, and opened it. It was three thirty-seven in the afternoon. The screen said there were twenty-seven voicemails and forty-eight text messages, probably all from Collin.

Groaning, he pressed buttons, opening up the text app. He'd decided when they started coming in, he wouldn't read them, but he couldn't help himself. He scrolled down the messages, all from Collin.

> Please call me. We need to talk.

> I'm sorry.

> Call me.

> Are you Okay?

> Where are you?

> Call me.
>
> Talk to me.
>
> Don't do this, you're killing me.
>
> Call me.
>
> Fucking call me.
>
> Where are you?
>
> I'm sorry!
>
> Call me!
>
> Call me!
>
> Talk to me!

Tears pricked his eyes, and he snuck his lower lip between his teeth. Should he listen to the voicemails? No, he couldn't stand to hear Collin's voice. He glanced at Collin's empty bed, still mussed from the argument of two nights ago. He just didn't have the energy to do anything since Collin left, let alone get Collin's things together to give to him. *Fuck him. He can do it himself.*

Hot Tears rolled down his cheeks and he swiped at them. "Shit." When would he quit crying?

Pounding sounded at the door. "Tristan?" A female voice filtered in from the hallway.

Who the hell was that? He sat up in bed and pushed snarled bangs out of his face.

"Tristan? Are you in there?"

"Yeah. Who is it?" He knitted his brows.

"It's Ally."

"Just a minute." What was she doing here? How did she even know where his room was? He climbed out of bed, still wearing the sweatpants and wool shirt he'd dressed in on Sunday. As he padded to the door, he looked down, wrinkles littering his clothing. *I must look like shit.* He pulled his necklaces out of his shirt, so they rested over it and opened the door.

Ally stood in the hallway with a dark hooded sweatshirt over her small frame and a black skirt covering her legs. As she looked him over, her eyes widened. "Oh my God, Tristan." She covered her open mouth with her hand. "What's going on?"

"I uh, n-nothing..." He pursed his lips, hanging his head.

"Yeah, right." She pushed by him and entered the room, stopped between the beds, and looked around. "What happened?" Her gaze met his.

After closing the door, he stepped into the room and sat on the edge of his bed. "It's a long story."

Bending over, she inspected him. "Your eyes are all puffy and your clothes are a mess." Her brows furrowed. "Have you been crying?"

"No." He bowed his head.

She sniffed at him. "You stink."

He looked up at her. "Thanks a lot." He thought a moment. "What are you doing here?"

"Oh, Collin sent me." She wrinkled her brows.

Pain pierced through his heart. He winced. "What? Why?"

She sat down next to him. "He found me in art class and told me you two had a fight on Sunday and you kicked him out. He said you won't talk to him, and he's worried about you, so he sent me to check on you. You haven't been coming to class, have you?"

"No." With a shake of his head, he pressed his lips together.

"Have you even been out of this room?" She turned toward him.

"No."

"Well, have you eaten anything?" She raised her brows.

He huffed. "No, I haven't. I can't." He wrung his hands in his lap as tears threatened to surface.

She tugged on his arm. "Look at me, Tristan."

"No." He shook his head. She didn't need to see him cry.

She puffed out an exhale. "You can't stay in here forever." She placed a hand on his forearm. "Listen, I know we're not like, best friends or anything, but you can talk to me. I'm actually a pretty good sounding board. All my friends always come to me with stuff."

"Great." He swallowed hard. She'd never understand this.

She tugged on him again. "Tristan, please, it's obvious you need to talk to someone, and you have to get out of this damned room and eat something." She bent forward to peek in his face.

He turned his head away.

"Let me help you. Obviously, Collin was right to worry."

"Like he really fucking cares. Why the fuck didn't he care enough about me to keep his fucking mouth shut?" As he thinned his lips, he glared at Ally.

"What? What did he do that was so horrible?" Her gaze searched his face.

"He betrayed me, that's what. The fucker was always so God damned demanding about having me trust him and then he goes and betrays my trust." The words spat out of his mouth, and he frowned. Ally didn't deserve his anger.

"How exactly did he betray you?" She tilted her head, studying him, her forehead wrinkling.

"I-I can't tell you that." He stared at the ground. He didn't need anyone else knowing about him.

"Did he cheat on you?"

He shook his head.

"Did he lie to you about something?"

Nodding, he shifted his focus to her. "He lied to me about his thesis. He, he..." Tears broke through and he blinked them back. "Shit." He clenched his jaw.

"Come on, Tristan. You can talk to me." She edged closer to him and wrapped an arm around his shoulders. "Please, I want to help."

He fought to keep the tears at bay. Her touch soothed him, and he relaxed into it. He did need someone right now. How his heart ached. "Listen, I can't tell you all the details, because,

because, well, it's too embarrassing. You see, I have, I mean, had, this...problem. Sort of a mental problem. And Collin's a psychology genius, so he was helping me with it. But then...but then I found out." His breath hitched.

"It's okay, go on." She squeezed him.

"I found out that he was just using me and writing his thesis about my problem and he told a bunch of people about it and now all these people—" His breath hitched again and he held his breath.

"Let it out, Tristan. Just let it go." She embraced him.

Wrapping his arms around her waist, he buried his face in her neck and wept softy for a minute. "I-I'm sorry. I'm so sorry."

"Shh..."

"I feel like an idiot." Sniffling, he pulled away from her and swiped his eyes with the back of his hand.

She kept an arm around him and leaned into him. "You're not an idiot. You've just been taken for a ride and had your heart broken by that asshole. You have a right to cry. Hell, you have a right to fucking scream, yell, and break things if it'll make you feel better."

He choked out a laugh. "I beat the shit out of him."

She chuckled softly. "You did?"

Straightening, his gaze cut to hers. "I sure did. Right on that bed there. I tackled him and punched the crap out of him."

She slid her arm from around his shoulders. "Good for you."

"Yeah." The smile on his face faded to a frown. "I loved him so much."

"I know. I could see it the day you two came into the shop." She shook her head. "It's funny though, either he's a really good faker, or I'd say he's just about as heartbroken as you are."

"He is?" His heart fluttered for a second. No, it can't be.

"Oh yeah. When he came to find me, he looked about as bad as you do now. Well, except he'd showered." She smiled at him.

"D-do you know, um, where he's staying?" He studied her face.

"Ah." She glanced away for a moment. "I think he said he was staying with some chick named Jennifer or Jamie or some *J* name anyways."

"Jessica," he said under his breath. His chest tightened. They could have each other now.

"Yes." She pointed at him. "That's it."

He gazed down at his hands, resting in his lap. "That figures. She's his thesis advisor and she's a fucking bitch."

"Why do you say that?" A smirk played on her face.

"Because she was always after Collin. I'm sure of it." With a huff, he wrinkled his nose. "Well, now she's got him, and they have their fucking thesis. I hope they're happy."

"You think they were together on this thing?" She arched a brow.

"Fuck yeah. I bet she's the one who put him up to it." He thought a minute. "I can't believe that bitch knows about me. God, I should have known." He slapped his thigh. "I should have known when he wouldn't talk about his thesis with me and was so guarded about his papers and stuff that something was up." He faced Ally. "Do you know that I saw things on his computer way before Thanksgiving and I asked him about them, and he flat out lied to me?"

"He did?" Her eyes widened.

"Yeah. God, I'm so stupid." Pressing his lips together, he hung his head.

Ally rested her hand on his shoulder. "You're not stupid, Tristan. You just put your trust in the wrong person. He's the one that's stupid, doing something like that to a great guy like you. No wonder he's devastated. Look at what he lost."

He snuck a peek at her.

"He lost you. And he'll never find a better guy than you. You really are a great catch, Tristan. And I believe there's going to be a lot of great things headed your way. I mean, my God, you're selling in one of the best galleries in the area. How cool is that?" She gave him a wide smile.

"Yeah, how cool is that." He gazed at the far wall. The pain subsided and his heart lightened.

She patted him on the back. "So why don't you get showered, and we'll get something to eat. I'm buying."

"Really?" He stared at her with a dumb smile on his face.

"Yep, really." Her smile widened.

Was he ready to go out? His stomach grumbled. Yes, he had to. With Ally it wouldn't be so hard. "Okay."

CHAPTER TWENTY-THREE

Tristan stood in front of the heavy metal doors to his sociology class in a black, long sleeve t-shirt and jeans. Collin was in there, he knew it, and he knew it because he was so late. But he'd promised Ally he'd start going to class today and so here he was. Late.

Taking a deep inhale, he grabbed the door with a shaky hand. If only he could quite trembling so hard. He tugged and the door opened.

The instructor had his back turned to the room and wrote on a white board with a black marker, making little squeaking noises.

He dashed in and took the closest open seat only a few rows back. Quickly, he unpacked his notebook and pen and straightened himself at his desk. His heart pounded and a wave of nausea rolled through him. He rubbed his palms on his thighs, wiping off the sweat.

The instructor turned around. "Mr. Tolken."

"Uh, y-yes?" His full attention drew to the instructor.

"I'll not ask you what time this class starts. Since the semester is almost over, I'll assume you're well aware of it." The instructor tapped the marker to his palm.

"Um, yes. I'm s-sorry." He held his breath.

"Well then, don't let it happen again." Flipping through some papers, the instructor went on with the lecture.

He freed his breath and sank in his seat. Thank God that was over. Now where was Collin? He chanced a few quick glances around the room, but didn't see him. Did he not come to class today? He focused on the lecture and relaxed as much as he could.

———

"SO THAT'S it for today. I'll see you all on Friday. And Mr. Tolken, please be on time." The instructor shut his folder of papers and gathered his things at the podium.

Bending over, he placed his notebook and pen into his backpack and zipped it up. A body came up from behind him.

"Hi, Tristan."

Collin's voice tore at his heart. His breath caught in his throat, and he held himself still for a second. "Uh, hi." He couldn't look up. He swallowed hard and rose to standing, throwing his backpack over one shoulder, keeping his gaze at the floor.

"We need to talk." Collin's voice was soft.

With another swallow, he lifted his gaze to meet with Collin's.

Red rimmed Collin's eyes and dark circles hovered below them. His face was paler than usual, and his auburn hair wasn't its usual perfect sweep around his cheeks and eyes. His clothes, cargo pants and a sweatshirt, even looked disheveled.

A deep ache flooded Tristan's heart. Collin did look as bad as Ally had said. As bad as he himself must look. "I-I don't know what there is to say." Other students filtered by them.

"Let's just go outside. It won't take long, I promise." He tensed his brows, then worried his lower lip.

"Okay." Tristan followed him outside, into a cloudy morning.

The sound of a far-off plane rumbled in the sky and the smell of the ocean hung on heavy air.

They walked down a cement path, past an archway with bougainvillea vines threatening to engulf it and into the overhang of a brick building's front door.

"So, where you been?" Collin studied him.

"At home." Tristan stared at the board shoes covering his feet and shoved his hands into his front pockets.

"Didn't you get my messages?"

"Some." Tristan pressed his lips together.

"Why didn't you call me?"

Lifting his head, he glared at Collin. "Why do you think? Maybe I wasn't ready. Maybe I didn't want to."

"I was worried about you." Collin's eyes grew shiny. "Fuck, Tristan, I still have feelings for you. I can't just turn it off like you can."

"Turn it off? Are you fucking kidding me?" He ripped his hands out of his pockets and fisted them.

"I'm sorry, that was wrong." Collin blew out a ragged exhale and rubbed his forehead with shaky fingers. "So, you still feel the same, I guess."

"About what? About what happened? Yeah, I do." Tristan swallowed against a growing lump in his throat. Pain and heartache threatened to rip him open, but he fought against it. "What do you want?"

"I-I guess I need to get the rest of my stuff." Collin winced, then shifted his stance.

Tristan nodded. "Okay, why don't you go get it now? I'll go to the library."

"You won't even come with me?" As Collin's brows wrinkled, he lifted his hands as if to reach out for Tristan, then dropped them at his sides.

"No. It, it hurts too much to see you." His voice trembled and hot tears spilled onto his cheeks. "Fuck." Twisting around, he took off at a run.

"Tristan, Wait." Collin called out.

Tristan stopped and turned back around, skipping. "Get your stuff and leave me alone." Swiping at his eyes, he continued his dash to the library.

———

TRISTAN WALKED the hallway to his dorm room and stopped at the door. It'd been two hours since he'd seen Collin. He had to be done packing and gone by now.

Pressing his ear up against the door, he listened. Only silence came back at him from the other side. What if Collin was just in there quietly waiting for him to come back? *He better not be*. But still, some fucked up thing inside him hoped he was there. Could he forgive Collin? Could he ever believe him again? No.

Pressing his lips together, he unlocked and opened the door. It swung and hit the stopper with a clap. He entered the room and shut the door. No movement. No Collin. The room was empty. His heart sank, despite everything he'd told himself.

He perused the contents of the room, taking in the empty desk and shelves on Collin's side, the naked mattress of Collin's bed and the vacant closet. Even all of Collin's posters that had hung over his bed were gone. *He's gone, really gone.*

He dropped to his knees and his backpack fell to the floor. Sudden agony overwhelmed him. He was alone, bitterly alone. He dropped his face into his hands and let the tears flow once again. After a few minutes, he stopped weeping. The bitter pain of what had happened was still there. No matter how much he cried or pretended it was getting better, it just wasn't.

He knew how to make it better. It's what helped when he had to deal with his mother and his feelings for boys. It's what helped when he was scared, upset, lonely, all of it.

He rose and went to the drawers inside his closet. Colin had made him throw out all his old briefs, but he'd saved one pair, just in case.

He snuck out a dark blue pair of silk briefs and held them up, studying them, admiring them. He hadn't worn these in over a month What would it feel like now? A grin crept over his lips. He stepped out of his shoes, socks and jeans and shoved his boxers down and off. He brushed his hand against his hardening cock as he bent to step into the briefs. It had been days since he and Collin had been together, and he'd been too upset to even think about touching himself since. But now? Why not. If it would ease the pain, he would do anything to ease the pain.

As the thin silk enveloped his now full erection, a feeling like being with an old friend washed over him. He slid his fingers up and down his shaft and closed his eyes. A wave of sweet sensation tingled through him. His body relaxed and the ache in his heart lessened.

He looked through his closet, found one of his baggy jeans and shucked them off the hanger. With his breath quickening, he slipped them on along with his socks and shoes, then dove his hand into his front pocket and let his fingers tease his cock, swirling the head and stroking the shaft. A soft moan escaped him. The pleasure washed away the hurt, the pain, the memory of betrayal. It was only him again, no Collin, no one trying to change him, no one making him face hurtful things, no one taking this away from him.

He rubbed harder, down over his balls and up to the tip of his erection, focusing on the spot just under the head. He rolled his hips, craving more. But he wouldn't give himself more. Not until he was satisfied the pain would be gone.

Smiling, he walked to the center of the room and picked up his backpack. After slinging it over his shoulder he strolled to the wall and grabbed his portfolio with his drawing supplies inside. It was time for art class, and he was ready. He turned and left the room. He could do this, he could.

A LITTLE WHILE LATER, Tristan strolled into his art class, set up his easel, drawing pad and charcoals and focused on the closest set-up of fake flowers in a vase, sitting on top of a black sheet. He toyed with the erection in his pocket, continuing the tickling and teasing he craved. If he was drawing already, maybe no one would bother him and he could go back to being the quiet Tristan nobody noticed.

As his gaze flicked from the set-up to the lines on his paper, students shuffled into the room with hushed voices and prepared for class.

Ally came in with a black blouse covering her top and jeans hugging her hips, her supplies in one hand and a black backpack over her shoulder, then scampered to Tristan. "Hey, how are you?

"Fine." He smudged some charcoal.

"Just fine?" She nudged his shoulder.

He stopped his fingers on his cock and smiled at her. "Yep."

She studied him. "You don't look fine. You look, I don't know, weird."

"What?" He dropped his hand from his drawing.

"You almost look too peaceful after what happened to you." She peered at him a second then grabbed his arm. "You aren't thinking about doing something stupid, are you?"

"Like what?" He yanked his arm away from her.

"Well, like commit suicide or something?" Her gaze searched his face.

"What? Why would you say that?" He scowled. "I may be upset, but I'm not *that* upset."

She placed a hand on her hip. "Well, it's just that Collin told me to watch out for strange behavior. He used to work on the suicide hotline, you know."

"Yeah, I know." He freed a soft sigh. An ache started in his chest. Why did she have to say his name? "Listen, I don't want to talk about Collin anymore, okay? And if he's still coming around asking you to check on me, tell him to forget it. I'm fine now. He got his things today and it's done."

"He did?" She looked around the class for a moment. "Are you sure you're okay with it?"

"Yes." He returned to his drawing.

"But...you were so upset yesterday." She cocked her head, studying him.

The instructor entered the room. "Hello, everyone. Flowers, it's all about flowers today." He chuckled and went to chat with a student in the corner of the room.

"Ally, just let me draw right now, okay? That's what I need." He focused on his paper and drew some shadow on the vase he'd outlined.

"Okay, but I'm here if you need me. Remember that." She left to get herself set up for class.

As he drew, he resumed the motions over his cock with his fingers, rubbing, stroking and swirling, sending waves of pleasure to wash over him, soothe him, make him numb.

———

TRISTAN TRUDGED into his dorm room and closed the door. He'd spent the last two hours drawing and touching himself. He used to be able to handle it, but now, it seemed he couldn't. He threw his backpack and portfolio on the floor and walked to his bed. Quickly, he undressed down to his briefs and lay on the bed in anticipation. Twice he almost came in class and how he'd stopped himself he hadn't a clue.

He lay on his back and placed long, even strokes over his brief-bound cock. pre-cum formed a wet spot in the thin silk. Sweet sensation teased him.

Wave after wave of need rolled through his body, but he didn't give in to it. He let out a soft moan and closed his eyes, keeping his mind free, letting himself feel.

He slid his fingers up to focus on the head of his cock, squeezing and rubbing as pulses rocked through him. He imagined a mouth, just any mouth taking him in and licking. He rocked his hips, skimmed his hand down to fondle his balls, then ran his palm up his shaft. That was good, so good.

Moaning, he stroked faster, harder over his dick. Need built inside him, each stroke bringing more and more pleasure. His sensitivity built to a dangerous edge. He stopped and shucked his briefs down and off, freeing his tortured cock. It was time.

Wrapping his fist around his seeping erection, he stroked up and down, letting his thumb swipe across the pearl of seed at the tip and rubbing it over the head of his cock. He jerked his hand faster, thrusting his hips, then cupped his balls and spread his legs wide. With a sharp gasp, his climax roared forward and the peak of sensation shuddered through him. He bucked and his toes curled, spurting cum over his hand and onto his chest while intense contractions rocked his body.

As it relaxed, a vision of Collin posing nude for him shoved its way through. "No," he groaned. Rolling to his side, he clutched the covers and clenched his eyes shut. How did Collin get back in? The ache in his heart started up again, maybe stronger than before. It didn't help, even this didn't help.

Taking the bedcovers with him, he rolled back and forth on the bed in agony. "No, no, no..." His gut clenched. What the hell had he done? His mother's voice shrieked in his head. *Freak, Tristan, you're nothing but a freak.* No, he was nothing but an addict, a sick and twisted sex addict. He'd never be right, never be normal. He didn't know how.

He stopped, keeping the covers wrapped around him, and stared at the ceiling. "Come on, God, tell me, what's wrong with me? Huh? Why can't anyone just love me? Why? Why did he have to do that?" He took a shuddering inhale. "Did you forget about me? Wasn't I born in your image, too? Don't I have a fucking right to be happy?" He blinked and tears streamed down his cheeks.

A deep blackness filled him, burrowed deep down into his soul. It all became very clear. Maybe his mother told the truth? Maybe he was never meant to be born. The thought came at him with stunning clarity and tragic certainty. It terrified and soothed him all at the same time. "Fuck. Oh my God."

He jumped from the bed onto his knees on the floor, found his backpack and rummaged in it for his phone. When he found it, he scrolled through his contacts. Ally, she was right. He pressed the call button.

"Hello? Tristan?" Ally's voice came through like a shining beacon on a foggy night.

His body trembled and his voice wavered. "A-ally? Hi, uh...I-I'm not, not so g-good."

"Where are you?" Determination rang out in her voice.

"A-at home." His lower lip trembled.

"I'm there."

The phone went dead.

Tristan exhaled and bent over, holding himself up on straight arms. He took a few slow, deep breaths. What the hell had just come over him? Was he really suicidal? Is that how it happened? Or was he just going absolutely crazy?

He shook his head. Clean up and get dressed, don't think about anything else.

He stood up, ambled into the bathroom, cleaned up with a wet washcloth and came out to his bedside to dress. Holding up the soiled briefs, he shuffled to the closet and threw them in the laundry basket. As he fished out a pair of boxers and slide them up his legs, knocking sounded at the door.

"Tristan? It's Ally. Let me in."

"Just a minute." He put on his jeans, walked to the door, and unlocked it.

Ally opened the door and stepped inside, looking him over. "What happened?" She shut the door.

He turned and paced into his room, rubbing the heels of his hands into his temples. "I-I don't know. I just got this horrible feeling. My mother, she told me she wished I was never born and so I got this idea that maybe, maybe she was right?"

Ally followed him in while he paced back and forth. "What?" She stopped.

He kept pacing. "A-and this, this feeling, it was dark, really dark and, and scary and I thought that maybe, maybe I might do something, you know, listen to my mom and—"

"Jesus, Tristan, slow down." She snatched his arm, stopping him.

With wide eyes, he stared at her. "Is that what happens when people commit suicide?"

"Hell if I know." She knitted her brows.

He looked away and huffed. Whatever had happened, it had been scary as hell.

She tugged at his arm.

He drew his attention to her.

"Hey, you didn't do it. You called me, so maybe it was some sort of warning. You know, your body telling you, you weren't as great as you thought you were." She scanned the room and led him to sit next to her on the edge of his bed. "So, what do you think happened that caused it?"

He drew a deep inhale. *I can't tell her the truth.* "Um..." He glanced at Collin's bare mattress. "I think it was just coming back here and seeing that all his stuff is gone."

"Uh-huh." She watched him for a moment. "What is this thing, this mental problem you were having that Collin used for his thesis?"

"What?" His breath caught and his heart quickened. "Why do you need to know that?"

Shrugging, she gave him a quick grin. "Well, I just think that it might be important as to how you're handling things. I mean, if you were bipolar or something, I could see it being dangerous for you right now."

He shook his head and wrapped his arms around his stomach. "No, I'm not bipolar or anything like that."

"Then what is it?" She placed her hand on his shoulder.

He glanced at her, then shifted his attention to the floor. "I-I can't tell you."

She squeezed his shoulder. "Come on, how am I supposed to help you if you have some weird mental problem that you won't tell me about?"

He pursed his lips. "It's not—well, it is sort of weird." A knot formed in his gut. "All I can tell you is that I have, had an addiction."

"You were on drugs?" She lifted her brows.

He huffed and met her gaze. "No, I was not on drugs and I'm not an alcoholic."

"What were you addicted to?" She chewed the corner of her mouth.

He sighed. Should he tell her all of it? "I..." The knot in his gut clenched. "I can't say. Look, in this case it doesn't matter."

"But my dad was an alcoholic. He's in AA now and I know that if you're stressed out or something you can have a relapse. Did you have a relapse?" She pressed her lips together.

Shifting his gaze to the floor, he nodded. "I feel horrible about it, like a failure."

She rubbed her hand over his back. "My dad starting drinking again when my mom left him. It took him two years to get sober again and I didn't speak to him that whole time. There were times when he just disappeared, and we didn't know if he was dead or alive. It was terrible. Addiction is a terrible disease."

"Yeah, it is." He took a deep, shuddering inhale.

"All I can tell you is that AA really worked for my dad. Maybe there's an AA type group for whatever your addiction is?" She took her hand off him and leaned back on straight arms.

"Maybe." He nodded, thinking on it. There had to be groups like that for him, right?

"Doesn't hurt to check it out." She sat upright. "You're going through a tough time. It's the smart people, the strong people that get help."

Parting his lips, he focused on her. "You're absolutely right."

He thought a moment. His heart didn't feel as heavy. Talking had helped. "I feel all right now. So, if you want to leave and get some studying done, it's okay."

"Yeah?" She furrowed her brows.

"Yeah." He nodded.

"You sure?" She eyed him.

"I'm sure. In fact, there's a bunch of studying I need to do after missing two days of classes." He looked at a pile of books on his desk. Maybe that would keep his mind off all of this.

She stood up and swiped her hands on her jeans. "Okay. If you need me again, call me. I'm not that far away. I'm in the apartment just across the way there." She pointed to his window and the building on the other side of a courtyard.

"You are?" He lifted his brows.

"Yeah." She gave him a warm smile.

He stood up and faced her. "Ally?"

"What?"

"I can't thank you enough for being there for me. You're a really good person." He rubbed his neck. "You've done a lot for me and I'm only now getting to really know you." If only he'd been able to figure this all out a long time ago.

She gave him a playful punch in the shoulder. "No problem. I love your art. And you're a pretty cool guy, too." She gave him a quick hug. "It'll get better. You'll see."

He nodded. "If you say so."

They parted and she smiled at him. "Remember to call me if you need anything else." She turned to leave and stopped at the door. Waving at him, she said, "Bye."

He waved. "Bye."

She opened the door and left.

CHAPTER TWENTY-FOUR

THURSDAY, DECEMBER 4

T ristan leaned back in his chair and stretched. He was tired of typing away at his paper for art history class. He checked his cell phone, sitting next to his laptop. No messages. His heart dropped a little. He had to stop thinking and feeling like that. Collin hadn't called or sent any texts since they'd talked, and it was over.

The afternoon sun streaked in through the window beside his desk, making it hard for him to see his monitor. He jumped up and shut the blinds.

When he sat back down, his hand brushed over his groin, and he rested his palm over it. Thoughts of touching himself, wearing his briefs, rushed into his head. He shoved them away. Pressing on his burgeoning erection, he let out a soft moan. But how good would it be? No, he couldn't think like that. He had to get into some program, like Ally had suggested.

Pounding sounded on the door.

He hopped up from his chair and strolled toward it. "Ally?" He wasn't expecting her.

"No, Jessica."

His heart clenched. This couldn't be good. He stopped at the door and sucked in a breath before opening it.

"Hello, Tristan, can I come in?" Her long blonde hair fell over her breasts in waves. A tight sweater and jeans revealed a curvy body.

"Why?" He threw her a glare.

"Because we need to talk." She put a hand on her hip.

"What could you possibly have to say to me?" He pursed his lips.

"Let me in and you'll find out, won't you?" She flashed him a smug grin.

He stepped aside. "Fine, but make it quick. I have a paper to finish." He huffed. He'd make her leave if he had to.

She sauntered past him and into the room. When she got to the area between the desks and beds, she stopped and turned around as if talking a turn on a catwalk.

Walking to her, he placed both hands on his hips. "Well?"

She put a lacquered fingernail to her painted lips and thought a moment. "We better sit down."

With a heavy sigh, he sat on Collin's mattress.

She dropped in next to him.

"So?" He eyed her. What sort of bullshit would she have to say?

"Listen, Tristan, despite what you may think, I'm not the enemy here." She shifted her attention to him.

"Really? 'Cause I figure you had a hand in the whole deception you and Collin cooked up regarding his thesis." He glared at her.

She shook her head, making the waves in her hair bounce. "Actually, I was against that."

"You were?" He hooked a brow. No way did he believe her.

"Remember that day we had the argument?" She lifted her chin.

"Yeah." He watched her. Maybe he should listen.

"We were arguing because I told him I wouldn't help him with his thesis anymore if he continued the way he was. I wanted him to get your consent." She glanced at the wall. "But he was certain it would destroy your progress." She pinched her lips. "At first, he found you fascinating for your, how shall I say it, interesting psychosis. He figured he could help you and maybe in the process have a fantastic real-life case study to do his thesis on."

Pain wrapped around Tristan's heart. "That fucker." He placed his elbows on his thighs and stared at his hands, gripping each other.

She leaned forward. "But he had feelings for you, Tristan, real feelings. He loved you and you fell in love with him," she said. "And he was afraid that telling you would send you back into your compulsion. You see, you were responding so well to his treatment, he didn't want you to relapse." She shrugged. "The treatment he came up with was ground-breaking, really. He thought it could help others with similar conditions, gay men or straight," she said. "I knew he never told you any of this."

He tilted his head away from her. Tears pricked his eyes. "He never loved me."

"Oh, but he did, and he does. He only decided to use your case for a thesis when he saw you getting better." She sighed. "I suppose then it was too late to tell you. In his mind, he was stuck, Tristan, stuck between losing you to addiction or continuing on for the greater good, finding a way to help others." She placed her hand on his shoulder. "So, he couldn't turn in his thesis without getting your consent and he was trying to find a way around it without hurting you. You know that only myself and our professor had access to your name. Others knew about it, but not *who* the subject was." She drew a deep inhale. "Anyways, I was concerned for your well-being then and I'm concerned for it now."

He shrugged her hand off and swiped at his eyes, staring at the window. Could he really believe that Collin was stuck like that and not just using him? "Why would you care about me? You always wanted him, didn't you?" He glanced at her, then focused on Collin's empty desk.

"No, of course not." She edged closer to him. "The truth is, Collin's never been in love before. You were the best thing that's ever happened to him. I could see that right away."

He faced her and straightened. "He's never been in love before?"

"No. His parents had a terrible divorce and I think it had a very negative effect on him, made him keep everyone at a distance." She huffed. "The only way he could get the intimacy he craved was to go around helping people with their psychological problems," she said. "He never let himself fall in love."

He dropped his mouth open, staring at her. No wonder he didn't want to say it.

"Listen, I know what he did was terrible, but he's a wreck. He loves you so much, he's literally heartbroken. He even collapsed at dinner last night and we almost took him to the hospital." She pursed her lips.

"Jesus, he did?" He raised his brow, his heart aching for him. Could it be he'd been too harsh with him?

"Yes. And what's worse is he's throwing away all his studies, all his dreams of being a great psychologist and quitting school." She watched him.

"What?" He sat back. Could he believe any of this?

"He quit all his classes, completely deleted all his thesis files and he's driving back to Phoenix on Friday, tomorrow."

He widened his eyes. "No fucking way."

"Yes." Sitting forward, she placed her hands over his. "I know it's asking a lot, but can't you forgive him and work something out? Can't you talk some sense into him and make him stay? He's really gone off the deep end and he needs you. He made a mistake, but he was working to make it right."

"I...uh..." He hung his mouth open. Forgive him? Make him stay? He shook his head while confusion ran rampant in his brain. Could he? "N-no, absolutely not."

She squeezed his hand. "But, Tristan—"

"Fuck no. No matter what you're telling me now, that asshole betrayed me. All he kept telling me was to trust him, that he was fucking trustworthy and then I find out about his thesis." His chest heated. How could he ever let him in again?

She wrinkled her brows. "Please."

"No way. Not only did he keep this thesis bullshit from me, but now I see he never let me in. He never told me half the stuff you know about. How the hell am I supposed to have something with a guy who I'll never trust again and won't confide in me? Who'll only say he loves me when I'm throwing him out?" He tossed his arms up and let them drop. "Jesus."

She sighed and sat back. "Okay then."

"Okay?" He stared at her. This might be the strangest conversation he'd ever had.

She stood up. "Okay, it's done. I did the best I could. I think you're making a mistake. I think you and Collin need each other and could be stronger after this, with some counseling of course, but if you're going to be bullheaded about it, there's nothing else I can do."

"Bullheaded? Are you kidding me?" He jumped up, glaring at her. As he slapped his hand on his chest, he said, "I'm looking out for me. *For me.* What he did fucked me up, too, you know. This whole thing..." His arms spread out around him. "Almost broke me, too. And you want me to stand here and feel sorry for Collin?"

"Tristan..." She shifted and cocked her head.

"No, don't Tristan me like I'm a child. Just get out." He pointed at the door.

"Very well." She hung her head and left the room.

I'm his first love...He didn't want to lose me to addiction. He was stuck. He loves me so much he deleted the files. He's leaving... The tears came with a rush, making his breath hitch and his chest heave with sobs. "Oh, fuck." He fell to sit on the floor, his back against his bed, his knees pulled up to his chest. "What should I do? God, what should I do?"

CHAPTER TWENTY-FIVE

FRIDAY, DECEMBER 5

Tristan rushed across the college campus through soft rain into his dorm, up the elevator, down the hallway and to his room. When he got inside, he slammed the door shut and leaned against it with his back. Soaked hair fell down around his shoulders and wet splotches marred his dark, long-sleeve t-shirt and jeans. Collin wasn't in class today. He must have quit like Jessica had said. Had he left already? His pulse kicked. He'd never asked Jessica what time he was leaving.

Knocking sounded on the door, startling him.

Who the hell was it now? It better be Ally and not Jessica again. He couldn't take another run in with her. He swiveled, his necklaces swaying on his chest, and opened the door.

A man stood in the hallway with short blond hair, gelled up at the top, wearing a long black trench coat and fashionable black pants. He appeared to be in his forties. Piercing blue eyes looked Tristan over. "Are you Tristan Tolken?"

He studied the older man. He looked familiar in a way. "Uh, yes. Wh-who are you?"

"Oh well, I'm um, well..." The man looked around him for a

moment as if lost, then his gaze met Tristan's. Taking a deep inhale, he rubbed his hands together and smiled a warm, inviting smile. Finally, he held his hand out. "Hello, son. I've waited a very long time to meet you."

The room spun. Blackness crept up on the outskirts of Tristan's vision. His knees buckled.

In a blur, the man reached for Tristan, threw his backpack to the floor and held Tristan up under his armpits. "I'm sorry. Let me help you." He guided Tristan into his room and sat him down on the edge of his bed, sinking in beside him. "Here, bend over." He gently pushed down on Tristan's back, putting Tristan's head between his knees.

Tristan took quick breaths, struggling for air. Did he really hear that right? *This man called me his son?* He fought harder to breath.

"Oh no, seems you're hyperventilating." The man rushed around the room, grabbed a plastic bag from the garbage, emptied its contents into the mesh can and put it over Tristan's mouth. "Here breath into this and slow your breath."

Tristan drew deep, slow breaths. In a few seconds, his breathing returned to normal and he sat up. A dizzy wave swept over him. "You, you're my, you said—"

"Yes, I'm your father, Tristan. My name is Steven Tolken. I'm sorry to have said it so abruptly like that, but I guess I don't believe in mincing words." He raised his hands as if wanting to touch Tristan, then set them in his lap.

"B-but you...my mother said you were..." Tristan swallowed hard, staring at the man whose facial features so closely resembled his own.

"Yes, I'm sure she told you I was dead." His father chuckled and swayed for a moment. "I can assure you I'm not, just excommunicated from that lovely church of hers."

Tristan's brows furrowed and his body trembled. He couldn't look hard enough at this man, this confident, stately looking man. It wasn't anything like he'd imagined his father to look.

"Um, what happened? How did you, um, find me? Why, why are—"

"Yes, seems I have a lot to tell you." His father clasped his hands together in his lap. "Let me just get it all out on the table, all right?"

Slowly, Tristan nodded, still staring at his father.

"I'll just assume you know nothing, because that's about what she'd have told you, and I'll start from the beginning." His father clapped his hands together. "Oh, I'm sorry, do you have someplace to be? Another class, maybe?"

Tristan blinked and wiped his eyes. When he opened them, the man was still there. His father was real. "No, no classes for, for a few hours." He continued staring.

"Good. Well, the beginning." His father pressed his lips together. "I met your mother when we were both very young, in high school. She was a very pretty girl, but never very much up here." He pointed at his head. "And I-I was a football player, trying desperately to be someone I was not. You see in those days in rural Utah, you married young, had lots of babies and well, was a good Mormon." He rocked once. "So, your mother and I dated and married right after our missionary work. She got pregnant right away, but I-I'd figured something out about myself while I was off doing my mission in Chicago." His gaze met Tristan's. "Tristan, I found out I was gay."

Tristan blinked a few times and nodded his head. Holy shit.

"Now, you know being gay is not tolerated in the Mormon Church, right?" His father studied him.

Tristan nodded again.

"So, like a good Mormon I went to be fixed, turned into a good husband and father and to be brought back to Christ. Do you know what they do to homosexuals, Tristan?" His father narrowed his eyes.

"Yeah," Tristan mumbled.

"After three of their horrible shock treatments, I gave up and during the process I lost all my faith in God and the church. I almost committed suicide. I went back to your mother, and I told her I was gay and quitting the church and that was that. And you know what she said to me?" He arched a brow.

"No." Tristan shook his head in slow motion.

"She told me I was dead to her and I'd never, ever be allowed to have any contact with my son, with you. And between the church and her ill will toward me, it became true." His brows furrowed. "I tried for years to find you, but she moved, and they hid you and her and finally, I gave up." He took Tristan's hand in his. "I'm so sorry. I never should have given up. My God..." His eyes glistened. "You've turned into such a fine young man."

Slowly, the magnitude of his father's words found their way to fit inside his head. "Y-you're gay?" Tristan dropped his mouth open and stared.

His father nodded, still holding his hand. "Yes, Tristan."

"I-I'm gay." Tristan pointed at his own chest.

"I know." His father gave him a warm smile. "And an artist, I hear? Selling at the Santa Barbara Gallery? A true chip off the old block, so they say. I'm actually an artist, too. I have my own gallery in The City, you know, San Fran." He let out an easy laugh.

The corners of Tristan's lips twitched with the start of a smile. "You are? H-how did you know about me? How did you find me?"

"Your boyfriend, Collin, got in touch with me. He sounds like a really great guy. He must really love you to have gone through so much trouble for you." His father squeezed Tristan's hand.

Nausea swept over Tristan in a heavy wave. He swallowed hard, fending it off and cutting his gaze to the window between the desks at the rain, now pelting the glass. "H-he's not my boyfriend anymore." His gaze dropped to his hand, entwined in his father's. How the hell had Collin pulled this off? Was that what all the ancestry papers were about that he'd found?

"Oh? Why not?" His father creased his brows.

"We, we had a, well, he betrayed my trust. It's a long story."

Trista's vision blurred. What a mess this was. Collin was gone and Collin, the bastard, loved him so much he'd seen through his mother's deception to find his father for him. Did finding his father have anything to do with Collin's plan to get Tristan's consent for the thesis without causing a relapse?

"Seems you've had a lot of that in your life. It happens, you know, that lovers will sometimes betray you. But it's something that can be overcome if you're strong enough and love each other enough." His father wrapped an arm around Tristan's shoulders. "You really do love him, don't you?"

Tristan nodded, clenching his jaw, his eyes stinging. He wasn't going to break down again.

"Where is he now?" His father's gaze searched his face.

"He left. He went back home and quit school." Tristan's voice cracked and his heart ached.

"Oh no. That explains why he was driving back to Phoenix this afternoon and couldn't meet me." His father shook his head and leaned back, releasing Tristan.

Blinking a few times, Tristan turned to his father and gazed into his eyes. "He was leaving this afternoon? He's still here?"

"That's what he told me this morning, when my flight came in from San Francisco." A warm smile spread on his father's lips. "You're going to find him, aren't you."

"Do you mind? I have to go. Now." If there was a chance, maybe he could forgive Collin and they would find a way to work through all this, together. Tristan jumped up and ripped his cell phone from his pocket. "Here's my cell number. Call me later and—"

"I already have it. Collin gave it to me." His father stood. "Come on, we have all weekend to talk and get reacquainted." He followed Tristan out of the room in a rush.

Tristan left his father standing in the hallway, racing to get out of the dorm, to somehow find Collin.

He sped across campus, running over grass and pathways, dialing Collin's number again and again, pressing his cell phone to his ear. No answer. Heavy raindrops fell on his face, his hair, his clothes. Where the hell had Collin said Jessica lived?

He ran through a mass of students with umbrellas and hoods over their heads, piling out of buildings, between classes, his mind rewinding his conversation with Collin. *The corner of Main and 3rd, that's it!*

He ran on, pushing past students and college personnel, the rain drenching him. His chest heaved and his lungs burned. He wouldn't stop, not until he saw Collin.

Speeding off campus, he made his way down Main Street, passed old craftsman and mission-style mansions with manicured yards and big oak trees to 3rd. As he came up on a two-story house with stucco the color of butter, he saw movement in the driveway. He jogged around to the driveway on the side of the house, bordered by large oleander bushes. The rain slowed to a drizzle, and he wiped the water from his eyes and face. His heart pounded as he looked beyond the bushes.

Collin stood bent over the back seat of his red Maxima. As he came out of the back door of the car, his auburn hair hung in dripping strands in his eyes and his leather jacket was wet on the shoulders.

"Collin?" He took tentative steps toward him and glanced in the car. It was packed with Collin's things. His pulse quickened. What if Collin didn't want to talk to him? What if it was too late?

Collin stood still, his back to Tristan, then tipped his head back for a moment and straightened.

Walking to him, Tristan stopped just behind him. "Collin? We need to talk. I don't want you to go."

Collin dipped his ahead, then twisted to face him. "It's a little late, don't you think? I'm supposed to meet my mother in Phoenix tonight." With pursed lips, tears shimmered in his eyes.

"But, Collin, you don't want to do this. You don't want to leave or, or quit school. I know you don't." Tristan held his palms up. Collin had to listen to him.

"How do you know about that?" Collin snuck his lower lip between his teeth, his brows wrinkling.

"Uh, J-Jessica told me. She told me the whole thing and then, then my dad showed up at my, I mean, our dorm room today. *My dad*, Collin. And that was because of you. You love me and you've never loved anyone before and I love you and well, I don't think I've ever loved anyone before either. And damn it, Collin, you did help me. You did so much for me I can't even tell you. I was such a mess, and you changed all that. You forced me from my shell and made me face my addiction and supported me while I got my art in a gallery and you just, you just loved me." Tristan's breath came in heavy spurts.

"I'm so sorry for betraying your trust, for not knowing how to handle this the right way, but I don't know how you could ever take me back or trust me again." Tears spilled over Collin's cheeks. "I made a terrible mistake, and *I* can barely live with me. How could you?"

Lunging at Collin, Tristan threw his arms around Collin's shoulders and yanked him to his chest, brushing his hand over the back of his wet hair. "I forgive you, Collin. We can work this thing out. We can both get counseling. We belong together. I became a new person because of you. You gave me so much. You gave my father back to me." His heart spilled over with emotion.

Collin buried his face in his neck. "I'm afraid, Tristan." His body shook.

"What are you afraid of?" Tristan kissed the side of his head.

"I'm afraid of loving you too much. I'm afraid of getting hurt even worse." Collin wrapped his arms around Tristan's waist.

"Remember what you told me when we first met?" Tristan held him tighter. He wouldn't let him go. They were both messed up, but they had to find a way to make this work.

"What?" Collin's voice was soft.

"There are no guarantees, but it's worth the risk. Take the risk, Collin, with me." Tristan's vision clouded.

Collin lifted his head and looked at Tristan with dark, wet eyes. "I love you, Tristan."

Tristan kissed him with all the passion and longing and love in his soul. Every emotion inside him turned back on as if it'd lay dormant though a long, cold winter.

As they kissed, warmth and light hit the top of their heads and their faces.

They pulled apart and squinted, peering up at a ray of sunshine breaking free from the clouds. Finally, they looked at each other and laughed.

———

A FEW HOURS LATER, Tristan hauled a huge black suitcase into the dorm room and sighed. "Shit, Collin, what did you put in this thing, bricks?" He swiped at sweat forming on his brow.

Collin turned from his desk, full of books and odds and ends. "It's just my clothes, I swear. Maybe you should start working out."

"Yeah, like that's my thing. I'd get even skinnier if I did that." Grunting, he tugged on the suitcase and let it fall in front of Collin's closet. "What are you going to do about your classes and your thesis?"

"I spoke with the dean while you were moving my car. He said he'd be happy to keep me here and we're going to meet on Monday. As far as the thesis goes, I'll think of something. My professor loves me." Collin smirked. "I am a prodigy, you know."

Tristan rolled his eyes. "Oh brother." Maybe, if Collin's case study of him really would help others like him, he would give his consent. Maybe. He'd still have to think on that, and counseling would definitely have to be included in that deal.

Collin walked past Tristan and shut the door behind him. When he strolled back, he wrapped his arms around Tristan from behind and kissed the back of his neck. "God, I missed you."

Smiling, Tristan swayed them, holding onto Collin's arms. "I missed you, too."

"So what time do we have to meet your father?" Collin bit at his shoulder.

Tristan glanced at his watch. "At seven, so we have another two hours." Collin's lips brushed against the nape of Tristan's neck. Little nibbles worked their way down to his shoulder and back up to his ear. Something hard pressed against his behind.

"I want you, Tristan. I don't think I've ever wanted anyone more," Collin said in a husky voice.

Tristan leaned his head back against Collin's, his cock pulsing and hardening. "Well good, 'cause I think we have plenty of time."

While Collin continued to kiss and nibble at Tristan's neck, his hand trailed down Tristan's stomach to fondle his sac and up to stroke his erection through his jeans.

Tristan freed a soft moan and rocked his hips, lost in the touch of his lover, his Collin. Tingling raced down his spine with the sweet kisses on his neck.

Stopping, Collin turned Tristan around. "Come on, let's get naked and get in bed. And this time, I want to see your face. No more hiding for me."

Placing his hands on Collin's cheeks, Tristan gave him a deep, penetrating kiss. "So, you *were* having intimacy issues when we had sex."

Collin blushed. "Yeah, you could say that. Let's not talk about it now, though. Right now, I want to prove to you how much I love you."

A wide smile spread over Tristan's lips. "I'm never going to get tired of hearing you say that. So, say it a lot."

"I love you, I love you, I love you, how's that?" A deep chuckle rumbled in Collin's chest.

"Great." Tristan placed another long, deep kiss on Collin's mouth. "Come on." Tugging on Collin's hand, he led him to his bed. Undressing, he watched Collin remove his clothing, admiring his muscled back and chest and toned abdomen and his cock, standing tall and thick and ready for only him.

Collin kicked off his boxers, climbed into bed and held the covers down for Tristan. "Hurry up, it's kind of cold in here."

"Could've fooled me." Tristan kicked off his jeans and boxers and lay down next to Collin.

"What did you mean by that?" Collin snapped a brow up. "Was that a penis size joke?"

Tristan smirked at him.

Collin smiled and rolled on top of Tristan, propping himself on his elbows, rubbing their cocks together and against their hips. "You're not exactly small, you know, for a guy your size." He kissed Tristan on the nose.

"Thanks, I think." Tristan cupped Collin's ass, then took a moment to look deeply into Collin's eyes. *He does love me. I can see it.*

With a mischievous grin, Collin kissed and licked his way down Tristan's chest and bit at a nipple.

Groaning, Tristan's back arched and his cock twitched, his breath quickening. He rutted against Collin and pleasure raced through him.

Collin moved lower, sucking at Tristan's stomach and licking in the crook between his inner thigh and groin, then shifted to Tristan's sac, taking it in his mouth and swirling his tongue over it.

Letting out a deep moan, Tristan writhed on the bed in raw pleasure. His cock ached to be taken in Collin's mouth. "Uh, please, Collin."

"Please Collin what?" Collin tipped his head to look up at Tristan.

He gazed down at Collin. "You know what I want."

"Just say it. I want to hear you say it." Collin flicked his tongue at the tip of his hard cock.

Tristan's cock twitched again as if straining to enter that sweet mouth all on its own. "Suck me, Collin."

Collin's slick tongue licked from the base of Tristan's erection to the tip and swirled.

A pulse of sensation bolted through Tristan, and he rocked his hips. "Do it. Now."

"Demanding little bastard," Collin mumbled. In one quick movement, he devoured Tristan's thick cock, all the way down to the base and slowly came back up again, running his tongue along the front.

"Oh shit." Pleasure seared through Tristan. He slapped his hands to the back of Collin's head, attempting to thrust into his mouth.

Collin only let the head of Tristan's erection enter with each rock of Tristan's hips. His tongue flicked at the slit and swirled over the head.

As sensitivity teased, Tristan became crazy with need, fisting his hands in Collin's hair, letting out sharp gasps.

Collin lifted off Tristan and looked down on him. "Where's the lube?"

"Oh shit, it's in the shower still, I think." Tristan pressed his lips together. Had that been the last time they'd been together? It had seemed so long ago now.

Collin climbed off the bed and rushed into the bathroom, his thick cock bobbing with each step. When he came back, he held up the lube and a condom with a coy grin on his mouth. He rolled the condom on, then opened the cap of the lube and squirted an ample amount on his fingers. As he came back into bed, he slicked his cock with long strokes and positioned himself between Tristan's legs.

Tristan's cock grew painfully hard. He wanted him and wanted him now.

Leaning down over Tristan, Collin held himself up on one straight arm. With his free hand, he dipped between Tristan's spread legs and circled his entrance, watching Tristan's reaction.

The ache in his groin grew unbearable. Collin teased him just enough. With a bite on his lower lip, he pulled Collin down and placed hungry kisses on his lips, thrusting his tongue inside Collin's mouth, tangling it with Collin's. "I'm ready."

"Now?" Collin pushed a finger inside and stroked his insides.

Collin's finger pad rubbed over his internal bundle of nerves, sending a jolt of sensation screaming through his body. He squirmed and cried out. "Fuck, Collin, now."

"Fuck you now?" Collin pumped his finger inside Tristan.

"Y-yes." Tristan clutched the sheet at either side of his hips and parted his lips as delicious pleasure shuddered through is body.

"Say it." Collin rubbed his slick cock on Tristan's thigh and groaned.

"F-fuck me now. Fuck me." Sensation welled up inside Tristan, dribbling pre-cum onto his stomach.

Trembling over Tristan, Collin pulled his finger out and placed his hard cock at Tristan's entrance, then came down on top of Tristan and claimed his lips, opening his mouth, penetrating him with his tongue. "Wrap your legs around me."

Tristan hooked his legs around Collin's hips and crossed his ankles, then he wrapped his arms around Collin's shoulders.

Collin thrust and the head of his cock entered Tristan, sliding it barely in and out, then gazed deeply into Tristan's eyes, caressing Tristan's forehead. "God, I love you."

With his heart swelling to near bursting, tears stung Tristan's eyes. At that moment, nothing stood between them. They were connected as one. "I love you, too."

Collin dropped his forehead to Tristan's, his gaze on his face, and thrust deep inside him. Moaning, he pulled out and pushed back in, cupping his arms around Tristan's head.

Rocking in a rhythm with Collin, over and over their hips came together and parted. Delicious internal friction drove Tristan's need to a sharp edge. Using his legs, he tugged down on Collin's hips and his aching cock rubbed over Collin's taut stomach.

Panting, Collin's thrusts grew ragged and more forceful.

A peak of sensation ripped forward and Tristan's climax

erupted out of him with a loud cry. Rippling waves of pleasure spurted his hot cum between them.

Collin's body grew rigid, and his hands fisted in Tristan's hair. Sharp gasps tore from his throat as he thrust hard and held his cock deep inside Tristan, filling him. As he pulled out and drove in hard again, he dropped his head to the pillow beside Tristan's cheek, His breathing coming in long, ragged draws.

Tristan's hold on Collin tightened and he buried his face in Collin's neck while the rush from his climax subsided. He'd never felt this close to anyone in his life, and it was amazing and terrifying. But he'd never have it any other way.

———

A FEW HOURS LATER, Tristan stepped out of Collin's car with a red dress shirt under his black jacket and a pair of his nicer jeans on. He looked over the pier and the water, sparkling in the early evening light given off by the lights of restaurants and bars.

Collin came up to stand beside him at the sidewalk and draped an arm around his shoulders. "You ready?"

Tristan gazed at his stunning lover, all wrapped up in a black turtleneck sweater and snug jeans. "Yeah, I'm ready. I can't believe my father is actually alive. Shit, I can't believe he's here and, and that he's gay. It's just..." He shook his head. "Unbelievable."

With a wide grin, Collin nodded. "I know. I couldn't believe it either when I found him." As they walked to the gay bar they now frequented, he gave Tristan a playful kiss on the cheek. "I'm nervous."

Tristan stopped and focused on Collin's face. A breeze blew a lock of auburn hair across Collin's eyes and Tristan brushed it out of the way. "Why are you nervous?"

"I'm meeting your father. Why wouldn't I be?" Collin curled the edge of his mouth.

With a snicker, Tristan said, "You didn't seem nervous to meet my mother and you sure as hell should have been."

Collin glanced out over the water, lapping at the pier. "Yeah, but that was different, somehow. I don't think I allowed myself to be quite as...invested as I am now. You know?"

Pulling Collin down by his shoulders, Tristan planted a deep kiss on his mouth. "You'll be fine. He already thinks you're the best guy ever for finding him."

Collin nodded, wrapped an arm around Tristan's shoulder and headed for the bar.

The bar bustled with a crowd of Friday night revelers, men all dressed up and nicely coiffed, mingling and flirting.

When they stepped inside the threshold, they looked around to find Tristan's father sitting at a table toward the back corner. He waved at them with a wide smile and as they strolled to him, he rose from his seat.

Tristan stood before his father. "Hi, uh, Dad." Saying that was strange and wonderful, all at once.

His father opened his arms. "Hello, son."

Tristan embraced his father for the first time in his life. As the strong arms tightened around him, his eyes pricked with tears. It was real, all of it. Collin was here and his father was here, and he had friends and a life, finally a real life. He sniffled and buried his face in his father's shoulder.

Collin coughed into his fist.

Releasing his father, Tristan stepped back, swiping at his eyes, and smiling. Nothing could ever take away his happiness now. "Um, Dad, this is my boyfriend, Collin." He held his hand out to Collin.

Collin stepped forward with his hand raised. "Hello, Mr. Tolken."

"Collin." His father took Collin's hand and after a brief shake, pulled him in for a warm hug.

They parted and sat at the table, Tristan next to his father and Collin next to Tristan.

Timmy, the waiter, waltzed up to their table. "What'll it be, boys?" He looked each one of them over in turn.

"I'll have a mojito, Timmy. Did you want one, too, Tristan?" Collin grinned at Tristan.

"Yep, me, too." Tristan met Collin's grin with his own.

"I'll have a glass of red wine, Timmy. Maybe a merlot? And one of your better vintages." Tristan's father smiled coyly at Timmy and gave him the once over.

"Do you like them full bodied?" Timmy tapped his index finger to his cheek.

"Always." His father smirked at Timmy and wagged his brows at him.

With a shake of his head, Collin chuckled.

"I know exactly what to bring you." Timmy patted his father on the shoulder and sauntered off.

Tristan stared at his father. "Dad..." Was he really flirting with Timmy?

"What?" His father's attention drew to Tristan.

Tapping the table in front of his father, Tristan said, "Did you just, are you flirting with—"

"Why not? I may be old but I'm not dead." Laughing, his father sunk back into his chair.

"Wow." With a wide grin, Tristan shook his head. Maybe someday he could be that sure of himself.

His father leaned in, his brows tensing. "Collin, listen, I can't thank you enough for finding me."

"Oh, you're welcome, Mr. Tolken. I uh, I love your son and like I said, when we visited his mother for Thanksgiving, she totally let on that you weren't quite as dead as she'd made Tristan believe all those years. And he needs you in his life, he really does." Gazing at Tristan, Collin squeezed his hand.

"So, Dad, tell me more about yourself. I'm dying to know what you've been doing all this time." Tristan wiggled in his seat.

Timmy showed up at the table and set their drinks down, getting close to Tristan's father.

His father took a sip of his wine. "Excellent choice, Timmy. Full of body."

Holding his hand up to his mouth, Timmy snickered. "There's more where that came from." After looking his father up and down, he walked away.

His father set his wine glass down. "Well, like I've already told you, I left your mother before you were born, thinking of course that once I was settled, I'd be able to see you. But anyways, I'd heard about the gay population in San Francisco and so I went up there and sort of reinvented myself. I was accepted into the Academy of Art University in San Francisco and when I graduated, I worked for a time doing ad campaigns for Gap. But then I tired of doing ads and my abstract paintings, that's what sells in my gallery now, well they started getting popular. So, I left The Gap with quite a few stock options and did well enough just painting."

Tristan sipped his mint and rum drink from a straw. "Wow, that's like a dream come true." If only his work sold that well.

"Yes, it is. Collin here told me you were a bit of a sensation down here."

With a shrug, heat rushed Tristan's face. "Yeah, well, I do charcoals of naked men." He looked up and they all laughed. He thought a moment of his mother. His gut knotted. "Not to change the subject, but what are we going to tell Mom?"

"I think you should tell her the truth." Collin gave Tristan's hand another squeeze.

"Yes, I think the truth would be best. And *you* better tell her. I doubt she'd take a call from me, even after all this time." His father rimmed his wine glass with his index finger.

Tristan let out a heavy sigh, peering at his drink. "She's going to be really upset." Maybe upset enough that she wouldn't want to talk to him for a while. Or ever.

"We'll do it together, Tristan. Don't worry about it." Collin wrinkled his brows.

"But what if she disowns me?" Tristan slipped his fingers up and down his glass. Was he gaining a father only to lose a mother?

"She won't," Collin said.

"How do you know?" Tristan shifted in his seat, eyeing him. "I won't let that happen." Collin pressed his lips together.

His father leaned in. "Neither will I. I'll be damned if I'll let that woman keep us apart or poison you again in any way."

Tristan's gaze met with his father's. "H-how much do you know about, about Mom and I?"

Collin blew out a breath and stared at the table.

With a glance at Collin, his father said, "Collin told me enough. Let's just leave it at that."

Tristan twisted his glass. "Oh." Did his father know about the emotional and physical abuse he'd suffered? Better to leave that discussion for another day.

"Anyways, what are you two doing for Christmas?" As a wide smile played over his father's mouth, he sat back.

Both Collin and Tristan shrugged.

"Okay then, you're coming to San Francisco, and I won't take no for an answer." His father patted the table between them.

With wide eyes and a growing grin, Tristan focused on Collin. "Can we? I mean, you don't have to see your parents, do you?"

"Nothing was set in stone and I'm sure they'd be fine with it. It's about time I had a boyfriend's family to visit. I've been with them every year since I've been born." He huffed a chuckle. "God knows they'll just be happy I finally found someone other than them to spend it with."

"It's settled then." His father clapped his hands together. "We have so much to talk about and to see, the galleries, The Haight, Union Square, The Tenderloin, the gay bars, oh the gay bars they have up there..." He looked around for a moment. "So do you think I can convince Timmy to join us?"

"Dad." Heat crept up Tristan's neck, and he gazed at Collin. "I can't believe this. I'm sitting in a gay bar with my boyfriend and my gay father, who I just met, is flirting with Timmy and wants to take him home."

Leaning forward, Collin placed his hand over Tristan's. "Well, get used to it."

EPILOGUE

SUNDAY, JANUARY 3

Tristan huffed, then planted his hands on his hips, standing behind Collin's desk chair. "I told you, Collin, I'm all right with it now." He peeked out the window at the sunny day lighting up the courtyard. Their therapy sessions were going well and while he'd begun to trust Collin again, Collin was learning to be open with him, really open. "I think you should try to write that thesis again, especially if it helps someone else like me."

Collin twisted from his desk chair to face him. "Tristan, are you sure about this?" He stood up, then grabbed Tristan's hands in his.

"Yes." Tristan gave a curt nod. "In my Sexaholic Anonymous meetings, there are so many people struggling like I was. I want to give back somehow." His gaze searched Collin's face.

"I'm proud of you, you know that, right?" Collin pressed a long kiss to his lips. "No matter if we do this or not." Collin glanced at Tristan's bed, strewn with a slew of new drawings. "Not to change the subject, but are those the ones you're sending to your dad?"

"Yeah, he thinks with his name backing me and the community up there, I won't be able to make drawings fast enough." With his heart skipping, a smile tugged at his lips. "I can't believe this is all happening."

"Me neither." Collin sighed. "You know what we have to do tonight. It's the last thing."

"Yeah, I know." Hanging his head, Tristan puffed out a breath. "Let's get this over with."

"I'll be right here beside you." Collins squeezed their hands. "No matter what she says, she can't hurt you, Tristan, not unless you let it. It's just words and—"

"Sticks and stones." Tristan raised a corner of his mouth. He'd learned that the saying was actually true. Words can't hurt unless you let them. His whole perception of the world had changed so much. He was still a work in progress, and he still slipped somedays, but each slip was not as bad as the last. "Okay, let's call her." He pursed his lips, then fished his cell phone out of the back pocket of his jeans.

Collin led him to the edge of his bed and sat down, pulling Tristan with him. Bumping his shoulder on Tristan's, he said, "I'm right here." He ticked his brows.

With a slight grin, Tristan dialed his mother and put the phone on speaker. It rang a few times, then clicked.

"Oh, hello, Tristan. How are you?" The clinking of ice in a glass sounded in the background.

Tristan pinched his lips and peeked at Collin. She was already drinking. They hadn't called soon enough.

Waving his hand in a circle, Collin mouthed, *go on.*

"Hi, Mom. Collin's on the line." Tristan drew a deep breath. "I have news."

"You do?"

"Yeah, um..." As his chest tightened, he worried his lower lip. "Um, well, I uh." He shut his eyes for a heartbeat. "I met my father. We uh, we found each other." They'd rehearsed this and he wasn't supposed to go into details that might upset her too much. They were breaking her in slowly to the idea of his father being in his life.

She scowled. "Oh."

"Mom, I'm going to try and get to know him. It's something I need to do." Tristan's heart pounded in his ears. "You understand, don't you?"

The clinking sounded through the phone again. "Sure, Tristan. I mean, he *is* your father, even though he's a no good—"

"Miss Tolken, don't you think that this could ease the burden on you? Not only will Tristan have you to count on, but his father can also be there for him. It seems to me that this could make things easier on you. Right?"

Her breath caught. "Well, I suppose so. I guess I never looked at it that way," she said. "Doesn't matter, really. Tristan's an adult and can do whatever he wants. He always did anyways, didn't he?" She scoffed.

Tristan rolled his eyes. *Here we go.* "Anyways, Mom, I just wanted you to know that. I'll need to go and um..." He glanced at the drawings on his bed. "Study for a test I have coming up." If he stayed on the phone any longer, things might turn ugly and they'd decided to cut things short before they did.

"Sure. I'll talk to you soon, okay?"

"Yeah, next Sunday." Tristan pursed his lips, throwing a glance at Collin, watching him.

"Sure, goodbye."

"Bye." Tristan hung up the call and freed a long breath, drooping his shoulders. "Holy shit, we did it. She didn't say anything about how he was supposed to be dead." He choked out a laugh. Maybe he'd never fully understand her.

"It's like I told you a long time ago, she'd rather pretend the bad shit never happened. We can use that to our advantage." Collin threw an arm over Tristan's shoulder and kissed his cheek. "I'll get started on that thesis and you get more drawings done. We're going to make it, Tristan. Both of us, together. I can feel it."

"Yeah, we are, aren't we." Tristan placed a long, deep kiss on his lips. "I love you, Collin."

"And I love you." Collin let out a soft snort. "Look, I can say it every time now."

"You can." Tristan rubbed his nose on Collin's.

———

WANT to read something lighter but still with college-age men? Try my Mesa Boys Series.

When a skater boy rooms with a hot college nerd, sparks fly. Will they give in to temptation? Read Catching His Fall to find out.

———

YOU CAN ALSO TRY the prequel chapter for the series in which a bad boy skater has a bi-awakening with his roommate. Claim your copy of Catching Him.

OR, buy it on Amazon: Catching Him

THANK YOU

Thank you for reading **The Obsession**. Helping other readers find new books to enjoy is easy when you share a review. If you want to share your love for Tristan and Collin, please leave a review. I'd really appreciate it!

Another huge help is recommending my work to others. Spread the word by giving this book a shout-out in your favorite book rec group if you like.

Find Christie and all her MM Romance books online at:
CHRISTIEGORDON.COM
Get exclusive content at Christie's Facebook reader's group:
Christie's Cocktale Cafe
Connect with Christie on social Media:

ABOUT THE AUTHOR

Christie Gordon started writing gay and MM romance books after finding Yaoi fanfiction by accident and falling in love with it. She's always had stories in her head and always enjoyed writing, so she decided to try her hand at it and took up fiction writing classes at a local community college. She published her first MM romance book with eXtasy Books back in 2009. She enjoys writing about men discovering themselves, overcoming obstacles and finding love in the process, along with a happy ending. Visit her website for a complete list of her books.

Christie's day job is in the high-tech industry with a Bachelor of Science in Electrical Engineering and a Master's in Business Administration. She currently lives in the Phoenix, Arizona metro area but has also lived in the Bay Area of California and grew up in Minnesota. If she isn't writing, she's watching boys love dramas or creating digital artwork. She's also a mother of two young-adult sons, whose antics keep her on her toes. Her one-eyed rescue pug is always by her side, snoring the day away.

Printed in Great Britain
by Amazon